THE MAX FARADAY
CHRONICLES

THE
MAX
FARADAY

CHRONICLES

JEFFREY SHURLOW GRAHAM

ARPress
45 Dan Road Suite 5
Canton MA 02021
Hotline: 1(888) 821-0229
Fax: 1(508) 545-7580

Ordering Information:

Quantity sales. Special discounts are available on quantity purchases by corporations, associations, and others. For details, contact the publisher at the address above.

Printed in the United States of America.

ISBN-13:   Softcover   979-8-89330-330-8
               eBook   979-8-89330-331-5
Library of Congress Control Number: 2024900542

Table of Contents

Chapter One

Never Let a Nuclear Scientist Go Hungry, or They Will Nuke for Food

My name is Max Faraday, Max to my friends. Nobody is going to believe me. Here I am putting it all on paper. It all began Thursday, July 11, 2002, the day before my twenty-year Cavanaugh City High School reunion. I have heard it said to always start your stories with a bang. But I'm starting mine with silence and shadows.

My training has given me the ability to be very quiet. I doubt if a stethoscope could even pick up my heartbeat.

My team and I have been here most of the night, and it is morning. I am the one up in the rafters of a warehouse listening to the ranting below. My team is scattered about the complex.

Since the adversary in question arrived, I have been up here crawling all over this place. The floor is littered with pressure-sensitive alarms, so when I ascend I dangle from a rope, leaving remote-controlled smoke bombs and noisemakers here and there in case I need a diversion.

Russians say, "Never let a nuclear scientist go hungry, knowing they will nuke for food. They are sore losers."

The one I am looking at used to be a Russian general. CIA operatives paid the general well, and he traded secrets. Both sides got what they wanted.

I didn't.

In my line of work, I have learned you can never trust a traitor. After you get what you want or need, it's best to terminate them. Otherwise, when or if you give them the chance, they will terminate you.

The general justifies his actions with a tirade of, "Russia will live again! Rise! Mother Russia will rise again!"

Excuse me, but didn't he sell Mother Russia down the hole to the highest bidder? Irony is, who I work for and swore an oath to was the highest bidder. Now I'll be cleaning up another fine mess that the powers that be got us all into.

I read in his file he sent his wife and son to the States, and the son went to a public school in Chicago. (As my good friend Ralph Shurlow would say, "The best terrorists in the world get a United States public school education.")

The general's son stands beside his father. I can see the diamond sparkle in his class ring. He graduated last spring and is planning on going to Harvard this fall, on a scholarship no less.

Speaking of graduation, tomorrow I'll be attending my twenty-year high school reunion.

But there is not a whole lot about my life I can tell them about.

I am relaying every word I hear via a wrist communicator. Since my middleman CIA agent named Graves back at base is ignorant of Russian, I tap the code giving him a *Reader's Digest* version. The wrist communicator has a camera and takes digital pictures. The computer then runs them through the system, and thankfully the middleman has a file on every one of them. I guess you could say, "Thank God for Big Brother watching us."

I get the feeling that the middleman is getting nervous. This was not supposed to happen.

A US senator was being blackmailed by the Russian Mafia, and they chose me to do some recon into the situation. But if all I had to do was recon, why did I have to bring backup?

As team leader, I type in the code for *assistance needed* and *request terminal authorization.*

The good general is now talking about the blow that the Arab world struck on 9-11, cheering, and hand-wringing and beating on their chests, saying we should have been the first to strike! Arab names are spoken, and I again ask in code for assistance and terminal authorization. A diagram is shown of the Sears Tower and how their allies will use a purchased Russian nuclear bomb. Then he shows the weapon to his men, unveiling it like it was a new car.

Great! Now the good general is selling a football-sized nuclear bomb to an Arab terrorist group.

The general then flips a switch that starts a countdown. In English he says, "It is done. There will be no turning back. The Arabs will seize the bomb, plant it, and in less than five days it will go off."

My communicator displays "Code for assistance needed received. Authorization number given. Terminal authorization granted." So it's the Russian Mafia and a father and son against me and my team.

Lord, I know I have prayed for retribution, but I'm beginning to feel like Sampson in the last moments of his life. Then again, I have learned I cannot do according to my feelings. I instead do according to my actions, like in chess.

And how many moves ahead do I play? Well, that's classified.

It has been a while since I have done a wetwork operation.

To my teammates in the field I'm known as Selah. I make the enemy stop and think about what they are doing; give them time to know that the anti-bully is back!

I push the button on my remote, and charges go off with multiple explosions, drawing attention away from me. Then, after opening fire on my way down, I drop to the floor from a bungee cord hung from a rafter, with the nuclear bomb right in front of me.

A .45 is my weapon of choice though I carry multiple guns during my missions. But my team uses a variety of firearms as they follow behind me and my explosive distraction, making every bullet count as we run a serpentine route through the Russians while one of them screams, "Don't shoot the bomb!" just before I rush past him and hit his bodyguard in the face.

The general's boy just stands there in shock as I pump two into his father's head and one into his chest, then keep on moving to the right. My body armor takes a few hits that kick like a mule (I should know, since I've been kicked by a mule before). I leave a bullet in each gun and holster them like an old habit. The team comes from behind the Russian Mafia and yells, "Drop your weapons and put your hands up!" in Russian.

Those who surrender drop to the floor and put their hands behind their heads. As for those who don't, well, suffice it to say, they fall dead after their bullets fly past my head. Then the scientist who was screaming, "Don't shoot the bomb!" clasps his hands over his eyes, then opens them just in time to receive a bullet between them.

As the general's son, the only one left of his gang, reaches for a nearby gun, I tell him in Russian, "Don't do it, boy. Get down on the floor now!"

He stands, stuttering in broken Russian how his father was a great man. And now that I killed him, my days on earth were numbered, and that his uncle would avenge the killing, and on and on and on in a barely understandable tirade that finally ended with him crying while shouting, "I loved my father! And now he's gone!"

For a moment I pause, and in that moment he reaches down to his father's side, pulls out his gun and prompts gunfire from my team— then me.

I see countless bullets in my peripheral vision as they leave their barrels before I fire, just once. The general's son shoots his automatic weapon wide as his expelled slugs tatter my clothing but fail to cut meat, while I finally observe my single .45 round hit him in the chest and drop him lifelessly to the floor beside his father.

Then silence resounds amidst numerous corpses as I think, *As my friends from Scotland Yard would say, 'What a bloody damn mess!'* But thank God my team aimed straight, or I'd be among those who are now living impaired.

The nuke's timer continues counting down, so I bend over to observe it before being distracted by a nearby door being bashed down under the force of several shouting men.

"FBI. What the hell is going on here?"

And to further clarify for the readers of this story who thought I was in Russia, you should realize you were mistaken. Thanks to the department of US Citizenship and Immigration Services, we have Russian terrorists right here at home and living in our neighborhoods.

Investigate and you'll find a former Iraqi Republican Guard soldier running an auto shop or 7-Eleven. Then, after that, you can have fun guessing if he or she is here attempting a better life in America or existing as part of a sleeper cell just waiting to make a terrorist strike when the time is right.

And all of this is thanks to the US government. The same people who brought you pedophiles out of prison on early release, an economy currently comparable to the Black Plague, and massive warfare in places such as Korea and Vietnam they still refer to as conflicts.

In the confusion of FBI agents yelling "What the hell is going on?!" another agent steps in, flashes a badge, and yells similarly, "CIA. We'll handle this!" prompting the lead FBI agent to ask for identification.

CIA Agent Smith then pulls me to the side and says, "You killed the Russian scientist and the general, Selah!"

I respond by saying, "There are more where they came from."

Smith taps me on the back of my head and informs me, "That is out of line! And you are bordering on insubordination!"

With my finger I motion the agent to come closer. I take him to the scientist's laptop computer. I wipe off the blood, turn it on, and say, "You know we have a few options here. One, we can send the bomb back to Russia and let them figure out how to shut it down. Or two, we can return it to Osama bin Laden in the next five days. Since he paid for it, I'm sure we could find a copy of his sales receipt with his mailing address around here somewhere."

The computer comes on, and I punch in the access code as Agent Smith grows angrier while I say, "Or three, you can go over there and act like a big CIA agent and punch in the disarm code so the FBI will be impressed. And after that you can really wow them by showing that the hard drive on this laptop contains the names of numerous Arab terrorists and what flight they are on so you can pick them up when they arrive at the airport."

I look at him, and it is like there is an imaginary "Dumb Guy" sign over his head as he goes over and put the codes in, causing the countdown to stop and causing me to breathe a sigh of relief. Then I wonder if there are any more nukes that we don't know of.

A CIA agent uses his trench coat and sunglasses to cover me as I stare at the bomb, and he whispers to me, "Let me get you out of here, Max. You did well."

And then I realize I did well while I look at 9:00 a.m. in a Chicago P.D. station house and Chief Cybulski wearing a Mr. Nobody T-shirt that reads, "It's hard to get people to invest in the stock market when they're too busy buying canned goods, shotgun shells, and running around screaming . . ."

"Faraday!" the chief calls out, "in my office."

He closes and locks the door behind us with me saying, "Be careful what you ask me."

This prompted the chief to respond, "Word on the street is we have a few less Russian Mafia guys to worry about."

It then becomes obvious that Cybulski in his latter years has come to mistrust computers as he fishes a folder from a nearby file cabinet and throws it down in front of me on the desk and says, "This is a list of people you've encountered that no longer exist among the living. Max, you're a detective now. CIA Black Ops should be in your past."

"Chief, stuff like that is never in your past," I tell him.

The chief run his fingers through what is left of his hair before replying, "It's like the sniper shot you did two years ago all over again."

I break the silence by saying, "Chief, I have a long six-hour-plus drive ahead of me, and I can't give you any more information."

Causing Cybulski to retort, "Max, you're full of surprises."

Then I leave unceremoniously to go to the one-room apartment I live in as I continue the process of rebuilding my life, relatively content while existing basically as a Chicago cop protecting the populous as I deal with the city's dregs.

I asked a guy once, "Why do you rob people in the city? I mean, there are people who can witness you doing the robbery. So why not do it in the middle of nowhere?"

Then he said, "In the city nobody cares about nobody or nothing. And chances are they don't have guns. In the country, if the dog don't get you, the owner will. With a gun he'll shoot you dead. Before calling the local cops, they will talk over your dead body, and then share coffee."

This is where I came from. This is what I call my hometown. This is the place I live and work in. The place where most people I encounter are the dregs of the earth with an excuse for every move they make, moves that change the lives of decent people every day due to the fact that such human trash haven't a clue about what being a decent human being is all about. And like it or not, I suspect they never will.

My friends James Scott "Jamie" and his wife, Ellen Gates Scott, invited me back to my old hometown for my twenty-year high school reunion. "Come home," they say, "and you will have a ball. See your old school before they knock it down."

I hated grade school. It was bunch of jerks. They tried to beat up on me, a string bean, and my friends, namely nerds, geeks, fat kids, and Connie Mack, a colored girl. I was taller than some of the other guys, brace-faced with glasses. Girls don't let a guy ask a girl out with those credentials. I say their loss. I was also the anti-bully; I beat up the jerks and jackasses. So I was like everyone's big brother. I was no Einstein, but I was no special ed case either. I fell in the middle. I was just your average kid.

A mile from town and the first thing I see is a sign that reads: "Cavanaugh City, Home of Reed Jackson, lead singer of Counting Tornadoes at a Trailer Park." The name of the band confuses some people because it's also the name of their first big hit song. But, I like it. Fits the song and the band perfectly.

Driving into my old hometown of Cavanaugh City, Michigan, is like going back in time. Main Street has not changed at all from what I remember, and even though they have a What's Its Name restaurant on the other side of town so it does not clutter the downtown area, or so I've been told.

That is where my old house used to be. It's Howard's Used Cars and Service now.

Oh, I gotta pull over and take a look. Oh, this is sweet. A black and gold 1982 Pontiac Firebird Trans Am, looks in mint condition. Whoa! Look at the price. Well, I'll come back and drool over it later.

So I take a right at Main Street. A few blocks down is the Scott residence. It kinda blows my mind, this used to be an old lady's house that we used to call Old Witch Horton's House. That was back when I was in first or second grade. After my mom introduced us to her, she began making cookies for us. Now it looks like something out of *Anne of Green Gables or This Old House*. Across the street is another impressive sight, Home Hearth's Bed-and-Breakfast. When I was a kid, it was a funeral home where we used to say Witch Horton used to get raw ingredients for potions or for midnight snacks. Like I said, it was back when I was a kid. I feel kinda stupid and ashamed about thinking that now.

Now it is a three-story Martha Stewart dream house. Stone-walled fence, manicured lawn with statues and flower gardens, and a volleyball net in the back.

The sign on the front gate says *vacancy full. Make reservations at www.website.*

Home Hearth is a booming chain of self-help and do-it-yourself fix-up books and a nationwide 1-800 radio call-in show. Now they are going after Martha Stewart and bed-and-breakfasts? All thanks to Steve Pearson. He came from a dysfunctional home; his father was a thief and a bank robber, and they were on the run most of the time.

Steve got caught, and that is how he came to the Pearson's Foster Home. He was a foster kid, orphaned when his dad was shot in a shootout with police. The Pearson family then adopts him. It is rags to riches *New York Times* best-seller autobiography.

As I pull in Jamie's driveway, a voice calls out, "Max?" I am still stunned at the Home Hearth's house. "Max? Is that you?" I come to attention at the question.

"Jamie? Your hair, it's gone?"

In stunned disbelief he says, "You look good."

I shrug my shoulders and smile, replying, "Well, I work out."

A big I-don't-know-what-it-is dog is happy to see me, barks in joy, and jumps on me.

Jamie yells, "Whoa! Max, down Max!"

I say to Jamie, "Let me get this straight, you named a mutt Max?"

"Well, he is loveable, good with kids, barks at strangers, and as you can see, a good judge of character. He loves you."

"I still don't like the idea of a dog being named after me. I have been called a son of a bitch, but this?"

"Well, actually, he is a junior. Big Paul has Big Mamma." "Remember what I said about if the dog does not get you, well, this is the dog."

Ellen comes out screaming my name! She gives me a big hug and then a kiss.

"What do you have on you? What? You have a gun, don't you?"

"I'm a police officer. I use a gun occasionally."

"Well, not in my house!"

I humor her and take off my holster and gun and whisper, "I feel naked." I open my trunk and put the gun in my mobile gun cabinet.

Jamie half-heartedly apologizes, "We don't allow guns in our house, Max. I will not even let the kids have a water pistol."

I then ask, "What do they do when they play cops and robbers, point their fingers and go bang?"

Ellen is happy now that my gun is put away, saying, "Now, isn't that better. Let's get inside; my boys and girls are going to be back together!" Her boys and girls meaning me, Connie, Jamie, Jason, Steve, Adam, Dr. Churchill Smith, Big Paul, Marcy, and Burney "Dan Outta Luck Cottager." Jamie and Ellen have some nice kids: Gilbert, age five, Anne, age three. What can I say, they like *Anne of Green Gables*. We talk football, basketball, and relive past glories.

***

Unknown to me, at about eleven o'clock this evening, this was happening on a highway lovingly called Deer Crossing Alley Valley Highway. On the stretch of highway outside of town going north and south, a shirtless male driver with tattoos and pierced body parts is driving close to seventy-five miles per hour. That is pretty dangerous in this neck of the woods. There is also a stupid man who has nothing better to do than jog at night wearing a black jogging suit. The locals call the idiot Stealth Jogger. He is also on the highway lovingly called Deer Crossing Alley Valley Highway. The shirtless male driver with tattoos and pierced body parts is now driving close to a hundred miles per hour, and he and the Stealth Jogger meet. The shirtless male driver with tattoos and pierced body parts that was driving puts on his brakes and comes to a stop.

He gets out of the car, screaming, "Oh shit, I hit something." He does not go looking for whatever he hit; he looks at the front of his car. "Ah damn, the boss is going to kill me!"

A short distance away, he hears a whispery voice call, "Help me." He follows the voice a distance and finds a man calling out in his dying breath. The driver throws up and runs back to his car and drives away, screaming, "This is not happening, man! This is not happening, man!"

He puts the gas pedal to the floor and pushes the nitro button in an urge to put some distance between the dead Stealth Jogger and himself. The driver then sees a deer, and before he realizes he should slow down, BANG! and a splat of blood over the windshield! He jerks from side to side trying to gain control of the car, my guess cursing all the way. Sliding into a ditch, he comes to a stop.

He banged his nose on the steering wheel and begins to bleed profusely. He can't open the door, so he rolls down the window and crawls out. Looking over the vehicle, he tries to see fire or smoke. He then crawls back into the car and retrieves a cell phone and a bandanna.

After he tears off a piece and shoves it up his nose to try and stop the bleeding, he wipes his face with the other half of the blood-soaked bandanna and tosses it out the window. Then crawling out of the car, cursing profanity left and right, he checks the cargo in the trunk. The door is still closed tight. He gets on the cell phone, and with one hand holds his nose, with the other makes the call, "Boss, we have a problem."

***

Before midnight, I try but can't get any rest, excited about tomorrow. I change my clothes, put on sweats, and find a basketball in Jamie's garage and get out of the house, and I just start walking the streets in the dark. It looks like a Norman Rockwell picture, just lit by streetlamps and the flicker of stars. The sound of crickets fills the night. I think I can manage walking out after midnight in my hometown; I do it all the time in Chicago.

This is where my old house used to be. Now it is Howard's Used Cars and Service. Oh, I already told you that. An ice cream stand manager is closing down his shop. I wonder if I can still get a cone, so I walk over. "Are you still open? I wonder if I could get a cone."

The manager says, "Oh there was a late double feature at the theater. I guess I can make up a cone for you. What do you like?"

"Chocolate dipped in chocolate would be great."

The manager looks at my hand and notices my ring. "You a Marine?"

"Yes, sir I was. Now I am a detective in Chicago."

He smiles, saying, "Retired Navy man."

As he prepares my cone, I ask, "Do you know anything about that Trans Am across the street?"

"Here is your cone. Ah yeah, it looks nice. I went over it with a magnet, and a lot of it is fiberglass."

I pass him the money and say, "Keep the change."

Other than that, it is a great car. I look to the other side of the street. A tow truck at Howard's Garage starts up and heads east of town. Something must have happened. The manager says, "Strange things happen in this little town."

I shake my head and wonder what is going on. Sometimes I get a gut feeling; cop instincts, you might call it.

As I walk to the park I remember the house that used to be where Howard's Garage is now. It was a big old red brick house with enough bedrooms that the Faraday family of seven kids and two parents were, at most, two kids to a bedroom. Plus a couple guest rooms for Grandpa and Grandma Faraday, who lived with the family and died in that house before I was born. That is not including three bathrooms, a huge dining room, den, and library, and a good-sized basement and backyard.

In 1944 Marcus and Maxine Faraday, my parents, were married. I am told they were a happy couple. Marcus was twenty-one and worked at the Cavanaugh City Bank. My mother was talented and gifted for her age, and she raced through school and college, and by age nineteen she was teaching school and married that year. By 1945, Connie, my oldest sister, was born. Let's see then. Marcus, Jr., my oldest brother, was born in '46. Keith was born in '47. Penelope was born in '50. Rachel was born in '52. Webster was born in '53. Then last, but not least, Corey Faraday was born in '54, the seventh child of the Faraday clan.

According to my older brothers and sisters, everything was great till I came along.

Wait, I take that back. Rachel calls me every now and again and asks, "How is my baby brother doing?"

She was pretty cool to be around till she left for college. Connie married a Lutheran minister in '75 and also moved to Illinois. Corey is a captain in the New York P.D. I left the CIA when he got shot, but that is a story for later. We get along pretty good now. It is amazing what a near-death experience can do for a brotherly relationship.

I was born in '64, with my father lovingly calling me *the accident*. One by one, they all left for college, leaving fewer reasons why Marcus Faraday should show himself sociable around me. I am not saying he beat me much, because I did compare my woes with my friends. When we would go on family outings, that was the only time he would say, "Come here, son. Why don't you get your father a . . .? In other words we were on a first-name basis: Come here, Max, go there, Max, and get out of my way, Max.

The chocolate ice cream cone was the best I have had in a long time. Real ice cream, none of that watered-down stuff. I lick my lips and know it was worth it. I wonder if I could get some real milk from Big Paul's dairy farm. The park is lit up. I dribble around to get the feel of the court. Nice, I like the feel, and when I shoot it goes in. I shout, "Two points!"

Then sheepishly I look around, remembering it is after midnight. People are sleeping. A dog barks. A man shouts, "Shut up!"

A voice from my past asks, "Can I play?"

"Connie, is that you?"

"Max! It is so good to see you, baby!" With tears of joy, she gives me a big hug and kiss! Connie Mack was, as far as I know, the first African American to go through the Cavanaugh City School System. Connie's father was an engineer, moved, or was relocated to C.C. Industries Cavanaugh City Division. Her middle class family that must have thought Cavanaugh City was Michigan's version of Mayberry. Her mother is an accomplished pianist and has recorded classical and religious music. When she was not on tour, she taught piano after school and played piano at the local Baptist church.

I yell to Connie, "Not bad for girls' all state! Three points!"

"Not bad for a run of the mill high school MVP! Three Points!" she shouts, then she says, "I was modeling in Paris. Three points!"

"What are you doing now?" I ask her.

Connie replies, "I missed the hoop, damn! I am the women's high school basketball coach for Cavanaugh City."

"You're kidding," I say.

"No, I love it here. I taught in Detroit and hated it," she continues. "One weekend, me and my husband visited my parents and liked what we saw and moved up here."

I ask, "You are married?"

She replies, "Don't look so shocked. Three points."

Some kids come onto the basketball court and say, "Hey, you mind? We'd like to play here."

"Yeah, but aren't you a little young to be up this late?" Connie says. "Boys, you don't know who you are messing with here. How much you got?"

One kid pulls out a wad of ones with a rubber band around it and says, "Thirty."

"All right," Connie replies. "Me and Max against you. First to reach thirty gets the court and the wad."

"Deal," the kid says.

"And if you keep mouthing off, you might also get my foot up your—" Connie adds.

Holding Connie back, I say, "You get a fifty."

As we play, a Carter County police cruiser's lights come on, and one of the biggest African Americans I have ever seen gets out of the car and barks, "You boys! I told you, NO playing basketball all night. You're disturbing the peace! And Connie! What are you doing?"

"Baby, I'm playing basketball with my old friend, Max. What do you think I'm doing?"

"Would you people shut up, *I'm trying to get some sleep!*" sounds from an apartment window nearby and draws laughter from the late-night street-ball players on the court.

Later, as I walk back to Jamie's, the Howard's Garage truck comes back into town.

The car it is towing is banged up pretty bad in the front, and the windshield is cracked with blood on it. The truck does not pull into the garage and keeps going out of town.

I wonder where the city police are. They should arrest them for not having their lights on.

I find a pay phone and look up the number and call the police. "Yes, I would like to make a report. My name is Max Faraday."

"Okay, Mr. Faraday, we will look into it. Thank you."

As I start walking back to Jamie's, something in my head says something just ain't right.

Chapter Two

My So-called Dysfunctional Youth

In '72 I was eight, and while I was in second grade my older brother Corey left for college only to come back to visit. All the brothers and sisters were more than welcome to visit. We do throw a mean Christmas and Fourth of July here in Cavanaugh City.

Fourth of July is parades and fireworks. Christmas is colorful blinking lights, Jesus in the manger, Santa Claus, elves, the reindeer—the works. A regular Christmas wonderland. Heck, Mom had kept their bedrooms a shrine or museum to their achievements for when and if they return. I know, I lived in Corey's room till I left. They could talk about the good years.

In 1975 I was eleven and in the fifth grade when a new kid came into my life.

His name was Steve; he never told me his last name. At the time, the family court thought it best to try and give him a fresh start in a new life. As the story went, Steve and his dad were bank robbers. At age nine, he was already driving the getaway car. Somewhere in between then and age eleven, he was caught, and his dad got away.

He was placed in a foster home. Mr. and Mrs. Pearson took him in, and in time he became a big brother for their daughter Wendy and their other foster kids. In school he was making up for lost time. I mean, he was not getting an education playing Butch Cassidy and the Sundance Kid with his dad.

After I was asked by my mom to help get him up to speed, Steve and I became quick friends. Steve had a way with numbers; being a former bank robber, he must have counted the money I guess. Math was no problem. He also could read and write and comprehend a few grades above where the school placed him. I think it helped keep him on the honor roll. He could also size a person up. He was playing poker with high school kids and winning, but it finally caught up with him. One high school senior was a poor loser and wanted his money back. He had just lost all his money, and as Steve was getting up to leave, the senior realized he was beaten by a kid. "Come back here, kid, I want my money back!"

The chase was on! As the senior was running after Steve, a few of his friends were helping him corner Steve in an alley.

Wendy found me and told me some seniors were after Steve. I yelled back to her as I ran to Steve's aid, "I told him he should not be playing with seniors!"

Wendy pleaded, "Help him, Max!"

As I went to help Steve, she went to get Mr. Pearson. By the time I got there, the senior was throwing Steve up against the wall, knocking him around. I tried to get the guy to let him go. "Leave him alone," I shouted!

"Get out of here, you little bastard!"

I knocked him and his partner upside the face and gave them a good fight, then their size and weight of a tag team wrestler got the best of me. They tossed me aside like I was nothing, and down on the ground I went. I looked up from the ground, and Steve was receiving gut punches, and the senior reached in his pocket and got his money back.

By the time Mr. Pearson and Wendy got there, Steve was bloody nosed and bruised.

Me, I was just bruised. Mr. Pearson was silent; silence speaks volumes. We brought him home and he cleaned Steve up and bandaged him, and Mr. Pearson said, "I am very disappointed in you, Steve. It is dangerous what you did."

Steve whispered a sheepish, "I was just trying to help." "By getting you killed?" I and Mr. Pearson both murmured.

He got off the stool in the bathroom and came back with a shoebox full of ones and fives and a few twenties and a lot of change. Mr. Pearson eyes go wide, and he asks, "Did you steal this?"

"No, I won it. Here, you can have it. I heard you and Mrs. Pearson say you needed money because you were laid off at the factory."

"We will get by, Steve. We can't gamble in order to make money."

Steve counters with, "Churches play Bingo. We might not be a church, but we need charity."

Mr. Pearson counters, "No, we are a family, and you can call me Dad, Steve. You call Mrs. Pearson Mom."

Steve answers, "I have a dad, Mr. Pearson. He might not be a saint like you, but he is my dad. I don't have a mom, so it is okay to call Mrs. Pearson Mom."

Mrs. Pearson came into the bathroom. She had overheard the conversation, and tears trickled down her cheek, now that she knew why Steve had opened his heart and called her Mom.

Mr. Pearson asked, "So what are we going to do, Steve? Honestly, we do need the money, but can you promise never to gamble again?" After pause, he says, "Please, not in this house. Do you know that gambling is wrong?

"Yes," Steve answers.

Mr. Pearson shrugs his shoulders. "Well, I guess that will have to do for now."

The Pearsons took the money that they really did need. Mrs. Pearson thanked Steve by whispering," This is a gift from God, and you are a gift from God." Then she kissed him on the cheek.

Steve never gambled inside their house. As for gambling outside of their house, that is another story.

Monopoly was Steve's game; he always won at it. He liked the idea of starting out even or equally because in real life it was never equal. The high school champ from the Monopoly club played him and it took a week of on and off play.

"Did I mention Marcus was a poor loser?"

It was 4:00 p.m., raining cats and dogs outside. We were setting up the game at my house, and the TV went up, and Marcus had the day off and was bored. Mom had the car and was out doing PTA or something, and my father Marcus was left to watch me.

"What are you doing?" Marcus asks.

I reply, "Monopoly. Steve is going to beat us again, but it is something to do."

Marcus asks, "Mind if I play?"

Steve says with confidence, "If you don't mind losing."

Around six Mom came home and started dinner. Wendy is out, bankrupt. Marcus laughs, and Wendy, holding back tears, asks, "Do you treat your bank customers this way?"

We keep playing through dinner, and Jamie is out by eight. Churchill is called home by nine and makes a few deals with Marcus. I think he got a real microscope out of it. Marcus calls Mr. Pearson, asking if Steve can spend the night. It's a Friday, so he will have to come home and get a change of clothes. When he is gone, Mom and I watch the table. Marcus hovers like a vulture, ready to steal a hotel or move a game piece.

By midnight Mom says that was enough and to go to bed.

Saturday morning Marcus wakes us up at six. I don't think he slept that night.

He had the coffee pitcher and cigars to wake him up. By noon, Mom woke up to see us playing. Marcus kept his legs together because he did not trust us to be left alone with the game. When he sees Mom, he shouts, "Maxine, watch the table. I have to go!"

Marcus comes back with a change of clothes. We chuckle to ourselves, thinking he had an accident.

About five that afternoon I fold. Whatever I owned is now Marcus's and Steve's.

About six that night, Marcus sneaks alcoholic drinks in his Coca-Cola.

By ten o'clock, it becomes evident Marcus is drunk.

Ten forty-five. "You damn bastard foster kid, get out of my house!"

In shock, Steve asks, "What?!"

"You heard me, get out of my house! Before you steal something, you bastard!"

I yell, "Steve, get out of here!"

Mom gets up. "I will not have you—"

Marcus slaps Mom across the face! "Don't talk back to me, woman! As for you, you little bastard," and he slaps my face! "Don't you ever let him back in this house ever again, you hear me!"

Marcus kicks the table over, breaking his toe in the process and smashes the table lamp! Cursing a blue streak at the pain! Electrical sparks start a fire!

Mom goes to put it out! She could do it with her tears by now. Marcus picks her up, tosses her around, yelling, "OUT OF MY WAY, BITCH!" He smothers the fire with the tablecloth.

He is left alone in his anger. We go for our hiding places. Marcus comes upstairs, and I am in my closet. I have it locked from the inside. He comes into my room and looks at my shelf and asks where my model airplane is. I call out from inside the closet, "Steve helped me build it and asked if he could have it for a week."

Marcus yells, "Don't you ever give that son of a bitch anything!"

Marcus storms out of the house and gets in the car and drives off. In the silence, I can hear Mom crying in the closet on the other side of the wall.

I was not big enough at that time to defend her against Marcus, but I could put a lock on the inside of her closet door.

Marcus composed himself when he got to the Pearson's home. "Max loaned your son something, and I have come to get it back."

Mrs. Pearson says, "Fine. I will get Steve and we will see about this."

Marcus enters the house and goes upstairs. "That is breaking and entering home invasion." Mrs. Pearson goes to the garage where Mr. Pearson and Steve are talking. "He said what? He called you what! Honey, Mr. Faraday is here and—"

Marcus walks down the stairs with the model, and Steve sees him with it and runs after him, calling out, "Hey, you can't have that! It is mine!"

Marcus strikes Steve, and he tumbles down a few stairs. Mr. Pearson can't run; he lost his leg in Vietnam, and Wendy is and will be his only biological daughter because the explosion that took his leg and also took his ability to father children.

Marcus blurts out in rage, "You son of a bitch, you broke the damn model. And you, you broken-down baby killer, what are you going to do?!"

I ran to Steve's house to warn him that Marcus might be coming. By the time I get there, Mr. Pearson was beating the crap out of Marcus! Marcus was trying to crawl out the door, and Mr. Pearson was on the floor punching him, and when his artificial leg came off, he grabbed it and started whacking Marcus with it! Jamie's dad, Mr. Scott, tried to get Mr. Pearson off Marcus, but once Mr. Pearson started swinging his artificial leg around, Mr. Scott gave up trying. Rabbi Hyman, the Pearson's next-door neighbor, is trying to shelter Mrs. Pearson from the violence and console her in her weeping.

Police sirens! Mr. Pearson yells to a young rookie officer Indigo McGraw, "Lock his ass UP!"

The young junior officer McGraw asks what the charges are.

Mr. Pearson yells, "Breaking and entering! Assault! Drunk and disorderly! Theft!"

And Steve yells, "And being a jackass!"

Mr. Pearson looks at Steve, and in agreement we all yell, "AND BEING A JACKASS!"

Mr. Scott says to Mr. Pearson, "I have to go and tell Maxine we will be praying for her and Max." As he leaves he sees me just standing around and watching things happen. He reaches down to me and hugs me and whispers gently, "We will be praying for you."

As the ambulance arrives, so does thirty-five-year-old just out of the seminary Father Michaels. As they bandage Marcus and strap him to the stretcher, he sees the good father and whispers with a broken jaw and missing teeth and an eye swelled shut, "Forgive me, Father, for I have sinned."

The good father is too angered to cry and too damn disappointed to care.

The good father waves him away in disgust. "Just get out of my face! I don't want to see you anymore."

Mr. Pearson hangs his head, "This is not good. This was not a good example for the kids."

Police Officer McGraw comes by and asks, "How are you doing, Mr. Pearson?"

He asks, "Aren't you going to arrest me?

The cop says, "Hell no. The bastard broke into your house; you were just defending yourself. Heck, you could have shot him in your own house."

Mr. Cooper asks, "Do you want to bring him back into the house? I know where he keeps his gun."

The officer thinks about it for a moment. "Well, he did force an auction on my daddy's farm equipment, The son of a . . . no, once they make it to the ambulance, the kill or maim option goes out the window."

Father Michaels adds, "There will be no killing or maiming around here. Max, run home, your mother is worried about you."

I add a, "But," but with a stern, staring look that only a priest can give, he says, "But nothing, go home."

I left but I didn't go home, just yet.

Mrs. Pearson says, "I'll be taking Steve to the emergency room, just to make sure nothing is broken."

Steve comments, "Mom, I think it just a sprain."

"Listen to your mother, Steve," Father Michaels tells him.

Father Michaels then bends down and tends to Mr. Pearson's artificial leg and asks, "How did you get the bend in your leg?"

Mr. Cooper, Jason's dad, says, "Marcus's head, would be my guess."

I am hiding quietly in the bushes looking through the window, and I just smile.

Mr. Pearson asks Father Michaels, "You must know about artificial legs, right?"

The good father places his foot on the metal pipe to apply pressure to straighten it, explaining, "I worked at a VA hospital after Vietnam and then heeded the call to the ministry."

Mr. Pearson asks, "Vietnam, what did you do?"

The priest replies, "Sniper recon, things I still do not wish to talk about. You?"

"Army Corps of Engineers, land mine got my leg."

Jason's dad, Mr. Cooper, says, "Flat feet 4-F. I went to Woodstock and went to college."

The two give him dirty looks.

Rabbi Hyman comes by, asking, "What happened, neighbor? I heard the commotion. I open the door, and you are beating Faraday to a pulp on the floor."

Mr. Pearson hangs his head, saying, "Marcus was drunk and came and broke into my house. Slapped up Steve, and we got into a fight. Thanks for consoling my wife."

The rabbi places his hand on his neighbor's shoulder. "Women should not see such things, and Marcus should not have broken into a man's home looking to pick a fight. Oh, poor Max, he is such a good boy. I'll keep him and his mother in my prayers."

Father Michaels adds, "I have been holding it back. I am going to suggest to Maxine to get a divorce."

Rabbi Hyman rubs his beard and adds, "About time."

Father Michaels asks, "I beg your pardon?"

"This is a small town, young father; everyone knows that Marcus—"

"That may be, but Jesus taught us forgiveness."

The rabbi reaffirms, "Yes, that may be, but God taught us to repent and atonement. Without that, what good is free forgiveness?"

Father Michaels hangs his head.

Mr. Cooper, Jason's dad, says, "Father, I am not Catholic, but isn't faith without works dead? By faith, Marcus might think he is forgiven, but without working out his belief, he just stays the same jerk. It was his job to repent and find atonement."

In astonishment at the wisdom Mr. Cooper just gave, Mr. Pearson says, "I have to agree."

A deep sigh comes from Father Michaels. "I believe God has brought us together in this moment. Marcus has failed as a father, and Max needs a fatherly figure. I can't do it alone."

Jason's dad, Mr. Cooper, says, "He spends enough time at my home. I might as well adopt him outright."

Mr. Pearson adds, "Same here, he is a good kid."

Rabbi Hyman adds, "I love this. A priest, a rabbi … are any of you Baptist?"

Mr. Pearson says, "No, we are United Brethren in Christ."

The rabbi says, "A good joke does not work without a Baptist. But this is not a joke, so I am in. By the way, Maxine is going to need a good lawyer for the divorce." Rabbi Hyman hands over a card. "He is the best. Tell her I sent him."

The next day was Sunday. The sermon was on fathers, and I had a hard time getting into the sermon. The goodness and wholesomeness of fathers is hard to agree with when your own experience is jaded by your personal history. When it is time to leave, I shake the pastor's hand, not looking directly at him, and I head out to the Pearson's van.

The pastor asked Mr. Pearson what the problem was, and Mr. Pearson gave the details.

The pastor gave up his time to shake hands with his congregation to come out and talk to me. "So Max, I hear you had a rough time last night."

I look at him straight in the face, saying, "You could say that."

His smile turns to a frown when he sees my bruise where Marcus slapped me last night. "Do you mind if I take you home today so we can talk?"

I shrug my shoulders and say, "Why not?"

In the pastor's car I ask why he said that Jesus knows what we are feeling.

He replied, "Because he does. How? He is God. He was also a man for a time, Max, fully man and fully God."

I ask, "Then why does he let it happen?"

The pastor lowers his head for a moment and says, "Because he trusts you with the pain. In many ways, Max, I know what you are going through, because I went through it with my father when I was about your age. But you are a United Brethren. Just because I am a United Brethren minister, and our laws do not allow us to drink, but that does not mean I can't relate. Besides, I was brought up in another Christian faith and doctrine, and my father also drank and beat me and my mother, brothers, and sister."

I ask, "How did you do it?"

He replied, "My father died in a car accident in my early teens. In many ways, I had adopted other fathers. The experience has helped me be able to help others. And I hope help you."

I ask, "Who gave God the right to allow people like Marcus and your dad to screw around with our lives."

The pastor answered, "People like Marcus and my dad have a free will to do so. God loves us so much that we don't have to stay screwed up, Max. Through our pain and difficulties, God can reshape our life into something beautiful. But we have to ask him. You have asked the

Lord into your heart and to take away your sins. Have you asked him in your heart, Max?"

I answer yes.

"Then ask Jesus to take away your pain and anger towards Marcus, your father. Because it will only destroy you if you keep it. You are going to have a life, and you can't spend a minute hating him. When you come through this, you will be there for others, as others have been there for you."

The pastor drove me home and walked me to my door. My mom is there with sunglasses.

"Hello, Mrs. Faraday, I just wanted to let you know my wife and I will be praying for you. I will not share it with anyone unless you wish it."

Mom says, "Thank you, Pastor."

"As I was telling Max, I went through similar experiences with my father. If you have need of anyone to talk to, my mother counsels people in need," and he passes a telephone number to her. "See you next Sunday, Max."

***

In 1978 I started an investigation into drug dealing at my school and found that Jack Hammer, a classmate of my big brother Jake Hammer, to be the ringleader of the gang. I collected the evidence and passed it to the Cavanaugh City Police.

Before they could arrest the leader and the crew, Jack's big brother Jake left town. Or so we thought. I got the cold shoulder from Jack and verbal threats.

One day Jake's crew, minus Jake, shows up during recess. Although I put up a fight, I got seriously beat up. At the same time, Jake, who we thought left town, was able to sneak onto school grounds. Jake was safely watching the fight from the third-story greenhouse room. When the fight was over, he left. Big Paul Chapel saw him on floor and beat him up by punching and knocking him down the stairs. Paul had his own reasons for hating Jake; two or three days before, a young farmer friend Tommy had an accident that killed him. The grief almost killed the boy's father. When the family went through his things, they found the drugs. Paul helped me to put two and two together. I was in the hospital for weeks. I missed my piano recital and so many days from school that I almost had to take eighth grade over again.

Uncle Sherman and my mom nursed me back to health. I kept the information private that Jack was in on the pounding. Revenge maybe?

I was taught forgiveness and second chances. In time, I let Jack into my circle of friends.

***

Dale Chapel was a Vietnam Air Force pilot and local hero. His wife, Faith, died of a rare bone cancer. My mom and Faith had been friends for years. In the good years, we used to take vacations together. They had only one daughter, Kathy, who was born with scoliosis and walked with braces and crutches. We had been in the same class since kindergarten.

Faith fought it hard, and through the worst of it, Kathy stayed with us till the end.

Dale ran the Cavanaugh City Chapel Air Strip, known as Chapel Air. Besides being an ace, he was a heck of a mechanic. After school sometimes, Paul Chapel, his nephew, and I would go there and help him repair all sorts of aircraft. I wanted to be a mechanic for the Marines, and Paul wanted to join the Air Force. I can honestly say I worked a lot of frustrations out trying to figure out how to fix stuff in general. I think in a way Dale adopted me as a son he never had. He would rib me about wanting to join the Marines.

Whenever we would play lost or Marco Polo in the tool or parts shed, I would call out Marines! He would call out Air Force! Dale took me under his wing and taught me how to fly. So when I received my learner's permit for driving a car, I also had a pilot's license.

***

In 1980 I was sixteen, and Marcus Faraday Sr., who was at this time *not* my father, got shot and killed while working at Carter City Bank. A Max Faraday quote, "Couldn't happen to a nicer guy."

26

I wasn't supposed to, but I went to the trial. When the murderer bank robber started laughing how Marcus just stood there in shock and peed his pants, "Bang! The son of a bitch went down!" Judge Tailor yelled, "Order in the court!"

I had nothing in me. Not even a single tear.

In the will, Mom received enough money to keep the house free and clear.

Not much left over for me on paper, but the other kids made out pretty good.

One thing about Marcus Faraday, he knew how to manage his money.

A penny saved is a penny earned. Now I like Ben Franklin's saying and all, but it was a part of Marcus's Holy Trinity. For him it was a statue of Mother Mary on the window: "A Penny Saved is a Penny Earned," on the doorpost, and a Jesus crucifix on the wall. Between Mary and Jesus, I think they were shaking their heads most of the time.

***

The gambling habit started pretty much during my senior year in high school, back in '82. Pool, poker, dice—I played the odds. It almost cost me my high school diploma. Odd jobs, basketball, and shop class helped me keep out of trouble most of the time. After high school graduation, I joined the Marines and picked up the gambling bug again. When I won, I sent my winnings to my rabbi, Papa Abba Hyman.

I never really cared for managing money, so I let Papa Abba tend to that for me.

When I lost, I was broke and chalked it up to education. Sore losers that wanted a fight usually walked away walking funny.

Chapter Three

Welcome to the Marines and the World of Black Operations

I was sat down by my commanding officer. Behind him in the shadows were several higher-ranking officers, or suits, and at least one or two spooks. My CO told me, "Max, I have been looking at your record. You are a fine mechanic, a good Marine, and you could be great, but your gambling is going to get you in a world of hurt someday. I want you to stop. By the way, Max, have you ever thought of losing your glasses or your contacts?"

I ask, "What do you mean, sir?"

"I have been looking over your records. With your glasses, you are an expert marksman, and I have knowledge of an eye operation that could eliminate your need for glasses. It is very new, and the results are promising."

"Yes, sir. I would be very interested."

"Your uncle has also informed me that you would like to look into Special Operations."

An officer behind my CO, who I would later learn to be a CIA agent spook named Titus, asks in Russian, "How did you learn to speak Russian?"

I answer back in Russian, "With my Catholic priest Father Michaels, who wanted to be called to the ministry in Russia and learned the language in hopes of going there someday. I asked him to teach me, and he did, and I like reading *War and Peace* in the original tongue."

Another spoke in Hebrew, "And it says you can speak and read in Hebrew."

I answer, "The Torah Bible is more than just religion, it is where stories begin. Our whole culture is rooted in Bible references. The Book of Joshua is taught as military tactics. I have a rabbi friend that I call Abba Father."

"You speak French?

"I have a good friend, Big Paul, who used to get French comic books from his grandma in France. He shared them with me, and before long I learned the language for myself."

"It says here you speak Aramaic?"

I speak in Aramaic, "I worked at a grocery store, and one of the workers used to be an Iraqi citizen. He left with his family and is now working toward his citizenship. His son told me he wants to join the Marines like me."

"You are the kind of recruit we are looking for in the CIA."

My CO adds, "Take care of your gambling, and I can help make it happen, Max."

The CIA agent adds, "You take care of your gambling, and we will consider you."

I was scheduled to begin Special Operations Training, and my CO, I liked and respected him. If he did not like me gambling he could halt my training, perfect record or not. I tried cold turkey, and I had a desire I needed to fill. Gambling filled that need. I never hit rock bottom, so I could not justify the need to quit. So I was sent to a twelve-step gambling program and showed everyone what a good actor I could be, then I was cleared, and I put my energy into my training. I excelled at everything they put me through. When they asked for more I gave them more. And as for my eyes, after preliminary Special Training I got the eye operation.

Now I have better than twenty-twenty vision.

***

In 1984 my mom turned sixty-seven and married Dale Chapel. It was about time; they had been holding each other up as friends since Dale's first wife, Faith, died. The problem was, I couldn't get time off for the wedding. Dale's daughter Kathy understood and sent a letter saying welcome to the family.

***

In 1988 I was twenty-four, and I received the call that my mother had died of a heart attack. Her poor health was because of her lifelong smoking habit. The funeral was different; it was like two different families and only one mother. As I told you, Marcus and my mother Maxine Faraday were married back in '44. Connie, my oldest sister, was born in 1945. Corey, my youngest older brother, was born the seventh child in 1954, and I was born in 1964, so there was ten-year difference between us. The ones before me had a family history all their own, and by the time I came around, most of them were in college. When Marcus and Maxine Faraday divorced, they went their separate ways. The Chapels were here for me. Paul was home from the Air Force and gave me a bear hug and whispered, "How you doing, cousin?"

It was kind of strange, and in a good way life goes on. My old high school friends were either married or making plans or they were holding hands and kissing. Me, I was alone, unless you could say I was married to the Marine Corps and having an affair with CIA Black Ops. After the funeral, I went back to training Special Forces and Black Ops.

***

Before the birth of Maggie Maxine Chapel, Big Paul calls me up. "Max, I need to call in a favor."

"What is it?"

"The Air Force won't let me off for the birth of my next kid."

"Let's see, what are you up to, Paul junior, Pete junior (after Paul's good friend, Pete Cortez) . . . Any chance you could name your next kid after me?"

Paul replies, "No, Marcy says it is going to be a girl, and she likes Maggie."

"Well, how about Maggie Max Chapel? I'll settle for a middle name."

"You would, ha. I'll ask Marcy and see what she thinks. Anyway, the Air Force won't give me time to go home and be with her. I am too valuable, I guess. Any chance you could get a week or two off and help out?"

"Gee, Paul, I would love to, but I can't. I'm on call at a moment's notice unless it is a death in the family or something; all I can do is ask."

So I talk to my commanding officer. "Sir, I wondered if I could get some time off?"

He asks, "To do what, Max?"

"I have a friend in the Air Force, a mechanic. His wife is about to have a baby. The Air Force won't give him leave to be there for the birth. He wondered if I could take time off and be his substitute for him."

The CO says, "Max, sit down. You are the best. The instructors are amazed at your skills. You work hard. You give it all you have. Nobody questions the fact you give 100 percent. So why are you coming to me asking the impossible?"

"Because Paul is family, sir, and I thought it would not hurt to ask."

My CO scratches his chin. "Your records tell me you played poker and had to give it up as part of your training."

"Yes, it was viewed as a weakness and I should quit."

The CO's fist hits the desk. "Bull crap, I can't trust a man who won't play poker. How good are you, Marine?

I ask, "Sir, how good are you? Do you have a deck of cards?"

The CO gets out a deck. "Now show me the cards. I'll commit them to memory. Now display the cards facedown."

As he does, I begin to name the cards and turn them over. A smile comes over his face and he says, "You can count cards?"

"To some degree, yes. My buddy Steve and I went to Vegas in high school and—"

The CO stops me and says, "I play with some guys on the base. I lost big time last month. If I bring you in, and you help me get some payback, I'll get you two weeks off."

For two weeks, I was a Chapel; I milked cows, drove Marcy to the doctor's, worked on equipment, and loved every minute of it.

"Max, it is time!"

I carry Marcy to the pickup. I have everything, and we are on our way to the hospital. Marcy even had me train with her in natural childbirth classes. That was a waste of time; Marcy had a C-section.

I shed tears of joy as I hold this precious life in my hands. "Marcy, you were right; it's a girl!"

Maggie Maxine Chapel is born. My little Marine. I send her Marine T-shirts and other memorabilia. Paul gets a good chuckle out of it, him being in the Air Force and all.

***

It's 1989. I can't go into too much detail about that, so just use your imagination, throw in a lot of dead bodies, explosions, gunfire, and files stamped TOP SECRET NATIONAL SECURITY. Let's just put it this way. It is hard to get people to invest in the stock market or buy a new car if they are too busy buying shotguns and canned goods, screaming it is The END OF THE WORLD! If the world or the average guy on the street knew what really went on, they would be yelling, it is all over and we haven't got a prayer!

And those files stamped TOP SECRET NATIONAL SECURITY and the fact nobody knows what is going on in the world keeps the world turning in the so-called great scheme of things. The truth is, the purpose of the military is to kill people and break things. I do that very well. That is how I got the code name Selah, meaning pause, stop, and think about it. Do you really want to die?

Gone to Russia. Can't talk about it. Avenge my death if I don't come back. It was a dark and stormy night; cliché as it might sound, that is what it was. Thunder and lightning. The rain was coming down so heavy that it could drown turkeys. All they would have to do is look up and open their mouths in shock. Shakespeare, eat your heart out.

I have to be vague in this story because, well, we both want to live to see tomorrow.

I think you can figure it out. Me, I am trying to figure this time in my life's history as well.

It is like a mystery that I just can't fathom what it all means, so I replay it in my mind from time to time. We are dressed in Russian military uniforms complete with perfect fake papers and documents. "When in Rome."

My team leader Jackson is on point. We just went through the military base checkpoint.

We are meeting with a general. My final meeting with him and his son you already read.

Agent Graves leads this mission. The head spook, if you will. Graves is a tall, thin white male who you might think was an undertaker, and you would not be too far wrong. The stench of death and deception reek all over him. I guess I am thankful he is on our side. He points to Jackson and says that is where we will meet him.

"A warehouse is always a warehouse." Graves goes to the door, knocks, gives the password, and we enter. A makeshift barrel stove heats this dark corner of the building.

The general speaks in Russian. Graves politely says he does not speak Russian and points to me as his interpreter. The general goes over the terms, and I translate, holding in my disgust for him. Money is handed over, and the general's expression says it all.

He is at ease with talking with me. I was told my Russian accent was good, when you put it all to the test. The general takes a moment and asks questions about me. "Who are you?" he asks. That's the nice thing about all my training, and multiple fake identities come in handy. I have a Russian identity that I am carrying, a passport that should get me home if the worst-case scenario should happen. I give the name and smile.

"What are you doing with this CIA, Russian swearword man?"

He thinks I am Russian, so I play along. I tell the general I am like him; I am trying to make a little money.

"Where were you born?"

I tell him the history about my family that a CIA intelligence guy made up. And I pray to God that he will forgive me for telling a string of lies.

The when and how, maybe I'll go into greater detail some other day.

He hands over documents to Graves and adds that we will place the sum we agreed to in his brother's account in America. After I translate, Graves nods his head. More documents are provided. Graves asks the secondary request about the location of our pilot who crashed less than a week ago. This inquiry makes the general nervous even before I translate it. The general says in English, "That information will cost you."

Graves says to name it, and I am waved away from the table.

I walk over to Jackson. He and the others are watching the windows. I whisper to him, "I can't believe we trust this guy."

Jackson chuckles, "Who, the general or Graves?"

"Both."

Jackson adds, "In our line of work, I have learned you can never trust a traitor. After you get what you want or need from them, it is best to terminate. Because if you give them the chance, they will terminate you." Prophetic words if I ever heard them.

Graves gets up from the table. The two shake hands, and then Graves walks toward us whispering, "This information must get to the sub tonight." Then Graves hands over a map of a building. "And I would like to bring along an extra passenger."

Jackson's eyes go wide and he whispers, "He is here in the city?"

I murmur, "This is too tempting; it feels like a setup."

Graves adds, "You will be taking this mission. The pilot has been beaten and tortured and has not talked. He has valuable information in his head, and the Soviet Union's KGB will do all it can to get it out of him. If you can't get him out alive, someone has to put a bullet in him before he talks. Understood."

Now you have an idea why I save a bullet.

Jackson adds, "Yes, sir. We will have surprise on our side."

Graves orders, "Then get out of here. You have less than six hours to plan an escape and get the pilot on the sub."

No one has to say it; we just know it—or else.

As Jackson and the boys load the car with documents, Graves pulls me to the side, saying, "I am very proud of you, Faraday. We could not have pulled this off without you."

I add, "Jackson said in our line of work you can never trust a traitor. After you get what you want or need from them, it is best to terminate, because when or if you give them the chance, they will terminate you."

Graves nods, saying, "Agent Jackson speaks of truth. Tell you what, if the good general becomes a threat and I have the power, I'll have you terminate him."

"Gee, Graves, I feel all warm and fuzzy inside, thanks." Well, on some things Graves can keep his promises.

Then he places something to my ear. A sound goes off, and then Jackson yells, "Come on!"

A sound, why can't I remember what that sound was? Why do I think it is important?

We leave in separate vehicles, and I go into the facility. I am told I can play the perfect Russian. The general gave us forged papers to get me in. Getting out?

The Marines taught me never leave anyone behind. Believe it or not, we are one big dysfunctional family. CIA argues with the FBI, and we all argue with locals on jurisdiction. Hell yeah, we argue and fight, but when one of our own falls, usually we stop fighting and sit up and take notice. This pilot is like a big brother that I have never met. If fortunes favor the lucky, after today we will never meet again.

The papers get me in, and I walk to his cell. A guard lets me in to take a look at him. They think I am in the Russian Air Force here to ask more questions. He has been beaten to a pulp. I check his vitals; they are weak but stable. I can say beaten to a pulp because I have seen the satellite footage of his plane coming down in Russia, and he was able to walk away from the crash. I whisper to him, "Big brother, little brother is going to get you out of here. Can you walk?"

With a broken jaw, he whispers back, "Broken legs, bag of marbles."

I also note a bullet hole in his side. It went clean through, and the bleeding stopped. I give him a syringe full of painkiller, and he is out. Sweet dreams.

There is not enough money that Graves could hand over to get him out.

CNN has not reported a missing pilot. Chances are they will never know.

If it didn't happen on the six or the eleven-o'clock news, then it didn't happen. After looking him over, I push a button on my wristwatch. Jackson and the others provide a disturbance; explosions go off! The guard grabs his revolver, turning for the door, and I grab his head, snapping his neck like a chicken bone. I grab his revolver and grab the pilot, lugging him over my shoulders. I am not a big guy, and he is a sack of potatoes.

I yell in Russian, "The Americans are here to get the pilot! We must get him out of here!"

You can never truly know what you can get done in confusion till it happens.

Everyone else is going for the explosion, leaving me and nappy boy staggering out of the building. When someone recognizes the pilot on my back, they begin to ask questions.

"Put him down!"

As I do, I reach for the revolver and shoot the one with the AK 47, grab the rifle, roll to the ground, spin, and fire at the ones that surround me. I am running on adrenaline or something. Broken glass from the surrounding offices shatter, with shards coming across my face and body like snowflakes in a blizzard and bullets flying from everywhere!

In all this confusion I can't miss. Besides the fact they are too damn close to begin with, I am moving too damn fast for them before they can take a shot. The last of them are dead.

Click! Out! I am out of ammo. Dead all around me! I double-check the pilot to see if he is still alive—still alive with no more bullet holes than he had when we left his cell.

A lone Russian is shouting obscenities that I care not to translate, wielding a knife, yelling, "Come on!" in Russian A long shard of glass is at my fingertips, and I fling it at him with the simplicity of throwing a paper airplane. He tosses his knife at me as my glass spear passes it in midair. Blood spurts from his skull between his eyes and he falls back. I catch his knife. A souvenir?

I grab grenades from a dead soldier and toss them down a door headed for the basement.

I pick up the pilot and head for the door. Jackson and the boys cover me as I carry the pilot. Explosion! Jackson yells, "What was that!"

I smile and say I threw grenades into the basement. They must have had weapons in storage down there. Shots are fired from above. I grab an AK-47 and fire at the snipers. They fall to the ground from the roof. Jackson yells, "Get in! Get in the car!" We burn rubber leaving the parking lot, and the building behind us explodes with a chain reaction.

As the tensions relax, high fives are given all around. I guess I am one of the boys now.

We get out of the city and meet Graves by the docks. A fishing boat takes us out to the ocean, a sub picks us up, and we are off to parts unknown.

***

I got drunk one night after returning from a successful mission that I can't go into.

Being the youngest on the team, I got drunk with the guys more than I should. Trying to fit in, I guess.

I must have gotten plastered, because I woke up with a tattoo on my left arm: *Selah*. I had time coming, so I drove back to Cavanaugh City, homesick I guess. It was late, and I went to the only place I could call home, Big Paul's Dairy Farm.

I pulled in the drive. It was way after midnight. The dogs didn't even bark; somehow the good dogs know who the good and the bad are. I walked into the house and crashed on the living room couch.

About four in the morning Paul wakes up and comes downstairs in the dark in his underwear. He sits down on the couch and fumbles around looking for the TV remote. When he accidentally places his hand on my throat, I snap into action. Rolling him onto the floor, I punch his jaw and almost break his neck in a choke hold. *FART!* OH God, that stinks! I loosen my grip because of the stench! *WHAM!* Paul hurls me against the wall! We just wrestle like we did when we were kids in grade school. Big Paul yells, "You know, Max, if this wasn't playing, I would think you were trying to kill me!"

The commotion wakes up the house, and Marcy and the kids come out of the woodwork.

By late morning, Paul had the farm chores done, and I and Marcy had a good laugh.

Paul asks, "So what brings you here in the middle of the night?"

My answer is, "I guess I was anointed by my teammates, and I got drunk, and they gave me a tattoo."

Paul puts on his glasses to get a better look. "SELAH? What does that mean?"

"It's my code name. Kind of like Dirty Harry, you know, the one who said, "Go ahead, make my day." Only mine is shorter, and it means *stop and think about it; do you really want to die?*"

"That sounds like a comic book character. How did you get that name?"

I smile and give Paul a wink, saying, "Sniper rifle, C-4, hand-to-hand combat. People die around me. What can I say?"

Marcy looks stunned. A big grin comes over Paul's face and he says, "That's my boy. Kicking ass and taking names, heartbreakers, and widow-makers. See, Marcy, we have a professional in the house. I knew taking you deer hunting with me would help you someday. So, when are you going to go over and kill Saddam?"

I state plainly that we don't do assassinations in the CIA. Paul and Marcy just laugh.

"Deniability. Oh, that is good. Next you are going to say you haven't been trying to get Castro!" Paul says.

"Listen, forget whatever I just said. It is for your own good."

Marcy asks what my clearance level is. Do I know about the UFOs? Or where are they keeping JFK's brain? I love them and the questions they give me, but what am I supposed to say?

"If you must know, what is left of JFK's brain is the secret head of the CIA. It was saved by little green men who got a ride to Dallas by Santa Claus." Silence … they did not think that was funny.

Marcy says, "Oh, now you are just making fun of us."

Paul adds, "Yeah, everybody knows the aliens at Area 51 are gray."

"And I thought you were our friend," Marcy adds pouting.

After lunch, Paul sits down with paper and pencil and starts drawing. I sit next to him, and he is drawing me in a body armor outfit with the name Selah at the top. He whispers, "What is missing?"

I say, "I like .45 pistols."

Paul draws leather pants, then adds .45 pistols and utility belts. Then he finishes with a black marker. My eyes bug out. This is perfect! So cool! I take it to Marcy, and she looks at it and says, "Paul, I think you have a winner here."

He asks, "What?"

"You have been submitting your artwork to Wild Tail Comics. Why not submit your own character?"

Paul crosses his arms, saying, "Because I would have a better chance going independent. Plus, I would be able to keep ownership of my character."

Then Paul looks at me and says *our* character. Marcy asks what is his story, his origin? Paul replies, "I don't know? If I even make a comic book, it may only be a one-shot, so it better be all action."

Marcy adds, "Yeah, we can make up the story and plot as we go along."

I left them with their rendition of Selah, not really thinking about it. One day I get called into Agent Bent, my superior's office. He places the Selah comic in front of me. I chuckle. Paul and Marcy did it!

He murmurs, "You know these people?"

"Sure, I went to school with them. A few months back, when I got drunk and the guys gave me the tattoo, I had some time coming and I went home. The name kind of gave them an idea for a comic book character."

He picks up the comic, shaking it in his fist. "A gun-toting vigilante. Who goes around exacting bloody revenge on terrorists around the world?"

I ask, "Does the story have an origin?"

'No, from what I can tell, it is all action scenes. I don't like my agents being turned into comic book characters. Since there is no actual connection to you or this agency in this fictional character, there is not much I can do. Make sure you tell your friends to keep it that way."

It's 1991 during Desert Storm, so use your imagination. If I told you what I know, I would have to kill you.

***

It's 1992, my ten-year high school reunion. I get the invite to come home, and a part of me just does not want to make the trip. Success in my life is a dead bad guy and my team makes it home in one piece. I can't share my life with my high school graduation class. Paul and Marcy are on their fifth child. Selah is still an independent comic, with Wild Tail Comics wanting to buy but Paul won't sell. Churchill and Candy married, with a divorce soon down the line. Hyman is married and is a rabbi. Jason is married, with his video game business going strong.

Reed Jackson is a successful fireman and still single. Connie could not come home because she is training for the Olympics or something. Dan Cottager is working with his father, still trying to keep the family business going.

I get a chance to ask Wendy, "Do you ever think about getting married?"

"Are you proposing? I haven't had a serious relationship in years. This may sound pretty sad, but I think I am married to my kids."

"No, that sounds like you, always giving and all."

Less than a year later, to make a long story short, a Mr. Jimmy Thomson's gun kills Wendy. He walked into the school around lunchtime, just got out of prison. She vaguely remembers him from childhood, and during lunch says, "Come into my office and let's talk." That was the last time anyone saw her alive. Jimmy brought a gun to school and killed her and then himself. I get a call from Marcy, and all I can do is hit the floor screaming. Wendy is killed by Jimmy Thomson's gun. I vaguely remember Jimmy, a snot-nosed kid who Wendy used to share her lunch with.

A month later I get a call that my brother Corey was wounded as a New York P.D. detective. I was called because I was listed as a next of kin and there was a possible need for a kidney. The doctors were able to save both his kidneys, so I was just there for moral support. During the days Corey was in the hospital, we really became close. Near-death experiences can do that, I guess. I asked Jackson for time off, and he and the CIA reluctantly gave me leave to stay in New York and become a detective-in-training under Corey.

***

During 1993 through 1994, on and off again I became head of security for the band Counting Tornadoes at a Trailer Park after their song "Christ Taking Apart Anger Through Prayer" became a hit.

That was fun. How do I describe Ralph Shurlow? Well, I quote him enough I guess.

Ralph gave up his freshman year of high school to work on the family dairy farm.

He went to night school and met Connor Chapel, who was home working on his brother Paul Chapel's dairy farm, recouping his life after years on the road trying to become a country singer. Ralph was amazed with his stories and shared some of his poems and songs. Connor was a bit older than him and took the young pup under his wing and convinced Ralph to sneak out from time to time and together they would sing songs at the local bar called Sodom and Gomorrah. Reed Jackson joined the band and soon others.

After graduation, Ralph wrote a science fiction novel called *Ice Soldiers*.

The first country music hit the band had was called "Counting Tornadoes at a Trailer Park," which could be a bit confusing since it was also the name of the band. Their first Christian song was called "Christ Taking Apart Anger Through Prayer."

They had obligations and had to get on with their lives. Weekend bars, county fairs, dances, and church socials for "Christ Taking Apart Anger Through Prayer" were great but not paying all the bills. The band split up for a time. Ralph was sent out to New York.

When Ralph did radio interviews, he insisted that they play at least one of his band's songs, usually "Saga of the Ice Soldier" by Ralph Shurlow.

Little by little, the band made contacts, and they were touring again and making music. Ralph made friends in law enforcement too. I remember the first time we met. Ralph was a silent observer researching another novel via friends in the CIA.

A bomb went off in New York's subway system. The FBI has called the CIA for their assistance. Peterson says to Ralph to keep quiet and watch. Graves, his partner, hates the idea of Ralph going along for the ride and tells Peterson every chance he gets. The FBI agent reports they know the terrorists are an Arab group. They found a dead subway guard and were pretty sure he was killed by the guy who planted the bomb. Ralph looked the dead guard over. Graves asks, "Okay, Shurlow, what do you see?"

Ralph asks, "The crime scene has not been disturbed, right?" The FBI agent says it is clean. Ralph begins, "You can tell by the angle of the knife wound the attacker was left-handed. The struggle tells a story that they fought hard until the knife struck the victim's lung. The attacker was weak after the fight.

"Look here, hand, feet, and knee prints in the dust with blood. My guess he was about five five or six."

Graves asks, "How can you tell?"

Ralph answers, "By the distance between the feet and knee print. Look, here he falls again. He is either out of shape or . . ."

Peterson asks, "Or what?"

Ralph gets on the floor and looks for something.

"There is something under the heater. Give me a stick or something?"

One is passed to him. He reaches in, and blood pressure pills roll out. Graves yells, "Get prints on these!"

Ralph adds it is a bit late for that.

"Why?"

"If the killer did not get his pills, he is already dead by now. Better start calling the morgue."

I was the local New York police detective. I add, "We picked up an Arab guy of your description who must have died of a heart attack about an hour before the bomb went off."

The FBI agent is impressed and says, "Well, Sherlock Holmes, you called it."

Ralph smiles and adds, "Well, actually, my full name is Ralph Holmes Shurlow."

CIA Agent Peterson puts his hand on Ralph's shoulder. Ralph keeps quiet and does not say a word unless he is asked; that was their agreement.

When we gather information, a so-called know-it-all tells us "I know what is going through their minds! I know the bomb they used. I know the psychology of the terrorist. I know their mindset. And you are wrong, this is not a political issue! The bomb was an overall message!"

"And that message is?" the agents ask.

They argue back and forth who is right who is wrong, and Ralph sees something that the others and I do not see, and it is obvious to him. So why is it not obvious to us? He speaks up, "Ah, sir?"

Graves yells, "SHUT UP! When we want you to speak or want your opinion we will tell you! Now shut up!" Then it was back to arguing.

Ralph calls a cab on his cell phone, shakes his head, and says I don't need this. Then Graves says, "Hey, Max, why don't you get us some damn coffee?"

As I get up and walk by Ralph's desk, Ralph gets up, passes me a note, and says, "Can you give this to Peterson? I got to go," as I walk over to the coffee machine.

I mutter to myself, "Why don't you make your own damn coffee, you son of a bitch?"

As the water fills the pot I read the note. And I bump the coffee pot, almost knocking everything on the floor.

That causes the others to stop arguing for a second, then they continue. I return with coffee and set it down. I pass the note to Peterson. Peterson reads the note. "If he is such a know-it-all about the damn terrorists, it may be because he trained them." Peterson then gets up out of his seat.

"You trained them, didn't you?"

"Who?"

"The terrorists!"

"That is classified information."

***

After Ralph published his first sci-fi novel, *Ice Soldiers,* Reed Jackson, a lead singer and guitar player in the band Counting Tornadoes, suggested me as security. That is pretty high praise coming from him. Ralph brought me downstairs in the basement garage of his New York apartment building. "Mr. Faraday, I have heard a lot about you."

"Is that why you want to show me your basement?"

"Reed Jackson pitched your name, and I have a few friends in the CIA who backed up the idea."

"Oh really, what clinched it?"

"Agent Graves hated the idea. That made it a sure thing in my book; I don't know what it is, I just get a bad feeling around the guy." I like Ralph already; he has good instincts.

"I am starting up a research facility called Ice Works, and security, well, I would like that to be your department."

I chuckle. "You write science fiction, Mr. Shurlow. What do you have that really needs securing?"

Reed says, "You're a car guy; I have something I want to show you."

Ralph turns on the light, and I see a '92 red Dodge Viper with a coiled rattle snake and "Don't Tread on Me" on the hood. My jaw drops; this car is so sweet.

Ralph says, "Let me show you the engine." When Ralph lifts up the hood, there is no engine. He says, "This is a perpetual motion device I invented. It works off magnets. Basically, it charges the batteries, and the batteries run the electric motor connected to the power train to the wheels and so forth."

In shock I ask, "This thing doesn't run on gas?"

"No, and best of all, when it is parked here I can connect it to the apartment building's main power line. It almost brings my electric bill down to half of what it used to be. I have an uncle that is in the Navy, and he is using the application on old diesel subs and nuclear subs too. The way I look at it is, just because you can glow in the dark does not necessarily mean you should.

"You see I don't get along real well with my in-laws. Fact is, ever since I and my good friend Mack Sterns smoked them at a wedding reception. A few have tried to break in and see what my little boy "Ben Franklin" is made of. I need this car out of the country quick. Just say the word and I can have you and it shipped on an Air Force transport headed for a NATO base in Germany. By the way, how would you like to drive this baby on the Autobahn?"

***

In '94 I leave Counting Tornadoes for Chicago to be closer to my Uncle Sherman. I am thirty. That is sometimes considered old in my line of work. So I moved to Chicago and joined the police force and became a detective. I was engaged to be married to a beautiful Miss Kate Dent. I get shot on duty. She couldn't handle it, so she calls off the wedding. But she made me promise to always wear my bulletproof vest armor. Like what she did to me could be protected by my bulletproof vest— bullet right to the heart.

I get a job offer and I move back to New York, and I am a detective.

In 1995, with the success of Counting Tornadoes and *Ice Soldiers*, they are constantly on the road, doing tours. And I take time off to tour with them as security.

It is the drive home to Cavanaugh City. It is late, and we are traveling down Deer Crossing Alley Valley Highway. We are all tired, ready to call it an end. Bang! Out of nowhere, we hit a herd of deer.

We all get out and inspect the damage. Reed yells up and down, "I have told you time and time again, you don't go over forty-five on Deer Crossing Alley Valley Highway!"

We get out examining the damage. Big Bertha, the band's semi's cattle catcher is bashed in, and all the headlights are smashed out except for one. We are going to have to limp the rest of the way home.

Bob says to Reed, "I thought when you were talking about Deer Crossing Alley Valley Highway you were just joking."

Reed angrily replies, "Does this look like a joke to you?"

Ralph smiles and says, "Hey, Reed, I think you and me have a song to write."

Ralph starts out with the chorus:

"Deer Crossing Alley Valley Highway"

If you go faster than forty-five you will be lucky to make it out alive.

Deer Crossing Alley Valley Highway

Like a bad nightmare dream to see deer in your high beam

Deer Crossing Alley Valley Highway

You are out of luck when you hit an eight-point buck

Deer Crossing Alley Valley Highway

The guys yell we got another HIT!

Deer Crossing Alley Valley Highway

Deer Crossing Alley Valley Highway is a name we have given to a certain stretch of road.

If you don't watch what you are doing you will end up dead like a squashed toad.

Friendly farmer driving tractor pulling equipment that takes up a lot of space.

Amish in horse and buggy of course will slow down your pace.

When the sun goes down it is a real obstacle course to get to another town.

Deer Crossing Alley Valley Highway

If you go faster than forty-five you will be lucky to make it out alive.

Deer Crossing Alley Valley Highway

Like a bad nightmare dream to see deer in your high beam

Deer Crossing Alley Valley Highway

You are out of luck when you hit an eight-point buck

Deer Crossing Alley Valley Highway

Driving down the highway late at night you swerve to avoid a man in black, a Midnight Stealth Jogger who just put you in a fright!

You want to swear at that son of a gun!

An oncoming car with high beams blinds you and you have kids with you so shake your head and bite your tongue.

Deer Crossing Alley Valley Highway

If you go faster than forty-five you will be lucky to make it out alive.

Deer Crossing Alley Valley Highway.

Like a bad nightmare dream to see deer in your high beam

Deer Crossing Alley Valley Highway

You are out of luck when you hit an eight-point buck

Deer Crossing Alley Valley Highway

A so and so guy doing a hundred in a nitro rice rocket!

You are trying to make it to your girlfriend in one piece and there is a poacher shooting his gun doing an impersonation of Davy Crocket.

In this neck of the woods a tow truck driver laughs all the way to the bank.

As you hit a family of deer you call out you son of a blank!

Deer Crossing Alley Valley Highway

If you go faster than forty-five you will be lucky to make it out alive.

Deer Crossing Alley Valley Highway

Like a bad nightmare dream to see deer in your high beam

Deer Crossing Alley Valley Highway

You are out of luck when you hit an eight-point buck

Deer Crossing Alley Valley Highway

Reed prepares to leave the Counting Tornadoes. He has a fireman career in Cavanaugh City waiting for him. His wife is an upcoming Preacher Prophetess Deborah Debby from down South in the Bible Belt. When he brought her to his old hometown, she felt this was where the Lord wanted her. That was an answer to prayer for Reed.

Together they found his old church that had been left abandoned. Behind the church was the old church bus. Reed's time as a Counting Tornado and some good investments gave them the cash to start their ministry. Before leaving the band, Reed did one last song and a video.

"A Church Bus Named Hallelujah"

When I was a kid, my daddy didn't take any fuss.

He used to send me to church on the bus.

It was filled with little old ladies who couldn't drive.

Crazy kids and mad mothers with hair done up in a beehive.

The bus was noisy. Smoke came out of the exhaust. To say the least it was slow.

Church at times was the last place I wanted to go.

Instead of being washed and baptized in The Blood of The Lamb.

Sometimes I think we were washed in vinegar and baptized in formaldehyde.

Did I mention the pastor was sent to prison for running a scam?

Now I am grown up and I have been around the block and now I drive the church bus and if I am going to make it to church on time I am going to have to beat the clock.

In a church bus named Hallelujah

In the color scheme of lime

If we are running late for church hit the nitro we'll get to church on time

In a church bus named Hallelujah

In the color scheme of lime

If we are running late for church hit the nitro we'll get to church on time

In a church bus named Hallelujah

I am the fireman of the group called Counting Tornadoes at a Trailer Park

AKA Christ Taking Apart Anger Through Prayer

And one day at a concert she was there.

Blond hair and we make a good-looking pair.

The guys helped me write her a song to show her how much I care.

On the road I decided to go back home and be a fireman again, my wife joined me in my new life.

Did mention she is a preacher?

There are some things they really didn't teach us in Sunday school. And I have a lot of questions and she is a great teacher.

When I came back to my hometown I found my old church abandoned and run-down.

And I saw my old church bus out on the back lot.

Call me crazy, but I was getting visions of how to make that old girl look hot!

In a church bus named Hallelujah

In the color scheme of lime

If we are running late for church hit the nitro we'll get to church on time

In a church bus named Hallelujah

In the color scheme of lime

If we are running late for church hit the nitro we'll get to church on time

In a church bus named Hallelujah

I don't mind to brag.

I have even asked the Baptist church bus to drag

She is long and lime green in BIG letters is John three sixteen.

Written on the sides are sage inspired messages.

"I hope you know Jesus, and do you know where you are going when you die?"

And when you are looking in your rearview mirror you can read Hallelujah as we are passing you on by.

God bless you and bye, bye!

In a church bus named Hallelujah

In the color scheme of lime

If we are running late for church hit the nitro we'll get to church on time

In a church bus named Hallelujah In the color scheme of lime

If we are running late for church hit the nitro we'll get to church on time

In a church bus named Hallelujah

The love bug hit in '97. I am thirty-three and I fall in love agai$$n with Kate Dent. In '98 I am thirty-four. I propose marriage again and she accepts.

On a vacation in 1999, a few of my so-called buddies got together. I begin th$e gambling again and I begin to drink. Bad combination.

During the millennium, in 2000, we did not die at the stroke of midnight. What a letdown.

It's September 11, 2001. "Where were you when the world stopped turning …?" Alan Jackson asks in his song by the same name. His immortal words take me back to Chicago.

I just finished a murder case, and somebody turns on the TV, and I see it like the rest of us; I see it happen live on TV. The reality is, every day there is something like a World Trade Center disaster in the making. But it does not happen because there are people behind the scenes that keep it from happening. January 1, 2000, should have been a 9/11, but it was not. The world went forward, and we all got up and we go about our lives as if nothing ever happened. If you think that, fine, God bless you, please go about your life as normal as possible. Those who know better, for them please say a prayer.

I get a call and I am sent to Washington.

October 2001. I wake up in Chicago and I get a call on my phone.

It is the chief. "Max, our hostage case just got hot again! I'll be there to pick you up. One way or another, we are getting that bastard!"

The bastard in question is an armed murderer, slasher, child rapist, and kidnapper that a just society would kill on sight rather than let go on a technicality. This son of Beelzebub has been making up for lost time and claimed eight victims and is on number nine. The detective on the case has him cornered at a rundown apartment building on the West Side of Chicago. The day unfolds just like I lived it over and over again. Chief sets me up on the other side of the street anticipating the main escape route in case the arrest goes bad and the kidnapper escapes. I am one shot, one kill in the department.

I'm asked by the chief, "Are you ready, Faraday?"

"I am the only one who can get this right, Chief." I hold it in. I should have been on the case from the start. But I was called to Washington to help the CIA out on a case, and if they had their way I would still be there.

We hear gunfire and soon over the radio we hear "Officer down!" I pick up my rifle and get ready to take my shot.

We all hear the engine revving up. The car busts through a garage door coming right in front of me! The car is a convertible, and I see the whites in the driver's eyes.

I say, "Nobody takes it but me!" and I take the shot. Bang!

I see his head splatter, and the car crashes into trash containers.

Summers says, "The girl is not in the building. I have two wounded officers!"

Chief yells, "We got the driver, it's over!"

Summers was the first to open the trunk, and Chief is close by when I hear him whisper, "Oh my God, Max, what have we done?"

I have seen a lot of things in my line of duty, but this little girl …

The same bullet that killed the kidnapper went through his head and went straight through the backseat of the car and struck the girl tied up in the trunk. Summers adds, "He never transported a victim. He caught them, raped them, and then killed them."

In spite of all my training, I just break down and I sob. "She could've been Maggie, Max, or anyone's little girl." At that moment it could've been my little girl. I had enough.

Chief defended me and said, "I gave the order. You did no wrong here."

If I did no wrong, why can't I forgive myself? I am the one who has to live with this.

I was found innocent of killing the girl; it was an accident.

In time, I compartmentalize my grief and go on, or so I thought.

It's 2002 and a bad beginning of the year for me. Drinking and gambling have been my weaknesses. I am very good at gambling, and that is the problem.

When I win, I win big, and when I lose, I lose big too. I lost everything.

Some of my friends on the force put together some cash and bought me an old police cruiser since my other car was seized.

I was told to get another case and get a life. I get a call from my CIA manager Graves, asking if I could do some snooping into the Chicago Russian Mafia who was blackmailing a senator. And the opening of the story brings you up to speed.

CHAPTER FOUR

The World You Leave Behind Is the World You May Be Coming Back To

It's Friday, July 12, 2002, early in the morning, in a warehouse outside of Cavanaugh City.

The Boss, also known as the Mystery Man, has come to see why his delivery was not shipped. "What were you doing?'

'I was late, Boss, I was making up time."

The Mystery Man in his anger takes out his gun and shoots the driver. Just as he does the act, he realizes, *Oh my God, what did I do?* His body shakes. "Toney, take care of the body."

Toney asks, "What about the car?"

"Your family owns a junkyard. Take care of it."

Toney comments, "We may have another problem." "What?"

"We got word that Max Faraday saw the tow truck drive into town last night without its lights on and called the Cavanaugh City Police."

Toney is about to hit a brick in fear of what the Boss might do to him.

The boss says, "I'll take care of him."

***

It's 1982 and I'm attending my twenty-year high school reunion. The first to greet me is Dr. Churchill Smith. "How you doing, Max?"

"Good, can't complain, and you?"

"The hospital is growing under my tutelage. We are going to have five new specialties for the public. The hospital in Carter City is barely even basic. They don't even deliver babies anymore."

I ask, "How come the hospitals never merged? Carter City is a bigger town than Cavanaugh City."

The room goes silent in a hush. Churchill looks me in the eye and says, "Because they are Carter City and we are Cavanaugh City. There is a big difference; you would be well to remember that." I can hear Big Paul in the background saying damn right.

I ask Churchill, "Have you been drinking?"

"Hey, I'm not on duty tonight, so I can have a little fun."

I of course say I am always on duty.

"Hey, Max!"

It's Big Paul and Marcy! "How are you doing?" I ask them.

Paul starts off with, "Farming has its ups and downs, but life is a roller coaster."

"How many kids are you two up to? Last time I was here, it was five."

Paul proudly responds, "Well, you have been gone a while. We are up to ten. Our oldest is getting ready for The Air Force."

I look at Marcy. She is four feet, close to five if that, and Big Paul is, well, Big Paul, and the word *how* just comes out.

Paul answers, "Well, Dr. Churchill is working on a zipper, so we don't need a C-section again." I think it but don't say it— *again?* "See ya, Max. I got to talk to Reed about some organic smoked pork he wanted to buy."

I see Candy, Churchill's ex-wife. "So, what have you been doing?"

She hugs me, saying, "If you can believe it, I am a schoolteacher, eighth grade English."

I respond, "Lucky kids."

She sees someone else. "Nice talking to you. I'll be right back."

I see an old friend, Dan Cottager. "How you doing?"

Dan replies, "Not as good as I would like, but not bad, I guess." Dan unloads his troubles. "After the Wild-Mart Store came to Carter City, it just sucked the life of all the mom and pop stores in the area."

"So what are you doing now?"

"Good old Churchill has made it possible for me to get paramedic training, and now I am a paramedic. I just got off of two on-call shifts in a row. I am tired, but I wouldn't miss it for the world."

"Hey, that's good."

"Good to see you, Max."

From across the room I see Jason. You see, Mr. Hyman, Rabbi Hyman threw a bar mitzvah party for his son Burney. It was also a swim party. And Jason was not permitted to go, because it was an overnight party, and he did not keep his grades up or something. So he decided to take his chances and went anyway. Figuring he'll get grounded for a month, tops. His parents put two and two together and figured out what he did.

They even called the hotel to call Mr. Hyman and make sure he was not in a ditch somewhere dead or something. He was there at the party all right, and so was I, but I had permission, and I was on the honor roll for a change. While he was gone, his father took down all the posters in his room and painted the walls white. Then with a black marker marked off every day till his eighteenth birthday in July sometime, I think. When he got home his father said, 'Son, when you turn eighteen you are out of the house." He was pale white for over a week. I have to say, it shook him up in a good way.

"Jason, how are you doing?"

"Great, Max! You look great. I hear you beat some kids out of thirty bucks."

I smile. "Guilty as charged."

"One of those kids was my kid, Danny. Thanks. Now I have to hear, 'Dad, I got to have thirty bucks.'" We laugh hard about that one.

"What are you doing?"

"I got tired with the computer game business, so I sold it to Ice Works, and that kind of stuff is a hobby now. Last couple years I did what my dad did and now I am a gym teacher, can't you tell?"

Jason is a bit thick, has a receding hairline, and walks with a limp from falling out of a deer stand with a rifle.

"That is a no, no from what I am told. No, I can't."

Connie Mack, former high school and college basketball star, modeling, now young women's gym teacher, just laughs.

Jason says, "That is not funny, Connie!"

Burney Hyman comes over, opens his arms, and gives me a big hug. "Good to see you!" Burney grew up in our town but didn't graduate with us. He left in the ninth grade because he went to rabbinical school.

"What are you doing, Hyman?"

He hands me his card, which reads: Burney Hyman, Rabbi and Tax Management.

"Hey, there is Candy. I got to talk to her about her cottage industry."

"How you doing?" Reed Jackson asks. Reed sent me this e-mail, I think it defines him.

Definition of a Redneck. A redneck is a rural, lowland southerner. In other parts of the country we are called hillbillies, cowboys, bumpkins, hicks, or just plain country.

Rednecks are traditional Americans who work hard to support their families and go to church on Sunday. Rednecks volunteer as Sunday school teachers, youth leaders. firemen, and anything else their community needs. Rednecks usually drive pickup trucks, and they spend a lot more time than they would like using those trucks to haul things for neighbors, but they never complain, decline, or accept payment.

Rednecks pay their own way and spend their hard-earned money on clothes, insurance, food, and education for their kids. Rednecks won't take charity or welfare.

Rednecks mow their own lawns and work on their own vehicles, and they have every manner of tool imaginable (which they keep in a shed that they built themselves).

Rednecks don't spend their leisure time protesting, or at fancy cocktail parties criticizing President Bush's grammar. They hunt, fish, and enjoy sports with their friends and families.

Rednecks usually wear work boots or cowboy boots, but at the same point in their lives.

Most rednecks owned a pair of work boots or combat boots when they risked their lives to give the "pampered" the privilege of criticizing our "cowboy" president.

Rednecks show respect for veterans, say the Pledge of Allegiance with the words "under God," and stand when the national anthem is played. Rednecks may not have the best education, but they know what matters: faith, family, patriotism, self-sacrifice, and a strong work ethic. A redneck may not have much money, but he knows what is truly valuable. If you threaten a redneck, his family, his friends, or his country, he will not back down, surrender, or appease.

(As do the French, added beyond original text, because it just needs to be said.)

Reed pats me on the back, saying, "Not bad, you wild man!"

"Watch it, Reed, I am packing heat." I show him my gun. "I picked it up before getting in their car. Don't tell Ellen."

"Hey, Max, don't show it to Jamie or Ellen. They will flip out, man."

"I know, I had to sneak it on. Ellen watches me like a hawk. Nice talking to you."

Reed Jackson was an all-around SOB. He made little girls cry.

As he grew up he changed, his faults began to fade, and his redneck attitude and friendship grows on you. His one saving grace is he knows how to put out a fire. For that, the good people of Cavanaugh City tolerate him. He saved my house. He saved the hospital. He saved a guy trapped in a car with the Jaws of Life.

He would say things like: "You are so stupid, you had ten plugs in the same outlet! Don't let a lung cancer smoker in the hospital and have a cigarette in the damn hospital! Why didn't you stay at the bar's parking lot in the car and sleep off the hangover! Now you got your fat ass in a car upside down in a ditch!"

I even met him in Desert Storm. He was there putting out the oil well fires.

He had some choice words! To top it all off, in 1993, he was the lead singer and guitar player in the country rock 'n' roll band Counting Tornadoes at a Trailer Park.

Jason comes by and says, "For a firefighter, he starts more fires than he puts out." Then comes a poke to the ribs and a chuckle.

They were the happy couple, Steve and Kathy Pearson, high school sweethearts who married shortly after college. His psychology practice took off, and his self-help books became bestsellers. When his son was born, something happened to Steve.

Home Hearth, his own creation, started taking more of his time. He was helping people by the hundreds and then by the thousands in seminars. Books were selling. He did the talk shows and then a radio show of his own.

Kathy was his wife and manager, and she could see all the good he was doing. And after years of being the silent wife and partner, she gave him a way out to leave their marriage, and Steve took it. Kathy came home to Cavanaugh City to raise their son, and then she started going to school to become a lawyer. Now she is prosecuting attorney of Carter County. As for Steve, Home Hearth, as before mentioned, has become a bit of an empire, and Steve is still playing Monopoly. Steve sees me, puts out his hands, and we walk toward each other, and then we run and give each other a hug! "I missed you, Max!" Applause fills the room.

Then Adam comes in and the room goes silent.

Adam was a detective in Seattle, Washington, who was sent to prison, I feel, for a crime he did not commit. He was a marathon runner and long-distance jumper in high school. He was one of us, one of the guys. But most of our small town believed the hype, and no one has fully trusted him, a bad-cop-on-the-take reputation can do that. In our small town, prejudices exist. Steve asked him to come home to Cavanaugh City and help decorate his Home Hearth Homes. And as far as I know, he is his main decorator and carpenter.

Oh, here comes Reed Jackson. What is he going to say now? Reed says to Adam, "Hey, Cupid, how you doing?" and pats him on the back.

Adam sits down at a table, and no one sits with him. Reed goes over and asks, "Is this seat taken?" Then Steve and Kathy sit down with them. I see a chair waiting for me with Jamie, but I think I'll sit with Steve. The dinner was okay. And I am amazed Reed did not say or tell a stupid dirty joke about pigs, bad cops, or anything.

I ask Adam how he got the name Cupid. Reed jumps to the answer. "He does the damnedest stunt with the bow and arrow. He can shoot a dime or even an aspirin."

Adam smiles in modesty. Reed continues, "He is one hell of a decorator."

"Oh, it is what I do."

Steve adds, "He has designed and remodeled all the Home Hearth Homes."

I ponder the missing that are not here, and I ask without thinking to get an answer.

Why does it take death to wake us up? Silence comes to our table.

Reed says, "I think it is because until you have a dead body, it is hard to get the point sometimes. I mean, Jesus died on the cross, and that got people's attention. And then he rose again, and that really got people's attention." A silent pause in thought. "But maiming is good too. My dad was a son of a bitch when he made that crack about homosexuals at a biker bar. Who knew? It is amazing he is still alive. I mean, he was paralyzed from the neck down when he woke up from the coma. He has his right arm, and he can get around in that electric chair now, and he is going places."

Kathy says, "It was so good of Grandma to take you in when your father—"

Reed adds, "Bit off more than he could chew. She died shortly after I graduated from the firemen academy."

Steve asks, "Show her the picture."

"Of what?'

"Your grandma."

Reed shows the picture. Kathy whispers, "She looks like Elton John."

Reed responds, "Well, she was British. A lot of those British women look like men when you get right down to it. Just look at that Dame Edna."

Kathy asks, "Where is your wife?"

Reed replies, "She would have come tonight, but she had a revival meeting she was leading at the church."

Adam adds, "My wife is doing the praise and worship music there too."

I ask Reed, "Do you have any pictures?"

"Yeah, and I have a new one of her and my baby three-year-old girl." Reed pulls out his wallet to show pictures.

I can just smile when I think about Reed and his wife and say, "When 'Christ Taking Apart Anger through Prayer' did the revival concert, you two hit it off."

Reed comments, "Yeah, she has been knocking me upside the head ever since then, and I thank God every day. Yep and she is Pentecostal and has the same hair problem as Jan Crouch. Although I don't think it is a problem, I just think that when the fire of the Holy Spirit touches her, it gets her hair singed."

As my good friend Ralph Shurlow says, "You know there are some things they really didn't teach us in Sunday school."

As the night goes on I think again about the missing. Big Paul comes by, and I say, "I wonder where Jack is."

Big Paul says, "Jack, that son of a bitch, can crawl under a rock and die; it would do a world of good."

I ask, "Really?"

Paul continues, "Unemployed drug runner has five kids in foster care from three women. Blames everything on everybody else. Lost his license for DUI, but he still drives."

I whisper, "And poor K. Ray C."

Paul states, "Poor K. Ray C? That's your problem, Max, you care too damn much, it will get you killed. I love you man, but sometimes you care too damn much. Do you know, or remember what happened to K. Ray C? Well let me remind you. He got drunk one night and had the cops chasing him down a dirt road doing a hundred! He hits a tree, BANG! Sudden STOP! Goes through the windshield!"

Marcy says, "Don't talk about this, Paul."

"Woman, I will talk about it if I want to. The cops on duty can't find the body. Where did it go, where did it go? Come morning, I am taking a load of cattle to the stockyards, and what do I see smack dab on the roof of the Johnson house? Well, it's K. Ray C., smack on the Johnson's house like a bug on the windshield."

"Oh, God, Paul, I just ate! I think I am going to be SICK!"

I ask, "What about Smokey Joe?"

Reed Jackson steps in and yells, "That son of a bitch nearly burned the hospital down! He was on his deathbed, and his wife slips him a cigarette, lights it, and leaves the room to smoke outside. Next thing you know, the fire alarm goes off! Most likely he died smoking!"

Reed nudges me and says, "Didn't even get half price off for cremating him!"

Big Paul yells, "You tell him! I know, I was there. Marcy was having a baby!" Marcy is in the background covering her face.

"After the smoke cleared it looked like somebody threw a man on an open pit grill!"

Churchill yells, "We have just eaten. Do you mind?"

Reed calls back, "What was the cause of death?"

Churchill yells, "Stupidity!"

Reed asks me, "What you so happy about, Max?"

With a sinister snicker I exclaim, "Ever since Smokey Joe started smoking, I started a special savings account."

Jason says, "Hey, I remember that. For every cigarette pack Joe bought and smoked, you put that amount in cash money in the bank."

Churchill adds, "He had been smoking since the sixth grade. How much is that? I know where I can get a 1982 Trans AM in near refurbished condition and have some left over to put on a Harley."

Ellen says, "Oh, that is so sick and morbid. I think on the back I'll have the words "In Memory of Smokey Joe.""

Jamie asks, "What color?"

Ellen pinches him, "Jamie!"

As the night goes on, I walk the halls and pass the Wendy Pearson High School Library.

She was my best friend. Later that night, Ellen walks by and calmly says, "It's time to go."

They are locking the doors as we speak. So I take my flower off my tux and set it by the memorial. Ellen does likewise, and others who have not gone home yet do so.

"Welcome home, Max," they say as they walk by. The parking lot is lit up, and I see a sight and say, "Wow!" It is Reed Jackson's fire captain's pickup! The door depicts a firefighter twirling an axe above his head with one hand and with the other holding the fire hose and putting out the painted flames at the front and hood of the truck. That is so cool!

Reed says, "Yeah, Big Paul did it. The city is going to use the design on all our fire trucks."

Big Paul adds, "I'll be doing it in my spare time this winter. Detailing cars is a good side job for me since Selah is in hiatus."

We say our goodbyes and call it a night. I sit quietly in the back seat of their family car.

Jamie says, "I almost forgot, we have to pick up the kids at the babysitter's." The kids, half asleep, crawl in and over me. I was practically an only child, I think I could have been a big brother, and in a way I am.

We get back to Jamie's, and his little girl gets out. She bounces her ball up and down, up and down until it slips from her grasp and rolls out the drive and into the street. Jamie sees it in the mirror as he is just getting out of the seat. A car pulls out as the little girl goes from the driveway to the street to get her ball. The car steps on the gas!

I yell, "NO!" and run after her. Jamie and Ellen are both desperately fighting with their seatbelts. "Damn you, let me out of here!" Everything is in slow motion in my memory.

I have her. I pick her up and I try to keep running, but the car is coming too fast! She is up in the air flying as the front bumper tags my legs and I am on the hood.

The hood ornament gashes and slashes my left leg and my right shoulder hits the windshield—CRASH! I am flying over the car, and I see as I turn my head that she lands in the grass, hopefully a safe landing, and now I see pavement coming in hard and fast.

A snapshot, I got most of the license plate numbers. I am out.

I wake up for a minute. Jamie yells, "Hold on, Ma, help is on the way!"

Where is the ambulance?!

I hear the crying of Jamie's little girl and hear, "Is Max going to be okay?"

Jamie yells, "My God, it has been ten damn minutes!"

CHAPTER FIVE

History Revision Blackout

"**M**ax, are you ready for school? I am up! I am up!"

I look at myself in the mirror by my bed, and I am blurry. Oh my God, I? Sweet Jesus, Mother Mary, have mercy on me. I am in purgatory, and I am thirteen!

"Max, is something wrong?" "Nothing's wrong, Mom."

I say to myself, *Calm down, Max. You got hit by a car, and you are just dreaming.* I can barely see. I reach down and find my old pair of glasses.

I look in the mirror and see my glasses and open my mouth and see my braces.

Mom yells, "Well, then come down and get some breakfast, or you will be late for school!"

This has to be a dream. This has to be a dream. Just go along with it. The smell of fried eggs, sausage, and buttered toast mixed with cigarette smoke fills the house.

Mom died at seventy-two and should have lived longer if she quit smoking, cut out the fat, and ate a few more muffins, but as far as I know she died happy.

I look at the calendar and see Monday, September 25th, 1978. I look at her and she lovingly mutters, "Well, come on, Max, eat your breakfast." And all I can do is grab a hold of her and say, "I love you, Mom!"

"Oh, Max, I love you too. Now eat before it gets cold."

"Oh, thank God for the greasy food."

"Now that is not a proper prayer, Max, and you are going to need that grease to put fat on your skinny bones. I can tell right now it is going to be a cold winter."

I still can't get over how Mom looks, and I say, "Mom, you look good for fifty-two."

She replies, "Here is a tip, Max. Don't remind a girl about her age. You won't like it either when you get to my age, if you are so fortunate. Now get your books and get to school."

I try to save myself by saying, "I love you, Mom." "A little late, Max, it's a little late."

***

It is the end of September, and a bit of Indian summer is trying to hold on. As I make it to the sidewalk, I hear Jamie Scott asking, "What did you get for science question number …?" A future teacher of America's youth.

"I don't know, and if I don't keep my grades up, and don't get into a college, I will be working part-time at a McDonald's all my life because my dad is kicking me out when I turn eighteen.

"I wish you children would just grow up!"

Dan "Outta Luck" Cottager trips over his own two feet. "Ouch! Damn, I broke a pencil!"

Burney Hyman, who has braces, says, "What a putz."

Cough, hack, cough. "Hey, wait up!"

"Oh here comes Smokey Joe."

Churchill says, "When are you going to stop smoking? You are going to get yourself killed!"

"Churchill has a point. Shut up, there is a Trans Am in your future."

Smokey Joe's comeback is, "Why don't you stop sneaking drinks from your dad's liquor cabinet?"

I then say, "You've been in your dad's cabinet?"

Churchill insists, "Hey, it helps me relax."

Joe responds, "Well a cigarette helps me mellow out," as the chain-smoker and the alcoholic bicker.

"Hey, Max!" It's the girls, and we start casually walking, not noticing them.

Ellen yells, "Hey, Jamie, wait up."

I ask, "Hey, where is Steve?"

Wendy says, "Sick. Dr. Churchill Smith says it is his appendix. Didn't you know that already?"

Luckily to change the subject, we see K. Ray C. riding his bike into the street without looking where he is going and almost gets hit by a car! The driver yells out, "Damn kid!"

His full name is Karl Ray Chambers, and we call him K. Ray

C. for short because there are a lot of Karls in the Cavanaugh City school system: Karl Smith, Karl Jones, Karl Keller, Karl Edwards, Karl Graham, and Karl I can't remember his last name. There were a lot of Karls. K. Ray C. kind of stuck.

Smokey Joe says, "K. Ray C. must have a death wish or something."

Off in the distance comes "Jimmy Thomson" Kindergartner. He is little for his age, Dumbo ears and blond tangle hair, and the hint of a smell like pee. Wendy helps out in kindergarten as a teacher's aide instead of study hall and most of lunch. She is an angel. The big sister to everyone, even Jimmy Thomson. I break off and walk with the guys; this is too much to handle, even for a dream. The two of them walk over to Mrs. Horton's house. I can't believe we used to call her Old Witch Horton. She was a sweet old lady.

Half the time Jimmy's parents send the kid out the door without breakfast. When they don't, Wendy has an arrangement with Mrs. Horton to bring Jimmy for a visit and she will give him an egg sandwich. She has a bad heart and lives by herself.

***

The park is so wow like I remember it. Connie comes from behind, hitting me in the head with her basketball! "Come on, Max, let's play."

I drop my books for a little one-on-one. Wendy picks them up and carries them for me. Well, she is my semi-girlfriend at the time. And I play one-on-one, and they walk off. After a while, Connie says, "We are late!" and she takes off. I run after her because this is a dream, and I have to follow her.

As we are running to class, Pete's mom drops him off and says, "Have a nice day!"

Pete Cortez is a super smart kid of Mexican lineage who, if it went by his age, would be in the third grade. But no, he is super smart, and we have to pack him in with the eighth graders to stimulate his mind. He yells my name and grabs a hold of me. I am his protection, "The Bodyguard." I assure him it is okay. We are going in the school now.

We make it to class just in time for first-period history class. I get my bag from Wendy here and sit down. I open my bag, expecting not to have my homework like any good dream, and I find my homework all done. Something is wrong here. After sitting through a boring class, we start doing our assignment. In the silence I hear what could be described as a little motor running, but it is not a motor. It is Marcy farting. I look at the second hand on the clock. Now everyone looks around wondering where that sound is coming from.

Then K. Ray C. sees poor Marcy trying to hold it in. He hits the table tapping it as if to say, *I have something funny to say and I can't hold it in*. He yells out, "Marcy is farting! Somebody open a window!"

The teacher shouts, "K. Ray C. Shut up!"

Marcy goes POP! The second hand almost makes it to a minute. For such a little thing, how could she hold so much gas?

The teacher asks somebody to open a window, and everybody laughs. The teacher apologizes, "I am so sorry, Marcy."

K. Ray C. laughs until he turns around and sees Big Paul's face. And he shuts up, turns around, and faces forward.

Marcy and Big Paul might be just friends, but you don't make fun of Marcy when Big Paul is around. As the room goes silent, you can hear Big Paul crack his knuckles. That is Big Paul's way of saying, I will knock you a good one upside your head.

Kathy, Steve's future wife, is handicapped. She has braces on her teeth, braces on her legs, and a back brace to straighten her crooked spine due to scoliosis. She also has crutches on her arms. Kids call her Iron Maiden, though my favorite is Lightning Rod. The teacher as a rule gives her a five-minute head start to get her books and go to the next class. She then goes from the first floor to the second floor for English. As I leave the history class, I can't remember where my locker is, so I grab Pete's shoulder.

"Ah, Pete, can you help me find my locker?"

Pete asks, "Max, you can't find your locker?"

"I think my mom accidentally slipped a pain pill in my vitamins, and it is kind of taking effect."

Pete's eyes go big. "Well, don't tell anyone, or they might send you home. Big Paul can only protect me when he is not in special ed for Math and English. And if you are not here, I am doomed."

K Ray C. yells, "Marcy fartsy!" and runs away.

Big Paul waddles hurriedly after him saying, "I am going to get you! Pant! Little Pant! Mother Pant!"

I yell to Big Paul. "Run, don't yell, and save your energy for his beating!" Paul turns around and gives me the thumbs-up signal!

Pete adds, "K. Ray C. is just asking for it."

Study hall. I keep wondering when I am going to wake up. Then it is as if time stops. Nobody moves, silence, a paper airplane thrown by K. Ray C., now sporting a black eye, stops in midair. A man with a black robe that kind of looks like Moses appears out of nowhere, pulls out a seat, and sits down: "Hi there, my name is Bridge."

In shock I ask, "What is going on around here?"

"Oh, I forgot to tell you, I am the caretaker of the universe."

I say in shock and amazement, "No freaking way."

He continues, "I was sent to inform you that you have been given a special gift."

"What kind of gift?"

Bridge smiles, asking, "What do you remember about last night?

"It was July 12, 2002, my twenty-year high school reunion. I get hit by a car, and when I wake up, I am in September 1978."

"Well, when you go to bed tonight, you will wake up in a coma at Cavanaugh City Hospital, Saturday, July 13, 2002. I don't know how long you will be awake because it has not happened yet. But at some point you will go to sleep and wake up back in September 1978 tomorrow. And so on and so forth."

I implore why.

"My guess is God has time on his hands, and He really likes you." He pinches my cheek. "Think back to the hit-and-run, when Jamie's little girl ran into the street. What happened? That car sped up. Why did it speed up?"

"I don't know."

"Well, you are a detective. Find out."

"I am thirteen and in the eighth grade, and according to you I will be in a coma when I go to sleep tonight in the year 2002!" Bridge smiles, saying, "I like you. I didn't have to repeat it.

You got it all the first time. This is great. Details. You have the chance to change some things, right a few wrongs, and see the results of your actions twenty-four years in the future in less than twenty-four hours a day. Be happy, you have been blessed with a great gift. One catch, say you write to yourself a note, *Don't go to your twentieth high school reunion* and don't go. That car hits

Jamie's little girl, and you don't get your memories sent back in time."

I ask, "What kind of God would let a little girl get hit by a car?"

Bridge answers, "The same God that gave man dominion and free will to do good or evil. The choice is up to you and anyone else. You chose to risk your life to save that little girl. Another man chose to try and kill that little girl. Remember, Max, God does not put anything in motion that he does not already see the end results. The possibilities are endless."

"Then who was driving the damn car?"

"He also likes to give us a mystery from time to time. And you are a detective, so solve the mystery."

"Wendy."

"Yes, precious Wendy, and other lives you have come in contact with. You have helped so many people in the past. Imagine what might happen if you could see twenty-four years down the road, because you can, and will. I have to go now; the universe is a busy place."

Time resumes. Big Paul laughs as he reads his Wild Tail comic book. "I love this stuff. The funny thing about this is, Bridge is on the cover of the comic!"

"Oh sure, it is great to read about that kind of stuff, and it is another thing to live it."

***

Lunchtime Recess:

As I walk around the halls and look over the place, I just can't get that I am back in 1978. I look outside, and Jack is harassing Wendy. "Come on, Wendy, give me some. I don't see Max around. You know you want to!"

Wendy pleads, "Get away from me, Jack! Or you will get it!"

Jack says, "From who?" I yell, "From ME!"

Jack smiles and declares, "Oh, if it isn't Max Faraday, bastard supreme."

I motion and whisper to Wendy, "Get out of here, now." Jack laughs, jesting, "Oh, what are you going to do?"

I say to her, "Wendy, now" She runs!

Jake's gang comes out of the woods—high school dropouts and younger.

I remember this day. I got beat up pretty bad. Steve and I shared the same hospital room. Steve said if he had been there with me we could have taken them. Uncle Sherman nursed me back. I almost had to redo the eighth grade because I missed so many days.

***

A Ralph Shurlow/Maverick Robins quote: "One of the best ways to have peace is to remind possible enemies they are a little lower on the food chain."

Semper FI! I am a Marine! A lean, mean Killing Machine! I don't care if what I say scares the shit out of them or not. Actions speak louder than words. PUNCH! I have trained my body to be perfect! KICK! Although I am fourteen I have skills. Queue the music: "War, what is it good for?" This is too easy. There is no leadership, no tact, just a bunch of junkyard dogs wanting to perform for their master. WHAM! To the face! Knee to the 'nads!

Dodge and evade, counter and strike! Drop down, swing with the leg, knock down, they land on their ass on HARD concrete! Jack is about to run, so I grab him from behind. I could break his neck, and it is tempting. I hold him there as his gang watches him jerk around; I have him in a sleeper hold.

Jack's older brother Jake Hammer leaves the third-story greenhouse room when he sees his brother and his gang beaten up by Max Faraday. Big Paul and Pete are coming up the stairs because Paul is helping Pete move a science project. They match eyes, and calmly Paul says, "Peter, go downstairs and call the police, now."

Jake, a dropped-out high school senior, grits his teeth, saying, "I am going to get you, Paul."

Paul calls out, "Pete, call an ambulance too!"

With the stairs behind him, Paul guards the only way out. Jake starts throwing punches, and Paul knocks him upside the head.

Jake starts kicking, and Paul says only girls kick, and the first kick to Paul strikes his side, ouch. The second Paul grabs and hurls Jake back, where he lands on his ass. Jake screams, "I am going to get you, fat bastard!"

Jake gathers all his strength and charges Paul. Just before contact, Paul steps aside, and Jake loses control and tumbles ass over tea kettle down the stairs. Pete comes back screaming, "Paul, I called the police!"

Paul calls back, "Did you call the ambulance?"

"No, in all the excitement, I forgot."

"Go call the ambulance."

Teachers and students begin to show up. "Hey, that is Jake Hammer. Isn't he supposed to be wanted by the police?"

Paul comes beside Jake and sees his broken opponent.

Jake whispers, "I am going to get you."

Paul says back, "I hate leaving things unfinished."

Paul looks out the window and sees Jake's gang defeated around Max and leaves.

By now, Wendy has rounded up the guys. I drop Jack on the ground and say, "Who's next?"

One of the gang taps Jack with his foot. Jack coughs. He is still alive. Like the dogs they are, they limp away, and some stagger off. The teacher's aide shows up and asks, "What is going on around here?"

Jack says nothing and coughs. And I say, "Nothing, sir."

"Get back to school the bell is about to ring."

It was fun watching Jake's gang stagger to class. Apparently they all slipped on the waxed floor at the same time.

I have to tell the guys, "Keep it down about what happened, okay?"

"Sure, Max, whatever you say."

I see the Cavanaugh Police pull up to the school. A teacher's aide yells, "Paul, we want to talk to you!"

After the police were done with Paul, Jake was sent to the hospital and then to jail.

Paul catches up to us in gym class. Big Paul winks at me and says, "Kicked their asses for good." Paul was the hero as far as the police and his fellow students were concerned.

He would rather have his friend Tommy back than any award or praises.

The day went on like nothing ever happened, as far as I could tell. Okay, I can face Jack and his big-brother's gang, but I don't need to get in trouble with my mom.

After school I follow Dan to my after-school job at the C. Connection. The store is in good condition, but what strikes me is the food prices are so low. It just catches me off guard. Dan's dad asks, "Are you feeling okay, Max?"

"I have had a bit of a headache and haven't felt good since recess."

Mr. C. says, "Well, stock those shelves, will you? Then take a sick day."

My mom the prophet. When I get home from my after-school job at the C. Connection, Mom has dinner waiting for me. She rarely went to church, but when the spirit moved her she went to the closet in prayer and lifted up a name of family and friends or one of her students past or present. As a teacher, she could look at one of her students and see what they might be somewhere down the road in their life. I ask her, "What do you think of my friends?"

Mom says, "Jamie has such a kind heart, he will be a good teacher. He has a crush on that Ellen girl, doesn't he?"

I admit, "Yeah."

"They make a fine couple. Marcy wants a big family when she grows up. Paul is her protector. I love his artistic touch. Steve is a know-it-all and has a great mind of a scholar. I can only imagine the roads he has already had to travel in his life. Wendy, she's an angel, she carries burdens of others with such grace. Churchill, I hope he does not have to carry the burdens of his father. Jason, he has such a gift of joy."

I ask, "What about me?"

"Honey, you are a force to be reckoned with, and that is why Jesus has called you to be a defender. You have the strength to defend the weak and underprivileged and the tenderness to hold those who are scared. That is who you are."

After dinner I do my homework. It is not so hard; I did it over twenty-four years ago. I watch some TV. They may be first-runs to Mom, but they're reruns to me.

"Okay. Time for bed," she says. So I lay my head on my bed and . . .

75

CHAPTER SIX

Hello. I'm in a Coma

wake up Saturday, July 13, 2002. My body is in a semi-coma state. I cannot move or speak, but I can open my eyes and can hear loved ones who visit.

Ellen joyfully screams, "I think he is coming out of it. He is moving his eyes!"

Dr. Churchill, who looks like he has been up all night, says, "No, it is just a reflex."

I do the best I can to yell, "Reflex my ass!" but nothing comes out.

Jamie comes out with balloons, flowers, my favorite candy bars, and says, "Thank you, buddy, for saving my little girl" and hugs my limp body. The registers start blinking and beeping! Jamie screams, "Is he dying?"

Dr. Churchill rearranges the sensors, saying, "No, you moved the sensors when you were giving him a bear hug."

Jamie's comeback is, "Well, I have done more for him than you did! You were drunk, and I am tempted to call a lawyer because it took ten minutes for the ambulance to get my house. If I was not afraid he had a severe spinal injury, I could have dragged him in my car and drove him here in less than five!"

Ellen yells, "Stop arguing! You are not helping the situation!"

If I could talk, I would say I agree with Jamie, but I can't.

"I will have silence!"

My God, it is Father Michaels.

"You are acting like children!"

Churchill adds, "But—"

"Shut up!" The look on the pastor's face from where I am laying says, get out now!

Jamie says, "Come on, honey, let's go see what they have in the cafeteria."

As they leave, Father Michaels grabs my hands and then gets on his knees and says, "My son" and prays. For hours he prays over me, and then he composes himself and wipes tears from his eyes. After patting me on the head, he walks out.

Jason comes in and says, "Wow, what can I say after you have been visited by a priest?"

After pause of silence, he continues, "I went to the funeral of the Midnight Stealth Jogger. You remember the guy who ran up and down Deer Crossing Alley Valley Highway? He was hit the other night. Man, it looked painful. He was like a local legend. Do you remember, I put his likeness in my video game? How can we go on in this world without a Midnight Stealth Jogger? I talked to him once, tried to offer him money for using him in my video game. Get this, he can't sleep at night due to insomnia, so he jogs at night, hoping people will slow down on the highway so they don't hit a deer. Did I mention the guy was a vegetarian? It won't be the same without him. Hey, Max, you are not married and all. You like danger. You like staying up at night. You like to jog. When you wake up from your coma, why don't you become our new Midnight Stealth Jogger?"

I don't know where it came from, but instantly I punch Jason. WHAM!

I am back to coma mode as if nothing ever happened, while Jason massages his jaw "Ow! Max is coming out of his coma." They all gather around him, asking what happened.

"I asked him if he wanted to be the next Midnight Stealth Jogger, and he punched me."

And I can see out in the hallway one by one they all take a punch at Jason.

"That is so stupid! Ow! What is wrong with you? Hey?"

After they leave for the night, Father Michaels comes back and prays over me.

Paul Sr. and Jr. and Dale Chapel, come into my hospital room. Paul says, "Hey, buddy, how you doing? We had our air show today. You should have been there. We had all of William Wildtale's planes flying."

Paul Sr. adds, "Who knew connections with William Wildtale would get so much in return?"

Dale adds, "We just got a WWII Marine Corsair. We are going to need a good mechanic to put it back together. Remember the Marine Pappy Boynton, commander of the Black Sheep Squadron? That is what he flew."

Paul Sr. with tears says, "We opened the Chapel's Chapel at around four this morning, and before six the church was full. Prayer warriors from every Christian denomination, and even Father Michaels and Rabbi Hyman showed up.

Paul Jr. sniffs up tears. "We had to leave because of the air show, but it was something to see."

Dale puts his hand in mine and says, "We left the air show and drove by. There was still more than a handful of spoken and unspoken prayer requests shared. Kid, you get people together who would not get together on their own. Now, come on, Marine, get out of this bed and show us what you are made of."

Nothing.

They get on their knees, and one by one they pray for me.

"Dear Lord, be with your warrior and protect your defender of the innocent. Heal your servant. Please let it be your will that he makes a full recovery. In Jesus's name, amen. Son, would you help me with up? My knees."

CHAPTER SEVEN

I Wake Up on Tuesday, September 26, 1978; Who Says Grown Men Don't Cry?

I wake up crying. I love that man. And those men. Father Michael spent just about the whole day praying over me. Mom gets the morning paper and reads the exploits of Paul vs. Jake Hammer. "Max, there was a fight yesterday, and you did not tell me!"

I yell downstairs, "It was between Big Paul and Jake, not me!" I fought Jack and Jake's gang, but I am not telling her that.

"But you helped in the investigation and the arrest. Aren't you worried?"

"Not with Paul around."

As I come downstairs, Mom says, "Oh, honey, can you come home and help clean the house up after school? I forgot to tell you, Father Michaels is coming over for dinner tonight, and I would like to have the place picked up and neat and tidy. Have you been crying?"

"I love you, Mom," and I give her a big hug!

"I love you too, honey. Is there something wrong?"

"No, Mom," sniff, "everything is okay."

I go to school, take another night off from the C. Connection, and rush home that night to clean up the place. When Father Michaels comes in, the house is cleaned from top to bottom. Mom says to Father Michaels, "We should have you over more often."

When I see him, I just break down and cry, "I love you."

"Well, Max, you are such a good boy."

He strokes my head just like he does when I am in the coma. After dinner I decide to experiment. When I wake up in 2002 I can see my left arm in front of me raised and strapped to my bed. Is this all a dream, or what I have to find out? So I get one of Mom's lighters, light it, and hold it underneath my arm.

I bite my leather wallet. Damn, this hurts! Okay, that should leave a scar. I go to the bathroom and run cold water on the burn. It has to be a second-degree burn at least! Damn, I wish there was a better way. But I can't think of one. I then wrap it and put on some cream to soothe the pain. I turn out the light and go to sleep.

July 14, 2002, Sunday. I wake up and see the burn on my arm. The scar is there. Okay, I have my damn proof, now what? Still, I cannot move, and for the most part people think I am a vegetable. I hear a knock on the door.

"Hey, Max, is you up?"

It is too early for visitors. Reed must have had someone let him in. "Sorry to get you up so early. But I have to drive Hallelujah this morning, so I'll be going soon. You remember the times we had on the road with the guys? Ah man, I miss them something fierce. At the same time, I love the life I live too. I can't give up being a fireman to go back out on the road. I would like to, but I have responsibilities and such. I checked into it, if I was to leave and come back, I would have to start off at the bottom of the ladder and work my way back up. Hey, I like being the fire captain. Debby is getting on my nerves a bit too. I can't even go out and sing karaoke at Sodom and Gomorrah anymore. And I love their Better than Sex BBQ. Ah buddy, you got some drool." Reed gets a Kleenex and wipes the drool from my lips because I love their Better than Sex BBQ too. "Well I got to get going. I'll see you tonight."

A nurse turns on a TV and a TV minister says, "Today is your day for a miracle!"

By the same nurse and an aide I get a sponge bath, and monitoring devices get changed or cleaned. While doing this she hums "Amazing Grace" and a few other songs that I am not sure what they are.

Dr. Churchill comes in when they are done, looks at my chart, and looks me in the eyes, and then takes a deep sigh. He sits down in the chair next to me and watches the TV church service. I am for the most part out of it, but I catch the TV minister saying, "It is time to make a change! Confess one to another."

Tears come down Churchill's face, and he wipes them away with tissues and blows his nose. Churchill whispers, "I don't know if you can hear me or not. But I am in trouble with a certain Dr. Ho Chi Min."

That is Churchill's pet name for Dr. Sam, who is of Vietnamese descent.

"I came to work a few weeks ago with alcohol on my breath, and he sent me home and told me if I ever show up at the hospital again like that I would be relieved for a week.

"Well, you know how I was that night. Well, I am always on duty. I was off that night, but I got a call that you had an accident and I came to the hospital. His stool pigeon nurse passed it on that I had alcohol on my breath. So Dr. Ho Chi Min might be showing up today. You are in a coma, and I can still hear you say I am always on duty.

"My life is not as great as I make it appear, Max. Churchill Jr. rebels against authority. I have not had a serious relationship since Candy. The good news is I have been accepted to teach at the University of Michigan. I have done some heart research in my spare time and helped create a new operation and method. I spent my life trying to grow up and get away from this town, and when I finally become a doctor, where do I end up? Here in Cavanaugh City. I said to myself, I would never end up like my dad. And I am, my dad.

"I want to leave, but I hear my patients say, "What would we ever do without you?" and I am ashamed to think I ever wanted to leave.

Churchill gets up and leaves.

Adam shows up next. He comes in with balloons and candy. Sits them down and rearranges the cards and straightens up my room trying to make the place look homier, I guess. With a smile he says, "Now, isn't that better?"

Adam, what do you expect me to say? Oh no, that just won't do. Here, let me show you how to really do it.

The silence fills the room, and he sits down in the chair next to me. "You know, it's been hard for me to come home after I got out of prison. When Steve asked me to decorate his Home Hearth Homes, I thought I would be in New York, not Cavanaugh City. There are no Starbucks here. Reed Jackson, you would not think it, but next to Steve, he has been really a blessing to me. One day I was going to the hardware store to get some supplies, and these jerks treated me terribly. At the Cavanaugh City hardware store, the owner mutters, 'We don't want a dirty cop around here!' And that was the last straw. Just as I was going out the door, Reed was coming in. Sees my expression and asks what the problem is. I tell Reed the store owner won't let me purchase my supplies because he says I am a dirty cop.

"This was the first time I had seen Reed since our last reunion. I didn't know what he was going to do. Reed said, 'Let's go back in there and get your stuff' then asks the store owner, "Jerry, what is the problem?'

"'He is a dirty cop and has a prison record, and I don't want him in my store,' Jerry replies.

"Reed turns around and says, 'Damn son, what happened?' Jerry says I'm a thief and a dirty cop.

"'Well, thanks, Jerry, I would not have known that if you did not tell me," Reed tells him. "Now why won't you sell the good man his supplies?'

"'Because he's a crook and I don't want him in my store,' Jerry repeats.

"Reed ponders this because he had a history. 'What if I said I don't want to buy stuff here because you look at nude girls in your so-called private bathroom? I mean, there is a filth you can't wash off with soap and water. And you are a deacon in your church. How is that a good example of your Christian witness? What about forgiveness? As far as I am concerned, Adam was railroaded and framed. He may be dirty or guilty, and if he is, I pray that someday he will see the light. But he isn't going to see the light if we don't live it! Sometimes we are the only Bible people are going to read. You have a wife and kid, and you are a hypocrite.'

"Reed then turned to me and said, 'Adam, you and me, let's get out of here. I know another hardware store we can go to.'

"Reed Jackson stood up for me. He says he is praying for me. He and Hyman got together, and he took some of the money he made from Counting Tornadoes and bought the hardware store. They even bought an espresso machine and put in a coffee section.

"Max, he has changed over the years." Adam then suddenly changes the conversation. "Well, I hear somebody coming we can talk later."

Steve and Kathy come in just after noon. Adam and Steve hug, and then Kathy and Steve hug, and then they all hug; it is so cute it is sickening. Adam says, "I'm going to the cafeteria. Anybody want anything?"

Kathy adds, "Don't eat too much. Big Paul and Marcy are bringing food tonight for a cookout on the hospital's back lawn." Adam adds, "Fat farmer kills the fatted calf, sounds delicious."

Kathy chuckles and says be nice.

Adam snickers saying, "Well, I'll bring a fruit salad and see if anyone guesses who brought it."

Steve shakes his head and then asks, "How you doing, Max?"

If I could answer I would let you know.

Steve says, "The doctors here say you are a vegetable. I think you can hear every word we are saying."

You are correct, and just like on the game show *Jeopardy!* I think, *Johnny tell the man what he has won!*

"Come on, Max, fight damn it, fight. Get out of this bed!"

Kathy starts playing "Eye of the Tiger" from *Rocky*.

"Come on, Max, GET OUT OF THIS BED!"

Between the two of them, they shake the bed, making noise with whatever they can get their hands on! Dr. Sam/Dr. Ho Chi Min comes in asking, "What you are doing?"

Doctor Sam was born in South Vietnam. He came to the States to learn medicine at the University of Michigan the same time Churchill's dad is there, and they become good friends. Churchill Sr. helps Sam become a citizen of the US.

After he graduates, Sam feels he should return to Vietnam to help his family, who are in the middle of a civil war. Sam gets captured by the Vietcong, and when the Marines rescue him, guess who is there to identify him as an American citizen, Dr. Churchill Smith, Sr. He joined the Navy. In 1969 they came home from Vietnam. At age seventy-one he is still pushing Churchill's buttons.

Steve's reply is, "I am trying to wake the patient."

The impatient doctor's reply is, "Well, you are disturbing the other patients!"

Kathy adds, "Well, if he woke up, that would be a miracle, and that would really disturb the other patients!"

Dr. Ho Chi Min bends down and says in my ear, "I don't care if he wakes up or not. As far as I am concerned, he is on the organ donor list."

Oh, and I am supposed to wake up to that response. Give me a break! If my Uncle Sherman was here, he would kick your butt, and he can do it now that the restraining order is off. Dr. Ho Chi Min leaves.

Churchill comes back, "What are you doing now?"

Kathy says, "Trying to wake up sleeping beauty."

Dr. Churchill asks, "Did it work?"

"No."

Someone looks in the doorway as he is walking by, takes a double look, and says, "Hey, are you Steve Pearson?"

Steve pauses before answering, "Yes?"

"Oh. I have read all your books. You saved my marriage. Can you please come see my wife? She just got out of heart surgery. Your inspirational book *All Things Are Possible* and prayers really got us through it."

Steve takes a tired look at Kathy and then me. "Sure."

I can see out of the corner of my eye the pay phone and a guy making a call. "He is really here, Steve Pearson, at the hospital. Bring the books, maybe we can get him to sign them."

By this time Kathy closes the door. "Welcome to my world. I'll let you in on a little secret. Steve and I are not really divorced. He had a friend make up an alternate identity. He took his original father's name, Milton Roberts. Whenever he needs to get away from the public life, he puts on a wig and old clothes, and Milton comes to life. We thought coming home to our little town would take the world off his shoulders.

"But everyone needs Steve Pearson these days. Milton comes to visit. He helps people in so many ways. As Milton, he can be anyone; nobody notices him. He likes giving complete strangers money. I have watched him do it. It is like they think he is an angel. He can talk one-on-one with people. With Steve, one becomes a hundred, and then it becomes a thousand. Only with God can he keep up the schedule he puts himself through."

Although I am technically off life support, I still need a food tube for nourishment.

Why can't I move? The gash on my leg may leave a scar. Other than the bump on my head, I should get up out of bed. Churchill's nurses and orderlies put me in a chair, and I am wheeled outside. Picnic dinner is laid out with all the trimmings. Big Paul mans the BBQ grill, and I can cruelly smell the steaks and hotdogs and they sit me at the table right in front of the cherry pie. If I were in a full body cast, I could break out of it on sheer will alone, but this? Hey, it's Reed! Kathy turns me around so I can see Reed and his wife and little girl. Reed's wife, Debby or Deborah, has a Dolly Parton wig and makeup. Tammy Faye Baker and Jan Crouch would be proud.

Everyone goes to help Big Paul set tables. Reed and his wife come over to me.

She gets down on her knees and Reed does the same. She begins speaking or praying in another language. Reed agrees with her in prayer: "Yes Jesus, do this. Oh yes, Jesus, we agree. Let your will be done."

She then lifts her head and says, "I can see the Holy Spirit all over you, Max. You are healed, and when the time comes, you will walk out of that hospital as if nothing ever happened. In God's time."

Steve asks Big Paul, "Since you furnished the meal, will you say the blessing?"

"Dear Lord, we ask you to bless this food and nourish it to our bodies. And we ask that you touch our good friend, Max. He has been there when we needed him, and we are asking that you help us return the favor. Amen."

Big Paul lays a feast before me and says, "Dig in, brother, dig in."

Nothing.

They are all expecting me to come out of this coma, and I don't have any control of this.

They are my best friends, my family, my only family now.

Father Michaels says, "I see tears!"

Tears come down my face and cheers come from them. This is a sign they have been hoping for, and I guess they got it.

"You are coming back to us, Max. You are coming back!"

They stuff themselves, gluttons everyone. While I have a food tube.

Ribs. Adam is eating ribs my ribs! BBQ is all over his face. Oh this is so good! Oh I am making a little piggy of myself eating piggy. I wonder if this was Miss Piggy? Oh just pass the frog legs. Ha-ha.

As the meal concludes, Steve comments, "We have been in contact with my mom, Mrs. Martha Pearson, and Dad, Mr. Frank Pearson. And we are looking to set up a boys and girls home in this area. There is an old farming community, for the most part abandoned, and we are thinking of buying it and renovating it."

Jamie asks, "What you are going to call it?"

Kathy answers, "If it all pans out, Wendy's Place. Dad is retiring, and he wants to help keep the books."

Jason says, "I'll volunteer my dad to help layout plans."

Steve adds, "We are thinking about setting up a K-12 school there too.

Ellen says, "Well that might be fun."

Wednesday, September 27th, 1978. I wake up, bandage my burnt arm, put on a long-sleeve shirt, and go to school. What else can I do? Over study hall I look over to Dan and see him reading an anatomy book with fascination on his face. Of course, at first, I don't think it is fascination, I think he has a picture of a naked girl or a hot car and I should go over and check it out. So I scoot over to take a peek. It's anatomy all right. I ask him what he's looking at. He whispers back, "I like it. I don't want to be working for my dad's store all my life. I think I could be a doctor."

Dan wants to be a doctor instead of work at his father's store?

I come home from work at the C. Connection, and Mom says, "I have some bad news. Mrs. Horton has been put in the hospital."

I remember Mrs. Horton. "Oh, Mom, her heart. Make sure to say a prayer for her."

July 15, 2002, Monday. I wake up, and someone tries to kill me by putting a pillow over my head. I can't do anything. I am in a coma, damn! Dr. Churchill walks by on his rounds—what the …?! He grabs the man, lays a good one on him, and sprains his hand in the process, "OW! Damn, my hand. Security!" Now who would want to kill little old me?

The intruder runs down the hallway past Connie's husband, Officer John Henry Watson.

"Hey, slow down, man, or you will have an accident!"

Churchill yells, "Security! Officer, stop that man!"

Watson turns and runs after him and yells back, "What did he do?!"

Churchill pants, "Tried to smother Max with a pillow!"

"Get back there and check on him! This is Officer Watson requesting backup!"

The intruder made it to his car and he is off. Reed Jackson is just pulling in the hospital entrance, and he sees the fleeing car. He has been listening on the radio and heard the call for backup. "Son of a bitch, that bastard is not getting away!" Stepping on the accelerator, he hits his horn that plays Dixie, turns on the sirens, makes a left to the exit, and he is gone. Watson in his Carter County Police car is also in pursuit wondering, *What does he have in that pickup?*

They skid between cars, causing cars to go to either side of the street. Thankfully, no accidents thus far, and when they make it to the highway, the intruder's car accelerates when he hits the nitro!

Reed yells, "Your ass is mine!" and pushes his own little red button.

Officer Watson mutters to himself, "A bunch of damn rednecks think this is *The Dukes of Hazard!*"

The intruder with reckless abandon runs his car almost to the redline.

Reed is almost on top of him. Over the radio, a call is given on reports of a fire on the other side of town. Damn! He gets on his radio and calls Watson, giving license number and make and model, then hits the brakes and turns around. As Reed speeds back to town, all Watson can do is shake his head and say, "Damn, what the hell is in that thing?"

Around noon, the three of them, Churchill, Reed, and Watson, meet back at my room. Churchill's hand is in ice. Reed asks, "Did you get the car?"

Watson shakes his head no.

"What about the fire?"

"False alarm. Someone knew I was after that bastard and had to place that call. What is in that pickup of yours? The guy you were chasing must have had nitro."

Reed smiles and says, "I can't tell you. It is a Ralph Shurlow Ice Works special.

Churchill says, "Right, Max here has a few secrets I would like to know about. I can't get medical records from the time he joined the Marines till now."

Reed adds, "Black Ops cloak and dagger shit."

Watson says, "No shit?"

Reed reaffirms, "No shit. Max here is a sniper. Makes Chuck Norris look like an amateur."

Watson comments, "You are joking me, Reed."

Churchill says, "Max has seen combat. Just look at this scar; that is a bullet hole. Knife wound there—I can show you X-rays—and he has metal fragments in his bones. He has a history, and chances are, we won't know about it, because he can't tell us about it."

Churchill looks both ways to see if anyone is watching or listening to their conversation. Then he whispers, "The other night, I had a man in a black suit check up on him. He wanted to know if he was stable enough to be moved."

Reed asks, "What did you tell him?"

"Stable, but I would advise against it. Gave me a number and told me to call if there is any change. I asked for medical records, and he said, 'This conversation never happened.'"

Read whispers, "Don't be surprised if you get a call from that guy saying, 'I thought I told you this conversation never happened.' The Feds probably put a bug in the room."

Churchill laughs, "Yeah, right, you and your flying saucers stories."

That night, Churchill gets a call. "Just to let you know, Big Brother is watching you, and I thought I told you this conversation never happened." Churchill looks at his caller ID, and it is blank, then the caller hangs up.

September 28th, 1978, Thursday. I wake up to the fact that someone wants to kill me. It is refreshing. Even in a coma, life goes on.

Then it's back to my dream, or whatever you'd call it. After school I go to piano class and practice for an hour. Mrs. Mack says, "Max, you are showing great improvement."

My comeback is, "Well, I have had years of practice."

I then see Dan walking by, and I ask Mrs. Mack, "I have finished my exercises. Can I leave now?"

"Sure, Max, keep practicing."

I then follow Dan. He is stocking shelves for his father at the C. Connection store. In 1978 you can get anything here.

If they don't have it, his father knows somebody who does and will make the deal and haggle down the price for you. Every time Burney's dad comes in and sees him at work, he asks, "Are you sure you are not a Jew?"

Thursday is my usual day off. Connie is practicing for a recital, and I am looking for someone to play basketball with. Dan says, "I can't play basketball, Max. I have to stock the shelves."

"Okay, so what if I help you?"

"Go grab an apron, and let's get it done."

I ask him, "So you really want to be a doctor?"

"Yeah, I love the store, but ever since Mom died last year from cancer …"

I remember Dan's dad was ready to franchise the C. Connection out in three other stores, then his mom gets cancer. If you have money, doctors will get it one way or another in order to fight the cancer. A year after his mom died, the C. Connection is still in the red. I hate to tell him the Wal-Mart store is coming, and all their fine and loyal customers will run to Wal-Mart like it is the second coming of triple coupon days.

Mr. Cottager enters. "So …" he began as he looked at his son. "You want to be a doctor?"

Dan's dad overhears our conversation. Dan puts his head down, knowing that his dad would like him to take over the business. "Yeah, Dad, I do."

"Well, I have a savings account that can get you to college." That savings account was, to my best knowledge, to be used to keep the store going when Wal-Mart comes to town.

"I can get you to college, but you are going to have to work to get through medical school." They hug. "Now, if you are going to work here on your day off, Max, get to work."

"Yes, sir."

Back at the hospital, I go to bed that night not expecting anything, maybe lights and a tunnel. Cliché, I know.

***

We get back to Jamie's, and his little girl gets out. She bounces her ball up and down, up and down until it slips from her grasp and rolls out the drive and into the street. Jamie sees it in the mirror as he is just getting out of the seat. A car pulls out as the little girl goes from the drive to the street to get her ball. The car steps on the gas!

I yell, "NO!" and run after her. Jamie and Ellen are both fighting with their seatbelts. "Damn you, let me out of here!" Everything is in slow motion in my memory.

I have her. I pick her up, and I try to keep running, but the car in my side view is coming too fast! She is up in the air flying as the front bumper tags my legs and I am on the hood.

The hood ornament gashes and slashes my left leg and my right shoulder hits the windshield. CRASH! I am flying over the car, and I see as I turn my head that she lands in the grass, hopefully a safe landing, and now I see pavement coming in hard and fast. I am out.

I wake up for a minute. Jamie yells, "Hold on, Max! Help is on the way!"

Ellen cries, "Where is the AMBULANCE!?"

I hear the crying of Jamie's little girl and hear, "Is Uncle Max going to be okay?"

Ellen yells, "Get back to the house and keep calling 911!"

Jamie yells, "My God, it has been five damn minutes! Here it is!"

Black out.

I wake up in the hospital and see it is Dan in a doctor's uniform. I black out.

The ambulance got to the scene in five instead of ten minutes.

Dr. Dan Cottager takes charge.

CHAPTER EIGHT

I Wake Up on Tuesday, July 16, 2002, and History Changes

Dr. Dan Cottager has been waiting by my bedside. Churchill brings in coffee, holding it in his good hand. I whisper, "Hi guys, how is it going?"

Dan whispers, "Max has come out of the coma."

Churchill yells down the hall, "Max has come out the coma!"

Everyone runs down from the waiting room. I can hear Father Michaels praising God all the way down the hall to my room. Churchill yells, "Everyone relax! How is he?"

I call out, "I think I am all here. What do you think, docs?"

Connie's husband comes in, and I say, "You better be here to take a statement."

He asks, "Why?"

"That was no accident. That the car hit me was deliberate. Somebody wanted to get Jamie's little girl."

"How can you be sure?"

"He speeded up, not slowed down."

He gets out his book, and I give details of the hit-and-run. I give everything, from the car's description to the license plate numbers to the fifth digit.

Churchill makes the call, and before five that night the men in black show up.

"Hello, Max," Titus says.

"Hello, sir."

"I read in the paper you saved a little girl. Nice."

"A detective in Chicago. Do you really like it there?"

I reply, "It is honest work."

Titus sneers, "And what I have you do is not honest?"

"I don't know any bragging rights and secrets I can't speak of."

Titus scoffs, "Well, that is why they are called secrets. If they weren't, they would be tales of old or days of yore. So, are you going back to Chicago or what?"

I state, "Someone tried to run over a little girl. I take that personally."

"You never got this from me," Titus says as he hands me some documents. "James Gates is a man who could use a little help and protection."

***

September, Friday 29th, 1978.

As I walk to school and see Jamie off in the distance, I wonder how or if I should tell him that someone in his future is going to try and kill him. The nice thing is they are blissfully unaware of what will happen to them in the years to come. So what am I doing here? I am not in a coma anymore. How long am I going to be reliving my life? Or seeing people?

Wendy taps my shoulder asking, "Hey, Max, why are so quiet?"

Wendy is beautiful. She is my age, fourteen. I was so head over heels in love with her, me being brace-faced and glasses and all. She gives me a kiss from time to time. I guess I was too much of a big brother for her.

Off in the distance I see Jimmy walking alone, and Wendy runs to him, and he wipes the tears from his eyes and does his best to smile. As we walk closer, I hear her say to him, "I will always protect you."

Steve by this time asks, "What did I miss?"

I smile and I am happy for the change of conversation. "Well, Dan is going to be a doctor when he grows up. That is what I am hoping for, at least he stays sober. Churchill is going to have a drinking problem and be forced to go to an AA program."

Churchill yells, "Hey, that's not funny!"

I yell back, "It was not meant to be. Jason is going to become a gym teacher and computer programmer."

Jason says, "Cool."

"And Jamie is going to piss off some drug dealers."

Jamie yells, "Oh that will never happen; besides, you and Big Paul would kick their butt for me."

"I will have to, won't I? K. Ray C. is going to get himself killed."

"Hey, we all know that."

"Smokey Joe is going to fall asleep in the hospital and nearly burn it down."

"Hey, I am only smoking three cigarettes a day."

"You will be smoking three packs a day, well, two and a half when you die."

Wendy comes by me and asks with untainted joy, "What about me?"

I look at her smile and curls and all. "You. You will be my best friend."

Steve asks, "What about me?"

"Jesus has not come back, but when he does, he will want your autograph because even he will be asking you how to solve the world's problems."

Lunch time. Big Paul's birthday is today. He is sixteen and gets his official license to drive. "Look here, people, I am sixteen and I have my driver's license!"

K. Ray C. adds, "Yeah, all the years of planning, doing kindergarten twice, first grade twice. Just so you could be sixteen in the eighth grade."

This takes the thunder out of Big Paul's joy. "Well, I guess I won't be picking your ass up for school when I get my pickup running."

Our little group goes silent, thinking, *He has wheels, we are mobile.* Cheers of adoration begin: "Big Paul, Big Paul," and little by little they get stronger, "Big Paul, Big Paul, Big Paul, Big Paul, Big Paul! So when do we roll?"

Paul continues, "I said I have to get the pickup running first."

Chapter Nine

People Die in Hospitals

It's Wednesday, July 17, 2002.

The doctors want to do more tests on me, but I get my things together. I am dressed wearing my "I ask the right dumb questions that make smart people think" T-shirt. I'm thinking, *People die in hospitals*, so I'm out the door.

Churchill is in trouble for having alcohol on his breath the night of my accident. He is brought before the hospital board. Defending himself he says, "I was off duty. I just came in to see if I could do anything for moral support!"

Dr. Dan adds, "He was not staggering drunk; he just had alcohol on his breath."

Churchill murmurs, "Oh thanks, Dan, that will help."

Dr. Sam says, "When I say I have no tolerance for alcohol, I mean it! Churchill, I am suspending you for a week."

Churchill declares, "A week!"

"Two weeks. I don't want to see you till the thirty-first! Call it a vacation; call it whatever you want, but you are out of this hospital. And get in an AA program!"

As they leave, Dan says, "Hey, it won't be so bad. Besides, you need the break."

I ask what happened and Dan says, "Churchill got suspended from the hospital for being drunk," then he shifts his focus to me. "Hey, aren't you supposed to be in bed?"

Big Paul says, "Max is home. The anti-bully is back!"

I say, "Come on, Churchill, you don't have anything to do. You can come with me and Big Paul."

Churchill asks, "What are you doing?"

"Trying to solve a mystery. Thursday night, I went out to play basketball at the park. I walked from Jamie's to the park. I saw a tow truck leave Howard's Garage. It went east, and about an hour later it came back through town with a car with a smashed-up front end."

"So?"

"The tow truck did not have its emergency lights on. Went right through town, and did not stop at the garage."

Paul adds, "Howard's junkyard?"

"Possible," I say. "As I was driving into town, I noticed a dead deer alongside the road."

Churchill adds, "Yeah, they are an eyesore, aren't they? How much you want to bet the deer the driver hit could still be alongside the road?" Then he pauses and scratches his chin whispering, "Or human? In that case, it could be murder."

I give the keys to Paul, and he gets my cruiser and pulls to the door, and Churchill reluctantly gets in the back. We go east of town and take it easy going down the highway and then north on Deer Crossing Alley Valley Highway until we see a dead deer and piece of earth carved out of a ditch. Paul opens his mouth, "Well that's a dead deer; that's what we are looking for."

We pull over, stop, and get out. I open the trunk to put on rubber gloves and say, "Don't touch anything until you put on the gloves. This is a crime scene here, treat it as such."

Snap goes on Paul's glove. He says, "Cool. The good doctor says crime scene, don't you mean disturbing a crime scene?"

Before I have a chance to explain, Big Paul says, "Max does not trust the Cavanaugh City cops because if they were doing their duty, they should have pulled the tow truck over for not having their emergency lights on. But they didn't, so they are in on it, right, Max?"

I say to Paul, "You have been paying attention."

He smiles, saying, "Hey, I might look dumb, but I am not." Paul winks at me with a smile, and I don't have to explain.

Churchill ponders, "So you think the city cops are in on it. What about Carter County Police?"

I shrug my shoulders, saying, "Don't know yet. Doctor. I need a tissue sample of the deer. Give me an educated guess about how long it's been dead." Churchill also takes pictures of the scene.

Big Paul yells, "Hey, I found a bloody bandanna!"

I walk over to see it. Yeah, it is a bandanna. Churchill takes a picture. "Bag it, it could be the driver's."

Big Paul mutters, "Or what is left of him."

I look at Paul. He replies, "Hey, I listen to Tom Clancy and Dean Kuntz and other mystery books on tape in the tractor and when I am painting. There are ways to get rid of a body."

I smile because I should know. "Get the glass and paint chips. We will need them to compare when or if we find the car."

Big Paul mutters, "Ah damn, that had to be a ten-point or at least a twelve-point buck!"

Churchill declares, "You are crying because there is a dead deer?"

Paul yells back, "Well, if the guy hit the Midnight Stealth Jogger, that guy who wore nothing but a black sweat suit, you would say he was a stupid son of a—"

The good doctor stops him by saying, "Only if I was drinking. I try not to swear when I am sober."

I begin to make a plaster cast of the tire tread left on the ground alongside the road. Churchill adds, "Guessing this car had to be going seventy-five, ninety, or even a hundred to do this kind of damage to a deer, and the car? What kind of hurry was this guy in?"

Big Paul mutters, "Late for his own funeral, my guess."

"Meaning?"

"Big Paul explains, "Jamie has been on an anti-drug mission with the kids when that junior high school boy overdosed."

I and Paul say, "History repeats. If you don't learn from the past, you are destined to repeat it."

Churchill adds, "Yeah, he got a list from the FBI's most wanted of possible people to look for, and he spotted one. It was a driver, I think."

"Yeah, it happened a few months ago," Big Paul responds. "Jamie spotted the guy in the diner. The guy was eating. He calls the cops, and a Cavanaugh City rookie arrests him."

Churchill continues, "The drug runner is sent to prison.

Jamie is the local hero."

Big Paul adds, "Drug runner gets killed in prison. Jamie is silent."

I ask, "And the arresting officer?"

Churchill answers, "Moves out of the area, never to be heard from again."

I say, "We are going to need to cut that bloody bandanna up. I have a couple places we can send it to. Maybe the driver was a sex offender, and they might have his DNA on file."

Big Paul yells, "Hey, I found a hubcap, must have come off from when the car hit with the deer!"

I run over to look at it, and I see fingerprints and double-check to make sure Paul still has his gloves on. In the excitement, I pat him on the back. This could be a big key to this mystery.

Churchill calls out, "Hey, here is a cigarette pack."

"Bag it. We will dust it for prints."

Churchill asks, "Where are you staying?"

I would like to say Jamie's, but he hates guns. Churchill adds, "You know, you can stay in my guest room. I can use the company."

As Big Paul searches the ground for broken glass and paint chips, I say to Churchill, "You and me, we can find out where and when Alcoholics Anonymous meets. You and I need to make an appointment."

We drop Churchill off at the hospital so he can pick up his car, and I follow Big Paul to Chapel's Farm. The place has grown over the years. Hay harvest is in full swing.

Having a big family helps taking care of animals and fieldwork, so no one has time to get in trouble. South of the farm is an air strip, Chapel Air. Paul's uncle Dale still runs the local airstrip. The brothers Paul Sr. and Dale still build ultralight and experimental planes with cooperation of Ice Works. Chapel Air has a flight school, biplane rides, parachute jumping, and hot air balloon rides. Off in the distance, I see tourists fall by parachute; it is a beautiful thing. I got to do that sometime soon; it would be a nice change to jump out of a plane that was not on fire or is about to explode.

Big Paul Sr. semi-retired from the Air Force in late 1970 something. Came home and took care of the family farm. In 1978 he was asked, if he could get back in shape, would he be interested in flying an experimental aircraft, possibly an F-15?

After high school our Paul joined the Air Force and became a mechanic and played football. All was going great until his uncle Robert's diabetes almost took his leg and eyes in 1985. Complications of the disease caused his death in '86.

So Paul came home from the Air Force to take care of things on the farm, and when things were settled, he became an Air Force Reservist.

You can see the old guy Paul Sr. riding around in a golf cart supervising the airport and the farm activities, always ready to lend a hand and give his two cents worth and tell a joke or story. He still has a say in Ralph's Ice Works.

Paul brings me into the milking parlor and asks one of his kids, "How is my boy doing?"

The kid is spraying down the parlor with a high-pressure hose and listening to country music. He happily responds with, "Good, Daddy!"

"That's my boy. When you are done, tell your mama Max is here."

Big Paul reaches down to the faucet of the milk bulk tank and fills me up a cup. Hands it to me, and I savor it on this warm day. Ahhh …

Then a big dog walks in the parlor like she owned it. Big Paul says, "Hey Max, how you doing?"

I shake my head in wonder, saying, "So this is Max senior?" "Oh yeah, we gave Jamie one of the pups."

"Pups? How many are there?"

"Well, let's see, Reed, Connie, Jamie, and Jason."

I ask, "And are they all named Max?"

"Max or Maxine."

I add. "Lucky guess."

"Well, take it as a compliment. Old ma sassy Max here was in really bad shape when she got here. She had wire cable for a collar around her neck, and it was so tight it was growing into her skin."

With tears, Paul adds, "Missing a couple teeth, who knows how? Gashes in her skin; somebody whipped her, Max. She was dragging three feet of wire behind her. And somehow she made it to us. I didn't think she was going to make it, but I called the vet. That sweet thing Becky just cried when she seen her. She had a bullet lodged in her leg; that is why she limps. We thought she was going to lose her leg to gangrene. We didn't think she was going to make it. She had been through a hell of a lot. That is why we didn't have her fixed; otherwise, we would have had it done then because she is a horny dog.

"She is so protective of the kids. She is just one of the family." The dog Max leaves.

It is a shame how people treat animals. They get tired of them and then they drop them off in the middle of nowhere. And like Max, they somehow end up here.

I ask, "Is that why you have so many dogs and cats around here?"

"Yeah, and Marcy always wanted to have a big family. If she isn't having one, she adopts a foster kid for a while. We always have a full house."

"How did you get into painting cars? I knew you drew comics and stuff."

"Oh, I painted antique tractors in my spare time before, and after Uncle Robert died in '86. And in '92, after our reunion, I had the accident with the sugar beet truck. Couldn't walk for almost a year. I was on crutches. Thank God I was drawing *Selah*, but that is just one comic book a month, and the farm bills."

I ask, "How did you get through it?"

"Friends and family pitched in and helped out on the farm. Marcy was pregnant at the time, so she and Mom did the books. I was stuck in the bed, so I did *Selah* and painted and it felt good to be doing something again, and Mr. Cooper came by and encouraged me too. I was helping Uncle Robert out so much and Farm Co-op during high school, I never had time to draw or paint, and after the accident I was in bed and I got the time I needed to paint. I was ready to sell the farm and draw comics full time, but friends and family came out of the woodwork, and Troy helped manage the farm while I was out of it. I was just starting my garage for painting hotrod cars when Counting Tornadoes needed artwork for their album cover. Heck, we built Big Bertha in my shop! Can you believe Garth Brooks called Big Bertha a piece of shit!"

Paul opens his shop door, and I can't believe all the stuff I see. Wow.

"Yeah, I painted Big Bertha with a redheaded Dolly Parton riding sidesaddle on a lightning bolt horse. Then I started to get more work than I could do in my spare time. Marcy was cashing pretty good-sized checks from my paint jobs. She said, 'Pa Bare'—that is what she calls me when she is happy with me—'you are going to do this full time and like it!' She and Troy pretty much run the farm, and I stay out here and paint. I do everything from cars to comic book covers out here. I get a kick out of sci-fi novels and comic book covers; they are my favorite. Hey, man, God will make a way where there seems to be no way. "I just had to lose the use of my legs for a while to realize it and find out how rich I really am. Now my brothers and sisters spend their vacations on the farm and bring their families here. I turned my backyard into a campsite, and they bring tents and pullout camper trailers. They would rather drive a tractor or ride a quad runner back in the woods or around the farm than go to Disneyland. Like I said, farming is a roller coaster. I guess it is how you look at it."

We go into the house, and Marcy is on the computer.

"Marcy, you know computers?"

'Sure, Max, I do all the archival work for the Cavanaugh City paper and have a website for our family farms. It helps the family keep in touch. And Selah fans still buy T-shirts and action figures."

I am stunned at the computer she is using; it is a top-of-the-line system.

Marcy comments, "Oh this, Pete got it for us. He had an extra, and Ice Works let us use their server for free. I teach home school computer courses and for the adults. You have to know how to use a computer nowadays. Go help yourself to what is in the fridge."

On the door of the fridge is a picture of Jamie's "Just Say No" rally.

Everyone is smiling except the Cavanaugh City police sheriff. That answers a question.

"Mr. Pearson is in this picture?"

Paul answers, "Yeah, he practically runs C.C. Industries now. He is giving ten scholarships to kids if they stay off drugs from the seventh grade on up."

I add, "It is nice to see such great things from people in my little world. Paul, can we have a meeting tonight?

"Where?"

"Your campsite. I think it would be good to let a few others in on our investigation."

Paul hands me a phonebook and says, "Start dialing. I'll start thawing stuff for the cookout."

Milking cows, it is like riding a bike; it all comes back to you, right? By afternoon, Paul and I are in the milking parlor. Two of their Mexican milkers called and said they would be late, so Paul and I are reliving our childhood. During school vacation, if I was not being a kid getting into trouble, I would ride my bike or hitch a ride to the Chapel's farm.

Paul's dad was the best. We would talk sports. He was a big fan.

Paul hands me a hose with a sprayer at the end and says, "Just spray the teats with the iodine teat dip."

Now I like this better than carrying the old teat-dip bottle. I wipe it off with the towel so that it covers the teats and dries them off and put on the milkier. As I repeat the process, I ask, "You have a double twenty. That is forty milkers. How can you watch all the milkers?"

Paul explains, "I don't have to, the system has automatic takeoffs. When the cow is done, it takes off the milker, and all you have to do is spray teat dip again, and when all her sisters are done, the bar goes up, and they leave, and another group comes in. The weigh jars monitor the amount of milk, and the information is stored in the computer. For the most part, every cow is a number, and we know when a cow is born and its health records."

As the group of cows leave and another comes in, one cow stops and stares at Paul.

"Come on, Half and Half, you have seen me before, you big pet." Paul pats her on the bottom, and she moves forward.

I ask, "Are some more than a number than others?"

"Oh, she was the smallest premature baby calf when she was born. Born in winter and almost frozen. Brought her in the house to warm her up, and Marcy kept her alive and house-trained the little fart."

I laugh!

"You don't believe me? I have pictures in my wallet, I'll show you. Marcy is going to set up an old folk's home for cows just like her, you just wait and see."

"Hey, Boss, sorry we are late."

We come back to the farmhouse. The kids are watching *The Simpsons*. Paul says, "All right, let's change the channel. I like *The Simpsons* too, but every time Homer says something, I think I am killing brain cells. They may be dying happy, but they are still dying, and we all need our brain cells."

They change the channel to the Cartoon Network, *Cow and Chicken*. What kind of mental case would make a cow and a chicken brother and sister? They change the channel to The History Channel. Trebuchet is the subject, and the kids say, "Can we build that? Uncle Paul, can we build that!"

"When I saw a little Marine T-shirt or that stuffed bulldog, I sent it home to Maggie. I have no regrets that the love of the corps rubbed off on her.

Paul Sr. states, "I think she still sleeps with that stuffed bulldog."

We begin with a barrel roll, and he is laughing and looks in the mirror to see my expression. I think he is disappointed because I am not screaming my head off. Big Papa Paul goes inverted and salutes somebody's house, and without putting his hands on the controls, the plane turns upright and levels out.

I turn back to see an angry Vietnamese man coming out of his house screaming at the top of his lungs. Was that Dr. Sam's house?

"Dr. Ho Chi Min! Took my driver's and pilot's license away!"

"Tell your brother Dale his remote control system works great!"

"What?"

"Kind of hard to salute a guy and fly a plane at the same time!" I think I ruined the surprise, and he lowers his head and says, "Well, Maggie won't be the only Marine in the family." Then Dale's system takes us home.

When we land the biplane, Dale and Paul Sr. give me the guided tour of the hangar.

I ask, "Is that a Predator?"

Dale smiles with pride. "Basically yeah, a stripped-down version. Anyway, we are working with Ice Works to turn it into a crop duster.

"Unmanned, I can have the pilot in the control room, and he or she can be running any number of planes at the same time. We have satellite and GPS. I can fly a plane or drive a car from here. I have this stuff in my old truck. I can go to town and do errands. Mostly I like to drive by Dr. Ho Chi Min's house and show off."

I add, "You know that is disrespectful to call him Dr. Ho Chi Min."

Big Paul Sr. pouts. "Well, he took my driver's license away."

Dale adds, "Well, you won't wear your glasses to see the road ahead."

"Whose side are you on?"

"You hit the poor guy and totaled his car with your old pickup. That's what caused Dr. Sam to get your license taken away. Because you won't wear your glasses!"

"They make me look like an old man."

I interject, "I used to wear glasses!"

"And why did you quit?"

"I didn't, I got contacts when I graduated high school, and then the CIA offered me an eye operation. I have better than 20/20 vision now."

"Well, contacts are expensive."

"Are you that cheap? If I had the money, I would get you a pair of contacts since you're giving your granddaughter to the US Marines."

"That sounds like a deal, Semper Fi, carry on."

Dale shakes his head and chuckles, changing the subject back to the remote-control system. "We are thinking that a service like this could do some real good with all the baby boomers getting older. They may lose their license to drive. They can still be mobile and independent."

Big Paul Sr. says, "Baby boomers, ha."

"Think of it, a helicopter could be at a hospital and be remote-controlled to a specialty hospital with just EMTs on board."

I add, "A plane could be brought down safely, like when they have been taken over by terrorists. Instead of going down in flames, like on 9/11."

Dale smiles, saying, "Silicon Valley can be anywhere, Max. Like Ralph used to say, even somewhere near Deer Crossing Alley Valley Highway.

Boys Night Out! A second cookout is held at Big Paul's hunting shack.

All the guys are here. After the second fatted cow and pig and a good sum of local fish and a deep-fried turkey are eaten, me, Big Paul, and Churchill share what we know.

"Okay, Jamie, what is going on?"

He gets the shakes and says, "They have called and left notes in my mail. We are coming after you. I have changed my number twice, and they won't stop. When they tried to run down Max, that was the first time they tried to attack me or my family personally."

Reed says, "That you know of."

I ask, "Do you know what they look like?"

Jamie states, "No, and I can tell they change their voices electronically."

I think, *Now I know they have bugged my phone.*

I say, "You have gone to the FBI."

Jamie says, "Yes, but how do you know?"

"I have my ways."

Jamie lowers his head, saying, "They say they are too busy."

I look at the ground and murmur, "They probably are."

Reed quotes, "It is kind of hard to get people to invest in the stock market or buy a new car if they are too busy buying shotguns and shells and canned goods and waving their hands in the air yelling, 'We haven't got a prayer.'"

I say, "Is that another Ralph Shurlow quote?"

"Yep."

Churchill murmurs, "You think he is such a big shot, don't you?"

Reed's comeback is, "Doc, let me put it this way. He is on the hundred dollar bill and the fifty dollar bill; deal with it."

Jamie says, "I don't know how you guys can be so calm. These guys could be trying to kill me and my family."

Jason declares, "Don't worry, the only way they will get you is if they get my gun. And the only way they will get my gun is from my cold dead hands!"

"Bang!" It misses the target. Well, it would have been more impressive if it hit the target.

I say, "Jason, the real idea is to get the gun from out of the bad guy's cold dead hand."

The others and I pull out our weapons and take aim and fire hitting the target. Jason mutters, "Ah, a bunch of show-offs."

Steve asks, "What about Officer Watson? Can he be trusted?"

Reed adds, "He chased after me and the guy who tried to kill Max."

"Yeah, but somebody made a false alarm call."

I add, "Kind of hard to call on a cell phone in hot pursuit."

"Hey, that is not public knowledge?"

"I was in the room. I heard the whole thing." Steve states, "I told you he could hear everything."

I ask Burney, "What do you know about the Cavanaugh City Police?"

Burney gets up out of his chair and dusts himself off, saying, "Well, I would like to say thank you for providing this fine kosher meal."

Laughter comes from all of us. Paul mutters, "My bad. Have you tried the deep-fried kosher pickles?"

Burney continues, "They don't do any accounting with us. As far as I know, they get it all done out of town."

One thing you learn in our little town, if you want things done right, accounting, taxes, or a good lawyer, you go to Hyman, Hyman, and Hyman. If it isn't kosher, it isn't the three Hymans.

Big Paul says, "If it isn't kosher, it isn't the Hymans.

Burney smiles, saying, "Hey, that can be our new slogan."

I take point, saying, "Churchill, tomorrow we are going to look at those security tapes."

Churchill lowers his head. "Dan will have to do it. I am banned from the hospital. Remember?"

Reed asks, "When will we have an identity from the blood sample and fingerprints?"

"I just sent them in today."

"Estimated time of death of the deer?"

"With tissue decomposition; last Thursday."

"Who has time to look for a car at the Howard's junkyard?"

Big Paul steps in. "Me, I can do it tomorrow. From what you told us, I have five possible makes and models."

"What are you going to do?"

"Look at some video footage and see where the police chief of Carter County stands in this investigation."

"You have doubts of the chief?"

"As of right now, trust nobody."

"Jamie, I would be thinking of places to go. They may—no, they will—try to kill you and your family again.

Jamie shakes his head, saying, "I won't go, Max. I am not running. School is going to start soon, and I intend to be there." Mr. Cooper puts his hand on Jamie's shoulder, saying, "Jamie, you can be there in body or in spirit; the choice is yours." "Right now, they have singled you out, but as far as I am concerned, they could be going after any one of us. I was on the platform at the anti-drug rally, as was Jason and Fireman Reed Jackson and Father Michaels. If and when the time comes, we will sneak you out of town. Are you going to sneak Jason out?"

Mr. Pearson says, "Son, you are not a fighter, and we may have a fight on our hands."

AN EXPLOSION!

"What the?!"

Everyone gets their gun. Mr. Cooper and Adam have their bows and arrows, and Jason grabs Jamie and yells, "Get down!"

Silence.

"Oh man, that had a kick!" "Who?"

Paul yells, "Petey, I told you to stay away from the cannon!" "Petey?"

"Cannon?"

"Cannon!"

Pete is knocked on his back, saying, "Oh man, that was so cool!"

I ask, "Paul, why do you have a cannon?"

"Oh, I have a lot of stuff back here. We built the cannon after watching *Junkyard Wars*. Half the fun of building stuff with your kids is blowing it up."

Jason nudges Steve, saying, "Hey, that sounds like the title of your next family self-help book. 'Half the fun of building stuff with your kids is blowing it up.'"

Paul brags, "My oldest daughter, Maggie, and Danny Cooper make their own fireworks, puts M-80s to shame."

I say, "Pete, I didn't know you were around."

"Where else would I be? I live next to Big Paul. Sorry I was late, guys."

The cannon blasted whatever Big Paul and family used as a shell into an old school bus that was converted to carry pigs to market.

Adam replies, "Somewhere there is a very happy vegetarian in this world."

Reed adds, "Piglets won't be going to market in that bus, ouch."

Pete apologizes, saying, "Sorry, Paul, how 'bout I buy you a new bus?"

"Sure, Pete, I can turn this into another chicken coop."

"Remember what I said about in the country, if the dog does not get you, the owner will. And he has a gun and will shoot you dead in his house, and when the cop comes to pick up the body they talk about it over coffee. We also brag about the hole we put in the dead guy."

I go to Paul and say, "Paul, I love Pete as a friend and all, but what can he do?"

Paul says, "Hey, remember, he works for Ice Works. He can use computers and maybe he can track the people who are harassing Jamie on the phone. Pete here designs stuff for the CIA anyway.

I stop Paul. "Pete, you and me, we have to talk."

Pete adds, "Max, if you want, I may be able to get satellite video of the car in question hitting the deer."

I ask, "You can do that?"

"It is best you don't know how though."

CHAPTER TEN

Oh, to be a Kid on a Saturday

Saturday, September 30th, 1978. I wake up and I think it is Saturday, but I can't be sure.

"Max, after you are done sitting on your butt, go outside and mow the lawn, will you, honey?

Oh, it is Saturday alright. I smell breakfast downstairs, and I get dressed and dig in to fried eggs, toast, bacon, hash browns, and fresh milk from Big Paul's dairy farm. As Mom says, "Why go to the store when you can go to the farm and get fresh gossip?" And the milk and eggs are good too.

After watching Bugs and Daffy—I love that duck—I go out and take a look at the lawn mower. Now it is just about worn-out. This was a top-of-the-line lawn mower when my father Marcus bought it in 1975. In fact, Marcus wanted it in the divorce settlement. Why?

We had to put a big lock on the door because he tried to break in the garage.

I turn the key, and it grinds, trying to turn over. I learned a few things about repairing engines over the years, so I start going to work. Thinking back at this time, I think Mom had to call a repairman to work on it. I had to eat tuna fish and egg sandwiches for a week while imagining the repairman eating steak. So I think, *Let's get to work and see what I can do.*

An hour later I put it back together and find under the seat what looks like a piece of paper. Not paper, money. About a couple thousand dollars in hundreds and fifties.

This was Marcus's secret stash! I thought. Ah, what I could do with this money?

New lawn mower, nah, it would just break down. I put the money up in an empty can, replacing the money with old grease rags, and put the rest of the lawn mower back together.

I turn the key, and it starts like a race car, and I start mowing, happy and content with what I have done. It feels good, the smell of freshly cut lawn, and the fact this is my lawn, not a used car lot, is pretty good too. Some kids come by and ask if they can play football here.

"Max, a bunch of high school guys have taken the field."

I say, "You can stay if you rake the yard and put the grass clippings in the trash can."

"Sure! I'll go home and get a rake!"

"Yeah, me too! We have a field!"

I start doing the shrubs and the bushes. By noon the kids were playing football and Mom was on the sidelines watching and smiling and yells out, "The lawn looks great!"

The old lawn mower is about whipped. I just tightened it where it needed it and changed the oil. Mr. Smith's Lawn Care Perfection is just starting to franchise out. On the other side of town, Mr. McGraw has started his branch. He only goes as far as he can ride his tractor because the doctors say he can't drive a car because of his eyes. He gets around town on his bicycle. Maybe we can make a deal.

Mr. Grant, who works at the Cavanaugh City Bank, is watching his son play football.

He and Marcus don't like each other, and I can use this to my advantage. I tap him on the shoulder and ask him if I can talk to him in private. "Oh Max," he says, "I am glad you wanted to talk to me. Your special account, I just got it into a higher percentage rate. What do you think?"

I show him the money I found. "Tell me can we keep this between you and me."

"Sure, what do you want?"

"I want to invest it in Mr. Smith's Lawn Care Perfection stock."

"You could own a down payment on your own franchise with this."

"That would be too much work. I want stock. And can we set it up that if a rainy day comes for my mom, that some money could fall into her hands?"

"Max, I think that can be arranged."

Mr. Grant in a few years will run the Cavanaugh City Bank. It is tempting to use the knowledge I have of the future and make some money.

After doing my good deed I go for a bike ride. I get a tagalong. "Hey Max, wait up!"

It's Wendy. She asks, "Were you serious about what you were saying the other day about the future?"

I lower my head, telling her, "About the future, you should not be making promises you can't keep, Wendy."

"What do you mean?"

"About Jimmy, you can't protect him, and you shouldn't be saying you can."

"He doesn't have anybody, Max. His parents—"

I add, "Would do the world of good if a tornado hit their house while Jimmy was away at school, or a meteor hit them while Jimmy was away, and then all the little kids could dance around the destroyed house and sing, 'Ding dong, the parents are dead.'"

"Max, that is terrible!"

I also add, "It is kind of ironic that we see Jimmy every day in tattered clothes, with bruises, and it is like nobody notices."

Wendy drops her head and says, "Adults like my mom have looked into it. As long as they provide a house, and the social worker does not see anything, they can't do anything."

I add, "And there is no guarantee that if he is put in a foster home it will be your parents."

Wendy drops her head again, saying, "Not when we are full, as it is now."

"Wendy, when you make a promise you can't keep, especially to a kid like Jimmy who does not have much to go on as it is, he is going to feel betrayed if you can't deliver."

Wendy cries, "Don't talk to me, Max," and she rides away in tears. I hate making her cry. I look up into the sky praying, *So what do I do now, Lord? You put me here.*

A little help?

I ride past Ritz Ville—that is what we call the section of town filled with many thousand-dollar or even million-dollar homes where Churchill lives. I live in old Cavanaugh City myself. Keep going to the outskirts, and you can see farmland and what will become the suburbs.

The old McGraw farmhouse stands pretty much empty. I was here with Marcus when he had them auction off farm equipment to pay off a loan. "Father and son days," I believe some people call it. It takes a while for Mr. McGraw to focus his eyes to see me.

"Max, is that you? How you doing?"

"Good."

"Your dad took my tractors away, but I still have my land, and now people want to build on it. What can I do for you?"

"Our old lawn mower is not long for this world."

"Is that so? My wife and I drove by your place this morning, and you did a fine job of cutting it."

"Well, that is very kind. I wonder if we could come to an arrangement. I have a good-sized garage and a pretty big lawn. I was thinking you could store your lawn mower at my place, and when I need to mow my lawn I could use it.

Mr. McGraw strokes his chin. "I do have a good number of people on that side of town that ask me if I could mow their lawns. I could use a partner."

"I am already taken. I work as a bag and stock boy at the C. Connection, and sometimes in the summer I milk cows at the Chapel dairy farm. But maybe who knows?"

Mr. McGraw comments, "Well, I have a spare mower; you would have to drive it to your place."

I ask, "No trailer?"

"I just go where I can drive my mower."

"Well let me check it out and see what my mom thinks, okay?"

"You did this without asking your mom?"

"Sure, why not?"

"Well, you are a good businessman."

I ride my bike home in a way that is downhill. Steve sees me, and he is doing some light exercising, training for cross-country running. He says, "I saw Wendy today, and she was crying. What did you say to her?"

"I said, don't go making promises you can't keep."

Steve asks, "What promise is that?"

"That she can protect Jimmy." "From whom?" he asks.

I answer, "His parents and the world in general."

Steve replies, "It is what she does, Max. She is like a mom to everybody. She makes promises that she can't keep, and by the grace of God or something, her promises in the end are kept. Like mother like daughter."

I comment, "Just to be on the safe side, don't pick me up tomorrow for church. I think I am going to be Catholic tomorrow."

"You mean sleep in and not go to church?"

"No, I am going."

When I get home, I tell Mom about the idea I had with Mr. McGraw, and she liked it. She called him, and he agreed it was a great idea, and I would be by to pick up the lawn mower tomorrow.

July 18, 2002, Thursday.

I meet Dr. Dan Cottager at the hospital. I am still having a bit of trouble believing he is a doctor now. Dan comments, "Hey, Max, nice shirt."

If white people don't learn to talk with an accent, the only thing we will be known for is white bread, mayonnaise, and the funky chicken. I mean, the guy is a klutz, but he did get me out of the coma earlier maybe. Dan takes me to the security taping room. The guard who was on staff that day is also here, as is Dr. Sam.

The video monitor shows the intruder coming into my room and covering my head with a pillow. The guard says, "Come on, show us your face."

I say to the guard and anyone who will listen, "He knows where the cameras are. Churchill's punch caught the intruder off guard, but he is more concerned about covering his face."

As the guard switches camera angles, it becomes apparent this guy knows where all the cameras are. He has done his homework. The guard mumbles, "There is not a decent picture in the whole record. How can that be?"

I say, "One, he purchased the camera layout from somebody. Two, he is a government agent of some sorts; they would have the records already on file. And three, he was trying to assassinate me."

Dr. Sam asks, "Assassinate you? Why?"

I leave them asking questions.

Paul, on the other hand, goes to Howard's junkyard. He brings along Big Paul, Jr., or Big Paul 2.0, as his friends and mother call him—just don't call him late for dinner—who is home from the Air Force. They kind of expect him there at the junkyard every so often, getting parts for their projects and refurbishing. The kids and his headman Troy look in one direction, and he goes in another. Paul takes pictures, paint chip samples, and glass fragments of a couple cars that match my description. He starts looking at a car that is under a couple others and finds dried blood.

Toney asks, "What are you doing?"

Paul answers, "Oh, my boy is looking for a car to play with and restore. I am just looking for possible parts."

Toney yells, "I say get out of here now!"

Big Paul says, "Toney, just relax. I am just looking."

"Get out of here now!"

Big Paul 2.0 comes from behind Toney, asking, "Having a problem, Daddy?"

Toney turns around, looks up, and sees Big Paul 2.0. "Yes, son, but I am certain we can handle it. I was just telling Toney that you (*wink*) were looking for a car, and I thought this might be a good one to look at."

"Well, Dad, let me move the cars on top so we can get a better look at it."

Big Paul 2.0 moves the other cars, and I can imagine Toney *thinking to himself, We had to use a crane to move those cars on top of that car.*

"We grow them big and farm-fresh on the farm," says Big Paul as he starts taking pictures. "Yeah, this looks like a keeper. Hey, Toney, how much for the car?"

Toney grabs his head and walks away.

With a crowbar, Paul and Paul 2.0 open the trunk. White powder. I gave Paul a chemical stick that will change to a certain color if it comes in contact with certain drugs. Cocaine, for example, changes on contact. "Oh yeah, son, this is it alright."

I get a call on Dan's cell phone. Dan feels the vibration and checks his phone. It's Paul's number. "Hello. Oh, it's for you. Hi? You found it, are you sure?" Paul said Toney tried to get them out of there, but they made him change his mind.

With a smile I say, "I am sure you did."

"Do you want us to bring it back? I have the trailer."

"Paul, you are taking a risk here. The guy on the camera was no amateur. I don't know if he is a professional killer or a government agent with orders to kill me. They tried to kill Jamie. If you have any evidence, they may come after you."

Big Paul soberly states, "Well I would rather use a car for bait than a good friend."

"Besides, Toney is giving us the runaround, saying he doesn't have paperwork on the car right now, so until he finds it, he can't sell it to me."

I add, "Or crush it. Do what you feel you can do."

Paul replies, "Me and Paul 2.0 are getting fingerprints, and who knows, maybe we will get a match with the hub cap."

I then go to Pete's. Pete is renovating an old farmhouse. Pete is there and says, "Hey Max, come on in."

I say, "You said you could track the car and get satellite video."

Pete nods. "Yeah, and I also said it is best you don't know how. Okay?"

I hand over the make and model of the car and the time it was possibly on the road before it hit the deer. Pete starts punching keys and putting the information in. He then says, "Well, that is step one."

I ask, "How long before you get any information?"

He says, "When I get it, I'll call you."

I respond, "I don't have a phone."

"When you get one, call me. I'll let you know."

Later that day I meet with the Carter County police chief. "Tom, how are you doing?"

"Fine, the Mrs. and I were praying for you when you were in that coma."

"Thanks. I wonder if I could ask you some questions."

"Come, let's take a walk to my office. Questions about what?"

"As you may know, I am a detective, and I am starting an investigation on the murder attempt on James Scott and his daughter's life."

"Yes, I read the statement you gave to Officer Watson."

"I have also been given added information to make me believe Mr. Scott is in need of protection."

Tom asks, "Can you share this information?"

We enter his office. I pass it to him, and he puts on his glasses and looks it over.

I ask, "How well do you know the sheriff of Cavanaugh City?"

"Not very likeable. Keeps to himself. Does not like it when I suggest we do a joint investigation."

"Can he be trusted?"

"He calls this area home. Any chance he gets, he is parts unknown. I always wondered why."

"I believe late July the 12th and early the 13th, there was a drug shipment that had an accident."

"Where?"

"Deer Crossing Alley Valley Highway." "What happened?"

"Head-on with a deer at seventy-five to ninety miles per hour."

I show pictures. "I have fingerprints and blood samples, and I believe we found the car."

"The driver?"

"No hospitals in the area admitted anyone. It will take a while to see if anyone pops up on the fingerprint and DNA files. I have a bloody bandanna we found near the car."

"Max, I didn't know. I need the ability to ask questions and put the law behind it."

Tom ponders it aloud. "I almost lost the election to that guy, and he could be aiding in the smuggling of drugs."

"The car in question is at Howard's junkyard."

"Are you sure, Max?"

I pass the chemical sticks that Paul used on the trunk of the car. "I saw the tow truck leave the garage late Thursday night. I played some basketball and came back the same way and saw the truck drive back into town with the safety lights off and leave town."

"That is a violation right there, if anyone saw it." I add, "Or looked the other way."

Tom nods his head, saying, "Max, God has his hand on you in this situation, and when you were put in that coma, the devil thought he had you beat. The Lord is in this."

"Can you put me on the force?"

"It will take some time to get the paperwork going. You just came out of A coma. Are you fit to serve?"

"You wanna take me to the practice range? I can use your gun."

The chief gets up to go to the practice range and reaches for his gun, and it is gone.

Tom wonders, *What the—?* I pass it to him with his wallet. "I think I am up to the challenge."

"Reed said he thought you were in Delta Force or something."

I reply, "Reed says a lot of things. And yes, I have had some or something training."

CHAPTER ELEVEN

When Lost, Ask for Directions

Sunday, October 1, 1978.

I get ready and put on my Sunday best. I hate suits. Walking to church with my mom. She rarely goes, but decides if I am going, she might as well go too. I have been to just about every church and Hebrew temple in our little town. My mom calls me a searcher, and I guess I am. After service, I ask Father Michaels if we can talk. He says, "Sure, if you can wait."

I say, "I'll go home and get some lunch and come back."

He asks. "Can you bring me anything? All I have had today is a communion wafer."

I come back with a platter of leftovers, and he says, "You want to give your confession while I eat?"

So I go into the box. I can hear him munch and crunch on the other side.

I say, "Forgive me, Father, for I have sinned." Munch crunch.

"Oh what could you have done? It has only been how long since your last confession?"

"You can't discuss anything I tell you with anyone else, right?"

Munch crunch. "That is right." Burp. "Excuse me."

"I am going to need to confess soon. I am from the future."

Cough of food and a hack. "What?" from Father Michaels.

"When I go to bed tonight, I awake in the year two thousand two."

"Really? Who is the President?"

"George W. Bush, the forty-third president of the United States.'

"And the pope?"

"Pope John Paul."

"How did this happen?"

"I am not quite all sure. It started the night I got hit by a car, and then I woke up in 1978 a couple days ago. When I go to sleep here, I wake up in two thousand two. It kind of replaces my rapid eye movement or dreaming state when I sleep."

He asks, "Which is the dream and which is reality?" "Actually, both are reality. I put a scar on my arm here." I

show it to him. "And it is on my arm there in two thousand two. Don't be shocked, but my first day in 1978, Bridge from the Wild Tail comic books explained some of the details.

"In my future, someone tried to kill Jamie and Ellen Scott's little girl. I was there and saved her. That act and a car collision caused me to be put in a coma and possibly, I don't know, sent me back in time."

"You are pretty calm about all of this."

The priest states, "Man has done time travel before, why not God? I think he even sent John the Revelator through time to be able to write the Book of Revelation."

"So what do you do in the future?"

"Detective in Chicago P.D. I also have another life." "What kind of life?"

"After I graduated high school, I joined the Marines, and I was offered to receive special training, and it was an offer I could not turn down, literally."

"What kind of training?"

"CIA Black Ops. I can speak different languages."

"Like what?"

"Russian."

"It is good to be able to speak the language of a people you are spying on." Not too much to my amazement, because he taught me Russian as a child.

Father Michaels says in Russian, "Yes, and you speak it so well. I do not hear an American accent in your voice, like you used to have. That American accent will get you killed. You have to be able to play a good game of chess, and also let them win from time to time. They are damn sore losers."

"They are that. What?! How do you know?"

Now he says, "I served as a special agent during Vietnam. A spook, if you will. The Russians interrogated and imprisoned downed US pilots, and I interrogated the Russians whenever I got the chance. I became very good at what I did."

"What was your code name?"

Father Michaels taps the code out. "With your connections in the future, you could find out about me, and I would not want you to know a few things about my past."

I tap, "We don't have reunions, and we don't have old folks' homes, do we?"

"Rarely do we make deathbed confessions. And we are never retired from service." He chuckles, saying, "Though a few change their names and get book deals."

I ask in plain English, "If you had the chance to do it over again, would you still take that offer?"

The good father thinks about it then says, "Knowing what I know … yeah, who am I to know the countless lives I have touched. Allowing God to be used through you in any way is God being used through you." With tears he adds, "Now let me bless you, my son."

After we talk, he asks, "Do you need a ride or anything?" "Actually I do, to Mr. McGraw's farm. I have to drive a lawn mower from there to my place."

He chuckles. "Oh, this has to be a change of pace to a good car chase in Chicago."

"Yeah, it is. In the future, someone is trying to kill Jamie and me too, for that matter."

He holds up his hand to his lips till we get in the car. "You never know who is listening.

"I guess being a kid, I let my skills slip a bit."

"Is that how you beat the crap out of Jack and his brother's gang?" In my memory of the original event, Jack and his friends beat me so bad I was sharing a hospital room with my good friend Steve Pearson. I defended myself. Father adds, "You showed mercy then by not killing him.

"I admit it was tempting."

The priest replies, "Be friends with him, and share Jesus's love with him. What is he in your future?"

"Drunk drug runner, has some kids, different mothers, not a very nice guy."

"Then make him a friend and see what happens. Don't just make scars that last; make friends that will last."

We drive to a woodland setting. I see targets off in the distance.

As we get out, Father opens his trunk and hands me a .45 and says, "Shoot."

I take a look at the gun and twirl it for feel and balance. "Oh just—"

Bang!

I hit the targets until the gun is almost empty. Father says, "You left a bullet."

"No, that is mine."

Father Michaels says, "Nasty habit to save a bullet for yourself, Max."

My response was, "I have been in situations where I was tempted to use that bullet, sir. I am expendable."

"No, Max, you are very precious." He quotes Jesus: "No man or woman hath greater love than is willing to give your own life."

I add, "It is also called expendable."

He puts his hand on my head and around my shoulder and says, "Don't feel guilt for living. If your time on earth were through, I am sure God would have brought you home. Be encouraged, be of good cheer, God has a plan for your life! My God, you are a good shot!"

I add, "I have had a lot of practice."

We get back in the car, heading to McGraw's farmhouse.

"So, is your mom still alive?"

"She died in '88. Lung cancer and a bad heart. Ah, smoking, bad habit."

"And Marcus?"

"Died in '80, shot while somebody was robbing his bank in Carter City."

"Maybe you are here to influence a different result. I go to an interfaith prayer breakfast once a month with local pastors and even a rabbi. I have kept tabs on Marcus. He is going to a church in Carter City now, and I hope it is a genuine repentance. That is good news, Max."

I grit my teeth, saying, "It is hard to be happy for a guy who called me bastard to my face when he was drunk or sober. Slapped up my mother and . . . Fine, he found God. As far as I am concerned, he isn't my father. And he can stay out of my life."

"How do you know he is not your father?"

"What?"

"Yes, Marcus was an all-around SOB. I will not ask you to forgive him for that just now. But how do I say it? Ask me when I see you in two thousand two."

"Why?"

"Because, I am not supposed to share a confession. But I may share a history after your parents are dead. Wait, I am still alive in two thousand two, right?"

Tears come down my face. "Yeah, you prayed for me while I was in my coma."

"Then I will talk to you in two thousand two."

He drops me off at Mr. McGraw's farm.

Mr. McGraw comes out, and we exchange keys, and I start driving the lawn mower back into town. The slow ride makes me take it all in. The leaves are changing, the sun that will be setting, and it is a beautiful fall day. I see the guys, Jamie, Churchill, and Jason, at the park off in the distance. They see me coming down the street, and they run and get on my wagon and get a free ride. So I have a one-man parade. Cool. These are my friends through thick and thin. We have been through it all, and I guess we may be through it all again.

Friday, July 19, 2002.

Not a way to wake up in the morning. Churchill is great for putting up with me. I helped him clean out the house of booze, and he is going through d.t.'s, so I gather my things and load them into the car. The first thing I do is look up Father Michaels's number. He answers the phone, "Hello?"

"It is two thousand two, and we need to talk."

"Max, I have been waiting for you to call me."

We meet at the local diner and order breakfast to go, and then we sit in the park and eat. Another Norman Rockwell moment. After we eat at the picnic table, Father Michaels says,

"So let me get this straight. You talked to me in '78. You went to sleep and wake up it is 2002."

I add, "Something like that. You said, 'How do you know he is not your father?'"

"I did."

"What did you mean by that?"

"When I became a priest I came to Cavanaugh City. Marcus even then had a reputation for, well, you know. Your mother got tired of being sick and tired of Marcus. Well, you know, and well, one night she hires a babysitter and goes out for a night on the town. Marcus was already out on the town at the same time. Days later, Maxine gets morning sickness. Marcus comes to me, saying he wants a divorce! 'She is not getting a damn thing from me. I want a divorce!'

"I told him, 'You will not get the blessing for a divorce from me or the church. You have come to me and Father Gregory time and time again and asked forgiveness, but when your wife who has been faithful to you all these years goes out, gets drunk once, and gets pregnant, you want, no demand, a divorce! And if you think of divorcing her, I will leave the church and tell everything you have done!' That shut Marcus up."

I yell out, "You should have let him have his divorce!"

"Hindsight is greater than foresight, Max. From where I was standing, it was the only call to make. A few years later, I was drowning my sorrows at the bar. The barkeep says, 'Father I am not Catholic, but I have something that needs to be said.' What, I asked? 'Marcus got drunk and said Max was not his son, that he was a bastard child.'

"Half drunk I say, 'So what else is new?'"

"Well I got to thinking,' the barkeep continues, 'I was a temporary here at the bar, and I was bartending the one night Mrs. Faraday came into the bar. She was pretty sloshed to begin with."

"And?" I say to him.

"Well Marcus was here at the time, and he was three sheets to the wind himself. The two of them got to talking, and I thought they were just playing. I didn't know Marcus's reputation like the rest. And they both walked off."

I snap to attention. "Are you saying my mom and Marcus got drunk, and I was the result?"

"Your mother was too busy crucifying herself, so she probably never thought of it. And Marcus at that time was mad because people like me held him accountable for his actions. And he was too drunk to remember anyway."

I shake my head. "That ruins my dream of Mom having a one-night stand with a Marine."

"You would rather your mother have a one-night stand than to have a—"

"I can see your point."

"You know, with DNA technology today, you could find out if it could be true."

"Would I want to believe it, if it was true?"

I drop Father off at the church and go to take care of some personal business. Since I pretty much lost everything to gambling and the Mafia screwed up my credit, I have been doing everything on a cash basis. Gambling was only part of it. When the Mafia got involved, I was working on an underground gambling network in Chicago. I had a solid case, and then they destroyed my name and reputation, trying to get me to back off. I was told by my old partner to drop it. I didn't drop it. Besides my gambling debt I was just recovering from, they destroyed my name and reputation.

In the end, we shut down the Mafia's racket. I still have a bullet with my name on it and my picture on a dartboard. All I can say is, get in line.

"Do not put all your eggs in one basket," a phrase I have used over the years. Religiously, I have been sending money to "Abba" Rabbi Hyman and the Smokey Joe fund, and when Grant retired from the bank, Abba was given the account. I am not the money miser Marcus was. Just give me my pizza and pop money and pay my payments and tithe, and what is leftover send to Abba. I am down to my last five, and I don't want my friends in Chicago to send money to John Doe via Western Union in Cavanaugh City. That is right, just say Max Faraday, and red flags go up, and it is, what money, where did it go? Please, somebody give me a terrorist to shoot. That I can handle; finances, internet commerce, telephone identity fraud, I am screwed.

I come to Hyman, Hyman, and Hyman. Burney greets me, "Max, hi!"

"Burney, is Abba here?"

"What is the problem?"

"I am tired of dealing with this on my own. I need to talk to Abba."

Burney says to his secretary, "Hold my calls or take messages."

I am taken back to the study of Rabbi Hyman.

"Max! How is the Christian son I always wanted?"

"I could be better."

"Tell Abba, and I will make it better."

And I tell the whole sorted details.

"So you started gambling again, and these Mafia destroyed your finances?"

"Everything but what you have kept for me here."

Abba mutters, "We had a hacker try to break in about that time. Almost crashed what Burney calls a firewall."

"Oh no."

"But I called a few favors, and it was taken care of. No need to worry. Your money is safe with us, my child. Would you like to see it?"

"Sure, it has been a while."

Burney says, "I'll print it up." As he leaves, Abba reaches out his hand and says in Hebrew, "You are one of my sons, and nobody messes with one of my boys."

"Abba, these people are dangerous."

"The danger is to let them win and go unchallenged; an eye for an eye."

"I know what you did in Israel. I have friends, they tell me things. We have a few options."

"Now you know where I got that, we have a few options. I have a few favors I can use, let me call them in, and we can clear your name."

Burney comes back saying, "Whoa, here you go."

I look at it. I am rich. How? Don't tell me. I am not a money manager, it will just go over my head.

"You better talk to Rachel. She can help you find a nice home, somewhere in the country perhaps."

"I have been looking at the Trans Am over at Howard's. But that will take cash."

Abba says "I'll get you cash. And we will get you a phone, a cell phone at least, and a mailing address, a PO Box now, and they will not bother you because you are one of my children. You just figure out what is going on with Jamie, he is a good kid. And you will spend the Sabbath with us."

"I can't say no to that."

I leave the Hymans and head to Churchill's mansion. Dr. Churchill Smith, my friend, and I have more in common than I care to admit. He has gone without a drink for days, and he is cracking. I have gone less than a year. As he stands in the library holding a flask of whisky, I yell, "Put it down, Churchill! Now!"

"Max, I am my father's son. I am going to get someone killed, just like him!"

"Not if you get yourself killed first. Put the drink down now."

"One drink won't hurt me."

"It will if I break your arm."

Churchill put the drink down.

"Abstinence, sobriety, words to learn and live by! I know I have gone less than a year without a drink. I and you are going to get in an AA program, and we will beat this."

"I am a doctor. How is it going to look, me going to an AA program? I will be laughed out of practice!"

"I don't think that will happen. It is better than killing someone by misreading a syringe or giving a wrong prescription! You have been damn lucky, Churchill!"

"You are not your father's son. He never tried to get help; you can."

He places the flask down. I empty it in the sink in the bathroom along with the whisky bottle.

"We have to get all the alcohol out of the house now. You can't be trusted with yourself."

"You sound like you have had experience with this."

"I got this tattoo, Selah, because I was so plastered I could not even feel it when they put it on my arm! That was a moment I could have been called to defend myself, my country, or my teammates.

"I cannot let my guard down, not now or ever. Neither can you. Your father can't change his past, but you can make your future. Now let's rid this place of liquor."

Churchill yells, "That is the good wine, two hundred dollars a bottle!"

"How much is a human life, Dr. Smith? Thanksgiving, Christmas, New Year's Eve, Easter! No tolerance!"

"Can we give it away?"

"Just as long as it gets out of the house tonight!"

"You know, Max, you are a real bastard!"

I grab Churchill, tossing him to the ground, flipping him on his chest and rub my elbow in the back of his neck.

"That is right, I am a bastard, and I'll bust your ass if you try to get a drink!"

Churchill gets up off the floor, saying, "You look tired, Max, why don't you take a nap"? Take it easy."

"Yeah. I might as well." So I lie down, and I am out.

***

Monday, October 2nd, 1978.

I wake up wondering, *Could I be Marcus's son?* I have accepted as truth that I am a bastard and to deal with it. But to be lied to all my life is, I don't know? Would it ease Mom's heart if she knew the truth? And Marcus, how would he deal with it? He can kiss my ass.

Monday, go to school, do what I got to do, and come home and go to sleep. There has to be more to this life than that. Wendy is here, but she is dead in my future, or is it present?

I go downstairs, and Mom has breakfast for me waiting. And a small sack.

"What is the sack for?"

"Oh, Mrs. Horton told me about Jimmy. That is his breakfast if he didn't have one."

"So how is she?"

"She could be coming home tomorrow. Max, I might be staying with her till she is up and going."

Mom never had to ask me this before; I was in the hospital, thanks to Jack and company. And Uncle Sherman came to visit during that time to take care of me when I came home.

"Sure, Mom, stay with her. I can take care of myself."

"Max, I want you to stay with other people when or if I stay with Mrs. Horton. You need to see what it is like to be with a family."

"We are a family, Mom."

"Humor me, Max. I'll know a little more tonight."

So here I go to school, same old same old. Wendy and Jimmy. He grabs his belly and sheds a tear. And he looks at Mrs. Horton's house. My memory kicks in, *Give him his breakfast, dummy*, and I run to catch up to them.

"Hey, little guy, don't cry."

I hand him the little bag, and he smiles, giving me a hug. As I walk with them I hear Wendy say, "I missed you Sunday."

I shrug my shoulders, saying, "I had to sort things out with an old friend."

She asks, "Things sorted out?"

"Getting started, I think."

She kisses my cheek and says, "You are forgiven."

I ask, "For what?"

"You know."

"No, I don't, but I am not going to ruin it by trying to figure it out."

As I carry my stuff to the table at lunchtime, I see Jack sitting by himself. The phrase, *Make friends not scars that last*, repeats in my head. I sit down next to Jack. He takes a look at me and gets up, and I say, "Don't leave, everything is okay, man."

He uneasily sits back down, asking, "What you want?"

"To eat my lunch, conversation is good too. Where is your crew?"

"They left me, thanks to you beating me up."

I smile and say, "Well, I beat them up too, and the pleasure was all mine. Sorry, I am a jerk. Let's start over. My name is Max Faraday."

In stunned disbelief he says, "Jack."

I go for a handshake, and I ask, "So what do you do for fun?"

During recess, the guys ask me why I sat with him.

"Because I wanted to tell him the war between us is over. You should cut him some slack. His big brother just got put in prison for selling and distributing drugs.'

"So?"

"He also lost his mother two years before he moved here. His dad is a drunk half the time, and Jack has become an auto mechanic in between his father's drunken lapses. Top it off, his dad works third shift at the factory and sleeps during the day. I asked him some automotive questions. I think he might even be able to fix Paul's truck if you gave him half a chance."

Stunned, Big Paul mutters, "No shit."

"No shit. I told him what you told me, and I think he could fix it. He is smarter than people give him credit for. He rides a bike to school for something to do. If you asked him, he might even ride out to your place."

Big Paul says, "We live six miles out of town, and he lives four miles the other way."

I state, "He is hungry for a friend, Paul. Sixteen miles is not that long."

Big Paul adds, "If you come out with him, I'll let him look at my truck."

"Deal. I can use the pay phone and tell my mom, and Dan, can you tell your dad I won't be coming tonight?"

Dan says, "Sure, if it will get us a ride to the big city. I can do that."

I wonder, "Big city?"

Dan explains, "Yeah, Paul was talking about taking the truck to the city and getting some comics. Me and Churchill were thinking about books at the used books store, and the girls were talking about clothes for the dance coming up in October."

Big Paul adds, "Yeah, well we aren't going anywhere unless my truck is running."

Riding six miles out to the Chapel Farm makes me wish we had mountain bikes.

Jack is good company; we talk basketball and sports. There is a lot of stuff I would like to talk about. It makes me rely on my photographic memory. I do my best not to mention future basketball greats like Shaq, Michael Jordan, or the great white hope Larry Byrd. What can I say, the best is yet to come?

Farming is a never-ending job, and we see everybody doing something. You can't get in trouble if you have chores to do. They have cows, pigs, chickens, and dogs and cats. I have worked here in the summer before and during harvest, putting up bailed hay. My young hands have calluses from working here. Mrs. Chapel is the best cook. She fed me so well I can see where Big Paul gets his appetite. Just before we turn into the driveway, a McDonnell Douglas jet flies over and lands at the Chapel air strip.

Jack just says, "Wow, I never seen a jet land before."

I say, "Oh, McDonnell Douglas has come to the farm."

Jack asks, "What you mean?"

I smile and tell him, "Just be quiet and watch."

Paul comes out and says, "Hey, you come and follow me." He takes us to the back garage that has a bunch of old junk and stuff.

Jack asks, "Can you turn the key so I can hear how it sounds?"

When he does, *rumble crack thud sputter choke* comes out and a bit of smoke.

"Can you get me some tools and lights?" Jack asks.

"Sure, can you do this by yourself? I have some more chores to do. Max, you going to stay?"

"Sure." Big Paul leaves us, and I play nurse to Jack's doctor.

We watch what is going on. Two business-dressed McDonnell Douglas professionals come walking around, asking, "Is Paul Chapel around?"

I ask, "Junior or Senior?" He replies, "Senior."

"Ah, ask Uncle Robert," and I point him in his direction.

Jack asks, "What is going on?"

I answer with, "Where is the last place you would think some of the best McDonnell Douglas ideas come from?"

Jack shrugs his shoulders. "I don't know."

The two businessmen follow Paul Sr. upstairs to his office over the house garage. We go to work on the truck.

Three men come storming out of the office. Big Paul Sr. calls to his son Connor, "Tell your mom I have to go quick. I'll be back in a couple days. Start packing."

Jack asks again, "What is going on?"

"Jack, Mr. Chapel is an aircraft technician, expert even, who knows how to fly just about anything. Sometimes McDonnell Douglas calls on him and asks his opinion on stuff. I have been here before, and the Air Force called on him, and he was gone for weeks at a time."

About an hour later, Big Paul comes back and asks, "How is it going?"

"Turn the key and find out."

Choke Sputter Vroom!

Big Paul gets out, leaving the truck running. "Wow, man, that is cool."

Jack says, "You need parts. I wouldn't go too far as it is. Get me a pad of paper. and I'll get you a list."

Big Paul hands him his drawing pad and pencil. Jack stares at it. "Whoa, shit, you drew this?"

"Yeah, I would like to fix her up a little bit at a time and paint her up slick."

"You can paint?"

"See that John Deere? I did that."

Jack walks around the truck, writing down parts needed, then hands it to Paul. "I can get you parts at Howard's junkyard. He is a friend of my dad. But with my time to do the job and parts, I need at least a hundred."

Big Paul says, "Mind if I talk with Max a moment? Max, what do you think?"

"I think he can do it. Somebody needs to give this guy a chance. I can't do it alone."

Paul looks back at Jack, saying, "Yeah, he looks like he has had it rough. Okay. Here is seventy-five now. I get paid Wednesday. I can have twenty-five then. Hey, can I give you a ride?"

Jack looks at the money and says, "Hey, if Howard's junkyard is still open, we can get parts tonight."

I get dropped off at my place, and the two of them go looking for parts and dreaming of how they can fix up the truck. Note on the door says Mom is at Mrs. Horton's house and to meet her there for dinner. The door is unlocked, so I go in and Mom and Mrs. Horton are talking. "You know you can come and stay with me and Max."

"Thank you, but no, Maxine remember when you invited me to your house for Thanksgiving dinner? Too many memories came back to me."

You see, the house we live in now used to be Mrs. Horton's. She raised a good-sized family, and most of them were boys, and they gave their life defending this country in World War Two and Korea. Her daughters moved away, and she was left all alone. Marcus purchased the house in fifty-four when her husband died.

Mom looks at Mrs. Horton and says, "In a way, I know how you feel. I look at the house and see memories of what used to be too."

"Oh don't say that, dear, you and Max have had some—"

"Yeah, we have had some . . ."

This is not the way to enter, so I sneak back out and knock on the door and wait for Mom to answer it.

"Oh, Max, you should have just come in."

"I don't know, maybe you and Mrs. Horton needed time to talk."

"I'll make some soup and grilled cheese sandwiches. You go in and talk to Mrs. Horton."

"What am I supposed to say?"

Mom says, "Talk to her." Mrs. Horton was a schoolteacher when my mom was growing up, and I think she even had a hand in getting her a teacher's scholarship. She has set up scholarships over the years, and my mom is on the grant board.

I ask Mrs. Horton, "So how you doing?"

An elderly lady with eyes of an angel smiles and says, "Oh, I thought the Lord would have called me home by now. I guess he still has a few things for me to do. Dr. Churchill Smith Sr. I guess kept me going. I was told I died on the operating table, and I guess I did. You know, I have been praying for you, Max, and that little Jimmy boy." Tears come to her eyes. "Tell me you will help Wendy keep her promise to him."

I am silent in awe.

"I was ready to jump into Jesus's arms and stay in heaven. Jesus said, 'I am not done; you still have some unfinished work to do.' Max, He is so proud of you. You are a son to Him, that is why He has given you this gift. Listen to Him, don't just call it your cop instinct. It is the Holy Spirit whispering to you. The Good Lord does not put anything in motion that He has not seen the end to. You are going to fail at times, and that is okay, only God is perfect. He turns things that are imperfect and turns them into perfection.

"I know you have had bad dreams in the past. It was of the devil, not of God. He loves you."

In astonishment, I ask, "How?"

"When you been alone, as I have been over the years, you can either keep on going alone or keep going on with Him.

"He is a father when I needed a father, a mother when I needed a mother, a friend when I needed a friend. I won't be here long, Max. I hope you don't mind me having your mother close to me for a little while. Unfortunately, although I am thankful for the skill and knowledge of Dr. Churchill Smith Sr., I feel he will fail me somehow.

"When I go, it will be my time, and that is all right with me. You are going to be a fine Marine and a fine—oh my, God has you taking out some bad people; I will be praying for you— police officer."

My mom brings me dinner, soup and grilled cheese sandwiches, old people's food. And sitting by this saint, I have been fed in another way. I go back to my house alone, and Mom stays with Mrs. Horton. I am tired; it is a good tired, and I go to bed. I relive a section of my high school reunion.

As the night goes on, I think about the "missing." Big Paul comes by. and I ask, "Where is Jack?"

Big Paul says, "Jack … it is sad, Max, sad. Five years ago, his wife got cancer, and she fought it hard for about a year. He got lost in the bottle. Two years ago, the kids were taken away from him and placed in a foster home. He lost his license to DUI and works at Howard's Garage as a mechanic."

I did not know and reply, "Really?"

I wake up later that afternoon, and I get in my car and drive back into town.

I stop at Howard's Car Sales and Garage. There are memories in my head of Jack as if he is or was part of my little click, you might call it. But it is all fuzzy, as if, yeah, I know, but at the same time I don't know. I know that Jack after school started working on Mr. Smith's Lawn Care Perfection but not a whole lot more than that. I guess I am supposed to find out as I go along. I get out of my cruiser and go over to the Trans Am and look at the price. I can afford it, thanks to the Hymans. I also know how to deal, thanks to Abba too. I walk into the garage, and I see a mechanic under a car and ask, "Jack, is that you?"

"Yeah, who wants to know?"

"It is me, Max. I just wanted to—"

He rolls from underneath the car and says, "Max, it is so good to see you."

I say, "Wish you could've been at the reunion."

"No you don't. I haven't been myself since . . ."

"Yeah, I can imagine. I miss Wendy and your wife, Ruth Leanne. It does not help to say, things happen."

Jack dusts himself off, saying, "So what can I do for you?"

"I want to know a little about the Trans Am."

"Oh, I can help you there. She is just waiting to run wild, if somebody can give her a good home, that is.'

"Did you do work on it?"

"Yeah, some fiberglass, but hey, she is all there. Mr.—"

Howard comes out of his office. "Jack, isn't you supposed to be doing an overhaul?"

"Yes, Mr. Howard, I was just talking to my good friend Max Faraday about why the Trans Am is such a great deal."

"Well, get back to the garage. Max, it is a surprise to see you up walking around."

"I would like to buy the Trans Am, but I feel it is a bit much." I get out a pad and write out my amount and show it to Mr. Howard.

"Come on, Max, did you bang your head in that coma?" and he says as he writes a different amount.

"What about the extras what can you give me?"

"Well, you are a friend, and this car has been sitting here waiting for you to come along. If you can get the money today, I can throw in undercoating and three oil changes."

I write a new amount, show it to him, and say, "How about this?" He bites his lip, saying, "If you can get me the money today,

I mean cash, we have a deal."

I shake his hand; it is cold and clammy. I get back in my cruiser and head to the Hymans.

****

Abba says, "Max, I need to talk to you." He motions me back to his office.

"What did you do to piss off the Mafia?"

"I did not give up in my investigation." "What happened?"

I tell the story, and Burney says,

"Nobody messes with my little brother."

Burney is just a couple months older than me, but ever since Abba has called me one of his sons, he has never been jealous. "Ever since we started getting your name cleared, things have been happening. We have been attacked by someone on the net, so I called in some help."

Burney waves me back to the computer room, and Pete is going at it like a nerd possessed.

Pete looks up and says, "Max, you have some people who don't like you very much."

"Sometimes you are better judged by your enemies than by your friends."

"Well, a number of them have computers, and they don't like you."

Abba adds, "If they want a fight, we will give them a fight."

Pete smiles, saying, "Oh I can give them a fight. The nice thing about technology, it can be the great equalizer. I am a warrior in the digital battleground. I have just about all of them running for the hills."

Amazed at what all Pete can do, I say, "Pete, have you given them a good scare?"

"Oh yeah!"

"Pete, tell them to back off and leave me alone. Just restore what is mine. I want justice, not vengeance. Mess with me again, and I will have vengeance. Can you do that?"

"Sure, Max."

He almost looks sad. I think he really wanted to bite someone's head off.

"Thanks, Pete."

"Jamie is my friend too, Max."

"So why are you going the extra mile?"

"The kid who overdosed was no brain surgeon, but he liked computers. Jamie asked me to come in and do a presentation on computers, and the kid really liked what I had to show him. I saw a bunch of kids, and he was the one I remembered. I wanted to see his name in the paper as a decent man who grew up and did right by people. Instead, I read he overdosed and died. It was just somebody's stupid kid that overdosed until it became personal."

"Okay, Pete, you are in."

Abba asks, "So what are you going to do now?"

"I am going to be a pillar in the community, and go to Gamblers Anonymous and Alcoholics Anonymous. I guess if you can get my finances straightened out, I'll call my chief in Chicago and tell him I am staying."

Tom says he is looking into getting me on the county police force, but I have to be a resident in the county. "Rebecca will help you pick out a house."

Abba shouts, "Rebecca, come here, and bring your catalog."

"Here you go, Max," and she lays it before me. I flip through the pages, and the old McGraw Farm sticks out.

"That place is for sale?"

Abba says, "Yes, but it will take just about all you have in cash at hand."

I add, "Property in this area has gone up in value, and stocks have been flip-flopping, from what I have been told."

Rebecca says, "Let me make the arrangements. The house has been redone, and the barn, well, you could tear it down and sell the land."

"No, if I could fix it up, I can always use it as storage."

"They have been trying to sell the place for months. I can get the keys if you want to look at the place."

"Oh, that reminds me, I was at Howard's, and I got a great price on the Trans Am."

I hand over the memo pad to Abba. Abba says, "Ah, I can get a better deal. Let me make some calls."

"No, Howard's is a part of my investigation, and this gives me an excuse to snoop a round."

Burney adds, "You know, he has built that new showroom and expanded the garage."

"Where does he get money when we are in a bit of recession?"

I get back to Howard's Garage and buy the Trans Am, "In memory of Smokey Joe." Howard takes the money and asks no questions. I walk around the garage, and there is a map of the counties that the garage serves.

Jack comes by and says, "You are getting the Trans Am?"

"Yeah."

He bends his head down and shakes his head as if he is ashamed of me.

"What is the matter?"

"You are a cop, right?"

"Right, yeah, I am a cop."

"Where would an honest cop get money to buy a Trans Am?"

I answer, "My Smokey Joe fund."

"Smokey Joe Fund?" he says.

"It was a little fund I set up to put money in the bank. For every dollar Smokey Joe smoked, I put that amount in the bank. It has added up over the years. When I came back for the reunion, I found out Smokey Joe died, and now I can spend the money."

With a smile, Jack says, "That is sick! You got a cool car."

He high-fives me!

"Tell me about this map."

Jack explains, "Oh, that is our map of crashes that we have towed cars into the garage."

I ask, "Like deer accidents?"

"Yeah."

"Not too many around Deer Crossing Alley Valley Highway."

"Shit, only a jackass would hit a deer around there. Everyone knows you don't go fast through there."

"But you don't have a listing for July eleventh or twelfth there."

"No, why?"

Howard comes by and brings me paperwork and smiles from ear to ear. I say to Jack, "You and me, we need to talk."

Howard asks, "What you want us to do with your piece of crap there."

"Oh, I'll take it with me. I am thinking of buying the old McGraw Farm."

"Really, so you are staying?"

"Yeah, I am thinking about joining the Carter County Police." "With a crooked smile, Mr. Howard says, "Well I feel safer already."

I call Big Paul and Jason and Steve from the Hymans, telling them I am thinking of buying the McGraw Farm. Rebecca gives us a tour of the house, but Jason goes out to the barn. The house is in great condition; it just needs furniture. Rebecca says she has to go to another possible sale and hands me the keys. I ask them, "What do you think?"

Big Paul adds, "Thanks to the suburbs, you can't go out and take a piss if you want to."

Marcy says, "It wouldn't be that hard to get furniture and appliances."

I mention, "You know, we are not that far from the city's public walking trails and woods. I was wondering, maybe we could set up a horse stable here."

Marcy's eyes go big, and Paul goes, "Oh boy, you just had to bring in the damn hay burners, didn't you?"

Marcy spouts, "Shut up, Paul, let's do it."

Steve adds, "Hey, that is a pretty big barn. If you insulate it, I will rent space from you."

"We could look into that, I guess."

Adam says, "Oh I just love old country. It is new and full of life."

Big Paul murmurs, "And cheap too, just go to most garage sales, and you can find good stuff."

Adam adds, "It is called rustic patina."

A pretty woman comes into the house and says, "Oh, I love this place!"

I ask, "And who are you?"

"Oh, we never met. I am Adam's wife, Jessica."

Jason comes out of the barn with cell phone in hand. "Dad, get your butt in gear out to the old McGraw farm now. You got to see this place. Hurry!"

I ask Jason, "What do you think of the house?"

"Forget the house, I want to live in the barn!"

"Max, you got to see this."

Soon Mr. Cooper pulls in the drive and yells, "What is so important?"

"Come on, Dad!"

"Yes, son, I see, a little worn but fixable, what?"

Jason gets out his battery-powered electric sander and peals down the paint. "What do you see?" And he takes a sniff. "Maple, and here oak, walnut, and over here, cherry!"

Mr. Cooper realizes, "This is not a barn, it is a cathedral!"

I ask, "What you are saying?"

Jason states, "Max, if you wanted to, you could sell this place piece by piece, beam by beam, and make more money than what they are asking for at least twice over."

Mr. Cooper pleads, "Don't do it, Max. We can strip off the paint to the wood. Stain and varnish this place, and I could design bed-and-breakfast suites and put them in the barn."

Adam says, "Oh, I can visualize this. I see a spiral staircase right here!"

Paul looks tired and disgusted, saying, "You would."

Steve asks, "What is your problem?"

Big Paul declares, "I am sick of all you yuppies coming here and turning everything into a damn bed-and-breakfast! I am sick of you people running to the big city and then coming back here and buying up land from farming people who are desperate for money after making sure you have cheap milk and the most affordable food this world has ever known at the greatest quality, so you can bitch about the price at the store and buy your son's hundred-dollar sneakers made in China. A damn spotted owl, we got to save it, it is an endangered species. The American farmer, screw him once, watch him squirm, and screw him again! Fuck it, I am tired!"

Big Paul marches out, leaving Marcy behind. He gets in his pickup and drives away.

Steve asks, "Did I say something?"

Marcy says, "Damn it, Steve, the world does not revolve around you. Paul is mad because the Mitchell farm is sold."

Steve is struck by the news. "I didn't even know they had an auction."

The "Dutch" showed up at their door and told them they are putting in a thousand-plus herd dairy farm, and they wanted the land.

Steve responds, "Paul is just tired of seeing so many farmers go out of business. He feels guilty for surviving."

I say, "Yeah, maybe."

Marcy grits her teeth, saying, "But they won't get our place, that is for damn sure."

I ask, "They have made you offers?"

"We are debt-free, thank God, and staying that way, but there are so many farmers who are mortgaged up the wazoo. Another thing that has gotten Paul mad is your B and B visitors come by our farm and start taking pictures, asking us to hold their cameras, pick up their kids, and say they are so cute. They come into our barns, telling us our place is filthy. We run a farm, not a damn hospital! We can't leave keys in our tractors or trucks anymore because they think it is an amusement ride! A kid got in one of the tractors while his father was taking pictures, and the kid turned the key and started the tractor."

Steve utters, "Oh my God."

"Oh my God is right. The tractor went in gear, and the five-year-old ran over a calf hutch, and thank God Troy was there to jump in the tractor and stop it!

"The mother was screaming, and I was so mad at her I could have ripped her a new asshole, and they grabbed their kid and left. We have had to put up signs, beware of dogs, and it is just stupid what city people do. We had to put the Hymans on retainer because somebody peed on the electric fence."

All the guys say, "Ouch."

"And there were no warning signs."

Steve says, "I am sorry."

"I know you are, Steve, but the jackasses you bring from parts unknown are neither the smartest nor the brightest people in the world. I was out planting our garden, and one of them stopped their car, got out, gave me a fifty-dollar bill, and said, 'This is for Farm Aid,' patted me on the head, and looked around and drove off. The kids asked, 'Mommy, what was that all about?' I said I didn't know.

"Under my breath I was saying, "Kiss my ass!" but I put the fifty in church. Paul and the Amish are getting sick of the tourists."

Paul heads for home but stops off at the farm and says, "Troy! Let's go, I need a drink, and I don't want to drink alone."

Troy asks, "Where are we going?"

"Sodom and Gomorrah's Saloon Bar and Grill."

Big Paul Jr. asks, "When will you get back?"

Papa's answer is, "When I get back." And they are off.

After Marcy let it out, things cooled down a bit, and she started making plans for setting up a stable. She isn't going to let a few dumb tourists ruin her dream of having a horse riding stable. Adam asks while he and Mr. Cooper are taking measurements, "So have all the tourists been jackasses?"

"No, actually some are okay. They get a kick seeing how a calf is born or the sunset and sunrise in the morning, the simple things you or me can take for granted. You don't realize how great this place is until you find people who never been out of their big city. And they say wow."

I leave them and go and spend time with the Hyman family. I am welcomed as if I was one of their own children. I speak the Hebrew language and put on my skull cap.

I sit at the table and Rebecca sits across from me while Burney is to my left sitting next to his wife and kids. Rebecca asks, "Well what do you think of the place?"

I say, "I think we like it, and please get the paperwork going. I'll take it."

She gets out of her seat, reaches over the table, and hugs and kisses me in her excitement. She is two years older than me. She was sent to boarding school for her education. So I really did not see her much until the summer of '79. She was a bookworm, and we did not get along whenever I came over. I guess I was too immature for her. Now she is a divorcée, no kids. I better watch it; in her eyes I am available. She asks me, "How did you learn all our customs?"

I smile, saying, "Well, I have spent time in this house."

Abba says, "That is my boy." I give Burney a high five.

She asks, "But you take our mannerisms as if they are second nature?"

I take a sip of water and say, "I have been to Israel a time or two."

She puts her elbow on the table and her chin on her hand and asks, "Business, tourist, what?"

"The answer is classified, and yes, I had some time to be a tourist."

"Are you still a Catholic, or have you converted to Judaism?"

The room goes silent.

My answer is, "I consider myself a searcher." It didn't answer the question most of them wanted to hear.

I get a call on my new cell phone. Abba asks, "Who brought a cell phone to the table?"

I sheepishly answer it. "Hello? Okay, Marcy, I'll go look for him. Sodom and Gomorrah? That is in Lincoln County? Okay, I'll bring him home."

As I put the phone away, I make sure to shut it off this time. "Thanks again for the phone, Abba."

Abba asks, "So what is the matter?'

"Paul is disgusted at the tourists and farms in the area being sold in general."

Abba sympathizes. "Oh, Paul, he is an artist, they are so sensitive. You come to the synagogue tomorrow. He did our beautiful mural."

"Paul?'

"Of ancient Jerusalem, it is beautiful."

"Paul? He does hot rods and John Deere tractors, Selah, and sci-fi book covers."

Burney adds, "And his brother Connor is a musician, Counting Tornadoes."

I remind them Paul gave up a lot so that Connor could do music for a living. Connor left high school to play for a country band that really didn't go all that far while Paul supported him. When Paul's uncle Robert died, Connor came home for a while and then left, and from what Marcy told me, he should have stayed, because Paul was doing too much. But Paul supported him. When Paul had his accident,

Connor was late coming home, but he eventually stayed. Paul made him go back to school, and Connor enrolled at Lincoln City because they had a night school there. He met Ralph Shurlow at night school, and a year later they started Counting Tornadoes.

Abba says, "Isn't it wonderful how God works. Paul went through some hard times after his uncle died. The first person he went to was Burney, and they put their finances in order. It was criminal what was going on."

"Well, I got to go and make sure Paul and Troy behave themselves. Excuse me."

Rebecca asks, "You will be here for synagogue tomorrow?"

I give her a hug, saying, "Wouldn't miss it."

Mrs. Hyman kisses me and says, "You will be there; there are a lot of people who were praying for you when you were in that coma."

I kiss her back and say thank you.

It feels good to drive the Trans Am, and I just turn up the music, put the windows down, and put the pedal to the floor. "You are now entering Lincoln County. Be warned."

"Gee officer, I just got the car, and I was just—" "Let me see your license."

I give him my license, and he goes back to his car and runs it through.

He returns with a look of, *I am giving you a warning*. The officer drives off and I am surprised. That patrol car came out of nowhere. I mean from zero to light speed.

Then it hits me, Ralph's electric car. He probably has that system in the Lincoln City patrol cars.

As I drive down the highway, I keep it at fifty-five, just to be safe. My radar detector did not go off or anything. Sodom and Gomorrah is in the middle of nowhere, a first-rate complex with dance hall, BBQ, grill, light show, and sound system. This is where the Counting Tornadoes got their start. The jukebox plays their first number-one hit, "Counting Tornadoes at a Trailer Park." The jukebox then plays "Daddy Won't Sell the Farm!"

C.C. and T-Roy are the only original members of the Counting Tornadoes still touring.

Ralph Shallow and his wife, Tatyana, were the first to leave for writing their *Ice Soldiers* novels and movies and coproducing the Generation Gap, and unexplained reasons.

Reed Jackson left because he felt he only had so many years to be physically fit to fight fires, and he shouldn't be playing a guitar when he should be saving lives.

Good answer, but I think his new wife had something to do with it.

Dusty, a singer and guitar player, started a family and works on cars and started his own body shop garage in Lincoln City East. Another member started up Christ Taking Apart Anger through Prayer 2.0., a Christian rock band. Both groups are doing quite well, from what I understand. Fans want the originals to tour again for old times' sake. I find Big Paul whooping it up, eating BBQ ribs, and getting drunk. I don't know about the getting drunk, but after eating kosher food, those ribs look pretty good.

I sit down, flag the waitress, and ask for an order of ribs. She calls back, "Coming up, honey!" I like being called honey.

"So guys, how you doing?"

Paul murmurs, "Marcy sent you, didn't she?"

"Yes. Your family is worried about you."

"Max, half the fun of having so many kids and raising your kids is so you can leave them and know you can have some fun and know that the work will be done whether you are there or not. I am not worried. The farm will be there when I get back."

My ribs come and I take a bite. "Oh God, these are good! Marcy can wait. I am going to eat my ribs."

Paul drinks a beer and offers me one.

"No beer for me, thank you."

"Max, all the time I have known you, you have never had a beer. Why?"

"I had an alcoholic Marcus for a reason not to drink. And a few of my own."

Paul puts his beer down and says, "Can we have a couple Dews over here?"

I eat ribs until I have to get a doggie bag. "Hey, you want to go for a ride in my Trans Am?"

Like kids, they call for shotgun. Troy gets in the back. I put the windows down, hoping the fresh air will do them good. And I'll have some fun too.

Not far down the road, the same officer that pulled me over earlier stops me again. "Listen, Mr. Faraday, I said I would give you a warning." He gives me a ticket and drives off.

Paul and Troy laugh their heads off. "Did you see him? Where did he come from? Did you see him? He came from out of nowhere."

Paul laughs. "Nobody speeds in Lincoln County." I take them back to the bar, and I follow them home.

Marcy waves at me from the door as I help Paul inside, while my namesake dog gets in my car and devours my ribs. I yell at her, "Hey, get out of my car!"

Paul yells back, "Take her, Max, you need a dog!"

I go back to the McGraw Farm, and I turn on the light. I left the dog outside, but she finds a doggie door and comes in. *I didn't know I had a doggie door?* And a good-sized one too. I look at my watch and see it is about midnight. I unroll my sleeping bag and turn out the light and go to sleep. The dog sleeps at my feet.

Chapter Twelve

Tuesday, October 3, 1978

I can see why Paul can get so mad at the world sometimes. I still have the hint of calluses I earned from August when I helped him load and stack hay bales. I have to get up and make my own breakfast; tonight I am supposed to stay with the Pearsons. I am late getting out the door, so I run to school.

At lunchtime, the guys huddle around Paul as if he is a general and we are the troops. "Okay, the plan is Friday. We leave for the big city right after school."

Burney asks, "Paul, can it be Thursday? I have the Sabbath starting on Friday."

Paul murmurs, "Thursday, Burney, that is a school night."

Burney puts his head down.

My guess, Paul remembers the birthday bar mitzvah and the kindness that was shown to him then. "If you can go on a school night, maybe we all can."

Pete asks, "Can I go?" Everybody says no.

"Why?"

"Because you are too little, you probably have an early bedtime."

Pete's comeback is, "Well, your mom and my mom are friends, so if I can't go, maybe you won't be able to go either."

As Pete runs off to the school pay phone, Paul realizes, "That is going to put a crimp in our plans."

Jamie asks, "You think he will be able to go?"

Jason says, "Oh, he's his mommy's little baby. Wherever he wants to go, he is going."

Paul says, "Steve, do the math. Top speed of the truck."

Jack says, "Forty-five, we can't run the truck hot until we replace the radiator."

I add, "And we don't want to draw attention to ourselves."

Steve agrees. "Yeah, Paul, you may be sixteen, but if we get pulled over, that will really cause us to be late. Pete's bedtime?"

"Eight eight-thirty."

"Why does he need that much sleep? We would leave here by, what, three fifteen?"

"The time it takes to get there and back. We have how long to shop?"

"Little over an hour, maybe two, but that is cutting it close."

I add, "And that is not factoring in train crossings on the railroad or bathroom breaks."

Paul remembers, "Oh, gas, everybody has to chip in."

"How much?"

"Five dollars, maybe six." "Five Dollars?"

"Do you have any other rides to the big city?'

"No."

"Then shut up."

Pete comes back and says, "My mom talked to your mom, and they said you had to take me."

Paul's comeback is, "Then you better have five dollars and babysitting money."

The other girls come over. "Can we come too?"

Paul declares, "Listen, we are not going to stop every fifteen minutes so you can go to the bathroom. We are only getting an hour for dropping people off at the mall, and I got to go to the bread store, the farm supply store, and the comic shop. And then turn around, pick people up at the mall, and come home."

The girls huddle together and come back, "We can do that."

"This goes for everybody. "If you are not ready to go, I am leaving your ass at the mall. No ifs ands or buts. I am on a time schedule."

The girls look at each other and say with a little less assurance, "We can do that."

"You are going to have to ride in the back of a pickup, and it could get chilly."

They go back into a huddle. "We will wear winter clothes."

Kathy comes by and asks, "Can I come too?"

Paul says, "Kathy, I don't think we will have enough time, and you will slow everybody down."

I can see it in Paul's eyes, he did not want to say what he just said.

Kathy bows her head and says, "I'll sit in a wheelchair. They loan them out at the mall."

Wendy says, "I'll push it."

And the other girls say, "We will take turns."

Paul smiles, saying, "Kathy, if you really want to go, I'll pick your butt up and load you on the back of the truck. Thursday, we leave here at the school by three ten."

After lunch I see Paul walking around by himself, and I say, "Paul, wait up. You were a bit hard on Kathy."

Paul looks at me, saying, "No, I wasn't. We were in Four-H, me, her, and Marcy, and we got to talking, and she said she didn't like being treated like she was special. So whenever given the chance, I treat her like she is nothing special."

"But still, Paul?"

"She wants to have a normal life as much as possible. She don't want to go to a special school that caters to the handicapped. The best thing you and I can do for her is ignore her difficulties, treat her as normal as we can, and pray that someday the doctors will be able to help her so she can have a normal life. Then again, what and who is normal?"

"Hey, Paul, you are a good friend. I got to thinking, with all the tools on the farm, you could have fixed the pickup all by yourself. Why are you letting Jack do it?"

"Ah, Max, do you remember before school started in August when you, me, and Connor picked up hay bales?"

I put out my hands. "I still have the calluses."

Paul admits, "You earned every one of them. Remember the Friday when the two jokers wanted to take the day and Saturday off?"

"Yeah, they said they would come back Sunday and finish the work of picking up bales. You know how my dad is, we don't work other than the necessary on Sunday."

"Yeah, and you asked your dad if we got the fieldwork done, if we could get their pay."

"He said that sounds fair, adult work deserves adult pay. And me you and Connor started hauling bales that morning. Steve, Jamie, and Jason helped part of Saturday."

"Yeah, Churchill couldn't get his hands dirty. Late in the afternoon, we had the bales off the field, and it was dark when we put it all in the barn. It took us till late Saturday night, but we got it in the barn. We filled it to the rafters."

"Sunday, those jackasses came by and wanted to go to work. But we had it all done and in the barn, and those guys were mad."

"Max, do you remember Teddy Bear? She was that mix-mutt dog, right? She followed us everywhere. One more mouth to feed, Dad called her. But he warmed up to her. Those bastards came back to our farm early Monday morning. They had a gas can and poured it on the barn. Just ready to light it, but old Teddy Bear made a ruckus and woke us all up! She and the other dogs scared them so bad, they stayed put."

"We all grabbed what we could before they could light the barn. Dad yelled at them with shotgun in hand, 'Light your lighter, and I'll light up your world!'

"The drunken SOB says, 'Now everyone just calm down!'

"Dad yelled, 'Get away from the barn!' Old Teddy Bear was barking up a storm.

"'Shut up that dog,' the SOB says. 'I hate dogs!'

"Well, Dad can bark too. He yells, 'I will shut *you* up, asshole. Get away from the barn!'

"Mom comes out of the house, saying, 'I have called the police, they should be here in—'

"The SOB yells, 'Damn! I am not going back to prison! Damn you, Chapel, you shouldn't have called the cops!' He reaches into his jacket and pulls out a knife and throws it!

"Old Teddy Bear jumps up in front of Dad and takes it in her side. All I could do is yell, 'NO!' I knew she was dying, just by looking at her.

"I turned around and had a shotgun ready to shoot, and my dad said, 'Son don't do it. It won't bring her back. Give me the gun.' I gave him the gun and that bastard tried to rush Dad, and Dad just whaled on him with the butt of the gun and down on the ground he went. The other guy just put his hands up and got on his knees till the police showed up.

"We were told by the police and the judge not to go or talk to the press till the case was done, that is why I never mentioned it till now. You know, Max, my dad rarely says anything to me, but that night when we finished the hay and it was all in the barn, after you and the others left, my dad said he was proud of me for getting the job done.

"You helped me, Max, you really came through. That is why I am helping you with Jack."

"Thanks, Paul."

After school I go to the C. Connection. Dan's dad is shaking his head saying, "I don't know ..."

I am stocking shelves as they discuss the trip. "Come on, Dad, please? I have been working hard here at the store, and you have seen my schoolwork."

"You are fourteen, and Paul is sixteen, and how many times has he been held back?"

After work I go to see Mom at Mrs. Horton's. She says, "I don't know about you and the guys going to the big city."

"Well, I am supposed to stay with Paul and the Chapels Thursday night anyway."

"Why not a Friday night?"

I answer, "Because Burney recognizes the Sabbath on Friday after sundown."

I start eating milk and cookies.

"Well, that was nice to consider that. I'll think about it. Now, go in and visit with Mrs. Horton. I think she is losing it. She says that you are going to buy Mr. McGraw's place someday."

Milk almost squirts out of my nose when I hear that. "Well, what is so wrong with that?" I ask.

"Well nothing, I like the place. She just is a little … Just go in and be nice and talk to her. I'll have dinner in a bit."

Mrs. Horton is sitting in her living room resting and gently wakes up as I enter. "Oh, Max, it is so nice to see you. Isn't your home wonderful?"

I ask, "You can see me in the McGraw place?"

"Oh, it is nothing like your mansion in heaven, but I like it. It even has a big doggie door for, what kind of dog is she, Max?"

In astonishment I say, "I don't know."

"Oh, Max, she has been through so much. She loves you. Pay attention to her. She can tell if a person is lying to you, but you must pay attention to her. Max, in Jesus's name, you must pray a hedge of protection around yourself. The devil and his minions are coming to kill and destroy. They don't like the good you are doing, and they will try to kill you and the ones you love. You are here to protect them, but they must also learn to protect themselves."

I add, "Jamie better learn to use a gun to defend himself, because there will come a time, and you won't be there to protect him." I then say, "I always wondered why Jamie has such a problem with guns."

Mrs. Horton explains, "Jamie's father has the problem and has forced his grief on his son."

"Grief?"

During Vietnam, Jamie's father was a cocky sharpshooter. One night he got scared and fired his rifle without fully knowing what he was doing. He thought he was shooting at VCs; instead, he accidentally killed members of his own unit. They sent him home after he had a nervous breakdown.

"It was an accident," Mrs. Horton continues. "Jesus forgave him at his first prayer, but he never forgave himself.

"It took time, and he restarted his life again, but he swore to never hold or look at a gun again. He forbade guns in the house, and like father like son, they share the burden both the father and son carry the grief and knowledge.

"You have burdens of your own, Max. It was the devil that told that bad man to put that girl in the trunk of the car, the devil himself."

"Yeah, but I was the one who pulled the trigger that killed the driver, and the bullet went through the driver's head and through the back seat and through the hostage."

Mrs. Horton instructs, "Next time, shoot the engine first, let the car roll, and shoot the driver from behind the car. It will stop before it comes to anyone's danger. Max, you really need to pray more. You need to come to your Heavenly Father. He loves you, Max. All the answers to the questions you seek are in His word and in His spirit. The rules of man confuse, don't they?"

"I agree, they have their moments."

And it comes to me—Seek ye first the kingdom of God and his righteousness and all these things shall be added unto you.

Mrs. Horton smiles, saying, "It is not so complicated, is it, Max?"

My mom brings ham sandwiches and soup. Old people's food, and again I am fed and again I want more. I say my goodbyes and head to the Pearsons.

Mrs. Pearson says, 'Hi Max, any chance that you might want some leftover pizza?"

"Oh, you are a godsend, Mrs. Pearson. All I have had lately is old-people food!"

She asks, "How are you coming on your presidents? You have to know them all at the end of the year in your history class."

Steve and Wendy come by, and Steve says, "Max has probably already memorized them. Well Max, let's hear it."

I start with George Washington, and when I get to Jimmy Carter, Ronald Reagan, and George Bush, Mr. Pearson looks confused and says, "Ronald Reagan, George Bush?'

"Ah, yeah, I, um, am, um, a Republican, and I just can't decide who I want to be my next president."

Everyone is stunned at my answer. Mr. Pearson says, "You are always welcome in my house."

Mr. Pearson reads the paper looking for part-time work. He has been let go—factory cutbacks, layoffs, and all. He is getting concerned. The rest of the house is full of the sounds of life, of children running up and down the halls, and the call goes out, "It is time to go to bed!" I can hear Wendy praying with the kids in the next room.

As I enter after Steve is done praying, he gives me his bed and he sleeps on the floor. There is no use arguing with him, so I say thank you and go to sleep. I love this family.

Chapter Thirteen

Saturday, July 20, 2002—A Rude Awakening

I hear the sound of barking outside, and I look at my watch; it is two in the morning.

I had experienced a whole day in about two hours sleep. I grab my revolver and find a perpetrator cornered. He goes for his gun, and I say, "Don't worry about the dog, worry about the owner. Max, heel!" And she stops barking. I can see neighbors turning on their lights, and I say, "Get in the house."

He says, "I didn't know you had a dog."

I chuckle and say, "You are still behind in your intelligence." Max watches the guy intently; she does not trust him, and neither do I. His codename is Badger, a favorite brown-nose of CIA agent Graves. We have had our moments.

He states, "Here, I have the info on the fingerprint sample you sent us."

I ask how he found me.

Badger responds, "Your cell phone in your own name, for starters. And the Hyman Reality, nice house you are buying. Oh yeah, I forgot, 'Welcome to America the Free.' By the way, you are being watched."

I begin looking it over. "Bob Black. Prison time for trafficking drugs."

"Missed his meeting with his parole officer two days ago."

I add, "You could have called me, and I could have given you a number, and you could have faxed this."

Badger murmurs, "Yes, but it would go through channels."

I wonder aloud, "Someone is watching me besides you?"

He continues, "Since you started buying things in your own name, a lot of red flags have been popping up on the net. The Chicago Mafia is running scared and has dropped you from their hit list. From what I have been told, you or a friend of yours crashed one of their porn sites."

I give a smile, stating, "Ah, isn't that a shame."

Badger asks, "Who you have working for you?"

I tell him, "I Protect my friends. You leave yours behind."

Badger's heart is broken, then I see crocodile tears, and he says, "I would never."

Max the dog growls.

"Max, what happened in South America was not my fault."

Max the dog barks violently at Badger.

"Hey, call off your dog!"

"Down, Max!"

"So, Max, can tell when someone is lying?" Badger continues, "We are very impressed with your current investigation."

Max the dog sits down and is calm. Does this mean Badger is telling the truth? Or is it "If you can't tell by now, you are on your own."

"The company would like to set up a small crime lab so you would not need to involve the locals in your investigation."

"You think they are involved in the drug smuggling?"

"Don't you?"

"Yes, but how far does it go? Cavanaugh City Police, FBI, who?"

Badger smiles. "We think there is an FBI connection. Too early to tell, we will let you know if we find anything."

I ponder out loud. "If the FBI gets a black eye, it won't hurt you any?"

Badger justifies himself. "Hey, we need the big bucks. If we get it from taking it from the FBI because they have people doing criminal acts, so be it. Our slate is clean." Max the dog growls. "Max, we want you back. We can help you; you can help us." Max the dog growls.

***

I go back to bed and wake up on Wednesday, October 4th, 1978.

The commotion of children running around and saying, "I want to take a shower."

"You were supposed to take one last night."

"Do I have to go to school?"

"Yes, you do!"

Steve and Wendy help with the younger kids. Mrs. Pearson says, "Thanks, you two. I'll make breakfast."

I, on the other hand, wonder if my dream of wanting to be a part of a big family is such a good idea.

Mr. Pearson has the morning paper and gently swats a kid saying, "Come on, now, let's get it together. Help your sister tie her shoes."

"Yes, sir."

I am dressed and ready to go, so I help them round up the little doggies and keep them from stampeding down the stairs. Mrs. P. calls out, "Breakfast is served! Well, sort of. Eggs and toast. Get in line. Sausages will be a few minutes."

I kind of like being the only kid now that I see what herd mentality can do.

Survival of the fittest is what it all comes down to. Mrs. P says, "You have been pretty quiet, Max."

I smile politely and say, "I thought I would give you a break and be the quiet child that keeps you wondering."

She smiles. "Thanks, I think."

As we leave for school, Wendy has a bag for little Jimmy in her hands.

At lunchtime recess, Big Paul asks, "So who is going?"

Jamie says, "My dad says it is okay as long as we don't get into any trouble."

"I'm in," says Churchill.

"Same here," Jason responds. "My dad likes you and thinks you can keep me out of trouble."

With a smile, Paul adds, "Oh, I will."

"I'm in too," Dan tells him.

"I'm in," says Steve. "This will be a blast!"

Jack says, "My dad doesn't care. He says it's okay."

Pete shouts, "I can't wait I get to go!"

"You are going under protest," Paul adds.

I say, "And me, count me in."

K. Ray C. says. "My mom is cool with it. I can go."

Paul asks, "Are you sure now?"

"Sure."

"Because I don't want to get in trouble if you get sick."

"Can I ride in the truck?"

"No, I'm driving. Pete is with me, and Jack is going to be watching the gauges."

"I'll ride in the back."

We all look at Burney who says, "My dad appreciates the day change and said I can go.

Reed Jackson adds, "My dad said I can go too."

Paul warns, "Then you better behave yourself, Reed."

Reed asks, "What would I do?"

We all say, "Open your big mouth."

The girls come by and say, "Our parents said we could go."

Paul says, "Now hold on, this is a pickup, not a bus. Wendy, Connie, Candy, Kathy, and Marcy, that is five of you, and eleven guys, that is seventeen! I am getting a bad feeling about this. If you can't fit in the cab, you aren't going."

Steve says, "Wait, Paul, Mr. Pearson has a van. Maybe we can borrow it for the night."

"To a sixteen-year-old and a bunch of fourteen-year-olds?"

"Well, everyone has five dollars to put in the for gas, right? Maybe Mr. Pearson can drive us."

"It might be cramped, but we can all fit in our van. And we have a luggage rack on top."

Paul asks, "You really want to go?" Steve asks, "Yeah, don't you?"

I just got one of my funny feelings, but if it is okay with Mr.

Pearson, it is alright with me.

Steve gets up to make the call, saying, "I'll ask him, and I should have an answer."

Steve calls home. Mr. Pearson picks up the phone. "Hello."

"Ah, hi Dad, I was wondering if we could use the van."

Mr. Pearson thinks, *Did he just call me dad?* Then he hears the rest and says, "The van?"

"The Thursday after-school trip, there are more people who want to go to the big city than can ride in Paul's truck."

"How many?"

"Seventeen guys and girls, and five bucks a person for gas."

A pause for thought. "See if you can get ten, and we may have a deal, and I get to chaperone."

"I'll see if they will go for it."

Steve comes back to us, saying, "My dad will go for it if we chip in five extra bucks, and he's going to chaperone."

I smile and say, "You are calling him dad now?"

Steve shrugs his shoulders, saying, "Yeah, I guess it just kind of came out when I asked for the van. They want to adopt me and all and make it official. I have had a problem of calling him my dad because my real dad is out there somewhere. I just don't know where. So I guess he is my dad now."

Reed pats him on the back and says, "Hey, that is cool, man!"

K. Ray C. mutters, "Ten bucks? That is a lot of money."

Paul adds, "Then you can stay home."

"No, I can get it."

After school I go to the C. Connection and then to Dan's house to drop off my things, and then we go to Wednesday night services at the United Brethren in Christ Church.

Aunt Peg and Uncle Hal make a cute couple. He was attracted to her, and she thought he was handsome. He taught her sign language, and she could talk all night in her sleep, and he could not hear a word. For that, all are thankful. Or, as she would say, "Isn't it wonderful how God works?"

We say our Bible verses for candy bars. Hal teaches the Wednesday night class, and Aunt Peg interprets. "Well, who has a prayer request or a praise report?"

Jason says, "Prayer request, my little sister has been sick, and my mom and dad are getting worried."

Steve says, "I guess I have a praise report. Mr. Pearson is going to adopt me."

Joy fills the class, and Steve says, "I guess in a few weeks you can call me Steve Pearson."

Hal asks, "Why, you are not happy?"

Steve replies, "I really don't know what it all means."

"Well, son, we are all adopted."

Hal opens his Bible and passes it to Steve.

Ephesians 1

1. Paul, an apostle of Jesus Christ by the will of God, to the saints which are at Ephesus, and to the faithful in Christ Jesus.

2. Grace is to you, and peace, from God our Father, and from the Lord Jesus Christ.

3. Blessed be the God and Father of our Lord Jesus Christ, who hath blessed us with all spiritual blessings in heavenly places in Christ.

4. According as he hath chosen us in him before the foundation of the world, that we should be holy and without blame before him in love.

5. Having predestinated us unto "the adoption of children by Jesus Christ to himself, according to the good pleasure of his will."

6. To the praise of the glory of his grace, wherein he hath made us accepted in the beloved.

7. In whom we have redemption through his blood, the forgiveness of sins, according to the riches of his grace.

8. Wherein he hath abounded toward us in all wisdom and prudence.

9. Having made known unto us the mystery of his will, according to his good pleasure which he hath purposed in himself.

10. That in the dispensation of the fullness of times he might gather together in one all things in Christ, both which are in heaven, and which are on earth; even in him.

11. In whom also we have obtained an inheritance, being predestinated according to the purpose of him who worked all things after the counsel of his own will.

12. That we should be to the praise of his glory, which first trusted in Christ.

13. In whom ye also trusted, after that ye heard the word of truth, the gospel of your salvation: in whom also after that ye believed, ye were sealed with that Holy Spirit of promise.

14. *Which is the earnest of our inheritance until the redemption of the purchased possession, unto the praise of his glory.*

15. *Wherefore I also, after I heard of your faith in the Lord Jesus, and love unto all the saints.*

16. *Cease not to give thanks for you, making mention of you in my prayers.*

17. *That the God of our Lord Jesus Christ, the Father of glory, may give unto you the spirit of wisdom and revelation in the knowledge of him.*

18. *The eyes of your understanding being enlightened; that ye may know what the hope of his calling is, and what the riches of the glory of his inheritance in the saints.*

19. *And what is the exceeding greatness of his power to usward who believe, according to the working of his mighty power.*

20. *Which he wrought in Christ, when he raised him from the dead, and set him at his own right hand in the heavenly places.*

21. *Far above all principality, and power, and might, and dominion, and every name that is named, not only in this world, but also in that which is to come.*

Hal signs, "You see, the moment you have asked the Lord Jesus Christ into your heart, you are adopted into the family of God."

Steve asks, "Well that is all well and good, but what about my real dad?"

Hal signs, "I don't know about your real dad, son. He is in God's hands, and we will continue to pray for your real dad as we do every week. Let us rejoice in your earthly adoption, and we can all rejoice in our heavenly adoption through Jesus Christ."

After class, when it is about time to go I overhear Mr. Pearson and Mr. Cooper talking. "Hey, Pearson, glad I found you. I have some good news for you."

"Well, I could use some, Cooper."

"How would you like to be the foreman at the plant on third shift starting Monday?"

"Foreman, that's great, but third shift?"

"I put the good word in if you. Want the job?"

"No problem, I'll take it, thanks."

"I know third shift is not the greatest, but right now."

"Cooper, thanks, this is a real blessing. So what do you think about the company merger?"

"They have been keeping me busy, and the new company won't let me take non-company drafting jobs. I had some good Wildtale Corporation side jobs I had to turn down."

"I don't know if I want to stay much longer. I have had to do a lot more prayer on this subject than it ought to be."

Mr. Pearson comments, "I have been praying for work, and you have been praying about too much. That is about what it adds up to. My wife has been in a good law firm, and she has just about paid off her loans from law school. I have been promising myself to take time off for the kids. I have just two, and you have how many? Sometimes I wonder if too many. Ouch, sorry. Thanks, Cooper, for the good word."

Mr. Cooper catches Dan's dad, Mr. Cottager. "Hey, I looked into the old C. Industries Warehouse." He hands over a piece of paper.

"Whoa, Ben, that is a lot of space."

"The place is in great shape. It even has a generator and a place for tools in the back."

"I was thinking about buying the place myself. It is too big for me to putter around with."

"I could rent space to you, and you could use it as your C. Connection Warehouse."

"You would do that, Cooper?"

"Hey, you have given me good deals over the years. What are friends for? I have a few ideas of my own. Thanks, I'll give you an answer tomorrow."

When we get back to Dan's place, the lights are on, and it hits me, as a kid it has been years since I visited Dan's home, and that was when his mother was alive. Now the place looks like a wall-to-wall storage for the C. Connection, and it is. The old warehouse had to be sold to help pay for the cancer treatments. Except for Dan's bedroom, there is not a room in the house that is not filled to the ceiling with C. Connection stuff. Canned goods, furniture still in boxes, some appliances, you name it, it might just be here. Dan says, "Max, I have a list of stuff that needs to be moved to the van tonight, so let's do it now."

Jokingly I ask, "Will I get overtime pay for this?"

***

I wake up again around 8:00 a.m., Saturday, July 20, 2002.

I look at my watch and say, "This is new. I had a whole day again in just a few hours."

It hits me, *Don't try to figure it out. Just say Praise the Lord and Amen and get your bare naked butt out of bed.* Actually, I was sleeping in a sleeping bag, and I always wear underwear. As I get up and get dressed, I wonder where Max the dog is.

I then get a wake-up call from a guy dressed in a blue long-john suit.

Max is just enjoying getting her belly rubbed by the stranger. I shout, "Who are you!"

The intruder says, "You can call me Blue Bomber."

"Oh, great, a guy who thinks he is the Wild Tail comic book character the Blue Bomber!"

Blue Bomber comments, "I like what you have done with the house, very minimalist."

Anger fills me, who is this guy? "Ah, I just moved in. I'll hire a decorator. Look, I don't like strangers in my house!"

The stranger asks, "And Badger, a butt-kisser of CIA Agent Graves is a welcomed guest?"

I ask, "How do you know about Graves or Badger?"

Blue Bomber chuckles, "Oh, you would be surprised what I know, little brother."

Now I *am* mad! I grab a hanger pole out of the closet and yell, "Get out of my house now!"

He reaches behind himself to his backpack and brings out two red staffs. "I don't want to fight you, really, but I was asked to see what kind of shape you were in, or who is in the driver's seat mentally."

I begin swinging and strike his red staffs. He is fast, I mean master of kung fu arts fast! He is just playing with me. Sharp sounds of click clack are the racket that his staffs make as I try to hit him. I let my guard down and catch a swing of his staff and I land on my butt! He says, "Get up, Max, and try again."

He knows who I am, now I am really mad! Faster, I have to be faster! He is too fast, shadowboxing me in every move I make! Max the dog has left the house, probably hurts her ears more than it does mine. Damn these staffs of his make it annoying; the blare it is hurting my eardrums!

And I am on my butt again!

The guy in the Blue Bomber costume asks, "Do you really want to get involved with Graves and Badger again?"

I yell, "How do you know about me or Graves?!"

Blue Bomber comments, "Graves is not to be trusted; there are other people you can go to get answers to your questions."

"Like who?"

"Like me."

"I don't even know who you are."

"Listen, Max, I don't know what this means, but your dog didn't actually like it when Badger came to your home, did she? And she let me walk right in the front door. I don't know what that means, but Twilight said I should mention it."

"Oh, there is a guy wearing a Twilight suit too?"

"Sure, why not? And a Wild Tail and—"

"And why should I trust you?"

"Because at one time we were friends and we looked out for each other, and I don't want you to get hurt or used. So we thought it would be justifiable to check up on you."

"Were friends? What do you mean by that?"

Blue Bomber replies, "How do I say this? At one time, you had knowledge of who I was, and something happened, and you asked to have that memory and more erased because it was too painful to deal with and you could not take the responsibility."

I ask, "And at some point you and I were friends?"

"Yeah, something like that. When you took on the Russian Mafia, that was very impressive, almost too impressive. I was sent here to see if you still had those gifts."

"And now?"

"Not at the moment. Maybe if you thought I was a real threat. Maybe your powers have a subconscious trigger switch. I don't know, I am not a psych or telepath."

I ask, "You think I have powers?"

"I don't know."

"Who or what do you think I am?"

"A friend who asked me to help him forget the past. But you are getting yourself in a world of hurt if you hook up with Graves and Badger. I think a part of you knows that."

As Blue Bomber is about to leave, I think a part of me wishes he would stay.

I say, "Blindman's Bluff, please stay."

He turns around and asks, "What did you call me?"

"Blindman's Bluff."

He shakes his head, saying, "We were warned that a part of your old self might try to reemerge."

"What are you saying?"

"You have some multi personalities in you. Some good some bad."

"What do you mean?"

"Let's see, how do I describe this? Some people who were abused as children sometimes have a mental block of that incident, and then after time passes the memory comes back when they are older and can possibly deal with the trauma. You had memories or personalities erased because you thought it was for the best. And maybe those memories will come back. We don't know."

"Why, how, when?"

"Why, because you thought it was for the best, you wanted a fresh start. And I am being vague because you were very adamant about giving yourself a fresh start. And how? By telepathic means."

"Wow, this is news to me. Telepathic, you mean like a mutant power?"

"We don't like to be called mutant, nor do we like freak of nature. I am a genetic rarity, a Great One to be exact. Usually it happens during puberty, and for me it way later."

"You mean like in the Wild Tail comic books?"

"Yes, like in the comic books."

"When did this all happen?"

"I really can't or don't know if I should answer that."

"Listen, if you don't start giving me straight answers, I—"

"What, say you had a guy in blue Flex Cloth come and pay a visit?"

"I might!"

"Who is going to believe you, the tooth fairy? See, little brother, I have been doing this for a while, and I know in most cases, at first, nobody will take you seriously. They will say, yeah right, and I saw the Easter Bunny. For your own good, stay away from Badger and Graves, they are too dirty to trust."

"And you aren't?"

"We Wild Tail Champions are so good, we don't exist. Listen, dirty or not, I used to be CIA, and they helped me get information I needed. Where were you?"

"You wanted a fresh start, and to the best of our knowledge we gave you a fresh start. You have free will, and we respected that to the best of our ability. But when you shot up the Russian Mafia, red flags started to go off. We thought it was best to check up on you."

"Why you, why not someone else?"

"I am the closest."

"Can you help me in my investigation?"

"I can pass on information to what we call troubleshooters, sure."

"I just briefly read this before I went to sleep. Can you look at it?"

"I wish I could, but for the most part I am blind. I can see solid objects, but paper and video draw a blank in my normal ability."

"What?"

"My G or Gauntlet, my computer on my arm, will copy the files, and I can read it in braille form."

"Blindman's bluff?"

"Right, I made that one myself."

"When we fought my staffs made a bit of racket. I use that sound like a ping on radar. I also absorb the sound waves, and it energizes me. Explosions are the best, that is why things explode around me. It is like an adrenaline super boost and energy rush and then some, all in one. I can even heal myself to a certain degree using sound energy. Grew an arm back once. Channel the sound energy to be able to see in color. I have even focused my sight to the point I had like X-ray vision."

"Who are you?"

"Funny thing is, little brother, certain people in the CIA know who you are and were. They also agreed it was for the best you forget who you were."

"They don't know who I am, and I intend to keep it that way."

"I'll be in touch if I find anything that can help you in your investigation."

As I watch him, he just vanishes, leaving more questions than answers.

I dare not go back to sleep. Who knows what kind of visitors I might wake up to, so I look at the clock. It is past eight thirty, and I start making calls. I call my team of experts to meet in the barn at the McGraw Farm:

Steve Pearson, the psychologist;

Big Paul, the artistic farmer and Air Force reservist;

Churchill Smith, medical doctor;

Burney, the rabbi tax auditor;

Jason Cooper, wisecracking funny man, gym teacher, computer analyst programmer;

Dan Cottager, klutz medical doctor;

Pete, computer genius;

John Henry Watson, officer of the Carter County Police;

Reed Jackson, fireman, professional singer, performer;

Jamie Scott, scared little pacifist man; and

Adam, the decorator, detective, and archer.

Gathering, I share the info. They are all looking tired and fresh out of bed except for Paul, who just looks tired; he has a little hangover.

I am bringing them up to speed, but I will not tell them about the Blue Bomber.

Although Big Paul would get a big kick out of the idea of Wild Tail being real.

"Okay, boys, this is who came up in the fingerprint check: Bob Black. Has anybody seen him?"

Jason Cooper asks, "Can we put his face on milk cartons, or is that only reserved for missing children?"

John Henry Watson says, "If I give you a ride in my patrol car, sonny, will you stop asking dumb questions?"

Jason asks, "Can I run the siren?"

"No."

"Then I will keep asking dumb questions as I see fit."

I shake my head and just smile. It is all I can do to keep from punching him.

The file also states his connection to organized crime.

Steve adds, "I have done studies on the criminal mind. His history tells us, if this guy could have made it, he would have gone to meet with his parole officer."

John says, "Now if he shows up, he is automatically going back to prison."

"Big Paul adds, "So he is either dead or on the run."

"Oh he's dead, he is pushing up daisies by now," Jason tells them.

John joins the party. "White boy has a point."

Reed comes up with a plan. "We need to set up a stakeout on Deer Crossing Alley Valley Highway. At least see if there are certain days that they are running on."

John adds, "That is a lot of highway, and we don't know if that is the only route the traffickers take."

"How about we get the damn car from the junkyard?" asks Paul. "Maybe there is something still on it."

John asks, "Like what?"

"Some kind of radar detection device or something," Paul adds "These guys have never been pulled over for speeding but hit a deer going ninety?"

"Dead deer tell no tales," Jason says.

Everyone looks at Jason. "What?"

Pete adds, "Paul, you have a point. They might have some kind of device that can monitor police."

Reed includes, "It would have been stripped, and all they would have to do is monitor police bands. I do it all the time."

"I will forget you said that," Officer John tells him.

Reed adds, "Hey, I listen to the radio, I have a Radio Shack credit card, and I know how to use it."

I look him in the eyes and say, "Jamie, I want you and your family to be able to get out of here soon."

Jamie responds, "I am not leaving, Max. Maybe they just wanted to scare me. And maybe they were not after me at all; they could be after you. For all we know, the two incidents may be not even related."

Churchill looks at me and says, "Yeah, someone tried to get you at the hospital. Since you were hit by the car, no one has tried to get Jamie."

"I don't get the kind of intel I get from people in the know unless there is something to it. I produced it in black or white for you all to see. Someone is after Jamie. And me. I can justify taking care of myself, but Jamie, you need help."

Jamie responds, "I won't be chased out of my home. I am staying!"

"You won't arm yourself, but you want to be a happy martyr, well, fine! What does your life cost you or the lives of your family and friends?"

"No man hath greater love than to be willing to give his own life, but no one said you had to do your best impersonation of a sacrificial lamb!" Jamie walks out of the barn.

Paul says, "I'll check the junkyard. That car is not going anywhere."

John says, "See if you can get serial numbers. We don't want to scare them away."

As Paul leaves, I ask, "Anyone up for jogging? John Henry and I are leading the way."

Churchill and Jason are, at best, power walking. Adam, Pete, Steve, and Reed are aggravating the slowpokes on by literally running circles around them. I ask John Henry, "So what do you think of my little town?"

John huffs and puffs and answers, "At first I didn't like it, but then little by little it kinda grows on you. Paul has set me up with a few of his farmer friends, and I hunt and fish whenever I get the chance. Shot a turkey last spring. Damn, it was good eating! I think in the old days I could have lived off the land. Between Paul and his farmers, I get my beef and chicken and eggs right from the source. I like it fresh. I hear you are thinking of joining the Carter County Police."

"It is part of the investigation. I don't know if it will be permanent."

John adds, "Connie wants it to be."

"I know that."

As we jog into the park, I see a car off in the distance. The engine starts, and it comes toward us! A handgun comes out of the passenger window!

John gets down behind a rock. He does not have a service weapon on him.

I have one of my .45s, and I pull it out. The passenger starts shooting! I get down on one knee and take aim! John yells into his cell phone, "Drive-by. Hit in the park. Send backup!"

I pull my trigger and fire, striking the passenger in the head through the windshield. He drops the weapon on the street. The driver then pulls his out, and with one hand on the wheel and one out the window, begins firing at random!

I start emptying my gun on him, and just before he could run me down, Reed comes in, tackles me and picks me up, and we are out of the way. The car takes a turn onto the football field and crashes into the scoreboard. The car then explodes!

The rest of the guys show up. John Henry walks over to the dropped handgun and stands by it. He does not have gloves on, so he doesn't pick it up.

The sheriff of Cavanaugh City comes by and asks, 'What the hell is going on around here?!"

John Henry shows his badge, saying, "I am John Henry Watson, officer of the Carter County Police. I am off duty. and I and my friends were jogging through the park. The car's occupants fired on us."

He then looks at me. "You are that Max Faraday from Chicago, aren't you? Hand over your weapon!"

I demand, "On whose authority?" The sheriff of Cavanaugh City puts his hand on me.

Chief Tom of Carter County Police comes to my defense. "Hold it! Get your hand off him, he is mine! He is one of my people now! I want him in on this investigation! Nothing held back!"

Reed flags down the fire department, and they start putting out the fire.

The gun is bagged and the paperwork is done at the crime scene.

Chief Tom snorts, "Watson, you seen it all?"

"Yes, Chief!"

"Then finish gathering testimony! Max, you are with me!"

He takes me to his car, saying, "I don't know what kind of damned pull you have, Max. You are an observer, and I will assign Officer John Henry Watson to drive you around."

"Thank you, sir."

"Max, I like you. We have history. I made a few calls to check out your record. Until you pissed off the Mafia, you could have had any law enforcement job you wanted, and you chose to be a detective in Chicago, no less. That takes grit."

"I don't like anyone telling me how to do my job, Feds or anyone. I am clean."

"The ball was already rolling to make you an officer. It doesn't need any outside help."

"I did not ask for it. I just asked for fingerprint identification, and they got on board."

Tom asks, "Why?"

I answer, "Because they think it might give the FBI a black eye."

"Why do they care?"

"If it does, more money will be sent in their direction with a terrorist war going on. They are still looking for the big bucks. Or if they have anything to hide, I will walk right into it and find it and get myself killed. Welcome to my world. Sorry I brought you into it, Chief."

The chief shakes his head, saying, "The sooner you get this case done, the sooner they will be out of my hair, what is left of it."

I ask, "Can you give me a ride to the Cavanaugh Synagogue?"

"I didn't know you are Jewish."

"Only through Jesus Christ. I was asked to go, and Abba Rabbi Hyman is family to me."

I get dropped off, and I run into the house for a shower and a change of clothes.

Abba asks, "Max, are you late?"

As I run upstairs to the bathroom, I yell, "There was a drive-by shooting at the park!"

"Is anyone hurt?"

"Just the shooters. They're dead."

Before I go in the bathroom, I turn to Abba, and I see him whisper, "That's my boy."

"Sabbath comes on a Saturday, well, duh?"

It is times like these I wish I brought more and better clothes. I'm wearing a business suit, not a real nice one, to wear to church or temple. I feel like I stick out. Burney's wife finds me and asks me to sit with them.

After service, I have a meal with them, making up for the one I had to leave so abruptly.

After the meal, Burney walks me around town, and we see an old park bench.

Burney says, "Remember when we were kids. It takes me a few minutes to remember those two old guys. There was a feud between two old guys when we were kids."

Every year around fall, the Christians would get together and organize a Bach concert.

And every year around the same time, the Jews in our community would have a Broadway-type show. Usually, it was *Fiddler on the Roof.* Of course, they would allow a few Gentiles in, being there were not enough Jews in our small town for the entire cast. Even I got into the act. An old Christian man would sit on a park bench waiting for the bus or something and say, "Ah Bach." Then an old Jewish man sitting on another park bench would say, "Ah, *Fiddler on the Roof.* Ah Bach. Ah, *Fiddler on the Roof.* Ah, Bach. Ah, *Fiddler on the Roof.* Ah,

Bach! Ah, *Fiddler on the Roof!*" And this would go on and on until the Fourth of July, and they would look at each other and say, "God Bless America." Then it starts back up again in the fall.

Burney adds, "Now they do Ralph Shurlow's, help, I am trapped in an elevator with a bunch of dysfunctional people."

I say to Burney, "You know how people say once you leave town you can never come back?"

"Yeah. I think a part of me wants to come back."

As I come back to the Hymans, Abba is cleaning and loading my .45. I felt so comfortable around Burney, I didn't think about needing it. "You should take better care of your gun, my son. Your Uncle Sherman would be angry if he saw it."

I ask Abba, "Where did you learn so much about guns?"

He smiles. "Israel, during the Six-Day War." And he becomes emotionless, like I am not going to tell you. "Maybe someday, but not right now."

I get a call from Pete. "Max, I got something you have to see."

I ask Burney, "Can you loan me your car? I need to talk to Pete in person."

I drive out to Pete's, and he sits me down and starts the program. "I factored in all the information about the car and the time and the stretch of highway into our Ice Works experimental program. This is what I got."

I see it happen. A speeding car strikes a deer. Smash! And there it is all before me.

"Now, you can't use this in a court of law, but I thought you would at least want to see it."

"How about the cell phone? Can you trace it?"

"Not enough time to trace, and not my department, but if I could call in a few favors."

I ask, "If another car was speeding through like that car, could you trace it?"

Pete taps his chin, stating, "We are working on a program that will enable a satellite to recognize a speeding car within five seconds or less, then send that information to a police dispatch, who can notify a patrol car to watch for a car."

"So that is how."

Pete smiles. "Got a speeding ticket in Lincoln County. We are working with L.A. So far, it is paying for itself."

"Can you set it up to monitor Deer Crossing Alley Highway?"

"Maybe, but this stuff does not come cheap, Max."

"How about for an old friend and the former head of Ice Works security?"

"I'll get the program set up for tonight, but I can't promise you anything."

I leave Pete's and head back to town and park Burney's car.

It is getting dark, so I begin walking to Jamie's. When I walk up to the door, Jamie comes to greet me. Jamie sees my gun and says, "No guns, Max."

"I have my gun holstered."

"Then you are not coming in my house."

"Fine, I'll stay out here and keep watch."

"Do you really think they are going to attack so soon?

"I know I would."

"Have you had dinner?"

"I have, over at the Hymans."

"I'll get you some water."

In less than an hour, like a bad recurring dream, the car that ran me down comes back.

Rapid fire! I shoot the windshield, and I think I hit one off the bat, screaming, "Get down. CALL 911!" A lit Molotov cocktail is thrown at the house and explodes in the garage! I empty my gun in the car, yelling, "Damn, it is the same damn car that hit me!" Its tires squeal as it strikes a car on the way out of town! Reed and the fire department show up and do their best to save the house, then I get a beep on my cell phone. Damn it. "Hello!"

"Ah, Max, it is me, Pete. Another deer got hit and didn't make it across the road! Hit it damn fast again. You told me to call."

I see Reed's fire truck and run to it. Pete continues, "I can see they have pulled over to the side to look at the damage."

"Reed, I got to have the truck!"

"I am kind of busy right now, Max!"

"Reed, there has been another deer accident, and the car has pulled over to the side of the road!"

"Damn it, Max, you don't make easy requests!"

"Uh, guys, I got to go!"

Pete is watching from his computer monitor, and another car pulls alongside, and the damaged car's driver starts loading. He calls again. "Max, there is another car, and they are loading the other car!"

Reed is moving his truck with his siren and horn playing Dixie.

The trafficker's car is loaded. The damaged car is soaked with gas and set on fire.

Explosion! We see the flames. Reed pushes the little red button. "The speed is a kick in the ass! They hit their nitro!"

We get closer and closer, and somebody sticks their head and body out of the car, and I do the same, like jousting, and we get closer.

Rapid fire goes across the radiator, and Reed yells, "Shit, we are losing the main battery!"

I do my best to shoot, but my .45 just can't get penetration! I get back in the truck. Reed turns around. headed back to the burning car. Reed's fire truck coasts and then comes to a halt. You can smell what I know is the battery acid.

He gets out the fire extinguishers. I grab another one, and I help put out the fire before it can spread into the woods. The fire is out, leaving a melted car on the highway.

Then suddenly there's silence. Reed says, "Well, that was interesting."

I grit my teeth, murmuring, "I liked it better when you cursed a blue streak."

"Marry a good Christian woman and learn to count to ten first."

"I yell, "Well, I am still single!" So I curse for the both of us. "Son of a bitch, we almost had them! Motherfuckers! Anyhow! Damn!"

"Feel better?"

"Yeah, I feel better."

Reed says, "Good, let it out."

Reed gets on his cell phone and calls Dusty.

Dusty was one of the Counting Tornadoes. Now he owns a garage in Lincoln City.

"Hey, Dusty, we have a problem."

He gets out of the truck and lifts the hood. "Shot the battery. The perpetual motion device is off balance. Shit, it's cracked apart. Damn!"

"Oh, I was chasing some drug runners with Max."

Dusty says, "Hi."

I yell, "Hi, Dusty! Oh shit. Let it out, brother, let it out."

"Can you get out here?"

"Yeah, isn't that GPS shit great, or what? We also need a tow for the trafficker's car too. Hot rod, midsize car. When the nitro exploded, it spread some of the parts around. See you, Dusty."

Ticked off, I say, "Dusty is coming. When he gets here, maybe I'll ask him if I can get a police cruiser."

Reed sarcastically comments, "Oh, that would be nice. Then I can have my fire truck for fighting fires!"

"I thought you were counting to ten."

"I just hit one hundred, and I want someone's ass."

"Welcome back to the dark side." I call John Henry, and he will be coming out to take pictures.

CHAPTER FOURTEEN

Thursday, October 5, 1978—The Road Trip

It is the last hour of the day in science class. We are staring at the clock, and it is 3:00 p.m. The school bell rings, and we are headed for the door. Mr. Pearson is waiting by the van in the parking lot and taking the money for the trip. He hands the keys to Big Paul, saying, "You're driving. I am just riding shotgun."

Kathy comes with crutches, and Paul and I help her in the van. Pete is jumping up and down, gleefully yelling, "I get to go, I get to go!"

Jason, Jamie, Ellen, Steve, Churchill, Dan, Reed, Jackson, and Burney are all ready to leave. Jack is standing off to the side, so I go over to talk to him. "Come on, Jack, let's go."

Jack shrugs his shoulders, saying. "I don't know if I should go."

"Why?"

"I was a real jerk to Wendy, and she has been decent to me since you and the others let me in."

I reassure him with, "Don't worry about it. That is her way, Jack. You are doing okay, just relax. The guys are cool about you coming, and when Paul gives you a chance, the rest will follow his lead, trust me."

"Well, I don't want to screw up."

"Then don't, just relax."

Wendy, Candy, and Connie are talking about dresses and material they are going to buy.

I gave them some cash. I don't like shopping for dressy church clothes myself.

I'll be going to the novelty and comic book store with Paul and get some baseball cards and neat T-shirts. That reminds me, fast forward to 2002, I should have my collectable stuff still stored at the Chapel farm. Before I went off to the Marines, I asked Paul if I could store it someplace on the farm so my mom wouldn't give it away or sell it in a garage sale.

Twenty years have passed. Better check on it when I wake up.

K. Ray C. looks nervous. Mr. Pearson asks, "K. Ray C., are you sure you have permission from your mother to come?"

He answers with an uneasy, "Sure, Mr. Pearson, no problem."

"I heard what happened when you went on the field trip to the Detroit Zoo without your mother's say-so."

"Hey, that is in the past. We are going to be back by eight, right"?

Mr. P. shakes his head.

The gang is loaded up to go, and Smokey Joe is sucking up a few puffs before the trip.

Paul yells, "Smokey Joe, get your ass in the van, or we'll leave you here!'

He replies, "I'm coming I'm coming!"

Mr. P. shakes his head again. Connie is the last to get in. She is a little phobic, and the only seat available is next to Reed Jackson. She still has some bad memories of him, but she sits next to him anyway. We are crammed in the van. Paul told us at lunchtime the first person to complain about being cramped or carsick is walking. Now, with our parents, we would most likely abuse that and start complaining right off the bat. But with Big Paul, you take him seriously from the word go.

As we leave town, Mr. P. says, "Paul, you know how to drive."

Paul reaches into his pocket and pulls out his wallet, handing it to him. A shocked look on Mr. P's face as he sees a CDL and aircraft pilot's learner's permits, boat, and other licenses, and a good amount of cash. "My dad is going to have me learn how to do crop dusting with my uncle. You name it, I can drive it or have driven it."

Pete talks to me in Spanish. "Hey, let's get Reed mad by talking in Spanish." We go on talking for a minute, then Paul asks in French, "What are you two talking about?"

I respond in French, "We are talking in another language to piss off Reed."

Paul says, "He is about to burst. His face is beet red."

Mr. P says in French, "Paul, watch the road."

Paul asks, "Where did you learn French?"

Mr. P answers, "High school, and I used it in Vietnam."

Burney says in Hebrew, "He is about to burst."

Reed bursts, saying, "Learn to speak English. You are an American, ain't you?"

We all say, "Ain't you?"

"You know what I mean."

Connie asks, "Can we have some music back here?"

The music is the song "Soul Man," and K. Ray C. says, "Turn that monkey music down!

Reed turns to him and states, "Do you want to walk home, or do you want to limp?"

Everyone applauds, and K. Ray C. is silent. Paul gives him a stern stare from the rearview mirror to back it up. This the first time Connie and Reed have been in the same room or vehicle since we were kids. As the song ends and goes to a commercial, Reed says, "Connie, I am sorry for the things I said when I was a kid. I am my father's son, and sometimes we say things that aren't too bright. Can you ever forgive me?"

Connie is about to say, yes, but "Johnny B. Goode" comes on! Reed yells, "Hey, turn it up. Turn it up!"

So far so good. We get to the mall as planned. Paul declares, "Now remember!"

Candy runs inside to get a wheelchair for Kathy and returns by the time we have her out.

Paul reminds us, "You people are only getting an hour and a half at the mall. I got to go to the farm supply store and the bread store and the comic book shop. And then I will return and pick you people up at the mall, and that is it. Have your shopping, your eating, and your bathroom visits done. We will not be stopping on the way back. Got that? We are on a time schedule!"

Everyone looks at Pete. "If you are not ready to go, I will leave your ass here, got that?"

And we are off.

I go with Paul, and we drop Churchill and Dan at the book store, and then we are headed off to the farm supply store and the bread store and then the comic book shop.

Mr. Pearson went into the supply store for dog and cat food and other stuff. I help him stack the stuff on the roof of the van's rack. He chuckles, "Paul thinks that they will be waiting for him when we get back to the mall."

I ask, "How much do you want to bet that they will be ready and on time to leave?"

Mr. P chuckles, "I am not a betting man, Max, but if they are ready, I will buy everyone an ice cream cone. At the bread store, we fill up our carts with all kinds of breads and some fruit pies and other stuff. Mr. Pearson just shakes his head. "Won't that go bad in a few days?"

Paul says, "No, we have a big chest freezer, and Mom will be making sandwiches for school. And if it does go bad and moldy, it is still cheap chicken food. The way Mom figures it, buying the bread here and freezing it pays for the freezer in the long run."

Mr. P agrees. "Your mom does know how to stretch a dollar."

Paul adds, "You have to, being a farmer and having a big family."

When we go to the comic book store, Paul has his order list and cash ready to make deals. He knows the comics he wants and has a few to sell, autographed copies from the time he went to the comic book show. The manager says, "You are a big Wild Tail comics fan, I see."

Paul admits, "Yeah, I read DC and Marvel, but I get my kicks out of Wild Tail and the other Wild Tail Champions."

I ask Paul, "Can I borrow some cash? I found some great cards. Especially for the price, they will get me twenty years down the road."

"You get paid on Friday?"

"Yeah."

"I'll hold them until then, so put them on my bill. We offer shipping and handling services. If you have a big enough order, I can give you a discount."

"Better than subscription?"

"And guaranteed mint condition. Where you from anyway?"

Paul replies, "Cavanaugh City."

"Really? That is a bit of a travel for you. Shipping and handling would come in handy. Would you like to be on our mailing list?"

Paul gets his stuff, and we pile it on top, putting a moving blanket on it, tying it down. We pick up Dan and Churchill, and they have their noses stuck in the books.

Dan asks, "Can we have lights back here?"

Mr. P. says, "They won't be ready."

I smile saying, "Oh, they will be ready."

As we pull in to pick them up, all are ready to go. Steve and Jason say, "You are late."

Paul snorts back, "Driver's privilege, and only by five minutes."

Mr. P. looks out the window in shock. "You are all ready to go. Why?"

Steve says, "Because we did not want to be left behind."

Mr. P. says, "I have heard sermon after sermon, and people hear the gospel and about the rapture and don't heed the Lord's call. And when Paul tells you to do something, you do it. Why?"

Jason says, "How many pastors, or even Jesus for that matter, say, if you are not ready to go, I will leave you here, got that?"

Paul smiles and says, "My sheep know my voice."

The ice cream tasted good, and we were on time. The girls are talking about the clothes they got. "Oh, Max, we got you the nicest suit for you."

Suit, great. Although I can't wear my KISS T-shirt to church or school, for that matter, it was worth the trip to get it. Jason got a book about computers. Pete is explaining the terms as usual. Jack has relaxed a bit, and I think, no I know, he is fitting in.

As we get out of town on the highway, Paul slows down a bit. Mr. Pearson asks what the problem is. Paul responds, "I think there is a drunk driver ahead of us. I want to put some distance between us. Maybe he will take a side road. The way he is swerving, I don't want to try and pass him."

"Good eyes, Mr. Chapel."

Other cars pass us in a hurry to go somewhere, but Paul slows down. Something is in the air, and the good shepherd that he is senses it. The car loses control! Oh shit, it is happening! The car behind tries to pass, but it is clipped in the rear, and it loses control and rolls over. A semitruck coming from the opposite direction can't avoid hitting the cars coming through!

Paul steps on the gas. We are moving! We rush past the oncoming semi, and we just make it past, and cars that were behind us and did not slow down to avoid the accident are getting their front bumpers bashed by the semi! Paul puts some distance between us and the calamity and then stops, sticking his head out of the window, asking, "Okay people, what now?"

Reed yells, "Let me out. I have first aid training!"

Before Mr. Pearson could say no, Churchill opens the door, and we are out! Mr. P. yells, "Pete, you get back here!"

Mr. Pearson, Pete, Wendy, Candy, Kathy, Connie, and K. Ray C. are left at the van, and K. Ray is huddled in the back. Candy is scared, crying, "What can we do?"

Wendy says, "We can pray!"

Mr. P. says, "K. Ray C., you don't look so good. Let's get out and get some air."

Pete helps me with K. Ray C.

Churchill runs for the drunk driver's car, and it is on its side. He gets to it first and he yells, "Oh My God! He didn't have a seatbelt and went through the windshield. The body is a bloody mess!"

I can tell at first glance the driver is dead. Churchill reaches down to touch it anyway. As he glances back into the car, a liquor bottle stares back at him. It is the brand he and his father secretly drink. He gets up to run away; he can't do anything here.

I hear a voice. "Max, we are coming for you."

Smokey Joe is taking pictures and at the same time yells, "Max!" and I run to him.

A car is turned upside down, and the driver is stuck hanging from his seatbelt.

The door is crinkled. I can't get it opened! "Joe, see if you can find Paul. Maybe he can get it open! Hurry!" The driver turns his bloody head to look at me.

"Max, we are coming for you."

The smell of gas is in the air. The driver of the upside-down car puts a cigarette in his mouth, and instantly I start running! As I run, my lungs take it in, and my heart could run on the gas fumes. I look back. He lights his cigarette and EXPLOSION!

I can see flames surround me and a flash of heat. and then I am out. I see Reed helping the trucker out of his cab, and he sees the flames. He yells, "Move your busted ass, or we are going to get flash fried!"

Then I see Dan and Churchill and the others helping a pregnant woman out of her car and putting her on a blanket because of her broken legs, and everyone taking a corner and as I run by I grab a corner and we just beat the flames!

As we come to safety, Jason says, "Max, do you want BBQ with that, or do you like your hair well-done?" My hair is on fire! I just pat the fire out.

The police and fire department come and take it from there. They just can't get over how we did first aid and did it right. Police and ambulance and fire department ask, "Who are you kids, anyway?"

We answer the question with, "Boy Scouts, a future Marine, and Future Farmer of America."

Then the TV news crew comes by and asks the same question.

We answer again, "Boy Scouts, a future Marine, and Future Farmer of America."

"Where are you from?"

"Cavanaugh City."

"Never heard of it."

When they ask Mr. Pearson how he got through this unscratched, he explained, "I was not the driver, Paul was, and it was a good thing too, because I only have one leg, and he was using both, one on the gas and one on the brakes."

The reporter says, "I must call this in. It will be on the eleven o'clock news!" He gets out a cell phone.

Mr. P. asks, "Is there any way I could make a call? Tell my wife we are going to be late?"

"Sure, be my guest. Just dial it like a phone."

"Hello, honey, we are going to be a bit late. There was an accident. Oh no, we are fine. I'll have to talk to you when I get home."

They get excited talking on the phone, and I walk over to Dan and Churchill working with the paramedics. They can't get over how well they have handled the accident, and they just chalk it up to Boy Scout first aid training. Smokey Joe is a shutterbug, camera in one hand and cigarette in the other, whispering, "Oh this is great!"

On the ride home we are all pretty quiet. We came to the big city thinking that we could get, stuff mostly. And that is okay and all, but what we did not know is what we could give by being where and when we were at that time.

A baby was born tonight. Remember the lady with the broken legs?

They say it came a bit early, a healthy baby boy. A baby was also born tonight in the spirit: baby Candy. I would like to say it was right on time.

We pull into town about nine thirty. Parents have come to pick up their kids, thanking God for their safe return mostly. K. Ray C's mom is furious, to say the least!

"K. Ray C., how dare you pull a stunt like this and not tell me where you were!"

He looks really sick. We had to pull over for him to puke a couple times; that is another reason why we're so late. He pleads, "Mom, please, just let me get in the car."

I pack my stuff and put it in the back of Paul's truck. "You are going to pick me up at Mrs. Horton's, right?"

"Yeah, go see your mom. I'll get you there."

I run there and don't bother to knock on the door. I just run in to let Mom know we are all right. "When we got the news, we were assured by the good news. Mrs. Horton was resting, and then she shouted, 'Maxine, we have to pray!' We didn't know what to pray for, we just prayed."

Mrs. Horton says, "Max, you are back. The Lord answers prayer."

With tears I break down, "I really needed prayer too! Oh, Mom."

She holds me, saying, "There, there, you are safe at home. Do you want to stay here tonight?

"No, I am a big boy," I say sniffing. "I like the Chapels, and Paul's dad will probably have me milking cows before school."

Mom shakes her head. I can't tell her that compared to the Marine basic training, Marines get to sleep in. "Well, I'll make a list for you to give to Mrs. Chapel."

As Mom leaves, Mrs. Horton says, "Max, you seen the demon, didn't you?"

"Yes, he said, 'Max, we are coming for you.'"

"Oh, my child, the devil is a thief and a murderer. Cover yourself with the blood of Jesus Christ and pray a hedge of protection around you wherever you go!"

I add, "I wouldn't be alive in this world if I didn't, because I know it works."

She smiles and giggles, saying, "But he, meaning Satan, does not know you know it works. He thinks you are a fourteen-year-old snot-nosed little boy. Don't get cocky and cling ever so close to the Lord, my child."

I ask, "There were deaths tonight, why? Why would God allow death?"

With tears she says, "Baby, everyone dies, it is what you leave behind. Hopefully, Churchill will wise up and stay away from booze. He saw the end results, now it is his time to choose. God is doing a new thing. There was great rejoicing in heaven when Candy accepted Jesus Christ."

"Yeah, I never really thought she took God seriously."

Mrs. Horton adds, "It is hard to take God seriously when it has never been seriously presented. Life and death can do that."

Paul pulls up, and my mom hands me the list. Paul picks me up and takes me to the Chapel farm. Mr. and Mrs. Chapel are happy to see us, as are all of Paul's brothers and sisters.

Mrs. Chapel makes a bed for me on the couch, and the eleven o'clock news comes on.

"Earlier tonight, there was a major accident on the highway. Kids from the small town of Cavanaugh City were heroes in treating victims. Son, can you describe what happened?"

Mrs. Chapel squeals, "Paul is on TV!"

"Hey, that's me!"

"A son of a *bleep* was drunk and lost control and his bloody *bleep* was spread all over the *bleeping highway.*" Paul's mom's mouth is wide open!

"That caused a chain reaction of death and destruction that you see before you," the reporter says. "Paul and his friends were responsible in giving first aid, comfort, and moral support to the needy. What are you kids, anyway?"

We answer the question with, "Boy Scouts, a Marine, and Future Farmer of America."

"Where are you from?"

"Cavanaugh City.

The reporter says, "Never heard of it." Then he continues to the camera, "This was a night of hope in the midst of tragedy; and next, the weather."

Mrs. Chapel yells, "Paul, they had to bleep you!"

Mr. Chapel responds with, "That guy was a drunken son of a bitch, and Paul just told it like he saw it."

"But they had to bleep him," Mrs. Chapel stresses. "How is that going to make me, us, look at church?"

Paul's dad defends him again with, "If they have a problem with my boy calling a drunken son of a bitch, a drunken son of a bitch, maybe we should find another church. Let your no be no, and your yes be yes. If the jackass was a drunken son of a bitch, he is a drunken son of a bitch."

Dirty looks and stares from Mrs. Chapel to Mr. Chapel.

"I will say good night, Max. It is time to get to sleep."

CHAPTER FIFTEEN

Sunday, July 21, 2002—Evil Licking Its Wounds

I am Bridge, Caretaker of the Universe. In my life, or by a better definition, "existence," I have had to learn when to act and when not to act. When to observe, and when to take action. On earth, my hand is for the most part held back, and I observe, because humanity must take charge of the situation they are in. Grow up, will you.

Be a caretaker yourself. It is your world. You are the one living in it. In all things, I ask for wisdom from my Heavenly Father, The Creator of the Universe. Find him for yourself; there is only one true lighthouse.

After the drug traffickers make their escape from Max's wrath, instead of having the good sense to get out of Cavanaugh City, vengeance payback is on their mind.

"I want his ass! He has cost me!"

"Who is he?"

"Max Faraday! I know you!"

"But what is he?"

"Get the word out. I want to know who he is, and what he has been doing all these years. I want that Jamie Scott dead. I need an example. No one messes with me!"

I am sure if Max could hear his enemy's threats, not promises. He would say, "Bring it on."

Max wakes up.

***

Going to church, I wake up with the knowledge of the road trip and the accident and the courage of us all. Then I remember I have to get up and go to church. Fumbling for the phone, I call Jamie. After several rings, I get a hello.

"Hi, it is me, Max."

"I don't want to talk to you right now," and Jamie hangs up. So I get a shower and put on the business suit I had on yesterday and head to church. I arrive and go in and then I look back to the parking lot, and Jason and his wife stop and talk to a young woman who has tattoos and body piercings all over her. They seem to be talking, and Jason's wife puts her arm around her, and they walk back to their car and get in and drive away.

I turn around and see Candy from a distance wearing a conservative church dress.

She looks my way, and she runs to me, giving me a hug, whispering, "Thank you for being there, for Churchill."

I can't control it. I am crying for joy. Candy is now my sister in Christ. With tears I say, "I love your dress."

"Oh, this old thing."

At Sunday school, Candy brings me into her class and shows me off as the miracle man. The teachers of the class are Uncle Hal and Aunt Peg; they have graduated to teaching the adult class. I say, "Thank you for all your prayers."

Jason, Big Paul, Marcy, and Dan applaud, and the rest say Amen! Candy says, "I would also like to thank you for your continued prayers. Churchill wants to join an AA group. Please continue in your prayers. This is a big step for him, he is not a churchgoer, and I have asked him to come. Last Friday night, we went out for dinner as friends. It was so . . . thank you for your prayers."

Amen! Praise The Lord.

Hal signs, and Aunt Peg speaks and hands out papers with information on alcohol products and the negative effects. Paul murmurs, "Are we going to bash Budweiser again?"

Hal asks, "Paul, why you are so defensive of the evil industry."

Paul states, "It is an industry, not evil or good. God gave people free will to choose to do evil and blame the particular industry for their actions, kind of like Adam and Eve blaming Satan in the garden."

Hal signs, "Yes, but they demean women and put thoughts in men's heads."

Paul responds, "Free will, and men are wired to have thoughts, and after ten kids and a hard day's work, it is a wonder I still get a thought from time to time."

Hal signs, "It is evil."

Paul says, "Let's look at it this way, a good Christian farmer like me grows the grain and sells it, and tithes on his profit. Another good Christian works at a plant that turns the grain into alcohol, gets paid, and tithes his pay also. Another good Christian owns the company, sells his product, and tithes his profits. A non-Christian gets drunk and gets pulled over by a Christian police officer. The Christian judge takes away his license or puts the offender on probation, sentencing the non-Christian to an AA twelve-step program, where the non-Christian in a roundabout way learns of Jesus Christ and accepts him as his or her savior. Excuse me, but the way I see it, we have them coming and we have them going."

Hal shakes his head. "Okay Paul, what drives you to drink?"

"I can drink if I want to or not, actually. And I sometimes offer to be the designated driver."

"The subject of the class today is to not bear false witness. When you go to the bar, are you not bearing false witness?"

Paul continues, "No. Because some people have been mentally and physically scared by the church, and if I shared Christ when they are sober, they might be mad enough to try to kick my butt. Get a few drinks down them the first time, and if they do get mad, I can make it to the door. Gradually, when we get to know each other, I don't need the beer and neither does he or she. And if your Christianity washes off going into a bar, you don't have much Christianity."

"Hey, I didn't grow up a United Brethren in Christ. I grew up a Christian, and you can have your beliefs, and I can have mine. What recently drove you to drink, Paul?"

Paul hangs his head. My guess is he does not want to hurt my feelings. "Max has bought the old McGraw farmhouse."

"Congratulations. Max comes from the rest of the class. And guess what they plan to do with the barn?"

"What?"

"Turn it into another bed-and-breakfast."

Hal didn't need to see the signing translation. He can read Paul's lips and does his best to say, "Cavanaugh City does not need another B&B."

Paul continues, "The Dutch are planning on building another thousand-cow dairy farm." The retired farmers in the class grit their teeth and bite their lips or tongues. "I was sick and tired, so I thought I would go have a beer with a friend and my brother." Hal has no comment for Paul's grief and anger.

A classmate taps Paul on the back and whispers, "Paul, next time you have a beer, have one for me too."

Paul nods his head and whispers, "Can do."

After church, Steve and Kathy meet us at the restaurant. Kathy grabs my arm and says, "You should have told me what was going on, Max." Her stern look is enough to tell me that we will be talking later, but this is not the time or place. They reserved the back room so we could all eat together. Paul and Marcy have brought their kids. Jason and family are here too, along with Reed Jackson and wife and the baby. At lunch, I ask, "Do you remember the road trip we took in the eighth grade?" For the adults, except for Reed's wife and Adam's wife, the room is silent.

Paul says, "Funny thing is, I dreamt about it last night."

And just about all of them say, "Yeah, me too."

Candy sheds tears, saying, "I miss Wendy. She led me in the sinner's prayer in that terrible moment."

During the meal I ask Jason, "What were you doing with that girl before church started?"

He says, "I looked at her, and I felt the need to talk to her, so I did. She is a new Christian from out of town, and she did not know her way around the area. I love our church and all, but it was not right for her. I felt our greeters could give her a hard time, and I did not want to take a chance. With a new Christian or a visitor, you may only get one chance. We have a great youth group; I felt she needed to be handled with kid gloves, so we offered a ride to Reed's church. I called Reed on his cell. We met on the road, and Reed picked her up with the rest of his bus ministry."

Reed pats Jason on the back, saying, "Oh, you guys missed her singing 'Amazing Grace.' It was so beautiful; people just stopped to listen to her sing."

Reed's wife, Debby, says, "Thank you for bringing her to our church. You really listened to the Holy Spirit, Jason."

Jason replies, "Well, just because we don't run around speaking in tongues does not mean we don't listen to the Holy Spirit."

After lunch, I head to Paul's. I find him lying down in his hammock on the front yard. I ask Paul where my stuff is.

"What stuff?"

"My stuff I had before I went into the Marines. I moved my stuff somewhere around here for storage."

Paul scratches his chin, saying, "I remember, and when you went to the CIA, you sent more stuff, and then you moved from there to New York, and you sent more stuff, and when you went to Chicago, you sent more stuff."

I smile and ask, "Where is it?"

Paul scratches his chin. "Let's see, garage sale? No. It is probably in the chicken coop."

"Where?" I look into the chicken coop and see a tarp covering a big container covered in chicken poop. My baseball cards!

"Don't worry, it is covered well and airtight with mothballs."

"We have to get it out!"

"It has been here; it will be there. Besides, those chickens are going to be slaughtered soon, and then you can get your stuff out."

"You sure?"

Paul shrugs his shoulders. "I don't know. You can get your punching bag that is in my work shed."

He takes me to the work shed, and there it is, my old punching bag. Still pretty worn and a few duct tape patches to cover up holes, so I give it a good kick to get the feel.

Paul murmurs, "You look like you need it more than I do."

I reply, "I have a lot to think about in my life, and this will help me get out some frustrations."

"Talking is good too, you know."

I put my hand on his shoulder and say, "That was kind of forced, wasn't it?"

"Hey, it is what friends are supposed to say. Go take your frustrations out on the bag, not your friends." He helps me take it apart and loads it in my car.

I come to Churchill's and find him drunk and on the floor. Candy has come by to visit and comes in with coffee. I come beside them and reassure them, "Don't worry, Churchill, tomorrow is another day."

I leave Churchill's and head to Jamie's. A Federal car is in the driveway, and an FBI agent comes out to talk to me. "You must be Max."

"I would like to go in and talk to my friend."

"I am afraid I can't let you do that. Mr. Scott does not wish to see you at this moment."

"You are a bit late. Mr. Scott has had death threats long before you arrived."

"How do you know?"

I hand over copies of my material. "Tell Jamie I said hi." I drive away. When I get home, I get out some tools. I find a place in the barn to mount the punching bag to the wall and just begin pounding it like it is an unseen enemy.

Chapter Sixteen

Friday, October 6, 1978—After the Road Trip

Up with the cows at 5:00 a.m. I used to get a ride to the farm and milk cows in the summer or spend the night in one of the beds that belonged to Paul's older sister who went to college.

So I am up and dressed and out the door hurriedly. I pitch in, feeding calves and milking cows, hooking up equipment, and being part of the Chapel family team.

Shortly after 7:00 a.m., I am back in the house getting ready for school.

Mrs. Chapel has breakfast ready to go, and before I leave for school, I give her Mom's list.

At 8:15, the school bell rings. The teacher says, "Big Paul, Big Paul! Class, calm down! Big Paul, Big Paul! Quiet!"

Paul retells the details minus the son of a . . . Candy is fresh meat now, it seems.

Her Presbyterian upbringing really didn't impact her life much, from what I remember.

You can play at being a Christian and have yourself and everyone fooled. When you make the choice, you make enemies. "So you are a Christian now, are you?"

Wendy steps in, yes, she is. Candy never really got in too much trouble, from what I remember. The girls persecuting her, one is pregnant by sixteen. Another arrested for intoxicated driving senior year, and that one died of a sexual disease. Bad life stories in general. I step in, saying, "Leave her alone."

"What are you going to do?"

"Support and defend my friend, because I can."

The bad girls walk away. Yes, there are bad girls. Me being taller than most guys, with glasses and braces, the girls never really let me ask them out on any dates growing up. Except Wendy, and she is like a sister to me, and I love her and all, but that is just weird. Wendy steps in, "You didn't have to threaten them, Max."

"Who said I was threatening them? I was making a promise."

Wendy, the good angel that she is, does not like my methods, and that is okay. In the background I hear the Lord saying to me, "That's my boy."

After school, I go to work at the C. Connection, and then I head to the Cooper's house.

Mr. Cottager has something in the works, but he is not telling. As I enter the house, Mr. Cooper looks worried, so I ask him what the problem is. He sits me down and says, "Lately my wife has been giving me that worried-mother look, especially since our daughter's checkup yesterday. We have been taking her foolishness of becoming a vegetarian with a slight chuckle here and there, laughing it off as a phase little girls go through. Nobody is laughing now."

At the dinner table everyone is quiet. After dinner, Jason and I play video games on his Atari 2600. Space Invaders is one of my favorites. Mr. Cooper has a younger brother who works for Atari and sends them video games. He comes by to check on us. "How are you kids doing?"

"This is great. Mr. Cooper! You are so lucky to have a brother who works for Atari."

"Yeah, he is studying how to be a programmer right now.

Listen you two, don't stay up too late, okay?"

Jason asks, "Dad, are you and mom fighting?"

"No, son, we are just not getting along with each other right now on about how to deal with your sister."

Jason asks, "So she caused it?"

"No, she is just being a kid, and I guess we had better act like adults and figure out how to cope with her choices. Now get to bed in a bit, will you?"

I ask, "So what are you going to do?"

Mr. Cooper looks at me and says, "When I married Jason's mother, we promised each other that we would never go to bed angry." With a crooked smile he says, "I'll see if I get any sleep tonight."

The Coopers are a decent family, even if Jason has to check off the days till he is eighteen and is kicked out of the house. The whole experience, it changed him in a good way. He went from a C student to honor roll. He has catalogs of colleges and ideas about careers that he would like to work in. I know he is a little scared now, but he will make a great teacher and computer game designer someday.

CHAPTER SEVENTEEN

All My Stuff Is in the Chicken Coop?

It's Monday, July 22, 2002.

I wake up automatically at ten to six, and it may sound stupid, but the first thing I think of is all my stuff is in a chicken coop. I feel bad about Reed's fire chief's truck.

But it was the only thing I knew at the time that could catch a trafficker's car.

Before I finish my thought, I hear my cell phone ring, and I gradually wake up and answer it. "Hello?"

"Hi, it is District Attorney Kathy Pearson. I have a busy day, so meet me for breakfast at S&G. We need to talk. Be there in thirty. Click.

Kathy sounds peeved. I guess I would be too if I was kept in the dark. Respectfully. she is the prosecuting attorney for the county. I'll have to explain it was for her own protection.

Kathy Chapel Pearson is a farm girl at heart, and as a kid she was known as Iron Maiden or Lightning Rod. Moving around the farm on crutches or a golf cart, she had an eye for taking care of the animals. She and Paul were in charge of the health of the calves growing up. Kathy would spot a sick pig, chicken, goat, or whatever, and Paul or Connor or whoever would treat it. She has always been a details person. I could use this skill, but for her own safety, she should be left in the dark.

Together, the Chapel farm family would bring home the blue and purple ribbons from the Four H county and, at times, state fairs. Before they would go on the wall of fame, they would be sent out to California to Grandpa. Grandpa Charles "Charles the Intimidator" Chapel, who was an Air Force mechanic/ace/ general/and commander of an Air Force base out in California until he retired. He was a World War II ace and patriarch of the Air Force traditions. He was also the only Chapel who was born without a green thumb.

I get a move on to S&G for breakfast, and I am a bit perplexed at what I see. A Sam and Gertrude's sign takes the place of Sodom & Gomorrah's neon lights. I was just here Friday night. What the heck?

It is just after six, and I see Kathy ready to go in the restaurant. As I open the door for Kathy, I say, "This is not Sodom & Gomorrah."

Kathy smiles. "No, this is Sam and Gertrude's from five in the morning to five in the afternoon, and from five in the afternoon till two a.m. it is Sodom and Gomorrah, just call it S&G for short."

"How? Why?"

Kathy explains, "Oh, Sam's sister Gertrude came back to the area after her restaurant went up in flames a couple years ago. Adam did a great job, don't you think? In about twenty minutes they can set up either way."

The walls are covered with local memorabilia, newspaper clippings like the tornado of '76 that took out Sam's farm and killed his wife. Celebrities like Ralph Shurlow of Counting Tornadoes got his start here as a part-time bouncer. I even spot a picture of William Wildtale with BBQ on his face. Paul must have invited him here or something. The menu is family oriented and is a hot spot for farmers, truckers, and yuppies on vacation that stay at the B&B's in Cavanaugh City. We get a corner booth in the back and sit down.

Kathy asks, "What is going on?"

"I am starting an investigation into drug smuggling and attempts on Jamie's life. And I guess somebody wants to stop me before I get started and for some reason maybe wants me dead."

She asks, "Can you give me any names?"

"I would rather not. Chances are you could be putting your life at risk just by sitting with me."

Our waitress comes by. "So sugar, what will it be?"

"Oh. I want an omelet with ham, cheese, mushrooms, onions, and a pinch of lemon garlic. I'd also like some buttered Texas toast and today's paper if you got it. And orange juice, fresh."

She smiles. "A William Wildtale special coming up."

I wonder, *William Wildtale has a special at SCG?*

"And you, honey?"

Kathy mutters, "Coffee and a bagel with light cream cheese." Then she turns to me. "You seem hungry."

"I am. I'll probably work it off today anyway."

"So you are not going to give me any names or leads?'

"If Steve thinks you need to know, you can talk to him, but as for me, think of me as a guy who has a bull's-eye painted on my back. The less you talk to me, the better."

Kathy sarcastically chuckles. "A bull's-eye painted on your back, where have I heard that before? What if I have information to give?"

"Pass it to Steve."

Kathy asks, "Are you seeing anyone?"

"No, right now I'm single and living with it. You and Steve faked your divorce?"

Kathy is stunned. "How?"

"You told me when I was in the coma. You played the theme from Rocky."

She was mad at me before, now she smiles with peace. I guess she is thanking God for how far I have come; I know I have. We talk about the pains of stardom that poor Mr. Right, Steve, has had to endure.

***

The nice thing about being the Caretaker of The Universe is I, Bridge, can change the subject. Through the night and early this morning, the

Bull's-Eye duo Red and Green have been tracking a drug lord/smuggler for the FBI. The criminal in question is named Keith.

Bull's-Eye Red is an expert with small arms and high-caliber rifles, a tracker and profiler without equal. Bull's-Eye Green is a detective too; his weapon of choice, bow and arrow.

And at handheld darts he is a trick shot. Keith has been hounded by our duo; it seems everywhere he has been, they have been there too. Shutting down operations, he made a hit on an FBI agent. Instead of the FBI waging war on Keith, they have had success farming cases out to the Wild Tail Champions, namely The Bull's-Eye Duo Red and Green, and our boys took the case with a vengeance.

A drug house was closed for business, a prostitution ring whose women were set free, and money laundering operation down the drain. They find Keith at a warehouse, scared shitless and cowering in a corner. Red declares, "It is all over, Keith."

Keith stutters, "I don't know how you made it here! My men are surrounding this place. You won't get out alive!"

Green drops Keith's bodyguard before him and says, "You mean like him? Tranquilizer darts will have them out for an hour."

"What do you want?"

"We want to know your connection to the T."

The T, Terror Thieves & Technology Organization, one of the Wild Tail Champions' many enemies. Led by a faceless man known only as The Man, they specialize in high-tech crime, like genetic manipulation.

Keith yells, "They will kill me if I talk! You may be tough, but you are no killers!"

Green murmurs, "Maybe we should change our reputation, starting with you?"

Kapow! Red and Green wonder aloud what that was. Kapow! Keith smirks. "I called for backup."

The warehouse doors are blasted open, and a freak of nature named Slam stands in the light, a mountain of a man standing eight feet plus tall. Their gauntlets identify the villain named Slam. Data comes across the duo's visors. giving them a brief bio of Slam.

When it comes to weakness, there is no listing.

Keith says, "Ha, payback is on. You two are dead meat!"

Slam raises his arms and violently slams them together, but the explosive force is directed at Keith! His body is turned to ash! Slam's sound wave could have ruptured their ears if not for their WTC (Wild Tail Champion) earplugs!

Green comments, "Not that I am complaining, Slam, but why did you kill Keith?"

Slam states, "My orders of The Man and The T. Keith was sloppy, and I needed to make an example out of him. Failure is not tolerated!"

Green says, "This guy went ten rounds with Brute."

Slam is angered by that memory. "That little firecracker will pay!" Then raises his arms and slams them together, aimed at Green! Red pushes his stunned partner out of the way! The explosion sends shrapnel and wood splinters flying! In the confusion, Red calls out, "Adam, are you okay?"

Green whispers, "Over here, Steve."

Green is bleeding, and my G is calling for backup.

Red changes his clip to high explosives and hollow points. "I'll buy some time till someone gets here!"

In agony, Green asks, "What do you mean? The med lab is full."

Red comes from behind a crate and sprays bullets across Slam's chest! Slam screams in pain. It hurts him, but his hide is almost bulletproof! "You see, I heal up pretty fast. I am not even bleeding now!"

Red takes two shots and strikes Slam in the eyes! The screams of pain. Slam, without thought, fires his sound waves at random, and Red takes cover in the debris and makes a run for his partner. "How you doing, Adam?"

"I thought we were not supposed to break our cover. I thought backup was coming. Oh man, that looks bad."

"WTC med lab is full. Something happened. I don't know the details. First aid will hold me together. What about Slam? He is bulletproof. I put a bullet in each eye."

Green in his pain smirks. "An eye for an eye. I like it. If it didn't crack the skull, he will grow new eyes. He can regenerate his own flesh-type powers."

"What?!"

"I have been reading his bio. It helps to keep my mind off the pain. OW!"

A steel beam comes crashing down, almost striking them both. Green adds, "If we can't take him out, we will have to leave now before Slam takes this place apart!"

Blue Bomber appears. "You are staying right here!"

Red asks, "Where is the backup?"

"You are looking at it."

"Then get him to the med lab!"

"Can't, the hospital is full!"

And Blue takes off his glove. "Green here has internal bleeding. I can see it with my X-ray vision. I have to heal him!"

Red questions, "But that will leave me here alone with that monster. You will most likely be drained out!"

Blue puts his hand on Red's shoulder, saying, "You are a born leader! I know you will figure something out."

Blue Bomber touches Green, passes his bioenergy to him, and then he is out. Red looks his partner over. The bleeding has stopped. "Wake up, Adam! I can't do this alone!"

Slam is making a lot of noise. Noise! Red grabs Blue Bomber and drags him towards Slam. "If I can just get Slam to fire close enough to Blue Bomber without getting him killed. This looks like a good spot. I'll try to draw his fire."

Slam yells, "Red! I am going to get you for what you did to my eyes!" Slam raises his arms and brings them together! The explosion takes that section of the warehouse down! Red is in fear for his friend Blue Bomber. "What have I done? You little Red rabbit, run!" And Red does his best to dodge Slam's blasts!

Kapow! What looks like Blue Bomber in rags shows up big time! Blue has become a giant in his own right and pounds on Slam relentlessly, tossing him like a rag doll!

Green staggers over the obstacles till he reaches his partner. Red asks, "Hey, are you okay?"

Green is still dazed, saying, "Yeah, but I feel I could sleep for a week."

"Come on, Blue is wearing down. We have to take Slam out!"

Slam is beaten but has tired Blue Bomber out, and he collapses on the ground. Slam raises his arms, and Red with pistols in both hands aims for Slam's palms and fires!

Firing into his palms until he has blasted through a gaping hole! Red's pistols click empty! Green fires two arrows through the holes in each hand!

The screams of pain from Slam awakens Blue Bomber, who looks at Red and says, "I knew you could do it!"

Blue takes his staffs and comes from behind Slam and choke holds him around his neck! Within moments, Slam settles down and is out. "I'll take him to Purgatory Prison for you. You don't need to be here when the Feds show up."

Red says to Green, "I still want to get you to the med lab," and they vanish.

The emergency room is filled with CIA agents. "What happened?" One of the orderlies explains, "One of the CIA secret prisons is not so secret anymore, and The T destroyed the place! Wild Tail offered our services, and we are neck deep in CIA agents and prison victims. Dr. Churchill Smith has been called in to help out, and Bull's-Eye Duo Red and Green lent a hand."

***

Back at S&G. "Oh this is good. I see a yuppie calling on his cell phone. Don, you don't know what you are missing here!" By the time we finish. Sam and Gertrude's is packed and a line is starting to form at the front door.

I need a car. I get out my personal phone book and find Ralph Shurlow's number.

I dial the number and get a secretary, and she transfers me.

"Hello?"

"Ralph, it so good to talk to you."

"Max? You don't call, you don't write, and you get one of our friend's trucks shot up. What can I do for you, friend?"

"I need a car."

"With you, you need a tank."

"I am going to be a Carter County police officer soon, and the kind of investigation I am doing, it would be good to have a fast car."

Ralph agrees. "Yeah, Dusty was telling me about Reed's truck. Let me talk to Chief Tom and set something up."

"Thanks, Ralph. Keep in touch."

I call Paul next. "Paul, I wonder if I could borrow a pickup?"

"Where you going?"

"Chicago. I'm moving. I figure with the FBI hanging around Jamie, now is about the best time to make the trip."

Paul replies, "Heck, I'll go. The sooner we get you moved in, the better."

"I'll buy lunch and take you out to dinner and top your tank off."

Paul agrees. "I am there."

We're going back to Chicago, making final arrangements for leaving. Paul and Paul 2.0 come to Chicago to help move. Paul 2.0 drives us to Chicago, leaving at 10:00 a.m.

Paul 2.0 is in the driver's seat, and Paul is in the back of the Ford 350 SuperCab.

I hop in and say, "Hi, guys! You guys had breakfast, right?"

"We are ready to go, Mr. Faraday."

"Paul 2.0, you can call me Max."

"Okay."

"You look comfy back there."

Paul is stretched out on the bench seat with a clipboard and drawing paper in one hand and a pencil in the other. I ask, "What you are doing?"

Paul replies, "I read the script last night, and I am putting the scenes to "The Exclamation!" comic, and whenever I get a chance I'll black ink them."

"You can ride and draw at the same time?"

"Sure. Junior, just make sure I know when there is a bump or if there is some sudden moves to be made, and I'll be alright."

I ask, "How come you're not doing Selah anymore?"

Paul answers, "Oh, the writer decided there was not much of a story and needed to do other things."

"But you and Marcy were the creators of the original comic."

"Well, yeah, but we sold the rights to William Wildtale, and when the new writer and the company say it's time to work on other projects, it's time to work on other projects."

"So what are you working on now?"

"Trash and Exclamation! And a few other side jobs."

"What are they about?"

"The Trash character was a Special Ops military engineer who specialized in surviving and making weapons behind enemy lines out of junk. The story is when he's semiretired from the military. He got married and then got divorced, and she got everything. He was living on the street when Wild Tail found him. He was fighting a gang that was hired to relocate a bunch of bums/homeless people. Wild Tail thought the guy had potential when he got a hold of his record and helped the guy with his comic book origin. He lives in the penthouse and fights crime using weapons he made himself or discarded guns he finds. He gets around, paying his wife's alimony by all the money he gets by being Trash. His butler is the hotel's manager. The butler took the money Trash gave him and now has the ownership of the hotel in his name. Little by little, they fix up the hotel, and he is fighting crime.

"Exclamation's origin happened when he was a little boy. A neck slasher was in Dexter City and Wild Tail was investigating the murders. Wild Tail was hot on the guy's trail when a young boy was at the wrong place at the right time. He was just going to the store for groceries and got caught by the slasher. The guy cut the boy's neck, but it was not deep as to kill him. Wild Tail was able to stop the bleeding and give first aid till paramedics got there.

"Wild Tail found the bastard and finished the job. The boy grew up, but he had no voice box; it was damaged by the slasher. The boy learned to speak in sign language. He became a history teacher at a school for deaf children. That is what most people know about him. Secretly, over the years, he learned martial arts, the art of hand-to-hand combat, and the ability to throw razor-sharp objects.

"There were some murders by a copycat neck slasher who came to his city, and the police couldn't get any leads on the guy. And by chance, he witnessed one of the murders. The murderer was talking to himself in sign language. The unnamed hero at that time followed the man to his home, where he had pictures of all his victims on the wall. Our unnamed hero beats the villain to a pulp and calls the police but can't tell them he has the murderer because he can't speak.

"So he pushes the buttons SOS until they trace his number and send a car out to pick up the bad guy. Then he starts fighting crime, first in a black jumpsuit beating up thieves, muggers, and the like. I like doing this comic. He doesn't talk about how he is going to kick your ass, he just does it. He gets to the point. When he is doing an investigation, all he can do is write questions on pieces of paper. And that does not help when the people you are asking questions of are illiterate. His brother is an inventor of sorts, and he developed sign language gloves that, when put on and connected to a computer, the speaker will translate sign language into English. His sister found out he was fighting crime and designed a suit for him and gave him the name Exclamation! I, of course, changed her design.

"Once he started making a name for himself, Wild Tail showed up, and he became one of the Wild Tail Champions."

I say, "Wow, that sounds a bit like real life, a family helping each other out."

"Yeah, I usually do two books a month and Trash and Exclamation! They are mine. I'll do a Wild Tail, or if I get a script and finish a comic for people who can't keep up with a deadline. Hey, some people golf, I make comic books."

It's noon, lunchtime. Paul Harvey comes on, and you cannot say a word or comment around Paul. He loves Paul Harvey, and then Rush Limbaugh comes on. We stop at a McDonald's and order lunch and I drive. It's 3:00 p.m. in Chicago. I called this place home, maybe for too long now. I am going home. We stop at a U-Haul rental and pick up a covered trailer.

It's four o'clock at my apartment building, and Paul says, "Max, this is your apartment?"

"Yes, Paul, this is my apartment."

Paul 2.0 whispers, "You live in the slums?"

Paul corrects his son, I think, by saying, "Don't say slums, 2.0, say projects."

A XXX bookstore is across the street. Paul just shakes his head.

"Son, maybe you should stay with the truck."

"Dad?"

"The truck, son."

We go up the stairs, and here is my apartment. I unlock several locks, and Paul shakes his head at the graffiti on the hallway walls. In my apartment, most things are still in boxes from when I had to move out of my last one.

"Paul, I hit rock bottom with my drinking and gambling. I'm ashamed of myself."

Paul holds me like the big brother he is, whispering, "Come on, boy. Paul and Jesus will make it right. Let's start taking this downstairs and get out of here."

As we come downstairs, people of many ages come out to the street. In shock, Paul 2.0 says, "Dad, they want your autograph."

"Well then, boy, follow Max upstairs and help carry his stuff down, and I'll stay here and sign autographs. Don't look so stunned, son, a prophet is not wanted in his own hometown."

After I leave the Pauls and get a ride to the station.

It's 5:00 p.m. at Chicago Police Station. Cybulski asks me to come into his office.

"So, you are moving out, are you?"

"Kind of looks that way, sir."

"Well, me too, I am thinking of retiring."

"Any plans?"

"I used to ride horses when I was a kid. It would be nice to work on a ranch."

I smile, holding back a chuckle, saying, "You and I got to talk."

I answer my cell phone. "Hello, Candy ... slow down, what happened?"

"Someone tried to kidnap one of Jamie's kids! The kids were just walking to the corner store, and a car pulled alongside. Thank God their babysitter was there and saw it happen! She yelled police, and then the car drove off! The kids are alright. Just everyone is spooked."

I grit my teeth, saying, "Candy, tell Jamie I am coming home, and if I have to, it will be guns blazing."

Cybulski is about to say something, and I put my finger up and speed dial Paul's cell. "Hello. Paul, someone has tried to kidnap one of Jamie's kids. We are about all loaded up and ready. I'll be finished up here soon."

Cybulski says, "Max, you have been through a lot lately, the coma and all. Be careful."

"If things get too boring, you can always come back here. You have a way of making things interesting."

I give Cybulski a handshake and begin to say my goodbyes.

A kid, one of Paul's fans, comes up to him.. "Mr. Chapel, I just want to thank you for doing the first few issues of Five Generations. Any chance you might do them and Cockroach again?"

Paul smiles, saying, "If I get time. I also have a farm back in Michigan. You wouldn't want me to let my calves go hungry, would you?"

The kids say, "No. I gotta do my chores too before I can play."

As kids come around to Paul to get their comics signed, one of the kids hands him a note.

Paul 2.0 has a few fans too for his Air Force football. "Hey, Paul, are you going to play professional?"

Paul 2.0 smiles, saying, "Just because I'm a big guy doesn't mean I am guaranteed a career in the NFL."

"Well, if you could, who would you play for?"

"My mom wants me to play for the Packers, and my dad says the Lions are a lost cause like the Tigers. It is kinda like they are saying we won't start winning games till you build us a new stadium. And when they do build the new stadium, it is like they are saying, suckers."

Paul sneaks to an alley and something comes out of the shadows. "Why didn't you tell me you were in town?"

"Cockroach, it has been a while, bro." Cockroach is the main Wild Tail Champion in Chicago. The legacy has passed from father to son. A former Army Corps Engineer and Chicago football quarterback. He found his father's Cockroach armor and fights crime on the streets. Cockroach asks, "When are you going to do my magazine again? Why are you doing Exclamation! and Trash?"

Paul sputters, "I get to say costume design changes, and they ask what color.

"You are a control freak, man. How is Max?"

"Max is coming home. Hopefully to stay."

"How much does he remember?"

"He is a blank."

"Well, that is what he wanted, a fresh start."

"Don't remind me." A police car comes down the street and before Paul can turn around to say see ya, Cockroach is gone.

Six o'clock at my rental storage unit. I drive them to the rental storage, and they are tired and getting hungry. "Boys, this is it last stop, and I am going to feed you."

Paul comments, "Take us to Wild Tail Champion World. We can eat for free."

"Free food, we are there."

I look both ways to make sure no one is watching us, open up the door, and then I motion them to come in the garage and close the door. I open a case, and their eyes go big. Paul whispers, "Max, you are little Mister NRA. Guns, rifles, battle body armor of all shapes and sizes, and ammunition, and Special Ops gear."

"I got this at a CIA warehouse going out of business sale."

Paul 2.0 says, "Wow."

Paul shakes his head, looks at me, and says, "You got baseball cards at my place, but you stick this kind of hardware in a storage rental?"

We load it up and we are gone.

Seven o'clock, dinner at Wild Tail Champions World. This place is a Wild Tail comic book collector's dream. They are packed, and we are standing in line from a block away.

"We will never get in, Paul." Paul gets on his cell phone and makes a call and two big guys escort us in, parting the people like Moses and the Red Sea. Inside, hanging from the walls and ceiling, are duplicates of Wild Tail Comics hero and villain equipment. The waiters and waitresses wear costumes from the comics and a Selah waiter escorts us to our seats.

Paul smiles and says, "All comic book artists should be treated this good."

"You mean they aren't?" We left Todd McFarland back at the end of the line.

Selah asks, "May I take your order?"

I look at the prices, and Paul & Paul 2.0 start naming stuff off—ribs, BBQ this, and BBQ that. "Uh, Paul, I don't have that kind of money."

Paul states, "Boy, I said we eat for free. It is on the house, and until they bring the food out, I'll be signing comic books left and right. Order your dinner, and you two go play some games. Look around, enjoy yourselves, and they will come and get you when the meal is ready."

As comics come to Paul and cameras start taking pictures, certain people start asking him questions. Friends of Paul's ask, "How is he?"

"Max, he does not remember a thing."

"Isn't that what he wanted?"

"Yeah, but it is what he might need to remember that I am wondering about."

One of the men Paul is talking to communicates in sign language. "So, he is moving back to Cavanaugh City?"

Paul recognizes him, then asks Bridge, "How you doing?"

"Tell me, Paul, are you trying to do something here?"

"If I was, it ain't working."

I go off by myself. I never got a real look at the Wild Tail Champions Digital Universe that Jason invented. Over a hundred players playing in the same digital universe at the same time, wow. Looks like fun. On the walls are pictures of the heroes in living color. They must be hired actors or comic book fans dressed like the heroes, or something.

As I look back at Paul, I see someone, but I just can't remember where I have seen him before. People begin to crowd around Paul, and then he is gone. Our meal is coming, and the guards that helped us with crowd control help us as we come back to our seats.

Paul bows his head and says grace. Even though the music and noise is louder than his prayer, I am sure God heard it. As we eat our meal, the chef comes out and says, "Hey, Paul, it is good to see you! When are you coming out for a cookout?"

"Oh, when I get a chance."

Another comes by and Paul asks, "Hey, what are you doing here?"

"I heard you were in Chicago, and I thought I would take the Magnetic Transport here."

Paul almost chokes on his BBQ chicken when the guy said, "Magnetic Transport."

"Oh, I am on business, and how you doing?" Paul sputters. "I almost needed a Heimlich!"

"Well, you behave yourself, Paul and Paul 2.0, and you too, Max."

"That is strange. How does he know me?"

Paul almost chokes again. "Eat slower, Paul." Paul 2.0 smiles and says, "You alright, Dad?"

It's 8:45 p.m. when we leave Chicago. Coming home, I drive. At 9:00 p.m., Paul and I switch, and he gets in the driver's seat. At 10:00 p.m., Paul Sr. is driving, so I go to sleep.

CHAPTER EIGHTEEN

Saturday, October 7, 1978—We Promised Each Other That We Would Never Go to Bed Angry

It's four o'clock Saturday morning. I am awake, and I can hear them talking in the next room.

Mrs. Cooper whispers, "Honey, the doctor says she is under her optimal weight for her age."

Mr. Cooper whispers back, "Well, you were little for your age, too. It is just genetics."

"She is not getting enough protein or energy. She is just not growing right."

Mr. Cooper murmurs back, "I don't care what Lucia's mother says, letting our daughter hang around with a bunch of hippie, tree-hugging vegetarians was your idea, not mine."

Mrs. Cooper is annoyed. "Grrrrrrrr. I was just trying to get her to meet new and interesting people."

Mr. Cooper says, "Remember the last Fourth of July when they invited us over to their pool party? There might have been fireworks going off, but that was not what I smelled. I know I could smell pot in the air."

Mrs. Cooper asks, "And how do you know what pot smells like?"

"I went to college, and lived in a dorm. I know."

Both of them say, "All they did all day was ask how you FEEL."

"Well, they are a younger couple in touch with their feelings and all," Mrs. Cooper tells her husband. "You were rude to him!"

"While you were enjoying your swim in funny air's pool, they both gave me a sermon on how I am killing my family by buying beef and dairy products, and I am cruel because I hunt deer in the fall. And when you got yourself out of the pool, you just gathered your little chicks like a good mother hen and left me. You know, you could have backed me up, Robin."

"Why, I think hunting is cruel."

"Well last year, you killed a whole family with your new sports car. I mean, you had deer and antlers in the front grill going through the radiator and out the tailpipe!"

I am holding back my laughter now as I listen. I love Mr. Cooper.

"Bambi's mama practically went through the windshield! Baby deer all over the place!"

"Do you mind?" Mrs. Cooper says.

"And when the insurance said, 'Sorry, your policy will not and does not cover this,' you went out and bought me a box of ammunition."

"I was mad then."

"Well, not much has changed. And I will tell you again as I told you then. Robin, I don't shoot with shotgun. I shoot with a bow and arrow. There is a big difference."

"You cared more for that car than you did me," Mrs. Cooper whines.

"No, I felt for your car. I cried when you took my truck."

"It was your stinky old hunting truck."

"I loved that old pickup truck. It was a stick shift, and you drive automatic. I saw you grinding gears to the oldies as you drove in the yard."

Here, my guess, comes dirty looks and silence.

It is a Saturday morning, and it was a fall, yucky-suck, early October day.

I watch them at the breakfast table. Mrs. Cooper makes breakfast, and Mr. Cooper, he tries to keep from tipping his head back and fall asleep and drown in his own mouth full of drool. He tries to be constructive in his own tired and exhausted way. Mr. Cooper says, "Honey, I can smell the burning toast and taste undercooked runny eggs that you set before me. And see my bloodshot eyes in the reflection of my spoon. I say spoon because I think …" he says yawning, "I was supposed to get a fork."

She grabs his plate of burnt toast, runny eggs, and a spoon, and shoves it into the microwave and slams the door. Blam!

Mr. Cooper turns to me and whispers, "Remember what I said about not going to bed angry. Well, we did not get any sleep last night, and it shows." Then he turns his attention to his angry wife, "Honey. Ah, Robin … the sparks are pretty. I think the eggs are done."

She says, "Oh, I put the metal spoon in the microwave!"

Kabang! The eggs exploded. She begins to cry, and Mr. Cooper stops his one liners and gets out of his seat and holds onto her, saying, "Shh. There, there. It's all right. I am here, everything's going to be all right."

I am silent. It is like I am not even here.

She cries, "Yeah, you're here. That is a big help."

So he decides to just shut up and let her cry.

She sniffs up a tear, wondering aloud, "What we are going to do?"

"What?"

"About our son Jason and daughter Jennifer."

"Wait, something is wrong with our son?"

"You don't talk to him."

Mr. Cooper says, "He never listens. I mean, he is from another planet. All he talks about is computers this and video game that. He hates baseball, and he is so-so at football."

Mrs. Cooper answers, "You should try bonding with him."

"Oh, it's not like you are doing such a great job with our daughter."

Then silence.

"That was cold."

He should have never looked into her eyes. He was a deer in her headlights. Before she starts crying, he holds on tight to her and says, "Listen, honey, I am sorry. I'll fix it. I don't know how, but I will."

I guess he has done enough damage here, so he goes outside. I also get dressed and go outside and find that it is damp and muggy, overcast, and just plain Michigan October outside. But it is colder inside, so I will stay out here for a while. I keep a distance and hear Mr. Cooper talking to himself, "What to do, what to do, what to do?"

He gets his bow and arrows that are hidden in the old pickup. I stay hidden in his pickup because somebody stole his deer target silhouette. He is not taking any chances. "Now what do I shoot at? Ah, I know, last New Year's Day, Robin told me to take down the Christmas decorations. I ran out of room in the attic, and I left the plastic snowman outside. I found it in the spring and stuck it in the tall grass. Here it is. The year has been hard on you, little guy. Better put you out of your misery."

The plastic snowman is sun-bleached white and the paint has faded. Now he has a target. So he sets it up about fifty to sixty feet away. He pulls back and takes aim.

"What are you doing?"

"Jason, you spooked me."

"The mighty hunter strikes again. Hey, is that our plastic snowman?"

"Yep, and it is about to become target practice."

"Hey, can you put an arrow through its head?"

"Yeah, why?"

"It would look cool, like Steve Martin in your *Saturday Night Live* videos."

So he amazes his son by shooting the arrow through the snowman's head.

"Now that is great, Dad. Wow, Dad, you did it! You did it! Hey, can we paint it and make a decoration out of it again. We have paint and stuff up in the attic."

The father adds, "That is my paint."

"Well, can we use them?"

"Go get them."

I walk over to Mr. Cooper and say, "You know, you are a pretty good dad."

He looks at me and smiles. "All I can do is try, Max."

A little while later, Jason returns. "Hey, Max, you got up early. Dad, did you paint all those pictures in the attic?"

"Yeah, I did, back in college."

Jason asks, "How come you don't paint anymore?

Mr. Cooper answers, "I kind of told myself I don't have the time over the years. A baby being born here and a job there. And little by little, I just left my paintings, and one day I packed them up and stored them up in the attic out of the way."

Jason says, "You were good."

Mr. Cooper says, "My college teacher said I was great, gifted in fact. Funny thing is, my grade schoolteacher used to come by my desk and say, 'Excuse me, it is not that you are doing anything wrong, I just want to show the rest of the class what not to do.'"

"Oh Dad, that was cold. Hey, can we paint red blood coming out of the snowman?"

"Son, let me tell you something. You and I are outnumbered in this family. Your mother has me walking on eggshells, and your sister is a vegetable head. There are only two of us, and two of them; we are outnumbered. If me and your mother have another brother or two for you to play with, we will still be outnumbered. So to appease the queen and princess, we have to make adjustments. One, when we paint this snowman, we have to make it cute. That means a rainbow scarf, black coal eyes, possibly a red top hat, and no blood coming out of the arrow because that is not cute. You can never go wrong with cute."

"Gee, Dad, we got it pretty bad, don't we?"

Mr. C smiles. "There is an upside."

Jason asks, "Yeah, what is it?"

"When you're eighteen, you're out of the house, and I get my den back."

A fatherly reminder to be sure of.

A few hours later, Robin, Mr. Cooper's wife, has gotten a good catnap and she and Jennifer make cookies, to freeze ahead of time for Halloween. Jason runs in the house and says, "Come on outside and see what me and Dad and Max made! With some old broken toys and some imagination, we put a light in the snowman and have him spinning slowly around with a little speaker and an old record playing Christmas songs."

Jennifer's eyes light up and declare, "Daddy, you did this?"

"I had some help."

"Oh, Daddy, it is so cute!"

"Hey, Jen, if you think that is cool, you should see Dad's paintings!"

"Dad paints?!"

"Come on, I'll show you."

Mrs. Cooper looks at Mr. Cooper with a smile and silently claps her hands, and when the kids are gone, she gives him a good wet one. A few minutes later, the kids bring his old paintings downstairs.

"Dad, this stuff is great!"

"They're young, what do they know about art?"

"Who cares?"

He cares, because in Jennifer's eyes, Mr. Cooper is not the mean, cruel hunter her friends say he is. He is her daddy.

Jennifer asks, "Dad, can you draw me a picture?"

"I'll make a deal with you," her dad says. "Your mom is making hot dogs tonight for dinner, and if you eat two hot dogs, I'll draw you a cow and a pig because I don't know where hot dogs come from."

That night, Jennifer ate two hot dogs with buns. Their doctor said she needs more protein; the vegetables were not enough for a growing girl's diet. Robin looks at him after dinner and says, "You look tired."

Mr. Cooper says, "I am."

She says with a smile, "Want to go to bed? I was going to watch TV with Jason. But Jason can run the VCR and tape it, and we can watch it after church."

Jennifer asks Jason, "What are Mom and Dad doing?"

Jason says, "I don't know. Dad said if he got lucky tonight he would see if he could even the odds, whatever that means."

Chapter Nineteen

Am I a Butterfly Dreaming I Am a Man, or Am I a Man Dreaming I Am a Butterfly?

We arrive home early, 2:00 a.m., Tuesday, July 23, 2002. Paul 2.0 unhitches the U-Haul trailer, and Paul walks me into the house. I am still half asleep, and I lay down on my sleeping bag and Paul says, "Rest easy, bro."

I kind of blank out, and he and Paul 2.0 drive away. I really don't sleep, kind of half awake, half asleep. About four, I get up and find a light bulb and some leftover blue paint from the previous owner of the farmhouse.

I paint the light bulb and replace the one on the front porch with it. Blue Bomber said he was close, just how close is he?

Blue Bomber shows up about 6:00 a.m. with information. "Nice touch, little brother. People who wanted to contact the Original Wild Tail in the old days put out a blue light bulb too."

I ask Blue Bomber, "Who or what am I?"

He shrugs his shoulders, saying, "I really can't answer your question."

I ask, "Can't or won't?"

"Not supposed to. I would if I could, but please forgive me if I don't."

"I would like the simple fact understood. Yes, I would if I could, but I won't."

"You have some people who really don't like you."

"Tell me something I don't already know."

I yawn. "Can you get the CIA off my back? Badger is pissing me off and making demands on me and people like Chief Tom."

Blue Bomber adds, "He is a good guy, isn't he?"

I ask, "How local are you?"

Blue Bomber is silent then asks, "You want out of the CIA?"

"Yeah, if it were possible."

"If it were possible, would you want to be rid of the CIA?"

I reply, "In my line of work, I am on call twenty-four-seven. I don't have reunions to go to. I don't have an old folks home to look forward to, do I?"

Rarely does anyone make deathbed confessions. I am never retired from service.

Blue Bomber states, "Sounds like my line of work, only I have a comic book deal. If I could make the CIA make you a free agent, would you?"

"Yeah, I did not know what I was getting myself into. At the same time, I would not be where I am if it weren't for the experience. Like a drug user, I keep going back to them, or they keep coming back to me. Maybe I need to separate myself from them."

Blue Bomber comments, "I'll see what I can do, little brother," and he is gone. I forgot to ask him how he does that.

I drive into town, and the people on the street look tense. Two drive-by shootings on Saturday, an attempted kidnapping on Monday, I guess fear would do it to anybody. I drive by the park, and hardly anyone is here. Norman Rockwell stopped painting and built a bomb shelter. The FBI agents are still here. They let me in, no questions asked, and I see Ellen has not taken away their guns. I give Jamie a hug and say nothing and pass him information.

Jamie is shocked as he finds out he has a price on his head for his stance against drugs. And that is the reason his family is in danger.

Paul comes in about noon, and Ellen gives him a big hug. Paul is like everyone's big brother. "Jamie, Ellen," he says, "I think it is time to get you out of the house."

Jamie replies, "Steve has been by and asked us to leave for the safety of the community."

Paul adds, "I know you won't leave, Jamie, but we should consider getting you out of town. I have an old farmhouse that I loan out in hunting season. You can use it till we figure out what to do." The FBI nods their head in agreement.

Paul takes us out to the farmhouse. One of his kids is mowing the foot-tall grass with a wind mower. At the same time, another is driving a tractor with a round baler. Another is with a weed eater. Paul reassures us, "The place will be cleaned up in a bit, and you could move in whenever you want."

The FBI agent says, "It is high enough; we can see from here to the horizon."

Paul adds, "The barn is full of hay bales, and all the doors are locked." He hands me the keys. "If you had to, you could put a sniper in the window, then you would have the high ground."

The FBI Agent smirks. "Thank you for your comments, Mr. Chapel. I really don't think we need snipers."

I look at Paul and say, "You must be beat."

"Yeah, I drove with one eye open and one eye shut, so I did get some sleep."

I chuckle.

Jamie walks over and says, "Thanks, Paul, this will work out just right."

Paul gives a tired, "Glad I can help."

"This isn't like when we were kids, Paul, when they used to steal lunch money from me, is it?"

"No, it is not, Jamie."

Jamie walks over to his wife and reassures her everything will be all right.

Paul says to me, "I wish it was like when we were kids, because I would have kicked somebody's ass and have it done by now."

***

Evil is planning. "You could not kidnap Jamie Scott's children, boss."

"Shut up. I have had a response to our Max Faraday information search. This is Vincent, a hit man who has a personal history with Max in Chicago. He comes very recommended."

"Uh, boss, we just got a call, Jamie has moved his family to a safe house out of town. The FBI is there."

"Vincent responds, "Get me a layout of the place. I'll make some calls."

***

Twilight meets with Graves.

In Washington, DC, Agent Graves is about to call it a night. His wife is fast asleep in their upscale mansion home. He finishes his last file and brushes his teeth. As he puts his head to the pillow, a whisper of wind brushes his face. It's Twilight the dark prophet dressed in a black trench coat, a black mask, and fedora hat. He is the prophet they don't talk about. He does not have a TV or radio or church ministry; he has a comic book. He whispers, "Graves." His eyes open and a shout of the voice of thunder is heard, "GRAVES!" By an invisible force, he is ripped out of his bed and slammed against the wall. He cannot move. His wife is still asleep, unaware of all that is happening.

From out of the shadows comes Twilight. "You and me, we have to talk."

Graves does his best to shake his fear. With gritted teeth he murmurs, "About what?"

"Agent Max Faraday. You had him on a Black Ops mission in Chicago."

Graves replies, "I promised him if the general becomes a threat, and I have the power, I would have him terminate him. I kept my promise. Max was able to do the mission. He wants out of the CIA."

"But," says Graves, "There's no way."

Pressure is applied, and Graves is pressed into the wall. He can hear his joints crack, or is it the plaster?

"Badger has been a pain in Max's side. He wants out, and we want him out. Make it so."

Graves asks, "What possession do you have that gives you the ability to make demands?!"

Graves falls to the floor. As he picks himself up, he sees files, and he opens them up, and then he closes them. Twilight leans down to get in his face and asks, "Do I have your attention now? I want Max to have honorable discharge benefits and all that is due him.

"Any retaliation, and I will nail your ass to the wall and put it in a jar of formaldehyde as a trophy in my office. You got me?"

Graves looks down at the files on the floor and then looks up, gritting his teeth, saying, "I'll have Agent Badger in my office in the morning."

When he looks down to the floor, the files are gone. And so is Twilight.

"That son of a . . ."

His wife wakes up, saying, "Honey, what is going on?"

***

October 8th, 1978, Sunday after church. We go out to dinner. Then Mrs. Cooper has Mr. Cooper stop at a garage. "Honey, I would like you to look at something." She puts a key in the lock and opens a door. We go in. She turns on a light and asks, "What do you think?"

He looks at the mechanical part and how it's configured. "This doohickey, they were supposed to take this design off the market years ago. It looks new."

She states, "It is new. They sold it to my client under another name and won't make the safety changes needed to bring it up to standard."

He recognizes the name on the product. "That company is owned by the same company that now owns Cavanaugh Industries." Reality hits him. "So, if you bring me in to testify, I could lose my job. Why couldn't you get someone else to look at this?"

"I did. They bought them out. I knew if anyone knew the truth about this design, it would be you, and you would tell me the truth."

I look from a distance, and I can see Mr. Cooper is concerned that this is his job he is talking about. "If you need me to testify, I'll be there."

On the ride home he does not say a word.

When we get home, Jennifer says, "Remember, Daddy, you promised."

It is time for a change.

Mr. Cooper takes down his trophies: the eight-point buck, his pheasant, and his pictures of animals he had killed over the years, and his kids put his old paintings up in their place. He made a deal with Jennifer, whatever food or animal she eats, he will draw a picture of it for her. After Sunday night church service, he takes Jennifer for a ride in his old pickup truck and takes her to an open field and teaches her how to drive a stick shift. When her friends get on her case about eating meat, she can proudly say, "I can drive a stick shift. Can you?" And her friends will think that is so cool.

CHAPTER TWENTY

Get Comfortable in the Boots You're in, You May Be in Them a While

It's Wednesday, July 24, 2002, and Jamie and family are moved into the safe house. I bring my sleeping bag, and the kids and I pretend we are camping out. After I make breakfast for everyone, Jack calls me on the cell. "Ah Max, I wonder if I could get a ride to Alcoholics Anonymous. My usual ride had, well, he had a prior engagement."

"When is the meeting?"

"Tonight."

"Kinda short notice, Jack. I'll see if I can get Churchill to come."

Why is the FBI circling the wagons around Jamie? The leader, FBI Agent Andrews, drinks his coffee as I walk toward him. "Thanks for breakfast, Max."

"You're welcome. Since we are on such good speaking terms, why are you going the extra mile to protect Jamie?"

"Somebody tried to kill him."

I add, "I saw the file. He called months ago and said that someone was trying to do harm to his family, and the FBI just did the 'We have you on file and we will keep in touch' routine." Andrews answers, "When you came by Sunday and shared your information on the drug trafficker's car and the driver Bob Black, flags started to pop up. We have been looking for this guy and his organization for over a year, and we don't know who the leader is. But your Bob Black, we are pretty sure was a driver for the network."

It hits me. "You are using Jamie as bait."

Andrews defends, "Jamie won't leave, and we are going to have to protect him, so call him what you want, Max. I need a live member of this mystery man's organization. For some reason, this guy is determined to get Jamie, and most likely, they will attack and we will be ready for them."

I compose myself. *As much as I want to smack this Fed upside the head, he is right.*

"We even got the car you found at Howard's junkyard. There was no serial number to track it with at the Department of Motor Vehicles. This guy covers his backside. As far as anyone knows, he does not exist."

I add, "Or learned enough in prison that he knows some of the mistakes others have made and avoids making them himself." "Or herself, Max, we don't know if this is a man or woman. We don't know if he or she has somebody working on the inside, giving him or her information either. What do you know about that?"

I reply, "One of the reasons I was not all forthcoming with information is a possible FBI link to the drug traffickers. The only people who know Jamie is here are your FBI agents and me and Paul's family. If I were you, I'd watch your people."

The agent asks, "When are you expecting an attack?"

"We just moved in, so my guess today they know where we are. Tomorrow all hell could break loose."

Churchill has a reality check and joins AA with Max and Jack.

"Hi, I am Jack. Most of you know my story. For the newcomers, I'll tell it again. On and off, I would drink just to enjoy life. After a game, drink some beer, no biggie. I always told myself, 'Watch it, you don't want to end up like your dad.' I stopped cold turkey after my first son was born because that is what a dad should do.

"In 1998, my wife got cancer. I had less than a year with her. As long as she was with me, I could hold back the demon of alcohol. In

'99, Ruth Leanne died of the cancer. She fought it so hard for our babies.

"I tried, but I lost the fight and began to drink.

"I went to pick up my kids from a babysitter, and I shouldn't have been driving. Thank God they were all buckled in. My oldest boy helped me do that, thank God. I had an accident and hit an oncoming car. Thank God, nobody was killed, but the other driver was injured.

"I was arrested on the spot. Thanks to the DUI and jail time, I lose my kids. I get sent to prison, and when I get out, I have to ask permission to see my own kids.

"Thanks to my friend Reed, who sponsored me, I have been sober for two years and some odd days. You can get help now before it is too late."

"Hi, I am Max, and I am an alcoholic. It started back when I was in the Marines. I vowed as a kid I would never be an alcoholic like Marcus. He was my mother's husband. But this is not about him, this is about me. I started to drink to be one of the guys. It was just sociable drinks. I only got plastered once, when I came back from a successful mission. I was so out of my mind I could not feel it when they tattooed my left arm." I show them my Selah tattoo. "I love the tattoo, though. I was engaged to marry Kate Dent, and she called it off when I got shot on duty. I guess I had a reason to drink then. We had this kidnapping. We found them, and I was set up to take the kill shot. I did it. I got the bastards. The bullet went through the son of a bitch's head and through the backseat and killed the kidnap victim, who was tied up in the trunk. I wanted to die that day. For a time, I tried to kill myself one bottle at a time. I had an intervention and slowly I began to live again, and I have been sober for about over a year. One day at a time, sweet Jesus."

"Hi, I am Churchill. I am an alcoholic. This is my first time, so I don't know what to say."

Jack says, "Start at the beginning."

"I started getting into my dad's liquor cabinet about the seventh grade. It tasted terrible. I could not see why my father drank the stuff.

"Now I am my father. I, I could have killed . . ." Churchill almost breaks down crying.

Jack comes by his side and says, "Churchill, that's a good start. You can come back next week."

After the meeting, we go to the local bar for a pop and hamburgers and fries.

A Kenny Chesney song comes out of the jukebox. That's why I'm here.

Churchill leaves us and goes to Candy's place.

After I come home from the AA meeting, I have a visitor. I look at him and say, "Didn't I lock the door?"

Bridge looks at me and says, "Do I look like I use doors?"

"What are you doing here?"

"You have been asking Blue Bomber questions that he can't or does not feel he can answer. Since the information you are about to partake is the kind you need to be sober for, I waited till after you're AA meeting was over."

"What kind of information?"

"The kind you cannot be told about, that you must be shown." Before I know it, I am whisked, floating away from my home, and we are traveling, and I notice the sky changing from day and night rapidly going from season to season in reverse.

"We are going back in time?"

"You are correct, Max, back to a beginning but not the beginning."

We end up on the streets of an American city. It is nighttime.

"Where and when are we?"

Bridge says, "New York City, January 1992. By the way, no one will be able to see you or touch you. You grand I are only observing the situation."

A man, a stranger to this city, tries to take a shortcut that if it was any shorter would get his throat cut. Muggers come from the shadows. Then from only my wildest imagination, he comes into the picture.

Dressed in blue, carrying a whip, a hero steps into the light. He is the Wild Tail! The muggers yell, "OH SHIT!" Oh shit is right! His whip strikes the one with the knife and it breaks the blade in two! One starts whirling around a chain, and Wild Tail shoots the chain link, and it snaps and strikes the other mugger, knocking him out cold! Stung full of disbelief, Wild Tail takes a flying leap kick, and the mugger with the knife is out. The stranger, happy to be alive, says, "Thank you!"

Wild Tail yells, "Would you please get a map before trying to take a shortcut?"

The stranger sees something and runs away for dear life. Wild Tail wonders, what?! A flying kick comes at him and knocks him down! A male presence wearing black stands over him. Wild Tail mutters aloud, "Oh this is going to be one of those nights." He rolls then stands up, and the man in black starts throwing punches, and he dodges them the best he can and strikes a few too.

I ask Bridge, "Who is this?" Then Wild Tail takes a punch across his face and pulls back part of his mask. The act of uncovering his face makes the stranger angry, and he takes off the kid gloves and opens up a can of whoop ass on Wild Tail. Bridge says to me, "You look perplexed, my friend."

"That face? That face, he is me!"

"Yes, he is known to certain people in the CIA as Black Phoenix."

I ask, "Black Phoenix?!"

Wild Tail yells, "G, I need backup ASAP!"

G comments, "All WTC are currently active at this time. I shall call up a reserve member." Wild Tail stands his ground and punches him!

Black Phoenix strikes him in the face, and Wild Tail falls down. As he comes close to him ,he kicks him in the chest and knocks him back off his feet and on the ground!

Wild Tail is spent. That kick took everything he had.

Then the one known as Infinity appears.

I look at Bridge and ask, "Are you telling me Infinity is for real!"

Bridge smiles, saying, "As real as you or me, child. In full dress uniform he is quite impressive, isn't he?"

In a way, I have to agree. He's in a red flex cloth suit with a white infinity emblem on the front and back. Infinity says, "Wild Tail, you look like—"

Wild Tail mutters, "Don't say it. Spit some blood, just do it!" Infinity and Black Phoenix look at each other, then they begin sparing. It is a game for the immortal. From what I remember of the comics, Infinity was sent from 1969 to the literal time period of the Book of Genesis. At least that is what I read in the comics? Living and fighting the good fight all those years apparently has given him skills of many martial arts. "He is good, Wild Tail. I can see why you needed help!"

"Don't get cocky, kid. He learns quickly!"

"Why do you keep calling me kid? I am older than dirt, and you keep calling me kid."

He strikes him across the face! Ow!

Wild Tail on the sidelines is bandaging himself, saying, "When you stop acting like a kid, I will stop calling you kid!"

Black Phoenix pauses and takes a step back. He then brings out swords! Wild Tail and Infinity both say, "I hate ninjas!" Infinity reaches for his own sword. Wild Tail says into his gauntlet, "This is a priority alert. Backup is needed."

Infinity's skill has given him opportunities to cut Black Phoenix down a bit. As the battle continues, bruises and slashes on appear on his arms and his body bleeds. He takes a leap back and he notices, as I do, his white extra layer of skin. It begins to automatically cover the injured parts of his body like a living bandage.

He grits his teeth, and the gloves are now off as far as Black Phoenix is concerned. Infinity replies, "I can handle this, Wild Tail," and for a few seconds he does. Then Black Phoenix pierces Infinity's chest, and Infinity falls dead to the ground.

I say in fright, "Oh my God, he killed Infinity!"

Bridge just says, "Oh, he will be back."

Then as he walks back to Wild Tail, the mighty midget called Brute appears.

"Sorry I was late; it was a late opera tonight." He tries his sword on him, and it shatters at first strike. Wild Tail asks his gauntlet, "Have we identified him yet?"

G responds with, "I have sent the description to our sources and have come up with no leads. The Questioner has a possible lead, though."

"Put him on! Questioner, what are we up against?"

"Boss, you have, to my best knowledge, a CIA sleeper agent assassin!"

"Come again?"

"I am just putting the details together myself. If it is who I think it is, he is called Black Phoenix! The CIA has their burners and shredders going. Someone is going to pay for this one."

Wild Tail responds back with, "Yeah, and a going-away prize is my dead body, right?"

"I don't know. Let me get back with you on that."

He tries to jump past Brute, but he keeps jumping, matching every move, keeping in his face. In the ghost form, I walk over to Infinity and see his wound mending before my eyes.

And not noticing him, I mean me, he walks right through me as if I am not there. Bridge asks me, "Are you remembering anything?"

"No, am I supposed to?"

Then he reaches into his pouch on his belt and places a C4 explosive on Brute! *Bang!*

Growls and sheer animal sounds of anger come from Brute. He is not holding back his strength! He swings his arm across his face and it also jabs his neck! The explosion tosses him twenty feet and he is out. Brute is still mad with rage and wants revenge! Wild Tail yells, "Brute, you don't know what you are doing!" He growls and looks to the sky, beating on his chest.

In that moment, Wild Tail gathers up his battered body and runs scooping him, I mean me, up before Brute can attack. Getting out his whip, he takes to the air, swinging from fire escape to fire escape. I turn to Bridge, asking, "Why?"

Bridge explains, "Wild Tail is not just a leader of the Wild Tail Champions. Wild Tail is not just a hero or vigilante. He is also a prayer warrior and has at times the ears and the voice of a prophet. When his mortal skills tell him this man is trying to kill me, he listens and hears The Great Shepherd say to him, he is one of my sheep, you must protect him. Then protect him he will."

In midair he awakens and sees Wild Tail and tries to strangle him! He breaks his hold, and he rolls to the ground. Brute has calmed down and pants, asking, "What did I miss?"

Wild Tail yells, "You tried to kill him in one of your crazy rages!"

Brute asks, "Hasn't he been trying to kill you?"

"Yeah, but I don't think he is responsible for his actions. Questioner said he was a sleeper agent. He could be programmed to kill me or us and not be doing this of his own free will."

Infinity has come back to the battle, saying, "Dead is dead, Wild Tail."

"No, there has to be another way! We have to protect him from himself and fast. We are drawing attention. Spit blood!"

"You are in no condition to fight. I'll take my round two!"

Infinity starts sparing again with him. Wild Tail says, "Brute, if you can't control yourself, spit blood."

Brute grits his teeth, murmuring, "I'll stay on the sidelines, but no one else shall die by his hands, Wild Tail."

Infinity has learned from his mistakes and has come back with a vengeance!

The sword Black Phoenix wields is beginning to crack. He runs away, then reaches for his .45 and turns around and shoots! With his skills, Infinity just dodges the bullets. Then they reach a dead end in the alley—there's no escape—and he has one bullet left!

He takes the revolver and begins to point it to his head. NO! A shot is fired, but it is not the .45, it came from above. Infinity looks up and sees the one known as Witness, and he comes down to see him. "Sorry I was late. It's a big universe, and you would not believe the traffic."

Brute brings a limping Wild Tail to the scene. Witness adds, "The tranquilizer should last long enough for Genetics Unlimited to get an idea what makes him tick."

Wild Tail spits blood and says, "G, you got that?"

G responds with, "They are waiting for you at GU labs. I can Magnetic Transport you there now."

"Do it."

They are gone.

***

I am back in my home, left with more questions. Who or what am I?

I get a change of clothes, and I head back to the safe house. Jamie and Ellen and the kids are asleep. I come in, lie down in my sleeping bag, and silently say my prayers, and before I can say or comprehend amen, I am asleep.

October 9th, 1978, Monday. I wave goodbye to Mr. and Mrs. Cooper as I walk to school.

Mr. Cooper goes to work at Cavanaugh Industries, and before ten he is called to his boss's office.

"Cooper, I just got the call from corporate. They received a call from your wife's law firm, and I guess they are going to have you testify against us."

Cooper nods his head. "Seems corporate scared or bought off everybody else."

Cooper's boss explains, "Son, this is not the company that my dad and I built. We are a multinational conglomerate now. Like it or lump it. One hand washes the other, son."

Cooper adds, "Or in my case, welcome to the new multinational conglomerate. You are fired."

"Son, they are putting the spurs to me as we speak. If you don't change your mind quick, I am going to have to let you go."

Cooper could stand there and give a speech about long hours and overtime and how good he has been, but instead, "I'll have my things out of my office before this afternoon."

"Cooper, I really hate doing this to you."

"Yeah, I know, Mike."

"Corporate is at fault, but they are going to fight it in the courtroom. Most likely it will get messy. I have to say, the foreman you suggested, Pearson, worked very well last night."

"I'll mention it to him; I am meeting him for lunch."

Mr. Cooper loses his job at Cavanaugh Industries. As he begins cleaning his office, he remembers a phrase: God closes a door and opens a window.

He meets with the guys for lunch. Mr. Pearson is astonished at the news, saying, "They fired you?"

Cooper says, "Welcome to the new multinational conglomerate. You are fired."

Jamie's dad, Mr. Scott, our middle school principal, asks, "So what are you going to do?"

"I just purchased a warehouse, and part of it is going to be rented by Cottager and the C. Connection. I have plans for the workshop in the back."

Dr. Churchill Smith asks, "And do what?"

"Doll houses for starters. After I built the first one for my daughter and yours, they told all their friends, and they in turn told their mothers and fathers, and I have about a hundred customers waiting. Cottager has found a doll furniture manufacturer that we can deal with, and I think it is going to work."

Mr. Scott adds, "Well, starting up a small business is one thing. Until it pays for itself, what are you going to do?"

"I have back pay coming. Mike hated to let me go, but I'll have some money coming."

"That won't last long. You still have a teaching career you could look into."

Pearson asks, "You can teach?"

"Yeah, I am a regular bookworm, jack of all trades. I have a teacher's license at home somewhere. I did about three weeks teaching summer school, then vacation came and I needed work, and I got the job at C. Industries. Got my wife pregnant and married that summer, and that is about my life's history so far. Now my wife's law firm got me out of the job I worked so hard at so she could afford to go to law school."

Mr. Scott pleads, "Come back to teaching; I can always use a good sub at the school. Maxine is out taking care of Mrs. Horton. I need help."

"Yeah, Jason said you had to teach gym last week."

"Oh don't remind me. Take a week off, and I'll set it up, and you can come back to school next Monday."

I see K. Ray C. at lunchtime. The guys are picking on him because he was sick, and he shouldn't have come on the trip without his mother's permission.

I yell, "Hey guys, lay off him." Then I pull him aside and say, "Let's go somewhere and talk."

We are alone as one can be in the playground. A couple of big painted tractor tires half in the ground is a good spot to talk. "Okay K. Ray C., what is the deal?"

"I don't know what you are talking about."

"You are sick. What are you hiding? Why do you have such a death wish? Do you have a disease or something?"

K. Ray C. makes a run out of the tires. I catch him and ask again, "What?"

"You have to promise not to tell anyone."

"I can't make a promise I can't keep. But I think you should tell someone, and I can help."

"The reason for my death wish. I have cancer."

"Is it in remission?"

"Yeah, how did you know?"

"Two of my friends want to be doctors. I pick up on terms now and again."

"I get weak every now and again, and I was beginning to get weak before the trip, and I thought I could handle it."

"But you couldn't."

K. Ray C. murmurs, "Yeah. What am I going to be remembered for, Max? I never really knew my dad, and he died when he was twenty-two. That is only eight years to go for me. My mom and I went to his old hometown to find out a little bit more about him. Nobody knew who he was or anything. I don't want to be a nobody. I want to be remembered."

I add, "Well, doctors are making strives every day to cure—"

"What am I going to be remembered for!" he shouts.

I look at the ground. "Well, you get drunk one night and have the cops chasing you down a dirt road doing a hundred. You hit a tree—BANG! Sudden STOP! You go through the windshield! The cops on duty can't find the body. They are wondering, where did it go, where did it go? Come morning, someone is taking a load of cattle to the stockyards, and what do they see smack dab on the roof of the Johnson's house? Well it's K. Ray C. smack dab on top of the Johnson's house, stuck like a bug on the windshield."

"That is not a good thing to be remembered for."

The school bell rings, and we go in.

***

I go to the C. Connection and Dan's dad has a surprise for him.

"We are moving!"

"What?"

"Come on, I have to show you. You too, Max. Mustafa can watch the store."

Mr. Cottager takes us out of town to a warehouse. He opens the door, and a long motor home is parked inside. Mr. Cottager places his hand on his son's shoulder, explaining, "Before your mother died, we talked about traveling the countryside. I hope this spring we can take to the road and travel."

"But what about our house?"

Mustafa's family is growing, and they can't stay in that apartment. I think we will have a yard sale and clean out the house, and they can move in."

Dan is between anger and disappointment, and his dad says, "Come in, look around. It is filled with family knickknacks and mementoes. You can have the back, and I'll have the living quarters. The couch pulls out into a bed."

I leave them in their family moment, and I find Mr. Cooper in the back setting up tools and supplies.

Sketches of dollhouses and specialty mailboxes are on the walls, and he looks over the orders and checks attached to them. I smile and say to Mr. Cooper, "You did well by buying this place."

Mr. Cooper agrees. "Yeah, now all I have to find a way to make it pay for itself, and pay the help I have hired."

Semi-trucks start arriving, and I and Dan start unloading merchandise.

People, possibly neighbors and friends of the Coppers and the Cottagers, come in and look around. Mr. Cottager gets to talking with a customer, and he comes by and opens a box to display a TV. Amazingly, they talk price, and they are about to buy then change their mind. Dan goes over and says, 'Hey, Dad, give them a wholesale price."

"What?"

"We didn't have to have to haul the TV back to the store, so why should they have to pay for shipping and handling?"

He pats his son on the shoulder and catches his potential customer. Next thing you know, somebody calls another friend on a CB, and a crowd shows up out of nowhere. When we are ready to call it a day, Mr. Cottager asks, "Hey, Cooper, your friend who's renting space for his hot dog stand, do you think he could work weekends?"

I go home with the Coopers, and Mrs. Cooper is angry at what has been done to her husband. "This is wrongful dismissal!"

"Robin, give it a rest."

"Why?"

He hands her his checks for the dollhouses. Churchill has some pretty rich friends with little girls who want dollhouses of their own. The niche market of making a duplicate dollhouse of the one they live in sells itself. "I have orders to fill, a company to run, we will be okay. Principal Scott even asked me to substitute teach at school.

"Hey, why don't we make plans for going to Disneyland over Thanksgiving vacation?"

CHAPTER TWENTY-ONE

Thursday, July 25, 2002

I wake up and wonder about K. Ray C. The kids are waking up, and they are enjoying the campout. The FBI is switching shifts. I get on the phone and call Churchill. "Good morning. I hope I didn't wake you."

Churchill responds groggily, "No, Candy was by and made me breakfast and thanked me for going to the AA meeting. Thanks, Max, for taking me."

Max asks, "I wonder if you could look up some medical information for me."

"About what?"

"K. Ray C."

Churchill ponders aloud, "I haven't really thought about him in years. I guess everybody thinking about our trip has gotten me to wonder why he was sick."

"Yeah, now that you mention it, he had a lot of sick days as a kid, didn't he? I always chalked it up to playing hooky."

"Listen, I'll buy you lunch if you can help me find his records. They might still have them down in the basement of the hospital."

"I could probably get in to look."

Steve Pearson and Adam come by, and the FBI stops them and checks them out.

"Hey, you are Steve Pearson, right? I have read a bunch of your books. Can I have your autograph?"

"Maybe later," Steve says, then turns to me and asks, "Max, how is everyone holding up?"

I give him a handshake. "The kids are taking it well I guess. Something is in the air. I feel it."

"Yeah, Paul called me and asked if I could pitch in. He said you needed a sniper, and the Feds wouldn't listen."

"Yeah, he said a sniper could get the high ground up in the barn window. He also said you had some high-powered rifles. Paul also talks too much."

Steve hands me his qualifications as his Milton Roberts persona. "I taught at the academy before I made psychology my full-time career. I still teach from time to time as Milton Roberts."

I shake my head and say, "Follow me." I take him to my place and the barn and uncover the crates.

Steve says, "Oh yeah, I can use this." He picks up the weapon, loads it, and handles it like it was a part of him. Then he adjusts the scope and takes aim. Finally, he takes the ammunition out, begins taking the gun apart, and commences to clean it.

"You know what you are doing. Mind telling where you learned that."

"You are not the only one with secrets, Mr. Faraday."

Adam asks, "When you are going to have me over to start decorating the house?"

"Actually, I am thinking of asking Paul if I could buy the house we are using as a safe house. That is an old farmhouse that the suburbs have taken over, and I like living in the country. Maybe when things get going I'll just stop by for breakfast."

Adam asks, "Why don't you and I get out of here and go to the C. Connection and see what kind of furniture selection they have?"

"The C. Connection? Sure Adam, that might be fun, just, uh, I am not feeling well right now. You want to drive?"

"For the life of me, I don't remember the C. Connection or where it is?"

"It went out of business, from what I remember."

Adam takes me in his truck out into the country and I see a sign: "Don't be a loony. Come out to the boonies and shop at the C. Connection." This is where Mr. Cooper's warehouse was. Cooper Manufactured Housing? He may have started with dollhouses and mailboxes, but he is making real homes now. You have come a long way baby.

This place is huge. We enter the C. Connection, and Mr. Cooper comes out to see us.

"Max, it is so good to see you, son. How long has it been?"

"Too long.'

He gives me a hug and says, "Come to get your old job back?" He taps me in the gut and keeps on smiling. "I hear you bought the old McGraw farm."

"Gee, news travels fast around here."

"Oh, what do you expect? We are all family. Hey, speaking of family, you are getting one heck of a discount."

Adam adds, "That is why I buy all of Home Hearth's furniture here."

As Adam and Mr. Cooper talk furniture, I just can't get over the history change. I look at the wall map of the US and Canada. There are over thirty C. Connection stores and about ten more planned for this year. I call Burney on my cell and ask, "Hey, Burney, do we have stock in the C. Connection?"

At the hospital, Churchill researches records down in the hospital's basement.

Dr. Sam comes up from behind him and spooks him. Churchill exclaims, "Don't do that!"

For Dr Sam, it is too much of a temptation not to. He chuckles, "Did I tell you I am proud of you."

Churchill lowers his head, murmuring, "Not in a long time."

"Well, you have been screwing up for a while, but going to AA, you are taking steps in the right direction. What are you doing down here?"

"I am looking up K. Ray C's records, if I can find them."

"Why are you looking for them?"

"Max will buy me lunch if I find them. He got to thinking about him and wondered why he had so many days absent from school."

Dr. Sam adds, "Your father was his doctor. I know a little about him," and Dr. Sam looks around and finds the file. "Luckily we never throw anything away around here." He blows the dust off the file and passes it to Churchill.

In astonishment, Churchill whispers, "He had cancer?"

Dr. Sam adds, "That and a death wish."

"You know, I know you call me Dr. Ho Chi Min behind my back."

Churchill's eyes go wide with surprise.

"Your dad told me once when he was drunk."

Churchill's cell beeps and he answers it. "Hello? Tonight at your place? Yeah, Paul, I can come."

Churchill changes the subject back to Dr. Sam. "Why did my dad drink?"

"Vietnam had a bit to do with it, I think." Dr. Sam explains, "My family sent me to the States to learn medicine. I met your father at the University of Michigan, and we became good friends. We went to the same teaching hospitals, and my family wrote me and asked me to come home. The war was already taking place. Your father pleaded with me to stay. He even helped me become a citizen during my schooling years. But I went home and was forced into the Vietcong medical core." Tears are flowing down now both their faces.

"Your father joined up too, and we were doctors mending our boys on both sides the best we could. The Marines captured the base I was at, and I became a prisoner of war. When I told them I was an

American citizen and I was forced to join the VC, who do you think they brought down to look at me?"

"Dad?"

"Your father fought so I could join the Navy Medical Corps. It took time, and I did.

"I wanted to stay. I am not a hero, Churchill. My home, my village was gone, most of my family were dead or disowned me, and your father said he lived in this nice little town in Michigan that could use two good doctors. When we came to the States, he rarely spoke of Vietnam, and I never spoke of it much either. Your father got his drinking habit there; I wish he could have left it there too."

We head back to the safe house, and I open the barn door with the key I got from Paul.

Steve, I mean Milton Roberts, and Adam climb the hay bales and take the high ground.

Steve to the north and Adam to the south. Paul comes by and looks things over from ground level. He asks me, "You getting the feeling something could happen tonight?"

I nod, "Yeah something is in the air."

"Prepare ye for tonight."

"What is that, Paul?"

"I got angry with your FBI guy Andrews, and I heard it in my spirit, 'Prepare ye for tonight.' Something is going to happen. The spirit is not particular about warnings, Max; we better heed them when they are given. Your FBI guy won't let me bring in volunteers to help out. Just letting you know, I am having my local firearms collectors meeting, and we will be staying late tonight. If you need anything, we will just be over that hill."

I am thankful Paul is on my side. "Thanks, your number is on my speed dial, Paul. You look beat. Go home and get some rest."

As I walk to the house I see Jamie. I look him straight in the eyes and say, "Jamie, you are going to have to defend yourself." I hand him a handgun. "Something may happen tonight, and I won't be there for you."

With trembling hands, he hands the gun back to me, whispering," I can't do this."

"Jamie, just point and shoot. This is your wife and kids we are talking about."

Jamie takes the weapon and walks toward the house. He then turns around and says, "Max, my dad—"

I then say, "I know. Your dad accidentally killed some of his fellow soldiers in Vietnam. You not fighting is not going to bring them back."

The sun is setting, and it begins to dim on the horizon. At the local firearms collectors meeting at Paul's farm, Paul give his two cents. "I am getting sick and tired of the Republicans kowtowing to the damn liberal tree-hugging Democrats! Why we have to give credentials to the peaceniks and flower-power screwups is beyond me."

Meanwhile, back at the safe house, Jamie's kids Gilbert and Anne can't get any rest, so they amuse themselves by telling a funny story.

Gilbert starts, "What are you doing?"

Anne answers with, "Eating chocolate."

"Where did you get it?"

"On the floor."

"Where did it come from?"

"Puppy made it."

"Where is the puppy?"

"Behind the door."

"What's he doing?"

"Making more."

They giggle to themselves as do the rest of us and shake their heads.

One of the agents says to himself, "I gotta remember that one and tell it to my kids."

Midnight's darkness sets in and it happens. Gunfire goes off in the distance at the safe house in front to the north of the house is a road going east and west. From the road, cars pull over and begin firing with machine gun fire. The FBI and I yell to Jamie and family, "Get down and get to the safe room!" FBI agents smash out windows, break out the rifles, and return fire. To the south, two off-road vehicles come up the hayfield.

Adam turns on his night-seeing goggles and comes down the hay elevator and starts taking shots with his bow and arrow, hitting tires of the oncoming vehicles. An FBI agent inside sees him passing under a yard light out of the corner of his eye as he is reloading. He then takes his rifle and starts shooting with him to the south.

Drive-by shooting at the Chapel farm! Two cars drive by and simultaneously machine guns open fire on the Chapel farmhouse. Everyone in the house, using everything from Kentucky rifles to machine guns and some in between, takes aim and fires! In seconds, the two cars end up looking like Swiss cheese and go into a ditch. EXPLOSION!

As the dust settles and things get quiet, Marcy yells, "Paul! Churchill! Benjamin is shot!"

In the confusion at the safe house, someone in an FBI uniform staggers in yelling, "I have been shot!" He is allowed in. Everybody who's firing, reloading, or dodging bullets want to know what is going on as the agent walks into the safe room with Jamie, Ellen, and the kids.

He pulls out a gun and points it at Jamie. I see him do this in slow motion out of the corner of my eye and I turn. Jamie has my pistol in his hand, but he just sits there!

The intruder fires at Jamie, *bang!* Jamie gets shot and killed, and the shooter makes a mad dash for the door. We fire at the intruder as he runs, but we can't penetrate his body armor. He fires at us as we shoot at him. Then right in the chest, something kicks me like a mule! I am out!

CHAPTER TWENTY-TWO

Tuesday, October 10, 1978

I wake up in a cold sweat, panting, "Jamie NO!"

Mrs. Cooper comes in and says, "Max, you had a bad dream. Are you sick? Do you want to see your mother?"

"No, Mrs. Cooper, I'll be okay."

"I'll call her just to let her know, Max."

As I walk to school with the guys, Jamie is alive and well, happy to all who see him. Me, I just can't get his face out of my mind when that SOB busted in and shot him. Jamie was lying there dead. As SOB fled, I emptied my gun in him, but his body armor. Damn! If Jamie only got a shot off at close range, he could have done it. I mean, with a hope and a prayer, he could have done it!

At lunchtime I come to him and say, "Jamie, you and me, we have to talk."

I have known Jamie since I was in kindergarten. He was being picked on, and Paul stepped in and saved him way back then. Over the years, if someone wanted his lunch money, it was up to Paul or me or one of the guys to save him. We warned him that one of these days we would not be there to save him. Even Paul pulled me back more than once and said, "No, he has to learn to fight his own battles."

He never fought back. When Mrs. Horton told me about his father, I could see a bit why he couldn't fight. His father raised him to be like a Christian Gandhi. Killing a brother soldier in friendly fire is one thing, but to mark your son with your own experience is another.

"Jamie, we have to talk."

"Sure, Max, about what?"

"You like Ellen, right?"

"Yeah, we are friends."

"But someday you want to be more than friends, right?"

"Yeah." Jamie smiles and shrugs his shoulders.

"I don't know how to tell you this, but sometimes I can see the future."

Wowed by this, Jamie says, "No way."

"Keep it down. You are going to get yourself in trouble, and me and Paul won't be able to protect you. I know about your father and Vietnam."

"How do you know about my father?"

"You tried to tell me, but I said I already knew. It will happen in the future. Jamie. You can't help your dad by getting yourself beaten up. It won't help your dad, and it won't bring the men he killed back. It was an accident."

With tears Jamie cries, "Fighting is wrong."

"Sometimes, Jamie, but sometimes you have to stand up for something or defend yourself or the ones you love. You can't bottle it up and let it kill you inside and out. Jamie, I don't know how to say this, but you and Ellen are going to have a family. You are going to do something that will piss somebody off. They are going to shoot you."

He pleads, "No!"

"Yes! Now listen to me. Paul, your friends, and I will protect you because we love you, but there is going to come a time you are going to have to defend yourself."

The recess bell rings. "Meet me after school, and we will talk some more."

After school, I tell Dan I need the night off.

I meet Jamie, I take him to my house, and I go to my room where I keep the .45 pistol Uncle Sherman gave me. Jamie freaks out when he sees it. We get on our bikes, and I take him to the firing range. "Jamie, for once in your life, you must fire this gun."

"No, Max, my dad—"

"Jamie, do it for Ellen and Gilbert and Anne."

"Who are Gilbert and Anne?"

"Ellen likes *Anne of Green Gables*. Now repeat after me:

What are you doing? What are you doing?

Eating chocolate. Eating chocolate.

Where did you get it? Where did you get it?

On the floor. On the floor.

Where did it come from? Where did it come from?

Puppy made it. Puppy made it.

Where is the puppy? Where is the puppy?

Behind the door. Behind the door.

What's he doing? What's he doing?

Making more. Making more.

Jamie chuckles a little bit and says, "That's funny, where did you hear it?"

"Your kids said it to each other just before the attack. *Your children.* Ellen is a big fan of *Anne of Green Gables*, so you named your kids after two of the characters. PBS is going to make a TV miniseries out of the books, and Ellen wants to make Mrs. Horton's house look like Green Gables."

"Mrs. Horton?"

"Will die someday soon, and you will remodel her old house."

"But it is next to the funeral home."

"Steve is going to buy it and make it what we call a bed-and-breakfast. I don't know how this prophecy works, but I have seen you dead, Jamie. I have seen you dead. I was there. I couldn't help you at that time because I was distracted by another shooter. At close range with a gun like this, you could pierce the intruder's armor.

"I saw you freeze up, and he just stood there. You had the gun in your hand because I gave it to you, and you did nothing, Jamie, and he shot you."

Jamie asks, "What did you do?"

"After he killed you, I shot at him, but his body armor was too thick at that distance. He turned at me, shot me, and I blanked out. I then woke up here in 1978. Jamie, you can change your future! For God's sake, for you and your family, pick up the gun and shoot."

Jamie's hand trembles as he takes the gun out of my hand. "Just point and shoot."

He fires and fires again. Then Jamie does it again! He continues firing till the gun is empty. He misses the targets completely, but he fired the gun. I grab hold of him and embrace him, weeping. "Thank you, thank you!"

Weeping he cries, "I'll do it for Ellen and my kids, Max, and you!"

I ride my bike back to my house and put the gun back in the safety box.

I was going to spend a night with the Pearsons, but I call and tell them I'll stay with my mom at Mrs. Horton's. My mom holds me tight and says, "Max, are you okay?"

"Just a little bit tired, Mom."

"Well if you are getting sick, we will take good care of you. Go and visit with Mrs. Horton. I'll bring dinner in a bit."

Mrs. Horton says, "Oh child, you carry a heavy burden, don't you?"

A tired yes comes out in agreement. With a confident smile, she opens her arms and holds me saying, "Well, set them at the altar and let Jesus have them. You have done all you can do. Give it to Jesus, and he will give you rest."

Before Mom can give me dinner, I am fast asleep in Mrs. Horton's arms.

CHAPTER TWENTY-THREE

Friday, July 26, 2002—Here We Go Again

Gilbert and Anne can't get any rest, so they amuse themselves by telling a funny story.

Gilbert starts, "What're you doing?"

Anne answers, "Eating chocolate."

"Where did you get it?"

"On the floor."

"Where did it come from?"

"Puppy made it."

"Where is the puppy?"

"Behind the door."

"What's he doing?" "Making more."

They giggle to themselves as do the rest of us and shake their heads.

One of the agents says to himself, "I got to remember that one to tell it to my kids."

Jamie has a pale white completion and whispers, "It is happening."

Midnight's darkness sets and it happens. Gunfire goes off in the distance! At the safe house in front to the north of the house is a road going east and west. From the road, cars pull over and begin firing with machine gun fire. The FBI and I yell to Jamie and family, "Get down and get to the safe room!" FBI agents smash out windows and break out the rifles and return fire. To the south, two off-road vehicles come up the hayfield.

Adam turns on his night-seeing goggles and comes down the hay elevator and starts taking shots with his bow and arrow, hitting tires of the oncoming vehicles. An FBI agent inside sees him passing under a yard light out of the corner of his eye as he is reloading. He then takes his rifle and starts shooting with him to the south.

Drive-by shooting at the Chapel farm! Two cars drive by, and simultaneously machine guns open fire on the Chapel farmhouse. Everyone in the house, using everything from Kentucky rifles to machine guns and some in between, takes aim and fires! In seconds, the two cars end up looking like Swiss cheese and go into a ditch.

EXPLOSION!

As the dust settles and things get quiet, Marcy yells, "Paul! Churchill! Benjamin is shot!"

In the confusion at the safe house, someone in an FBI uniform staggers in yelling, "I have been shot! He is allowed in. Everybody who's firing, reloading, or dodging bullets want to know what is going on as the agent walks into the safe room with Jamie, Ellen, and the kids.

He pulls out a gun and points it at Jamie. I see him do this out of the corner of my eye and I turn. Jamie has my pistol in his hand. He raises it and opens fire point-blank, and I see the shooter getting kicked back by the bullets!

The gun is empty, and Jamie is still pulling the trigger! Click!

The intruder places his hand down on his chest and raises it to his face and sees blood. He makes a mad dash, staggering for the door. We fire at him as he runs. Damn his body armor! We can't penetrate it. He fires at us as we shoot at him. Then right in the chest, something kicks me like a mule! I am out!

I wake up from the fight with bruised ribs. Ouch! The guns have stopped firing, and things begin to quiet down. I ask what happened while I was out. An agent explains, "The intruder made it out of the house and got to an escape car. Just as he was about to leave, the car exploded!"

I then get my bearings and go to the safe room. Jamie jumps to his feet and grabs a hold of me and yells, "I am going to join the NRA!"

Off in the distance, we hear ambulance sirens! Andrews asks, "Somebody call 911?"

I ponder, *No, they are not coming here, they are going to the Chapel farm!*

As I run out of the house, a hit man is just about ready to take a shot, and I hear a *peck*!

I look up, and Steve flashes a light from up in the barn, yelling, "That is the last of them, Max!"

I yell, "Something must have happened at Paul's!" Adam comes by with a car and I get in.

We get to Paul's and see the two smoldering cars in the ditch. The ambulance is backed up to the house. I plead, "Paul, what happened!?"

Paul yells back, "Somebody tried to shoot up my house! Can't you see!"

The FBI agents pull up, and Andrews yells, "What the hell happened here?!"

Paul yells at him, "Get the hell off my property, you!"

In stunned disbelief, Andrews yells, "You shot up those cars!"

Paul pulls back and lays a hard one into him, WHAM! The FBI agent goes down, then shakes it off, then yells. "You are under arrest!"

Everyone who came to the local arsenal and collectors meeting locks and cocks his or her weapon, aiming for the FBI agent.

Carter County Police Chief Tom says, "I would put your gun and badge down. These people are trigger-happy, and we might just let something happen to you. I am Chief Tom of Carter County. Thanks for letting me know what was going on over there."

"It was no concern to you, chief."

"Neither are those cars in the ditch to you."

"As for Paul and his friends, and I am one, we were defending ourselves when they opened fire on us."

Reed and the fire trucks have arrived and are putting out the car fires.

Tom continues, "When the fires are out and when and if we have dental records, we will let you know."

Churchill is there, among others, and he carries Benjamin into the ambulance.

Paul asks, "How is he, Doc?"

"The bullet cut his leg and broke his He will be alright. Let's just get him to the hospital."

Before Paul leaves in the ambulance, the FBI agent asks, "Hey, Paul, how did you know that you were going to have a drive-by shooting tonight?"

Paul grits his teeth and says, "When the Lord says, 'Prepare ye for tonight,' you better prepare for tonight! I called my pastor, my rabbis, the Hymans, and my priest, Father Michaels, and some of my closest friends, including my Army Ranger buddy and my small arms expert from the Navy Seal Academy who's my black powder rifle expert." And he keeps going down the list.

Stunned, Andrews asks, "Why do you need so many arms experts?"

"I write and draw comics, and it is good to be able to go to people who know things and get answers. They are also good prayer warriors. I am not sorry I punched you, because you have been rubbing me the wrong way. Take some advice, Andrews: listen to your Heavenly Father. If you can't hear him, maybe you ain't got one. Then you better get one."

Paul is off with the ambulance.

I come back to the safe house, and it does not take much to convince Jamie to get his family out of town and go to Illinois to Uncle Sherman's ranch for boys and girls.

We get Jamie packed to go. The FBI is pissed! Let them be. Andrews yells, "You have no right to interfere with my investigation!"

I angrily respond back, "I took a look at your sign-in sheet. While I was gone yesterday, who came by to check out the safe house?"

Andrews's looks dumbfounded.

"The sheriff of Cavanaugh City. That is our missing link. Jamie and his family are not your bait for some mystery man. I am getting them out of here now."

Andrews yells, "You do that, and I am out of here! I sent in fingerprints on our drive-by shooters and their hit men, and they are from a Chicago Mafia family that has a contract out on you. If I used tonight's evidence, I would have to say they were after you and not Jamie and his family. Mr. Scott just got in their way. I have seen the files and the records too, Mr. Faraday. You have a bounty on your head. You would be well advised to get out of town yourself."

I then tell him, "Don't you think I have already thought of that?"

At about 4:00 a.m., I meet Paul at the hospital. "How is Benjamin?'

With tears Paul stammers, whispering, "Broken leg. Marcy gave him blood. They are both B negative. Whoever they are, they picked the wrong—" Marcy comes by and consoles Paul.

Churchill motions to me, and I walk over to talk to him. "Ben will be alright. It is a miracle. I saw the bedroom. Max, there were bullet holes everywhere. It is a wonder how Paul's other kids didn't get shot. Oh, I forgot to tell you, I found some information on K. Ray C. in the basement storage files. I read it for myself. K. Ray C. had cancer, as if there were any doubts."

I ask, "What would you do if you could change K. Ray C.'s past?"

Churchill says, "Make sure he got, at least, a yearly checkup."

Paul leaves the hospital alone about 4:30 a.m. and goes home. His kids are all around him and they ask how Benjamin is. He breaks down a bit and tears come. "He is going to be okay. When he comes home, he is going to have a cast on his leg." Paul chuckles. "He said that is going to be cool, to go to school and have a cast. Keep your little brother in your prayers."

The kids go to their chores as best they can. Paul walks into the house and goes up to his office and locks the door. He said his prayers of thanks for protection.

"Lord, little Ben wanted a leg cast, and well, he got one. I guess you really should be careful of what you ask for. Lord, Max can't handle this kind of stuff like he used to. I am going to have to call on one of your servants to do the job. I ask it in your name. Amen."

He makes a phone call. "Hello, I would like to make an appointment with Raider as soon as possible. Thank you, I'll be waiting by the phone." Paul sets up his desk and gets out his drawing materials. He needs to find something to do.

Just as I am about to leave the hospital, Mr. Scott, Jamie's father, catches me on the fly. "Max, what is going on?"

I ask him, "How much do you know?"

"Jamie told me there were some people after him and his family, possibly because of a stand he took on drugs and that he identified one of the drug smugglers' drivers. And they were after you too." With tears he adds, "Thank you for rescuing my granddaughter."

I give some details. "I had the family set up a safe house with the FBI, and we were attacked last night."

"Anybody hurt?"

Paul's son Benjamin and a few agents were wounded, but could've been worse."

Mr. Scott comments, "Jamie has kept me in the dark about this."

I comfort him, saying, "He probably just didn't want you to worry."

Mr. Scott looks down and stares at my Marine Corps ring, a ring like he used to wear, and says, "He went to you before he talked to me. You must think of me as a weak man. I can't even defend my own family."

I reassure him. "No, sir. I don't. I believe you to be a strong man who fights in the way God intended him to. You put down one weapon and picked up another. I don't think any one of us would have made it through this alive if someone was not praying us through. You fought for my freedom before I was born. You comforted my mom when she needed comfort. Helping Jamie is my turn to carry the load. With you praying for me, it is not so heavy."

Mr. Scott just breaks down and grabs a hold of me and weeps. "Max, I have been praying for you. That the Lord would protect you and keep you safe. God bless you, son. God bless you."

I go home about 5:00 a.m. and put the blue light bulb out. Blue Bomber shows up around six thirty. "Maybe I should give you a cell number so you can get a hold of me," I tell him.

Blue Bomber adds, "Yeah, I heard through the grapevine you had an interesting night."

"That is an understatement. I am going to move Jamie out of town."

"Where?"

I pause for a moment. This is a matter of trust, and I still don't know about who or what Blue Bomber is. "My Uncle Sherman's camp for boys and girls in Illinois. Jamie and the family can hang low there. Churchill and Candy have volunteered to take them."

Blue Bomber adds, "I have friends who could keep watch over them along the way."

"That would be great."

Blue Bomber also adds, "That also means the FBI will be losing their bait for the mystery man."

I ask, "How do you know?"

"Oh brother, you would be surprised what all we know. Then that will mean you will be all on your own."

I smile. "Well, I will always have you."

Under Blue Bomber's mask I can see a smile. and he opens his arms and gives me a hug. "Yeah, you will always have me."

***

Churchill and Candy show up at the safe house with a minivan, and Jamie, Ellen, and the kids get in and they are off.

About 8:00 a.m., Paul receives a call. He then steps into his closet and lifts up a panel and pushes a few buttons and vanishes. Paul materializes at the Raider$'s HQ complex.

Raider$ are what we call retaliation-kept-on-retainer hired mercenaries.

Raider is their leader. His body is covered from head to toe in red, black, and white flex cloth. His other-than-human features are rarely seen. He and his twin brother, Mystery, are what you might call hybrids, part-human, part-alien life from another planet, time, or dimension. Or in his terms, a child of rape. That is a story for another time. Raider has human features, but where a tail bone ends for you or me, a tail of his just begins and if left untrimmed will keep on growing. Its length varies. At the end of the tail is a bone grappling-like hook with an eye for seeing and a mouth or snorkel for breathing. If cut, it will grow back in minutes.

He is an expert at many forms of combat and weapons of earth and beyond. Mystery is the silent one, the invisible guardian angel of the Raider$. Raider greets him, asking Paul, "How you doing?"

Paul responds, "I could be better."

"What brings you to my little world, Paul?"

Pool and video games are going on in the background as the rest of the other Raider$ take a break. They just came back from a mission from only God knows where.

Paul states, "Somebody attacked me and my family last light and put a hit out on my good friend Max Faraday, and I want to know who, and I want to know now.

Raider replies, "Yeah, you sent us a file on him, former CIA agent, former New York and Chicago cop. There are a lot of people who don't like him." And Raider hands Paul a list.

Paul asks, "How much would it cost to put a Raider$ protection on him?"

Raider says, "More than you have, Paul. You don't know it, but in his early years, the CIA sent Max to us for some training. He was pretty good even back then. If he wanted some protection with his skills, I might let him join up with us, maybe even do a couple hits on his enemies to thin them down a bit. Heck, some of them are wanted 'Dead or Alive' with pretty big prices on their heads. It would pay for him to join us."

Paul states, "What if I was to tell you he is Selah."

The Raider$ in the background go silent. Raider's eyes go wide and then his voice says, "No shit?"

"He does not remember who he was; all he knows is Max Faraday."

Raider wonders aloud,"He is a WTC, then he is automatically protected by us. Besides, Selah worked with us on a couple CIA Black Ops. Why all the—?"

"He wanted a fresh start, and that is what he gets. No contact with WTC, and no, 'for old time's sake.'"

Raider assures, "I'll keep my ears open."

Paul adds, "Oh, one more thing, my little boy got shot last night. He might walk with a limp."

Raider ponders. "Little Benjamin?"

"Yep."

"You are good people, Paul. I'll take care of it."

"Thanks." Paul walks back to the transporter.

The Raider$ are the stuff of shadows and mystery and automatic rifle nightmares.

They hunt their sport for the dollar, or so many might think. Wild Tail and his Champions play the good cop. Gladiator and his Genesis Agents are the good cops too, with great mystery. The Raider$, well, this is the way they put it: "If you are stupid enough to get yourself in trouble, we are going to be smart enough to make you pay to get out of it."

Every major governmental agency in the world keeps them on their speed dial or a little black book under "Pest control." The contacts the Raider$ have in the Wild Tail Champions keep them from offing or killing people in embarrassment. Like a freedom fighter or a witness to a trial. Oops sometimes happens.

Let's just put it this way, Raider chooses who he does or does not kill too.

A story told at the water cooler: A CIA agent comes to the Raider$ HQ to pay him to execute Cuba's Castro. A pile of untraceable US currency is placed before Raider. Raider asks, "Do you want a cigar?"

The CIA agent says, "No, I don't smoke."

"Really, they are Cubans," Raider confirms.

The CIA agent crosses his arms and says, "No, thank you."

"I have plenty," Raider says as he hands him a box. "Really, you can take a box back and share with your friends." Raider pushes a button, a door opens, and the agent can see a room full of Cuban cigars. The agent gets up and leaves.

Raider also has a soft spot. He likes good BBQ.

***

At a Mafia family mansion in Chicago, they have circled the wagons and are licking their wounds. From out of nowhere, the Raider$ bust in through windows and take out the armed guards without killing them and swiftly move on. The head godfather pushes buttons for backup, but they have already been taken out. An explosion occurs and a Raider comes bursting in, leaping to the air and landing on the meeting table. The Mafia sons leap to defend their fathers. Raider's twin brother, The Invisible Mystery, materializes, slapping their pistols out of their hands and kicks several across the room!

Raider picks one of the sons up by his feet, hanging him upside down with his tail.

The rest of the Raider$ have stopped firing their weapons by now and all is quiet.

Raider asks the godfather, "Do I have your attention? I have a message to give you. Max Faraday is under Raider$ protection. and I would like you to cancel your hit out on him now."

The Mafia godfather adds a "but—" and Raider drops his son on the floor. He lands on his head, and change and a cell phone pop out. Raider raises his voice. "I want answers and I want them now, or I will start dropping *you* on your head! Who gave you information on where Max was?"

The godfather stutters, "Vincent, one of my men, but he died last night."

"Who was Vincent working with?"

"I don't know. He had cash, and Vincent did it on his own. He even took some of my men with him. Now I have the Feds coming after me!"

"Leaving all the Fed's questions to you and the Mystery Man free and in the clear?"

The godfather slams his fist on the table. "Damn right, I should hire you to take him out for me!"

Raider asks, "Why did you strike at the farmhouse?" "Vincent called me on that. The Mystery Man, as you call it, explained Max would either be there at the safe house or at the farmhouse. It does not matter to me who dies, as long as I get Max Faraday."

Certain Raider$ come along the Mafia family and take snippets of their hair, putting them into little bottles along with blood samples, labeling the bottles and placing them before the godfather for a look-see. Raider declares, "Why should I work for you when Uncle Sam will pay me more to kill you? Funny thing is, you built this house with the entire latest quote unquote high-tech equipment. How did we get in undetected? We got in so undetected, what else might we leave behind when we go? Besides, when they come looking for you, they will need DNA samples to identify your corpses. You never know when something might explode in an old house like this. If anything happens to Max Faraday, I am coming after you."

The godfather pleads, "Hey, it could be that damn Mystery Man, not me!"

Raider yells, "I don't care, you better hope he stays alive, or I am coming after you! Oh, one more thing, one of your men wounded a little boy at the farmhouse, and he may walk with a limp." Raider takes his sidearm and shoots the godfather's son that he has been dangling upside down in the leg and drops him on the floor. "Now you know what it is like to watch someone shoot your son in the leg!" Smoke and explosions go off, and the Raider$ vanish into thin air!

As soon as they are sure the Raider$ are gone, the godfather yells, "Call off the hit on Max Faraday now, and I want that Mystery Man dead! I want you to tear this house apart. I want to know what Raider left behind!"

Paul asks Marcy, "Do you want me to rewind it, and we can watch it again?"

Marcy is disgusted with herself for what Paul has done, getting the Raider$ and the sheer joy of watching the Mafia family tear their house apart looking for a bomb that may or may not be there. With the Raider$, you never know.

***

In Illinois, at Uncle Sherman's camp for boys and girls, the woods and the lake and log cabins have a calming, otherworldly effect to troubled kids who come from the city. There are no TVs, any CDs, or video games, unless you earned privileges. There are chores to do and things to keep a kid out of trouble. All the kids here have a hard-luck story to tell. And sooner or later, they will have a story of their own recovery.

Churchill Sr. does not know what to expect. He whispers to his wife, "Candy, I don't know what will happen?"

Candy, the only person who got a full night's sleep, is driving and whispers back so not to wake the Scott family. "You and I did the best we could for our son."

"He is just like me, Candy, and he is just like my dad."

Tenderly, Candy whispers, "Churchill, I never met your dad, The best things I have heard of him is he was a caring man who tried to do his best for others. And you are like that, and our son is and was like that, and I pray he will be like that again. You are trying to make a difference before it is too late. And we both made the decision that if our son did not it would be too late. I have to believe we made the right choice bringing him here."

In the distance they can see campers and their chaperones coming. Running in front of them is their son. They pull up to the cabin and park the minivan. Churchill gets out and wipes his tears and grabs hold of his son.

"How is my boy?"

Sherman helps get the Scott family settled in. He puts his hand on Jamie's shoulder and asks, "Can you and me talk?"

They take a walk into the woods. "Jamie, I knew your dad. He was the best shot I ever seen. Things happen in war. Your dad should be proud of what you did to save your family."

Jamie with tears and a bit of shock in his voice says, "I shot a man last night."

Sherman reaffirms him. "Who was about to kill you and your family. What your dad did, he was a soldier. We are family. Your dad was good at protecting his family. Every day we were put in harm's way, and sometimes things happen. All the brothers in arms that your dad protected, thank God your father was there to watch their back. And the ones he accidentally killed? I have to believe the moment those boys entered heaven, they already forgave your dad for what he did."

"But my dad can't forgive himself for what he did."

Sherman states, "Well, living in this flesh, we have to ask the Good Lord to help us, especially when we can't or won't forgive ourselves."

Churchill Sr. and Jr. talk. "Son, I am sorry I could not be strong enough to help you get through this."

"You were strong enough to let me go so I could get help," Jr. tells him.

"I have not told you, son, we Churchill Smiths have a bit of a tradition. I hope you can break it I really do."

Jr. puts his hand in his father's hand and says, "One day at a time, Dad, one day at a time."

It has been a long day for me, being grilled by the FBI. As I call it a day, I no sooner put my head down and Blue Bomber shows up. Jamie and family have arrived safe and sound, and Churchill and Candy are spending a night in Chicago. I smile, thinking they are safe. Maybe I should go for the underground till things cool down.

"You have some friends out there that want you to be protected. Somebody put a Raider$ protection out on you."

"Raider$? What?"

"The Mafia dropped their hit contract on you. And so have a number of others."

"So the only one that should be after me is our so-called Mystery Man."

Chapter Twenty-Four

Wednesday, October 11, 1978

I sleep in and miss the start of school. When I awake, I look at the clock and see I missed the beginning of school. "Mom, how come you didn't wake me?"

"Because you looked tired, and I thought you needed to sleep in."

"Thanks."

"Get a shower and get dressed. I'll have breakfast ready, and you can be back to school before lunchtime. I already called the school and told them you would be absent, if you don't want to go to school."

I tell Mom, "I could use a sick-day break, but I'll go to school anyway."

Churchill says, "You should have stayed home today. You look tired."

I say, "Spoken like a future doctor. Churchill. What would you do if someone had cancer?"

"Depends on what kind. I am no doctor yet, but I would say get a checkup once a year."

"What if the patient in question didn't care if he lived or died?"

Churchill says, "Offhand, I would say make him get a checkup."

I gather them in. "Okay guys, listen to me, and don't take it any further than this table. I have it on good authority that K. Ray C. has cancer. But he basically has a death wish and does not want to see a doctor."

Paul adds, "He was sick on the trip."

Churchill adds, "He is under eighteen. He has to if his mother makes him."

Dan whispers, "What if she is tired of fighting him and figures if he wants to die, let him. I mean, honestly, there can come a point where some people just let go."

Steve says, "I can't believe that."

I mention, "She is all alone. I don't even think they go to church anywhere. What support do they have but each other?"

Paul adds, "Well, he is not the easiest person to like. Would anybody miss him if he was gone?"

"That is terrible, Paul. Someone should care."

Churchill says, 'Okay, Max, you go and talk to K. Ray C.'s mother, and we will back you up on whatever you want to do.

Paul whispers, "Hey, I got my truck. I say after school we go for a ride and make it quick before he gets home."

Steve adds, "I can keep him a while at the arcade. Anybody want to join me?'

Jamie says, "Sure."

Jason says, "Count me in."

"Okay, but whatever you do, don't tell him we know he has cancer."

After school, the guys, Big Paul, Churchill, and I, go to talk to K. Ray C.'s mother.

"Hello, Mrs. C. We are friends of K. Ray C. I would like to apologize for the road trip. We all thought K. Ray C. had your permission."

She waves her hand. "That is all right. Boys will be boys and all."

We all chuckle an uneasy chuckle, trying to think of a way to talk to her, so I just let it out. "We know he has cancer. What can we do to help?"

"How?"

"It does not matter, we know. Although we have had times in the past, we want to help your son in the future. What can we do?"

She motions us in. "I am so tired of fighting him about going to the doctors. He has resigned himself to die young like his father."

"We were married in '63, and I became pregnant, and his father died before he was four. Not much you can say. When we moved, we stopped at the town where my husband grew up. Karl wanted to know about his father. Everything about the town had changed over the years. They tore down his old school to put up a mall. We tried to ask people on the street to see if anybody heard of his father; nobody said they knew of him. Between being in and out of hospitals with the cancer, I think that is where Karl really decided he did not care if he lived or died. I can't get him to go get a checkup. I just don't have it in me to fight him anymore." Paul says, "Ma'am, if you make an appointment with the hospital, if we have to, we will hog-tie your son to get him there."

Tears start to fall, and then she chuckles. "You may have to hog-tie him." She makes an appointment for a checkup on Friday.

I have dinner at Mrs. Horton's with Mom, and I go home to sleep in my own bed.

Chapter Twenty-Five

Saturday, July 27, 2002—A Whole New Ball Game

Phone rings and it is Ralph. "Hey, friend, I have a car, and I'll be in the neighborhood."

"Ralph, thanks for hiring the Raider$."

Ralph grits his teeth, saying, "Man, don't mention that name around me, and I did not hire them."

I ask, "Then who did?"

"I don't know, and that kind of information should not be spoken on the phone. I'll see you today at noon at the Carter County Police Station. Call your partner John Henry, and I'll walk you both through the car."

For the occasion, I put on my "Rednecks driving around in circles at a Hundred and Fifty miles per hour, not impressive. Rednecks at a Hundred and Fifty miles per hour going in a specific direction. Now That IS AWESOME!" T-shirt.

It's noon, and John Henry Watson is ready to relax and enjoy his day off when I called him. "So what's so great about this car?"

The car rolls out of an enclosed truck, Ralph salutes the driver of the truck, and he drives off. Ralph is wearing one of his novelty shirts: *I am not defined by what people think I can do. I am defined by what people don't know what I am capable of.*

I give him a handshake and say, "Thank you."

John Henry stands there just shaking his head.

Ralph says, "I see we don't impress very easily."

John spouts, "You got me out here on my day off for this piece of shit?"

Ralph gives a stern look. "Get in the car, Officer Watson. Max, you can drive." He hands me the keys and gets in the back and puts on his seatbelt.

The car takes off like any ordinary police car. When we get to the highway, Ralph says to John, "To put the cruiser in stealth mode, open the glove box and push the green switch to black." When he does, the police car's engine is silent. It is like we are riding on glass, just rolling along.

"What the … you had me shut off the engine?"

Ralph comments, "There is no gasoline engine in the car. What you heard was simulations of said devices."

Ralph smiles, saying, "I don't think we want to give ourselves a speeding ticket. Max, take us to the racetrack and let's shake up some dust."

I turn up the radio and play Sammy Haggar's "I Can't Drive 55."

We enter the racetrack and increase speed. A good thing too, we have it all to ourselves.

I get us up to a hundred, and John is smiling, then Ralph says, "Push the red button," and I do. We accelerate, 125, 130, 140, 150, 160, 170, and John looks at me, then at the MPH 180 and climbing!

Ralph shouts, "Are you impressed yet!?"

I slow it down a bit and I laugh, then I look at John. "Oh, we better get you a change of clothes."

John asks, "How come I don't have one of these at home?"

Ralph answers, "Because if you did and everyone else did, then we would not have an energy shortage, and because if there were no energy shortage, we would have war. Because Middle Eastern countries built up by oil would declare war on other nations, trying to keep what they already have instead of making a place in the world marketplace for themselves. We as a nation do not want all-out war at this time. So we will buy oil from terrorist-supporting countries instead of researching alternative sources or technologies. In the meantime, people will parade cars with a top speed of forty-five, and if you're lucky, a hundred-mile distance range as a miracle of science. Then they'll wonder, why aren't Americans buying these so-called cars of the future?"

"Cars of the damn future, my ass! It is like watching a forty-five-year-old man asking people to get excited if he can poop in the potty! Americans don't want cars with top speed of forty-five, and, if lucky, a hundred-mile distance range. They want a car that will go so fast that you will pee your pants, and they don't want to have to fill it up. Americans can't have that car. No, It would piss off too many people and start a war. Can't have that."

"We all have to die of smog and lung cancer because that is damn politically correct."

"Maybe someday, until then I can share the technology with a few of my friends that can keep a secret. Can you keep a secret, Mr. Watson?"

"You don't tell anyone I peed my pants in your car, and I'll be your friend."

I drop John Henry off to change his clothes. "It is really good to see you, Ralph."

"Likewise, Max."

"Do you know who got me out of the CIA?"

"No, if I did, I am not supposed to tell you anyway."

"So you know?'

"Know what?"

"I had a secret life."

Ralph looks down and whispers, "Who doesn't? Everyone has a secret life in our business. You are the detective, find out." John Henry comes back and says, "I am driving this thing." The noisemakers are working; it sounds like a normal police car again. He asks, "So all the police cars in Lincoln City are these cars?"

Ralph sits back, relaxes. "Yes, and a few CIA and FBI cars are too. I trust you can keep a secret."

"Reed Jackson's fire truck! That son of a—. He has this too?"

"Yes, but I trust you can keep a secret."

"Who would believe me if I did? How did you develop this?"

Ralph explains, "I created the first as a type of generator for my parent's dairy farm. My Uncle Rodger helped me with getting batteries from old Navy submarines, and we played with the system. It started as a way to cut the electric bill, and then we put an electric motor in an old Chevy pickup. We got to the point we could store enough power in the batteries to go twenty-four-seven hours. The problem was, how could we do it without drawing attention to us? As luck would have it, a tornado hit in our area, and the power was out all over the county. We were just waiting for the chance. Previously, we recorded audio of a tractor running a generator and played the recording on big loudspeakers, so if anybody came by, they would hear the tractor. Well, to make a long story short, after Ice Soldiers was published, I was making friends with the CIA. I drove my old pickup truck to show them how it worked. We agreed, the technology was simple and in the wrong hands.

"So I left it with them because I was using the system with the Navy in old diesel subs. One day I caught up with my old CIA friend and I asked him, so what are you doing with my old truck? He said we have it in a storage facility at the moment. I asked, what is it doing there? I mean, you could have it rigged up to your power grid and help lower the cost of your electric bill. 'Ralph, that could draw some attention,' he said.

"I say, 'You are the CIA. You are supposed to be able to do anything. You could take the money you saved to buy bullets or something.' I helped them and they helped me.

"I think never having to provide for yourself can really stifle one's imagination. Necessity is the mother of invention. No necessity, no invention."

We meet the guys at the diner. John sees Reed at his corner booth. "You son of a. you had this all the time!"

Reed murmurs, "Keep it down, or you will find out we have ways of making you forget what you think you know."

John is not taking any chances with Reed and sits down and puts his hands on the table like a little kid who is so excited but can't yell out of sheer joy of knowing what he knows.

Reed says, "When I say Ralph is on the hundred-and the fifty-dollar bill, deal with it." The two look at each other from across the room.

"Damn, you are looking good!" They hug like mighty hunters that have risked life and limb and conquered their prey and rejoice in the success of the adventure. "I got to go, man. It has been great seeing you."

"No, come on, Ralph, one song before you go, the one we have been working on."

"Okay."

As the two of them set up for the song. Jack comes in and sits by himself in the corner booth. A part of me wants to go over there and invite him to our lunch, but I am hesitant; besides, I have to talk to the guys about Jamie, and I don't know where Jack stands as far as the drug smuggling goes.

Then Ralph and Reed start singing their collaboration:

"Am I a Fool for Still Wanting You?"

I had a dream the other night about her, and I woke up and went to work.

On my lunch hour, I went to the diner where a friend of mine from school works.

She said that the girl you liked in high school just lost her boyfriend and maybe you should give her a call. And have some guts and ask her out.

And I think to myself, in my life there are many uncertainties.

There are answers and there are questions.

There are winners and there are losers.

There are saints and there are sinners.

There are heroes and there are villains.

There are men and there are sons of bitches.

There are ladies and there are not so ladylike.

And am I a fool for still wanting you?

So at five I gave her a call and said. Hi how are you doing?

She said it's good to hear a friendly voice, and I'm so glad you gave me call.

She told me about the guy she was going with, more than I really wanted to know.

She asked me is there anything for certain in this world, and all I could say.

Chorus-

There are answers and there are questions.

There are winners and there are losers.

There are saints and there are sinners.

There are heroes and there are villains.

There are men and there are sons of bitches.

There are ladies and there are not so ladylike.

And am I a fool for still wanting you?

I could hear silence on the other end of the phone. I can imagine her wiping the tears from her face. And then a sigh of mixed emotions.

Do you want to go on a date?

Because only thing certain in this world is.

There are answers and there are questions.

There are winners and there are losers.

There are saints and there are sinners.

There are heroes and there are villains.

There are men and there are sons of bitches.

There are ladies and there are not so ladylike.

And am I a fool for still wanting you?

A profound silence and then applause!

"Do another! Do another!"

"Okay, my wife likes this one, 'You left your bra on my bed in a dream I had last night.'"

Reed at the guitar smiles and says, "My wife likes that one too."

I woke up this morning with a smile on my face.

Then went to work at my office and sat down at my workspace.

I call you at lunchtime and I still have a smile on my face.

You say that you have a workload that could go till night, what a rat race.

Thanks for the call and I wish I could see your face.

I say you would see a smiling face.

I dreamed about you last night.

You say, what did you dream about?

You left your bra on my bed in a dream I had last night.

I woke up with a smile and when I looked in the mirror I had a goofy look on my face.

I must have done something right.

You left your bra on my bed in a dream I had last night.

I don't know what it means.

I hear over the phone laughter as you cover your lips.

I don't know anything about dream interpretation.

I can hear you laugh out loud now.

With a giggle and a covered smile

You say I'll see you tonight for dinner.

We met that night at our café that very day.

She still has a smile on her lips.

You left your bra on my bed in a dream I had last night.

I woke up with a smile and when I looked in the mirror I had a goofy look on my face.

I must have done something right.

You left your bra on my bed in a dream I had last night.

Simple smiles are on everyone's face now except for Jack, he has his head down and looks like he could cry. Ralph says one more song.

"Thanks for the Gift"

A young couple expecting their firstborn.

His wife at the eighth month has complications, she calls 911.

She prays on the way to the hospital, "Dear God, save this precious life."

This father's hopes and dreams are wrapped up in this little boy.

The doctor says, "He was born blind and paralyzed by a birth defect, and he won't live long."

The doctor gave him three days, it turned into three years.

The day his little boy passed away, I heard his father's prayer.

Thanks for the gift.

I know you will give me strength to carry on.

There has been good and bad times, in all it's been fun.

Although I miss him already, and he hasn't been gone long.

I'll miss holding his hands, giving him a hug, and the day will come I will see him in eternity.

Thanks for the gift.

Seeing through Matthew's eyes. "Thanks for the gift"

Being a tax collector I was shunned by my creed.

Your son showed me there was more to my life than my greed.

Your son came into my life and filled a need and planted a seed.

He taught it is more than doing a good deed.

I have watched him do miracles and learned it is hungry souls he wishes to feed

He hung from a cross and left the empty tomb.

Now he has gone to heaven to prepare a place for me.

I know I can say it best in a prayer.

Thanks for the gift. I know you will give me strength to carry on.

There has been good and bad times, in all it's been fun.

All though I miss him already, and he hasn't been gone long.

I'll miss holding his hands, giving him a hug, and the day will come I will see him in eternity.

Thanks for the gift.

Ralph gets up, waves goodbye, gives me and his close friends hugs, then he goes. Someone says, "Man, I hope you and the band get back together."

There are lot of people who don't know about Ralph and what he does or what he knows about, or what goes on behind the scenes. I guess I was a part of that life, and I don't know or just can't remember. We make our orders, and Churchill sits down with us.

"Did I miss anything?"

John says, "Yeah, Ralph and Reed just played some songs."

"No way, I would have loved to meet the guy."

Reed adds, "Hey, when you are late to a meeting, you miss out."

Churchill pouts. "I just got back from Chicago."

We stare at Churchill as if to say, keep it down, you doesn't know who might be listening.

Churchill adds, "Me and Candy had a great time. We are talking about starting over."

Tension eased with the good news and a pat on the back, and Reed says, "Don't screw it up; you don't get many second chances in this life."

As I get up to leave, I say, "Hey, Jack, if there is anything I can do, just give me a call, okay?"

He smiles and takes the number. When I get home, I get a call. "Hello? It is Jack. It has been so long since I have been out. Do you want to do anything tonight?"

After a short pause, and I say, "Sure."

Then Jack and I go out.

After eating hotdogs and pop from a vendor at the park, we walk through our little town and talk. Jack asks why God took Ruth Leann. "Why did my brother Jake, my own brother, try to make me just like him?"

Silence fills the void, and then I say, "Because he trusts you with the pain. History repeats itself. People like Jake do bad things; it is because they have a free will to do so. And God loves us so much that we don't have to stay screwed up, Jack. And through our pain and difficulties, God can reshape our life into something beautiful. But we have to ask him."

With tears Jack pleads, "Max, he took my wife. He took my children's mother. My brother took my innocence."

I ask, "Jack, have you asked the Lord into your heart and to take away your sins?"

He answers, "Yes. It was a long time ago, and I haven't really prayed to him in a long while."

"Then ask Jesus to take away your pain and anger toward Jake and even God himself for the death of Ruth Leann. Because it will only destroy you if you keep it. You are going to have a life, and you can't spend a minute hating him. When you come through this, you will be there for others, as others have been there for you. I have issues about my father and a bunch of other people. I have to give it to God every day because I have to go on with my life, and only He can make life happen. When I went to the AA meeting, I admitted to fighting alcohol and gambling all the way. The only way I could go without a drink is with God's help. As much as you hate to say it, Jack, you would not be here if it were not for God's spirit in your life."

With tears Jack pleads, "How can he heal one person and let another die, Max? Why did he let her die?"

"I don't know, Jack; I am not God. He is. Your pain is your ministry. Jack. The history you have lived has allowed you to be a part of other people's lives. and you having helped them as others have helped you. We are all interconnected when you come right down to it."

We keep walking and come to the local diner where we had lunch earlier today. He sits at one table, and I sit at another. "Okay Lord," I pray, asking, "what now?"

I see a woman. Her name is Missy. A part of me thinks I know her from somewhere.

Then she walks over to Jack, and he gets up, and they hold each other, and without knowing it, they begin to dance and then the song "You Had Me From Hello" begins to play.

When the song is finished, I see that Bridge is the bartender. I leave Jack to see him for myself.

"Where have you been?" Bridge pours me a glass of water, saying, "I thought you stayed in Cavanaugh City to solve Jamie's mystery, not your own."

"Why did you leave me at that moment? Why didn't you take me to the GU lab?"

Bridge answers, "I didn't want to overwhelm you. Relax and enjoy your night out, the pretzels are on the house."

"I am sorry, I have had a bit on my mind lately, and part of me just does not know where to begin, what to trust. I mean, having my mind sent back in time when I sleep and history rewriting itself when I wake up. And the fact I have possible multiple personalities."

Bridge puts his hand on my shoulder. "That is why I am trying not to overwhelm you. You are doing so well under these circumstances. God is so pleased in you, my boy."

I ask, "Why doesn't he say it instead of you?"

Bridge assures, 'Truth is he does, but you are so hard on yourself you don't hear it over your own doubts. He has been speaking to you. And you have been speaking. Give him time to answer and be still and listen. God has created us to look for the good in others and see the anointing of God in the light of their eyes. Where there is the anointing, there is Christ in our midst. Do I have the light of the anointing of God, Max? Yeah, I think I can see it. Then know that you have it too, and don't be so hard on yourself. Maybe you and me will talk later, but right now, let's enjoy each other's company."

When I come home, Bridge is waiting there for me. Instantly we are transplanted back in time to 1992 and to Genetics Unlimited. I see myself as Black Phoenix lying strapped on a table. Wild Tail is receiving first aid medical attention. He, I mean me, really did a number on him. And he risked his life to save me? Scanners and medical devices are going over him from head to toe.

Wild Tail asks, "Okay, Doc, it has been over an hour, what do we know about him?"

Doc adjusts his glasses. "We cannot get a fix on who he is right now because he has an extra layer of skin that covers his fingerprints."

"What about a blood sample?"

"There are measures that have been taken, that his blood will decay when it is out of the body, making it unable to be matched to anyone's known blood type or DNA."

Wild Tail's eyes go wide. Infinity asks, "I thought I was the only one who could do that?"

Wild Tail asks, "Doc, what are you not telling us?"

Doc explains, "Before creating the Infinity project, Palmer Tech's security was compromised. The Russians were able to steal certain technologies."

Questioner has been listening to all this and says, "But Black Phoenix was created by or for the CIA."

Wild Tail adds, "The Russians or KGB stole from Palmer Tech. The CIA stole it from the Russians, would be my guess."

Doc adds, "Now what we have are personalities to deal with. How many? This Black Phoenix and the original mind's personality."

Wild Tail asks, "So this isn't a clone that we are dealing with?" Doc answers, "No, a clone would not have so many memories. You can tell that by the structure of the brain cells. Even a Cain's Agent Clone is remote-controlled, and there are no or very few memory cells."

Doc looks over the data and says, "Let me change this, adjust this, and add a little of this."

And little by little the extra layer of Black Phoenix's white skin begins to crack and peel off.

"The white outer skin, it's peeling? Hopefully, he is reverting back to his original state of normality."

Wild Tail yells, "Get his fingerprints and ID him!"

Then my Selah tattoo appears.

Questioner says, "I have an ID, Max Faraday, CIA agent. Interesting history."

Infinity asks, "Do you think he is even aware this is all going on, this other life?"

Questioner places a file before Infinity that he was able to save from the shredder. "No, I think for the most part he is pretty much innocent."

Infinity asks, "So what do we do now?"

"Doc, can we reverse his condition?"

"His Max Faraday personality is completely normal. I have no signs of genetic manipulation."

"Then what causes the change?"

"My guess is a sound, a picture, a hypnotic suggestion."

Questioner asks, "His brain can do all that?"

Doc replies, "The normal human brain is less than 10 percent of normal usage. There is 90 percent that is untapped. I estimate in about twelve hours he will wake up in his normal state. My question is, what are we going to do with him?"

Wild Tail jumps in the leader's seat, saying, "We can't just give him back to the CIA. Questioner, dig deep and find everything you can about Max Faraday and Black Phoenix."

Doc adds, "I think I can rig up a device that will enable us to shift his personalities from Max to Black Phoenix. But I will need to bring in some help."

Wild Tail agrees. "Granted, but no one is to uncover their face to him. He is still CIA. There is good CIA, and there is bad CIA, and until we know what he was doing trying to kill us, it is best to treat him as a captured enemy."

Blue Bomber shows up and has overheard his teammates saying, "Now wait a minute, Wild Tail. I know this boy. He is from my hometown!"

Wild Tail replies, "Then fine, Blue Bomber, you can be his big brother and watch out for him, but don't give up your identity or anyone else's, got it?"

CHAPTER TWENTY-SIX

I Am Back in My Home; Who is Blue Bomber?

As I go to sleep, I turn on the radio, and Kiss's "God Gave Rock and Roll to You" plays, and then I fall to sleep.

Thursday, October 12th, 1978. Making plans for the kidnapping.

My clock radio wakes me up to Kiss's "Detroit Rock City."

I go to bed listening to Kiss. I wake up to Kiss. Life may not be good, but it is interesting.

At lunch, we make plans for K. Ray C. and circle the wagons.

K. Ray C.'s mom has made a doctor's appointment for Friday for after school. Paul smiles, saying, "I have a rope to tie the little bugger up with."

Steve whispers, "I have a gag to cover his big mouth."

Dan nods his head. "I'll help hold him down.'

Pete smiles, saying, "I have the duct tape.'

Churchill replies, "My dad is his doctor, and he is encouraged by what we are planning. He has been after his mom to get him a checkup."

I add, "I am so proud of you guys. This is really important for K. Ray C."

Jason adds, "Sure it is, but I am going to do it just to hog-tie the little sucker."

Jack says, "I am with Jason on that too."

Paul adds, "Hey, I want to be back there holding him down, but I gotta drive the truck."

I just shake my head and smile. These are my guys and I love them.

After school piano practice, one hour later, I go to my job at the C. Connection.

After work, I head home and get a change of clothes and I am invited to stay at Churchill's overnight. The Smith mansion is a thing of legend in our town. My mom says, "The Smiths are old money," whatever that means. As far as I know, they have been doctors and lawyers. Churchill's mom is at the door to greet me.

"Hello Max, it is such a pleasure to invite you to our home."

"Thanks, I feel a little out of my league. Hope I don't end up like a bull in a China shop."

She laughs. "Churchill is upstairs studying."

"Ah, a French version of *The Autobiography of Benjamin Franklin.* You speak French?"

We just start talking French as we walk upstairs like we are old friends. We talk about the weather, you name it, we talk about it. She is like starved for French, and she shows me to my guest room.

"Oh, are you sure about this? I'll take a broom closet and a sleeping bag."

She smiles and says, "I'll see you at dinner."

Churchill comes in and says, "Max, French paid off, this room is only for relatives and government officials who are on a campaign trip and need a place to stay."

"Republican or Democrat?"

"Oh Max, we are Republicans."

At dinner I sit down, and they use all the silverware, not just the spoon, knife, and fork. I look around and I try to remember, do I put my napkin on my lap or what?

Dinner conversation starts with Dr. Churchill Smith Sr. "I am so thankful your mother is taking such good care of Mrs. Horton. She was like a mother to me growing up.

"I offered to bring her here to take care of her, and she wouldn't hear of it. My mother died giving birth to my sister, and Mrs. Horton made meals and took charge over me and my brothers and sister. My father had a hard time with my mother's absence. He never remarried and kept to himself." He then looks to his wife and says, "I am thankful that we have been able to raise our children together."

I miss the fact they never say *I thank God.* In all my time with Churchill, he never mentioned a spiritual belief.

After dinner I look at photos, the old ones with Mrs. Horton. Dr. Smith comes by and says, "She is a very special woman, Max."

"Yeah, she is kinda like the mother you never had."

"Your sister was only ten months apart in your birthdays. I think Dad blamed himself for that. He blamed himself for a lot of things. Is that why he left the practice of being a doctor?"

A pause and then, "Yeah. Well, it is time to get to bed."

CHAPTER TWENTY-SEVEN

Sunday, July 28, 2002—And the Spirit Moved

Reed and Deborah's church is casual dress, so I put on my "There are some things they really did not teach me in Sunday school. Better ask The Good Lord to help me make it up as I go along" T-shirt.

This was the church that Reed grew up in. As Ralph would say, they were not washed and baptized in the Blood of The Lamb. They were washed in vinegar and baptized in formaldehyde. They were not alive, they were pickled. Reed joined Counting Tornadoes, and whenever Ralph and a few others of the band got the chance, they did Christian concerts as Christ Taking Apart Anger through Prayer. Some of the concerts, well, they got a little wild, and Reed and Ralph grew to like them. I remember one where a so-called prophet got on Ralph's case because he was doing Counting Tornadoes and Christ Taking Apart Anger through Prayer. A woman prophetess boldly came up to us and said a man cannot serve two masters. Ralph's comeback was, "I like to look at it as I am getting another man's master to become a servant to serve my master."

She adds, "You call yourself a shepherd and you go into bars."

Ralph interjects, "Jesus turned water into wine and went into bars as a doctor goes to seek out the sick. We are commanded, 'Go into the world and preach the Gospel.' Not create your own little world and anyone who wants to can come in and is possibly welcomed."

She was silent for once. Ralph continues, "Listen, I don't look at myself as a shepherd. I look at myself as a sheep gatherer. If anyone listens to my music or reads any of my books and comes to your church, try not to screw them up too badly. Because when you serve them in your own strength you fail them. When you do it with God's strength and Spirit. you cannot fail them."

She looks at him after the stark reality of his truth, asking, "Who are you?"

Ralph's response is, "If you are half the prophet you think you are, you can go right to God the Father and get your answer."

We played the concert and there was an altar call.

"Come To the Altar."

From my childhood, I remember that day

A preacher's sermon, the spirits calling to pray

A guiding hand, and I hear you say

You'll be a new creation today

Come to the altar, there's room for one more

Come to the altar -Jesus knocks at your hearts door

Come to the altar -as time slips away

Come to the altar, let Jesus in today

Now I'm older, and I still remember

Some it seems it's getting harder every day

I pray, oh Lord, don't let me go astray

I feel your presence; it's just a prayer away

Praise God for saints in this church who disciple

Praise God for prayer warriors that approach the throne each day

They're praying for you, won't you heed the Savior's call?

Come to the altar, there's room for one more.

Come to the altar, there's room for one more

Come to the altar - Jesus knocks at your heart's door

Come to the altar - as time slips away
Come to the altar, let Jesus in today
Now I'm older, and I still remember
Some it seems it's getting harder every day
I pray, oh Lord, don't let me go astray
I feel your presence; it's just a prayer away

Reed would later marry that minister/prophetess, and I guess that is a story for another time. He came back home on vacation from Counting Tornadoes, and he saw his old church run-down and abandoned. His wife says, "Let's rebuild it and start our church here."

The music is wonderful, and Reed plays the guitar, and things just move with life.

Healing takes place, old things are made new. Praise and worship flow like living water.

Missy, Jack's girlfriend from the other night, comes to the front of the church and asks Reed's wife, Deborah, if her son could be anointed for healing. Cancer has reared its head again and seeks to claim another victim. The praise and worship calms down. She anoints the boy and the elders of the church, and Reed come around the child and family, laying their hands on them and praying. This is a church of life; they have had experience with this before. Together they have grown their faith and have taken down strongholds of sickness and disease, curse and infliction, in the name of the Father, Jesus Christ, and the Holy Spirit and destroyed the enemy. This church lives.

When I get home, Bridge takes me back in time again, and I am watching myself waking up from a deep sleep. Wild Tail and Blue Bomber are watching over me.

I see myself strapped to a hospital bed. A mechanical headband covers my head. I wonder what that is for. Wild Tail states, "He is about to wake up."

Dopey, I yawn, and he/me wakes up, asking, "What is going on here?" I see him/me struggle in the restraints. Wild Tail looks at his gauntlet and sees normal brain function displayed on its screen. He/me asks, "Who are you?!"

"My name is Wild Tail, and this is the Blue Bomber."

"Oh, then I must be Goldie Locks. Why am I strapped to this bed?"

Wild Tail says, "It is for your own protection and ours."

Blue Bomber asks, "Max, do you know what date it is?"

"January 20, 1992?"

"Add another couple days and you have it. What were you doing on the date," Wild Tail coughs, 10:00 p.m. till now?"

"I went to bed early. I was not feeling well and left early."

"Think back, did you receive a phone call before you left your office at the New York P.D.?"

"It was a wrong number."

Wild Tail wonders, "Was it? And you felt ill after the call?"

"Come to think of it, yeah?"

"We would like to show you some video that you might find interesting." Wild Tail begins showing the video of the fight between him and Black Phoenix. It hits him when he sees his face when Black Phoenix is uncovered. "That is me!" He watches as the fight continues and is moved by Wild Tail rescuing him from Brute and then when he is about to shoot himself a tranquilizer puts him out. Wild Tail comments, "You have heard about us, haven't you?"

"The Wild Tail Champions in the comic books, sure as living, breathing, human beings, only in rumor by criminals and people who think they know, but not talked about openly, I guess."

Wild Tail smiles and says, "That is how we like it. We are trying to figure out this whole situation with you and what we have found out about Black Phoenix."

Wild Tail touches a button, and I see him begin to instantly change into Black Phoenix's white skin! Breaking the restraints and lunging forward to Wild Tail and Blue Bomber! Then he stops and calms down, and Blue Bomber keeps him from falling.

"What happened to me?"

Wild Tail explains, "I activated the brain wave pattern that turns on Black Phoenix's metamorphosis."

The other me responds, "I instantly had memories of, my God, of people he killed, my God, is that me?"

Wild Tail continues, "Max, we are going to need your help in figuring all this out. We have been truthful, and we are going to ask you to be truthful with us. Okay, Max? Just so we are all on the same page here. We know that you are a CIA agent, and we know you have an interesting history. In my line of work, I have found there are good CIA and bad CIA, and you have been with, for the most part, the bad CIA."

A door opens and Agent Titus comes in. "Hi, Max." He recognizes him.

I plead, "What is going on with me?"

Titus tells him, "You are with good people here. If anyone can find out what they have done to you, it is Wild Tail. You know about him?"

"Yeah, he and his people have worked with us before. They have a history of doing the impossible. You are in good hands. I have to get back to the company. I have been given some leads to go on. I'll contact you when I have anything."

Titus leaves. I am left alone with Wild Tail and Blue Bomber. Wild Tail says, "Your record is quite impressive. It is a wonder that we never looked into you as a troubleshooter in the CIA."

"I would never betray my country for you!"

"Excuse me?"

"You and your ego trip. Where do get your authority?'

Wild Tail points his finger, saying, "Listen, you don't know all the shit we go through every single day, and for the most part, that is a good thing."

Blue Bomber adds, "We Wild Tail Champions keep the world from blowing up on a daily basis! You, on the other hand, what do you do?"

"I can't tell you what I do or I have done. That is top secret, but chances are you have a file on me now! How many people have you killed?"

Wild Tail holds up a comic book, saying, "For the most part, it is all here, just some of the names have been changed."

"What?"

"You have black budget funding. I have kids and adults buying comic books, and it is all here for them to judge."

"Judge not lest ye yourself be judged."

"Funny how you cannot be judged for your actions as Agent Max Faraday or Black Phoenix, but you can judge me and my people, and I do things in secret, but in the end it is in the light. And you do all in secret, and it never sees the light of day.

"Because there are some things people just don't need to know about. We have different methods, yet in many ways we have similar goals. The problem is a disease, a cancer if you will, has infected the CIA, and if we are not careful, it could bring it all down."

"What do you mean?"

Blue Bomber says, "Get up to speed, little brother. You heard the name Agent Bent?"

"Yeah, he helped me get into Black Ops. Why?"

Wild Tail hands him files and pictures to look at, explaining, "Everyone in his confidence, his inner circle, to the Black Phoenix file is dead. Except for you and one CIA agent named Graves."

The pictures stun me as they drop to the floor. I whisper, "I have seen their faces for an instant when you turned Black Phoenix memories on in my head."

Blue Bomber explains, "To start from what we think is the beginning, KGB agents were able to get into Palmer Tech labs back in the mid to late sixties. Some of the information was technology and biology, the early research of the Infinity Project."

"The Infinity Project?"

"Immortality concepts and theories. Instead of destroying the research, Genetics Unlimited placed the research in Palmer Tech storage. Russian KGB agents broke into the facility, and besides a missile targeting system, they also got the Infinity theory that we think is part of your Black Phoenix makeup."

The other me wonders, "Am I an immortal?"

"We don't know. As Max Faraday you are mortal, but as Black Phoenix? Bent was able to get a CIA strike force into Russia. Agent Graves was part of that original team. This was the doctor that headed the research in Russia."

All he can do is stare at him, saying, "Bent had me kill her through Black Phoenix. I don't know how, I have seen her face in my Black Phoenix memories."

Wild Tail agrees. "Yeah, Bent had you kill a lot of people over the years as Black Phoenix. The good thing is they probably deserved to die."

"That doctor, did she deserve to die?"

"I don't know. The evidence is still coming in. She helped Bent get the information so the Black Phoenix creation could begin. She also came back to the US to be part of that creation."

Blue Bomber asks, "The question is, did Bent have you kill her and others hopefully to save his own ass? Dead men tell no tales."

The other me asks, "Then why did he have me sent to kill you?"

Wild Tail chuckles. "You know, it is hard to believe it, some people really don't like me. I want you to read up on yourself, learn what you can. Then rest up a bit, because you and me are going out tonight and see if we can nail down your Black Phoenix personality. When you are Black Phoenix, you are stuck in kill Wild Tail mode, and we can't get very far if you keep that up."

He/me asks a question. "Wild Tale?"

"Yes?"

"The comic book, everything about it is true?"

Wild Tale smiles. "For the most part, yes, names and dates are changed; the gist of it is true."

"Do you know how twisted that sounds?"

"Twisted works, Max, believe you me, it works."

"How did you get your start in doing it?"

"I was a young comic book writer who was having a case of writer's block. So I went outside of my office the night before my deadline to clear my head. A young woman was being attacked by some hoodlums, so I gathered up my courage and opened up a can of Whoop Ass, and I wrote my story using Wild Tale as my hero. The rest is history, you might say. Twisted works."

Time passes. I watch myself read about himself as Black Phoenix. Wild Tail comes by and asks, "Did you get any sleep?"

"I tried, but it is like reading about another person's life and not my own. I have seen some interesting brainwashing or memory tampering in my time."

"Some of the best people are working on your case."

"Some of the hits I did as Black Phoenix were not all CIA?"

"Yeah, we are cross-referencing your files with the agency."

"You mean the CIA, right?"

"No, THE AGENCY, the one you don't talk about, the one that does not exist, period."

His/my eyes go wide. "You know about them?"

"Yeah, we have had a bit of a love-hate relationship with them over the years."

"You say that so flippant and casually."

Wild Tail smirks, stating, "Because everyone puts their legs in one leg at a time, and it takes a bit to impress me. As Max Faraday, I did Black Ops for the CIA. We uncovered an Agency investigation, and they had the authority to tell us to hit the road."

Wild Tail adds, "Yeah, I know, I was there while you two were arguing and comparing alphabet soup recipes. I copied files. did the investigation. and passed the evidence to proper authorities. Ever hear the name Gather?"

"You know him?"

"My father was a member of a team called The A.M. Express. The Anti-Mafia Express of the forties. You heard about it?"

"Through legends and myth I guess."

"Gather was the Fed officer at the time."

In shock, Max replies, "He could not be that old."

Wild Tail says, "Ever heard of cloning? He is not the original Gather; we cloned him a new body in the late sixties."

I chuckle in disbelief. "And where did you get that kind of technology?"

Wild Tail sternly states, "Cain is not a fictional character. He is real too."

"He has a pale complexion on his face. And so do I because I read the comics with Paul during study hall and recess when I was a kid."

Wild Tail explains, "When Infinity went back in time, it was not to play good little boy, it was to learn about our enemy, The Devil Satan, and his son Cain, in all his forms and some of his known and lesser known children, even if he did not know it at the time. If you ever think you are doing anything for yourself, God has a way of putting you on the right track if He really wants you or anyone else for that matter. He will get you. And he had and has plans for Infinity. When you think of all the connections of the right people at the right time, it was a "God thing" that the Infinity Project happened."

I yells back, "But at the same time you or someone else threw away the immortality theories that the KGB found and then the CIA recreated me! Where was God in that?"

"History repeats itself."

"Then why does he let it happen?"

Wild Tail says, "Because he trusts you with the pain. People like Bent and Graves did it because they have a free will to do so. God loves us so much that we don't have to stay screwed up, Max. Through our pain and difficulties, God can reshape our life into something beautiful. But we have to ask him. You have asked the Lord into your heart and to take away your sins, haven't you, Max?"

"Yes."

"Then ask Jesus to take away your pain and anger towards Bent. Because it will only destroy you if you keep it. You are going to have a life, and you can't spend a minute hating him. When you come through this, you will be there for others, as others have been there for you."

With tears I say, "Do you know when I was a little boy, my dad got drunk and beat me and my mom up? The next day the pastor gave me a ride home from church and almost word for word he said exactly what you just said."

Wild Tail whispers and holds me in a fatherly embrace. "My guess is before he said one word to you, he talked to the Lord in prayer and the Holy Spirit gave him the words to say. I know I did. We are not just fighting flesh here, Max. We are also fighting spirit. I would like to think the Devil has pretty good fight on his hands. When God looks at you and sees and knows all you have done and will do, He looks down from heaven and says, That's my boy. He never said it would be easy. He never said there would be no trials or testing. He said he would be there with us through it."

The End

To be continued in *The Black Phoenix Selah Chronicles.*

"COUNTING TORNADOES AT A TRAILER PARK"

Story begins after high school graduation.

With me selling my Comic Book collection.

Then I bought Mr. Smith's Lawn Care Perfection.

Daddy didn't like it, he twisted my arm.

Daddy wanted me to work on the farm.

Milk prices went low, bankers said to Dad the farm had to go.

Dad started mowing at my Lawn Care Perfection.

After the pay and the tip he knew his milking career is taking a correction.

Dad traded his four-wheel-drive, air-conditioned John Deere.

For a lawn mower after mowing all day hurts his rear.

We turned the farm into storage space.

Video Rent All to cater to the home improvement Yuppie rat race.

A new factory is coming to our hometown.

Construction is going up all around.

A businessman had the keen idea of turning farmland into a trailer park.

Dad said I have seen enough.

That was that and packed his stuff.

Now I'm a lonely Bach living in the house that my great-grandpa made.

This old house is an island of a sea trailer houses.

Just me my Lawn Care Perfection crew and cute looking mouses.

Counting Tornadoes at a Trailer Park isn't that hard standing where
we are.

In the house that my great-grandpa made.

It is warm in winter, cool in summer.

Has a big porch, its own shade.

It was built with purpose and made with pride.

It is a house with a hard wood hide.

Counting Tornadoes at a Trailer Park isn't that hard standing where
we are.

It's Trailer Trash Judgment Day!

Weather Bulletins came over The TV and Radio

Tornado Warnings saying better get low!

Like a reoccurring bad dream that bumped their head.

They go instinctively to the Tornado Bunker Weather Shed.

They packed in there like cattle.

While everything outside began to rattle!

Friends and family stopped at my house.

We decided to have a hurricane party and wait the tornado out.

A spirit-filled friend was praying going a mile minute.

While we were counting tornadoes and looking at what was in it.

Then it was calm the sun came out.

A TV crew came by and they wanted to find out.

The only thing standing is the house and farm, The Trailer Park is
gone!

Counting Tornadoes at a Trailer Park isn't that hard standing where
we are.

In the house that my great-grandpa made.

It is warm in winter, cool in summer.

Has a big porch, its own shade.

It was built with purpose and made with pride.

It is a house with a hard wood hide.

Counting Tornadoes at a Trailer Park isn't that hard standing where
we are.

It's Trailer Trash Judgment Day!

"Christ Taking Apart Anger Through Prayer"

This is a personal testimony.

We were milking cows just my brother and me.

The day went bad and he was looking to take it out on somebody

He was yelling at me and the world for all it's worth.

A farmer carries a burden on this earth.

Like Job you almost curse your own birth.

He is a tired lion.

All people say is God bless you and keep trying.

At times it is enough to make a grown man start crying.

Filled with regret I see silhouette.

Praying hands in the markings of a cow standing in front of me.

And I take a moment and give it to God in prayer, let it be.

Little by little his ranting begins to cease.

I thank God for the peace.

I later come in the house after work and I give my mom my testimony.

She said I felt the need to pray about that time.

I'll end this praise on a rhyme.

Christ taking apart anger through prayer.

Even when you are alone He is there.

When you are going through despair.

He will pick you up and say I know, and I care.

Christ taking apart anger through prayer.

At an Anti-Abortion Rally they argue.

Until their faces turn blue.

One group is yelling for their right.

Another is yelling In the end you will get your just due.

One in the crowd listens above the voices of the loud and hears the call.

She takes a few steps back from the ruckus to focus.

Her Maker sends her on a mission to get some coffee and donuts from a baker.

She crosses the line to make peace.

For a moment or two they both cease.

Christ taking apart anger through prayer.

Even when you are alone He is there.

When you are going through despair.

He will pick you up and say I know, and I care.

Christ taking apart anger through prayer.

Review Requested:

We'd like to know if you enjoyed the book.

Please consider leaving a review on the platform from which you purchased the book.